Grave Witch

KALAYNA PRICE

BERKLEY UK
an imprint of
PENGUIN BOOKS

BERKLEY UK

Published by the Penguin Group
Penguin Books Ltd, 80 Strand, London WC2R ORL, England
Penguin Group (USA) Inc., 375 Hudson Street, New York, New York 10014, USA
Penguin Group (Canada), 90 Eglinton Avenue East, Suite 700, Toronto, Ontario, Canada M4P 2Y3
(a division of Pearson Penguin Canada Inc.)
Penguin Ireland, 25 St Stephen's Green, Dublin 2, Ireland
(a division of Penguin Books Ltd)
Penguin Group (Australia), 250 Camberwell Road, Camberwell, Victoria 3124, Australia
(a division of Pearson Australia Group Pty Ltd)
Penguin Books India Pvt Ltd, 11 Community Centre, Panchsheel Park, New Delhi – 110 017, India
Penguin Group (NZ), 67 Apollo Drive, Rosedale, Auckland 0632, New Zealand
(a division of Pearson New Zealand Ltd)
Penguin Books (South Africa) (Pty) Ltd, 24 Sturdee Avenue, Rosebank, Johannesburg 2196, South Africa

Penguin Books Ltd, Registered Offices: 80 Strand, London WC2R ORL, England

www.penguin.com

First published by Roc, an imprint of New American Library,
a division of Penguin Group (USA) Inc. 2010
First published in Great Britain by Berkley UK 2011

1

Printed in Great Britain by Clays Ltd, St Ives plc

ISBN: 978-0-241-95665-6

www.greenpenguin.co.uk

MIX
Paper from
responsible sources
FSC
www.fsc.org   FSC™ C018179

Penguin Books is committed to a sustainable
future for our business, our readers and our
planet. This book is made from paper certified
by the Forest Stewardship Council.

To abi, who's bossy for a little brother, but who always pushes me to chase my dreams

Acknowledgments

A first draft of a book might be written in a vacuum, but the final project is far from a solitary endeavor. As such, there are a lot of people to whom I am in debt. There are not thanks enough in the world for these people.

I'd like to thank my amazing agent, Lucienne Diver, who believed in my voice and my writing, and who got Alex's story out and into the right hands. I cannot express how grateful I am to my wonderful editor, Jessica Wade, who took the story and pushed me to make it the best it could possibly be. Special thanks to Aleta Rafton, who created the gorgeous cover art for the book, and to the team at Roc who helped create the final product.

A very important thank-you is due to my amazing critique group, the Modern Myth Makers. Christy, Nikki, Sarah, Vert, Vikki, this book wouldn't be here without your encouragement (and threats). I rely on you to tell me what works and what makes you want to throw a book across the room—you don't disappoint. Thank you!

A special thanks to Meredith, SaBrina, Gail, and Matt, who helped me work out a schedule to juggle my writing and my day job. And thanks to the Cruxshadows, my musical inspiration who kept me company though many solitary writing hours. Of course, no thank-you is complete without acknowledging the amazing support of my family and my friends, who encourage me and put up with me. You know who you are, and I wouldn't be here today without you.

And last but by far not least, thank you, the reader holding this book. I hope you enjoy Alex's story!

Chapter 1

The first time I encountered Death, I hurled my mother's medical chart at him. As far as impressions went, I blew it, but I was five at the time, so he eventually forgave me. Some days I wished he hadn't—particularly when we crossed paths on the job.

"Ms. Craft, this is beyond unacceptable." Henry Baker accented the statement with a plump fist slicing the air before his face. Behind him loomed Death.

Eighteen years of practice kept my gaze off the jeans-clad soul collector and on my client, whose face darkened from cherry red to bruised purple. I fingered the spray of funeral lilies at my side, dreading the direction this conversation was taking.

"Our contract stipulated I raise the shade. I did."

Baker swatted aside my protest. "You promised me results."

"I said you could ask your questions." I leaned against his father's coffin. It wasn't exactly respectful, but I'd just shoved the senior Baker's shade back into his body two hours before his funeral. Respect had nothing to do with this job. But hey, a paycheck is a paycheck.

Baker turned on his heel and stomped across the aisle. I waited. I knew what was coming. Baker was a fortune hunter—a failed one at that—and I'd worked with his like before.

Death followed in Baker's wake. He exaggerated each heavy step, mocking the chubby man's jerky movements. All the while, a grin clung to his lips, his dark eyes never leaving me.

This had better be a social visit. I met his gaze, pleading, warning—I didn't care which—him to leave my client alone. He flashed a row of perfectly straight teeth, which didn't tell me anything.

Baker continued to pace.

Well, best get this part over quickly. "According to our contract, you can pay by cash, check, or money order. Will you need a receipt?"

Baker jerked to a stop. His eyes bulged, the skin hanging from his cheeks shaking. "I refuse to pay for this."

Here we go. I shoved away from the casket. "Listen, mister, you wanted a shade raised. I raised a shade. If dear old dad didn't say what you wanted, well, that's your problem, not mine. We have a binding agreement and if—"

He dropped his fist, and his eyes flew wide, startled.

That was simpler than I expected. I let out a breath to purge the rant from my tongue and pasted on my professional smile. "Now, will you need a receipt?"

Baker gripped his chest and wheezed. Once. Twice. Then, in slow motion, his neck twisted and his gaze moved over his shoulder. The amusement melted from Death's face.

Oh crap.

Angel of Death, Soul Collector, Grim Reaper—whatever you called him, most people saw him only once. He strolled forward, and Baker stumbled back a step.

Crap. I jumped from the casket platform. "Don't."

Too late.

Death reached into Baker's pudgy torso, and the color leached from my client's face. He swayed. Death stepped back, and Baker blinked once more before crumpling.

A scream rang from the corner of the room, followed by the clatter of chairs. The funeral director sprinted up the aisle, Baker's wife and teenage son behind him. His assistant, her eyes already glistening, fumbled a phone from her waistband.

"Nine-one-one," she said as Baker the third—and last remaining—pumped his father's chest. Poor kid.

I crept away from the commotion. Giving the family space was all I could really do. Death had already collected the soul—there wasn't any way to revive Henry Baker now. Not that I was going to be the one to tell his family that fact.

Death leaned against the far wall, his muscular arms crossed over his wide chest. He smiled, all devilish innocence as his dark hair fell forward around his chin.

I glared at him and scooped my purse from the floor. I couldn't fault him for collecting Baker's soul—after all, he had a job to do—but . . .

"You could have waited until I got paid."

He shrugged. "Didn't seem like he planned to pay you."

True. Maybe. The frantic huddle around Baker's body churned. *This is so going to be bad for business.*

I shoved my hand in my purse and fished along the bottom. I ignored the billfold—I knew it was empty. Under the tube of chalk for casting my circle, a ceramic ritual knife, my cell phone, and my license, I discovered three pennies, a dime, a crumpled foil wrapper, and a paper clip.

Death glanced at the treasure spread over my palm. "Planning on buying a gumball?"

"Bus fare for the trip home."

We both frowned at my palm. Thirteen cents wasn't going to cut it. But an emergency vet bill had wiped out everything I had. Until a job actually paid out, I was broke.

"Aren't you working the Amanda Holliday trial with the DA?" Death asked.

I dumped the change into my purse. "The shade won't take the stand until tomorrow, and then I have to wait for the City, or whoever, to cut the check."

I was giving the prosecution their star witness, because for once, being dead wasn't going to stop the victim from accusing her murderer. So far the headlines were mixed on whether I was the "voice of the silenced" or the "corrupter of the dead," but one thing was certain: it was big news.

More important, as long as the defense didn't rip me apart, I might end up on Nekros City's permanent payroll instead of being just an occasional consultant for the police. Then I wouldn't have to deal with fortune hunters like Henry Baker.

"You staying for this?" Death nodded toward Baker's body.

Baker's son still pumped the dead man's chest, fighting to reclaim his father, but the new widow had abandoned hope. She clung to the funeral director, who steered her toward the seats in the front row. I didn't see the assistant.

"Yeah, I'm staying. I wouldn't want to be accused of fleeing the scene."

Death shrugged, his black-clad shoulders lifting slightly. As they dropped again he vanished. I hated when he did that. One minute here; the next gone. He'd turn up again. He always did.

In my purse, Queen's Freddie Mercury belted out the line "We will rock you," and I cringed. The widow's gaze snapped to me, her mascara-ringed eyes hard.

Maybe not the best ringtone for the current situation.

Turning away, I dug my phone out and glanced at the display. I didn't know the number. *Let this be a job, not a bill collector.* I flipped it open. "You've reached Tongues for the Dead. This is Alex Craft."

"Alexis?"

I pulled the phone from my ear and frowned at the display. I still didn't know the number. *Who would call me—*

"Alexis," the female voice repeated, "are you there? I need your help."

"Casey?"

Her affirmative was a choked sob. My sister never called me. What was I supposed to say to her?

"What do you need?" I asked, and then grimaced. The question had sounded a lot more sensitive in my head.

"Have you seen the paper?"

"Not today."

Casey's voice caught in her throat, and it took her two tries to whisper, "They found Teddy."

Teddy?

The angry click of high heels rang across the room, heading in my direction. *Uh-oh.* I covered the mouth of the phone with my palm as I turned. The new widow was a head shorter than me, but twice as wide, and right now it looked as if that extra weight was pure mean anger.

"You did this." Her finger drilled into my arm.

Oh good—she's found someone to blame. Me.

Clearing my throat, I ducked my head and said, "I'm very sorry for your loss."

She continued as though she hadn't heard me. "I told him not to hire a witch. I told him." Her voice turned shrill, and she collapsed into the wall. "I told him."

I backed away, allowing the director to ease Mrs. Baker onto a seat. In the distance, sirens hurtled down the street.

The phone squawked in my hand. "Alexis, are you there?"

"Yes, I'm here. You said something about a Teddy."

The line was silent long enough that I wondered if she'd hung up; then she said, "Theodore Coleman? Surely you've heard of him. The police found his body last night. I need to know who shot him and where he's been these past two weeks."

I almost dropped the phone. She *had* to be kidding. Vice presidential hopeful Governor Theodore Coleman? A restaurant's surveillance camera had caught the shooting, but then Coleman had disappeared. If his body had been found, it would be a big case. Considering Coleman's political affiliation with the Humans First Party—and the party's open disdain for witches—my interference wouldn't be appreciated. "Casey, I don't think—"

"Please." Her voice broke again. "The police think Daddy is involved. They've been by the house several times already."

I rolled my eyes. The police could look, but nothing stuck to Lieutenant Governor George Caine. *Well, I guess he's actually the governor now*. Our father had deep pockets and a wide reach. After all, he'd buried my name change from Caine to Craft—and the fact his daughter was a practicing witch—so deep the media hadn't managed to dig it up during his campaign. Besides, I'd barely spoken to him since I'd turned eighteen. I saw him more in the paper and on TV campaigning for the Humans First Party than in person. Why would I get involved now? "Casey, this really isn't—"

"Please. This is what you do—right? You're some sort of magic eye?"

My jaw clenched. "Magic eye" was slang for a witch with a private detective license who did very little "real" investigative work. While I might not trail leads through dark alleys, and my investigations typically went only as far as questioning the deceased, I did find answers for my clients.

I took a deep breath and forced a smile to spread across my face, to seep into my voice. "I'm sorry. I can't help you." The words came out sickly sweet, but I didn't talk to my sister enough for her to recognize the tone. "I can't get involved in an ongoing police investigation."

"I can pay you."

I frowned at the phone. Last I'd heard, Casey had bought into the antiwitch position of the Humans First Party. If she was willing to actually hire me, she must be truly worried.

"Please, Alexis. Please. I need your help."

"Okay." Damn. I was working for my little sister, but I'd look into the case. See what I could find. With a sigh, I rattled off my standard legal spiel, quoted my rates, and told Casey to expect an e-mailed copy of my contract later that afternoon. As I spoke, the sirens hurtled closer, and I shouldered my purse with its thirteen cents, gum wrapper, and paper clip.

"When will you talk to the ghost?"

Ghost? I suppressed a groan but didn't bother correcting her. After all these years, if she hadn't grasped the fact that ghosts were cognizant, wandering souls, but shades were just memories, she clearly hadn't been paying me any attention. Instead I said, "If you want to be present to question Coleman's shade, we'll have to wait until the police release the body and it's in the ground. If you want faster answers, I might be able to question him at the morgue, but you can't attend the ritual."

The line was silent except for soft, ragged breaths on the other side. I gave her a moment to think as the sound of sirens drew closer.

"The morgue." Casey's voice dropped in pitch. "How soon will you get back to me?"

Getting access to a high-profile body in an open case would be difficult, but I'd built connections during my three years of running Tongues for the Dead. "I have a friend at the station. I'll give him a call, but I can't make any promises. I'll contact you tonight if I get access to the morgue today. Otherwise, expect me to check in tomorrow afternoon."

Wrapping up the call, I saved Casey's number and moved to get the door for the paramedics. The ambulance pulled to a stop, and a black and white cop car jetted to the curb behind it. Good—maybe the cops could give me a ride. The chill of Mrs. Baker's glare crawled across my shoulders. I wanted to catch a ride in the front seat of the cop car—not in the back of the wagon, under arrest.

As the paramedics rushed up the stairs I scrolled through the contacts on my phone until I reached the number for my friendly neighborhood homicide detective. A gruff voice answered on the third ring.

"Hey, John," I said as I stepped clear of the emergency workers. "I need a favor."

The doors to the Nekros City Central Precinct slid open, allowing the sixty-degree air inside to escape. The sweat clinging to my skin from the short walk across the blacktop chilled instantly. Six p.m. and the temperature hadn't dropped under a hundred yet. The South in the summer—you had to love it.

I swiped the escaped blond curls plastered to my face back into a messy ponytail and turned to wave to the two officers who'd given me a ride. I hadn't been arrested in connection to Baker's death, but there had been some tense moments back at the funeral parlor. Luckily, when Tamara, the medical examiner, arrived, she'd been able to confirm the absence of magical influence on the body during her initial examination, which freed me to follow up with John at the morgue. My favorite homicide detective had agreed to get me in to see Coleman's body, but only if I did a favor for him in return. In this case, "a favor" translated into raising an extra shade.

The cops turned out of the parking lot, and I stepped between the automatic doors and headed for the security check. I dug my wallet and ceremonial knife from my purse before dropping the bag on the conveyer belt. As my purse disappeared under the X-ray machine I put the knife in the basket the guard gave me. Then I handed the basket and my wallet—open to display my PI license and my magical certification issued by the Organization for Magically Inclined Humans, OMIH for short—to the guard. He glanced over my credentials before confiscating the knife, which I'd pretty much expected. Turning, I walked through the metal detector. No issue there, but the spell detector beeped loudly as I stepped through.

The security guard motioned me to stop and grabbed a spellchecker wand. "Hands out, palms up."

I did as he instructed, tapping my toe inside my boot as he waved the wand with its rudimentary detection spell over me. The glass bead on the tip glowed green as it moved over my right hand and the obsidian ring I stored raw magic in. Green meant magic, but not an active spell. On my other wrist, the bead glowed yellow as it traced over my shield bracelet—active magic, but not a malicious charm. Malicious spells, even inactive ones, made the bead glow red. The bead didn't turn red.

With a nod, the guard motioned for me to drop my hands as he placed the wand back in its stand. I grabbed my purse, my wallet, and the ticket I'd need to reclaim my knife when I left. Then I made my way to the elevators.

Central Precinct was an austere but multipurpose building situated in the middle of downtown Nekros in what people tended to refer to as the judicial block because of the proximity of the statehouse, the state supreme court, and Central Precinct. Though it was not overly apparent from the back of the building, where I'd entered, the main floor housed Nekros City's central police station as well as the undersheriff's offices. Upper levels of the building boasted the central crime labs and the district attorney's suite, but I wasn't headed up. The basement level contained the medical examiner's administrative offices and her place of power—the morgue.

John Matthews, the best homicide detective Nekros City could ever ask for—at least, in my opinion; but then, he was also a good friend—waited outside the main morgue door. His grizzly bear–sized form looked uncomfortable hunched over in the orange plastic chair, but his chin touched his chest, his eyes closed. *Apparently not too uncomfortable for a nap.* Wrinkles creased deeper wrinkles in his brown jacket, so he must have worked though the night—Maria would have never let him leave the house so disheveled.

"You all right there, John?" I asked as I clipped my visitor badge to the strap of my tank top. I didn't yell—

at least, not quite. Still, my voice reverberated off the walls, the echo making me wince.

John's head jerked up, and the report in his lap hit the floor, pages scattering. "Alex? Geez, don't do that."

Okay, in hindsight, maybe I should have woken him more quietly.

I knelt, gathering pages. Several photos had also scattered, and I grabbed one that floated under the chair. A pale shoulder lay in sharp contrast to the black garbage bags dominating the picture. A limp hand had escaped the dark plastic; the long wrist was delicate, feminine.

I handed the photo and pages to John. "Body dump?"

He nodded, rubbing his palms against the dark shadows under his eyes. "Third girl this month with the same MO."

Third? The cops must have been keeping this case very quiet for the press not to have picked up on three connected murders. I itched to get a better look at the case file—morbid curiosity might have been a personality flaw, but I talked to the dead for a living. I didn't press John—at least not yet. He'd tell me as much as he was comfortable telling. I nodded at the file. "She the extra I'm raising?"

He nodded. "Yeah. My black-bag special."

As in a Jane Doe. "I'll take a guess that you have no leads from the first two bodies?"

"Wouldn't be a fair trade if I did." His tone was light, but his shoulders slumped forward. "You got a pen?"

I pulled out the pen I'd pilfered from the desk jockey who'd signed me in to the basement level. John thumbed through the pages on his lap, separating documents from the case file. I signed the normal assortment of nondisclosure agreements and official paperwork. My standard rate was crossed out; the words "pro bono" were scrawled in red pen. I bit my lip as I initialed the change.

Free hurt, but John was doing me a huge favor by letting me see Coleman's body. Having an official case I was working on legitimized my trip to the morgue. Didn't make the big zero feel any better, though.

I handed the signed documents to John, and he tucked them away before pushing open the morgue door. The fluorescents buzzed over our heads, mixing with the scrape of our footsteps on the linoleum floor. Trays of sterile equipment surrounded the two unoccupied autopsy stations on either side of the room. In the back waited the cold room—or corpserator, as I called it. Beside the cold room, yellow light filtered from the window looking into the medical examiner's office.

The office door opened, and a shaggy-haired intern in a white coat emerged. "Detective Matthews, Miss Craft. Can I help you with something?" His eyes flicked from John to me.

Miss Craft? I frowned at him. Tommy Stewart had spent the past year as the medical examiner's intern, and he hadn't called me by my last name since his second week. Granted, we'd gone out for drinks a month ago, and, well, one thing had led to another, but it hadn't been anything serious. Or at least, I hadn't thought so.

"Tommy," John said, "how about you take a cigarette break."

It wasn't a question.

Tommy shoved his hands in his pockets and rolled his shoulders back. "There a body you need?"

"I got it covered." John waited. "Now, how about that break . . . ?"

Tommy shook his head. "Detective Andrews said—"

John cut him off. "I'll take care of Andrews."

Tommy's mouth twisted, his eyes pinching, but all he said was "Right—a cigarette break."

He jerked into motion but paused at the door. His

gaze landed on me, the look hard. *Boy, do I know how to kill a friendship.* I sighed as the door swished closed behind him.

"Who's Detective Andrews?" I asked as John disappeared into the freezer.

He didn't even glance back. "Don't worry about it."

I rocked on my heels as I waited. Several white sheet–topped gurneys were visible beyond the thick doorframe—busy week at the morgue. A translucent figure walked among the bodies, muttering to himself. The baggy jeans and flannel shirt he wore were colorless, shimmering with each of his steps. If I had dropped my shields, I could have made out the color of his hair and heard what he was saying, but I wasn't that curious. Ghosts, at least true wandering souls, were rare, but as a whole they were an obnoxious bunch. After all, it took a severely stubborn personality to withstand Death's attempt to collect a soul. Unfortunately, most ghosts I'd encountered hadn't been pleased with their success. They were just pissed that their struggles hadn't kept them alive.

I must have made a noise, because the ghost looked up and saw me watching. He pushed a pair of shimmering glasses higher up his nose, then flipped me off. *Jerk.* I returned the rude gesture, and his mouth fell open. I was no lip reader, but the slow question *"You can see me?"* was obvious enough that I nodded.

His next words weren't nearly as easy to decipher as his lips dashed into motion. His hands flitted through the air, accenting his silent speech with extravagant motions. *Great—an excitable ghost. How long has he been dead?* Most ghosts took a while to realize that no one could see them. Well, no one but grave witches such as me.

I might have dropped my shields just a smidgen to hear what the ghost was saying, but John chose that moment to reemerge. Actually, the gurney he was pushing emerged first, sliding through the ghost's shimmering form. The ghost's mouth snapped closed as he glanced down at the gurney passing through his hips.

I looked away before John stepped through the ghost as well. It was disturbing to watch things like that.

"Which is this?" I asked, tossing a nod at the lumpy form under the sheet on the gurney.

"How about you tell me." John stopped in the center of the room, and his mustache twitched as he smiled. "So, you're going to make it to dinner tonight?"

Oh yeah, it's Tuesday. I nodded. "Can you give me a ride?"

"Course." He pushed out a second gurney, this one with a body still in a black transport bag. The ghost was nowhere in sight. John parked the gurney beside the first. "Maria is making pork chops. A couple of the boys from the station will be joining us."

My stomach gurgled, and I squeezed my abs, trying to silence it. *Way to go, stomach; let everyone know I skipped breakfast. And lunch.*

I set my purse by my feet and dug out the black lipstick tube I carried my oil chalk in. Crouching, I pressed the waxy chalk to the linoleum floor. I dragged it, duck-walking, around the two gurneys.

As I drew my circle John adjusted the digital equipment. The camera was meant for recording autopsies, but John borrowed it whenever I raised shades for a case.

"Heard you might be a murder suspect."

I dropped the chalk. "You what? No, I—" The tube rolled toward the drain in the floor, and I scrambled after it. "I mean, the widow thought I . . . but Tamara cleared me."

John's mustache twitched so fiercely with his attempt

not to smile, it nearly walked off his face. I frowned, and a deep-bellied laugh erupted from him.

It wasn't funny.

Still, he had an infectious laugh. I found myself grinning as I finished my circle.

"Seriously though," I said, capping my chalk. "If Tamara hadn't been the medical examiner at the scene, I could be in holding right now. Waiting for the autopsy." Being held under suspicion of death magic was *not* something I wanted. Nulls already had enough trouble understanding the difference between death magic and grave magic—my unfortunate specialty. Luckily, as well as being the lead ME, Tamara was a certified sensitive. She could locate a spell quicker and more accurately than any spellchecker charm, and unlike a charm, she could usually discern the purpose of the spell. The only magic she'd been able to sense at the scene had been the ritual I'd used to raise the shade and charms to keep the flowers fresh. No spell had been involved in Baker's death.

With my circle complete, I stood. Recapping my chalk, I tucked it away.

John flipped a switch, and the camera turned on. "Ready?"

I nodded, closed my eyes, and cleared my mind. The obsidian ring on my right hand throbbed with the raw energy I'd stored. I mentally tapped into it, drawing out a spindly string of magic. There wasn't much. I hadn't had time to recharge the ring after the ritual for Henry Baker, but there was enough. I channeled the energy into the wax circle, and it sprang to life, buzzing with pale blue power behind my eyelids.

Now for the fun part.

Releasing my connection to the magic stored in the obsidian ring, I unclasped the thin silver charm brace-

let on my wrist and shoved it in my pocket. The extra
defenses the charms gave me vanished. The chill of the
grave pressed against my mental shields like icy water
lapping at the edge of my consciousness. I drew in a
deep breath and sank deeper into a trance. The grave
essence lifting from the corpses within my circle per-
sisted, thundering against my mind. Beckoning. Taunting. Demanding.

I dropped my shields.

A racking wind rushed through me. The clammy touch
of the grave slid against my skin, beneath my flesh.

I opened my eyes.

My vision had narrowed, leaving the world covered
in a patina of gray. Flakes of rust covered the stainless-
steel gurneys on each side of me. The threadbare and
tattered linen sheet covering the body on the gurney to
my left rippled in the breeze blowing through me. The
linoleum floor under my boots had worn away, and the
cement beneath it crumbled. Outside the circle, John's
wrinkled jacket was pocked with holes, but he was filled
with light, his soul a dazzling shimmer of pale yellow. I
looked away.

The wind picked up, filling my ears with its roar and
blocking out any other sound. The chill buffeted me,
clawing under my skin, into my blood.

It hurt.

I was alive. A being of warmth and breath, not of cold
and stillness. Not of death. My life force burned against
the chill, warring against the grave essence wriggling
into the center of my being. Sweat beaded on my skin
even as I shivered.

I needed a reprieve.

The soulless husk in the body bag called to me. I
didn't need to guide the power. I stopped fighting it, and
my living heat spilled into the waiting corpse. As my

heat fled, the chill of the grave sank comfortably into my limbs. The roar of wind stilled. I blinked. I could feel only one body within the circle—the female in the black bag.

Strange.

I mentally reached for her, my innate magic following the trail my heat had burned. Even filled with my life force, the shade my mind touched was weak, tattered. *How could a shade who's never been raised fade so quickly?*

My magic trailed along large cuts in the feeble shade. The deep, gaping incisions nearly shredded her to pieces. I'd never felt anything like it.

I poured magic into the corpse, letting my power fill the holes in the broken shade. She still felt frail—barely remembered. But held together with both my heat and power, she was substantial enough to raise.

Taking a deep breath, I gave the shade a gentle push. My power coaxed her from the body, guided her across the chasm separating the living from the dead.

She emerged screaming.

Chapter 2

High, piercing wails shook the air, and my hands flew up to cover my ears. *What the—*

I stumbled back as the shade clawed free of the body. A gaseous head and shoulders emerged from the body bag. The screaming never dampened. Her face twisted, as if the agony of her death had reached beyond the grave.

I gasped, still plugging my ears. "Bethany?"

The shade didn't respond to the name. I searched her face. The sharp chin and high cheekbones were on an older face than I remembered, but the hard, almost cruel beauty of her features, as if she were distantly descended from court fae, was hard to miss. It had to be her.

I turned to John. "I know her."

John's mustache tugged down toward his chin. "You can ID her? Who is she?"

"Her name is Bethany Lane. We went to academy together. She is—was—a wyrd witch." I frowned. I'd never before raised a shade of someone I'd known in life. Not that I'd known Bethany well. But even in a city like Nekros, witches made up a small percentage of the population, and wyrd witches—those witches who, instead of needing to be taught to reach the Aetheric plane to gather magical energy, had to be taught *not* to use magic—were an even smaller percentage. "She was a touch clairvoyant, able to see the past, and sometimes the future, of an object when she touched it."

John opened the file clenched in his hands and jotted something. He winced as Bethany's screeching rose an octave. Glass would shatter soon. "What's wrong with her? Make it stop screaming."

"Be quiet," I commanded the shade, but the wailing didn't drop in volume. I gritted my teeth. My magic gave her form, made her visible, audible. She should have had no choice but to obey my command. Apparently no one had ever told her that. *Okay, time for a different approach.* "Tell us your name."

Bethany's shade continued screaming. Her hands moved to her face and began digging at her eyes. I grabbed the vaporous wrists, tugging them down. She flailed in my grasp.

"Alex?" John stepped closer.

The edge of the circle trembled as he crossed it, and a shiver of power crawled down my skin. It was meant to keep out magic, not John, who was a null and as magically dampened as could be. He probably didn't feel a thing. I felt the disturbance down to my bones. I held my breath, unsure if the already weak circle would hold.

I swayed, and the thrashing shade wrenched her wrist out of my grasp. She lashed out, her jagged nails slicing through the air like a scythe.

I jumped back. The crumbled cement under my boots shifted, throwing me off balance. John caught me before I hit the ground, and the shade's next slash passed through him, grazing my shoulder. Three shallow trenches split open.

"The hell?" John flipped around to grab her.

A futile effort. His hand passed through her wrist.

She lunged again, and I stumbled back. *This is so not normal.* I cut off the stream of magic giving the shade form, and her eyes bulged. The cold wind washed backward through me, but she didn't fade. I shoved with pure power. Bethany's scream kicked up a notch, then cut off with one last lingering note as the shade vanished. The sudden silence rang in my ears.

I gulped down air. *When had I lost my breath?* The cuts on my shoulder burned, and I pressed my palm against them. Damp. I dropped my hand back and stared. Three thin lines of blood dotted my palm.

Beside me, John let out a deep breath. "What made it do that?"

Crap. "I don't know. Shades aren't supposed to lash out. They aren't that real, that . . . emotional." I shook my head. "They're just memories. No will, no pain . . ." Or at least that was what I'd been taught. I looked at the black bag. It was perfectly still, silent.

I wiped my palm on my jeans. Tonight I'd send some e-mails. Maybe someone over at the Dead Club discussion board would know what went wrong, but I'd surely never heard of a shade screaming. I turned to the other body.

Or at least I thought it was a body, though it certainly didn't *feel* like one to my senses. I squinted. It was the right shape. An icy drop of sweat trailed down my spine. I reached with magic, my hands hovering over the sheet. My power slid around the body—or whatever it was—not touching it.

That is just weird. I bit my lip and probed with the sense that drew me to the dead. Nothing.

The power level of my circle surged, lifting goose bumps on my skin. My head shot up as the ghost bounced off my barrier. He turned and slammed his shoulder into the edge of my circle a second time, flickers of green and blue light exploding in the pale barrier. Not what I needed right now.

I drew on the small well of magic left in my ring and channeled a thin line of energy into the circle. The barrier quivered but held as the ghost hit it a third time. He jerked as if stung, his form more transparent than before.

"What is it?" John asked, stepping closer to the gurney.

I forced my attention away from the ghost. If he hadn't broken the circle yet, he probably wouldn't. I had other things to worry about, like the sheet-draped form on the gurney. "You're sure this is a body?"

John pulled the sheet back, and the skin on my arms crawled. Coleman's face was pale and expressionless in death—and completely free of decay.

I blinked. Crumbled cement crunched under my boots. Rust covered the gurney. My grave-sight was functioning, but .... "He looks exactly the way he did on TV."

John nodded. "Pretty good for a two-week-old corpse, huh?"

I frowned. I'd seen two-week-old bodies before. Hell, I'd smelled them too. Without being embalmed and with the heat index hitting 104 on cool days, Coleman should have been a mess. Instead, he would probably have an open-casket funeral.

"What were the autopsy results?"

John pulled a small notebook from his pocket. "One of the bullets perforated the spleen. That was the kill shot. His body poisoned itself. No indication how the body was preserved this long without signs of decomp." He shook his head. "When the media gets hold of this, they're going to spin it with him being some sort of saint. Incorruptible body and all."

Great—just what the world needed: a sainted witch hunter. I let out a sigh, and my strength rushed out of me with my breath. Between Baker and Bethany, I'd been in touch with the grave too much today. I needed to wrap this up, get Coleman talking, and get paid.

I studied his unmarred features. Even if he wasn't outwardly decayed, he should have been desiccated in my grave-sight. Everything natural decayed in my grave-sight.

John lifted the sheet to cover Coleman's face, but I held up a hand.

What is that?

Leaning forward, I motioned John to pull the sheet down farther. Thick blue and green lines curved over Coleman's shoulders, filling the hollow of his collarbone. "Are those tattoos? Let me see his chest."

John frowned but folded the sheet down to Coleman's hips. Vivid patterns decorated the governor's arms and chest in a swirl of colors and shapes. The curving lines were like nothing I'd seen before, as if an artist had taken liberties in depicting characterized runes or ancient tribal art.

I leaned closer. "Not exactly something I expected to see on a public figure."

John stared at me, not the corpse, and my stomach twisted.

"You can't see them?"

He shook his head.

Oh crap. The patterns were undisturbed by the Y incision from the autopsy—a regular tattoo would have been ruined. I turned and looked at the marks from the corner of my eye. In my peripheral vision, I could almost make sense of the twisting patterns, but if I focused on them, they jumbled toward random. *Magic glyphs?*

"Did Tamara check the body—or whatever this is—for spells?"

John nodded. "She did a full workup. Nothing."

I swallowed, and the fist in my stomach clenched tighter. Tamara was a natural bloodhound for rooting out spells. I'd never found anything she'd missed before, especially something this big. Not that I had a clue what the spell did.

Behind me, a door banged open. "What the hell is she doing with my body?"

My head snapped up, and I whirled around.

A man stormed into the room, his steps thundering through the sterile space. In my grave-sight, he was a blinding silver blur, his soul shimmering below the surface as though his skin could barely contain it.

"Damn," John swore.

He shoved Coleman's gurney back toward the cold room, but the spell on the body caught on the edge of my circle. Energy tingled over my skin, and the clenched fist in my stomach thrust upward, choking me as the circle fought to hold the foreign magic inside.

"John, no—"

Too late.

John shoved again, and the circle shattered. The backlash tore through me like spikes ripping through my veins. Bile filled my mouth. *Oh, this isn't good.* My knees buckled.

Gravel bit into my palms, and I found myself blinking at the broken linoleum. John and I were going to have to have another chat about magic circles. I pushed off the ground.

Cold wind raked over me, through me. I shivered.

Oh no. The grave essence from the other bodies in the morgue—it was reaching for me. Papers rustled in the gathering wind, and the equipment on trays rattled.

"What the hell is she doing?" the stranger yelled.

I ignored him. There wasn't enough time to recast my circle. Closing my eyes, I concentrated on my outermost mental shield. I visualized a wall of vines growing around me, blocking the grave essence. The wind calmed, becoming a light breeze, and I let out the breath I'd been holding. Most witches formed shields of stone or metal, but I'd long ago learned that visualizing living walls protected me better against the dead. I turned toward the remaining gurney.

My hand trembled as I extended my arm and reached both physically and magically for the life force I'd stored in the corpse. It rushed into me, burning a well-used route to my core. My vision dimmed, my gravesight faded, and the chill gripping me retreated. Goose bumps lifted on my skin. The heat I'd regained was only enough to emphasize how cold I'd been while filled with the grave.

My shoulder itched, and I rubbed at the scratches before fumbling the shield bracelet out of my pocket. I hated this part. The charm bracelet's silver clasp snapped closed, and the last of the grave essence reaching for me vanished. The psychic disconnect left me shivering and blind.

"I'll have your badge for this," the unfamiliar voice yelled.

I cringed. Well, we'd certainly pissed someone off. Now if only I could see who. A wheel squeaked at my side, and I blinked furiously. *Stupid adjustment period.*

I squinted, but I couldn't make anything out. My postritual vision was worse than normal, probably because I'd used my grave-sight twice today. Impatient, I knelt and groped for my purse. Under my fingers, the linoleum was once again solid, smooth. *Where is that bag?*

The shadows crawled apart, and I made out a blotch of red to my right. My purse. I snatched it from the floor and dug out my glasses case.

"This is an open investigation!"

I turned, willing my bad eyes to focus. The stranger leaned over Coleman's gurney as if checking to see if we'd tampered with the body. A shock of platinum hair fell forward over his shoulder, and he brushed it back with a swipe of his hand. He looked up and straightened as John wheeled Bethany into the cold room. He jerked the front of his suit jacket closed, stepping around the gurney and into John's path. I frowned. The fitted suit showed off an impressive swimmer's build while marking him as someone higher up in the police food chain than a beat cop. While I certainly didn't know all the homicide detectives in Nekros, I thought I knew all the ones important enough to have pulled Coleman's case.

John's knuckles flared white where he gripped the metal gurney, but his gaze didn't lift above the black body bag. I slung my purse over my shoulder. Now might be the time to make a discreet exit. John could sort this out.

I headed for the door.

"Witch, stay where you are," the detective barked behind me.

I flipped around. *Busted.*

What was the name of the cop Tommy had been worried about earlier? Andrews? This had to be the same detective. I hadn't meant to get John in trouble.

The detective balled his hands on his hips. His suit jacket gaped, exposing an expanse of pristine oxford shirt and the dull black butt of his gun. "If your pet magic eye compromised my investigation, I—"

Magic eye? He did *not* go there.

Thoughts of fading into the background fled from my mind, and I marched into his personal space. "Detective Andrews, is it?"

He turned, his jaw clenched, but he didn't answer. He also didn't back down.

I was tall, and in my ass-kicker boots I was pushing six feet, but this close, I had to look up to meet his eyes. Intense eyes at that—frost blue, but right now burning hot with outrage. I jutted out my chin, matching his glare.

"Detective Andrews?" I asked again, and received a grunt in reply. *Oh, yeah, he's a real conversationalist.*

"I'm Alex Craft with Tongues for the Dead." I held out my hand, letting it hang in the narrow space between us. We were much closer than we needed to be to shake, and his gaze flicked to my outstretched palm before he grasped it.

For a shocked moment, I didn't understand the press of material against my skin. *Gloves.* He wore gloves. The handshake started firm and grew to painful as he squeezed the bones in my hand.

I smiled at him. I wasn't male, and I wasn't interested in an immature squeezing game. I had my own childish game.

I thinned my shields, visualizing the mental vine wall uncoiling, creating small holes between my psyche and the land of the dead. I was still wearing the charm bracelet, but I sidestepped its beneficial defenses by actively reaching for grave essence. I siphoned enough chill to lift the hair off my neck, for it to crawl down my arm, over my hand, and into the detective's hand.

His blue eyes flew wide as the unexpected touch of

the grave wound up his arm. He jerked his hand from mine, falling back a step.

My smile never slipped as I slammed my shields back in place. "Since I'm just a hack magic eye, perhaps you can explain why Coleman's body was never alive, yes? No?"

He blinked, but I didn't wait for a reply. Turning on my heel, I marched out of the room.

He didn't stop me this time.

John caught up with me outside the elevator. The shiny bald spot in the center of his head glowed red, but his gaze dragged the floor. "That wasn't smart." His whisper was hoarse, as if he was choking down what he really wanted to say.

I tossed my visitor's badge on the front desk and rounded on him. "Why isn't this your case?"

He didn't answer. A cough sounded behind me. A shoe squeaked. Crap, I was yelling. I took a deep breath as the heavy metal doors of the elevator slid open.

I waited until we were inside the elevator and the doors were closed before speaking again. "Why didn't you just tell me it wasn't your case?"

"I've got my own curiosity, and you're lucky he didn't arrest you." John frowned but looked up to meet my eyes. "I see you finally started wearing the glasses."

My fingers moved to the thick black frames. "I'm a fan of seeing. I just need them the first hour or two after using grave-sight." I paused. He'd changed the subject. Twice. Did I really want to push it? Yes, I did. "Who is this Andrews guy?"

John slipped between the doors before they were fully open and set a quick pace to the police station lobby. He reached the front door before pausing. "Falin Andrews transferred into the department a week and a half ago. You want to know how he got this case? Ask the chief. Now, are you coming to dinner?" He glanced over his shoulder, and his mustache twitched. "Maybe Maria will let us snag some of her upside-down cake before the meal." He winked and rubbed a hand over his expanding middle.

I smiled despite myself. Leave it to John to go from angry to thinking with his stomach. I had to admit, though—cake sounded divine. My steps were lighter as I walked to the door. *Cake might actually make this whole day better.*

I got a good look out the window in the door, and my optimism died. Outside, reporters crowded the steps. News vans lined the road.

"Should we try to sneak out the back?"

John shook his head. "I'm parked out front. You remember the magic words?"

"Yeah. 'No comment.'" And since the press got wind of my part in Amanda Holliday's trial, I'd had a lot of practice saying them. But walking into an onslaught of microphones? Not exactly my idea of fun. John waited, watching me. I made a last-ditch effort to smooth my unruly dishwater blond curls and forced what I hoped was a camera-worthy smile. At least I had on a halfway decent outfit—my favorite pair of black leather hip-huggers and a red lacy tank top—so I wouldn't look terrible on camera. "I'm ready."

He pushed open the door, and the reporters surged forward.

"Detective Matthews, are there any new developments in the Coleman case?" A perky redhead shoved her mic forward.

John stepped around it without a word.

"Are the police seeking magical consultation on the governor's death?"

A mic appeared in my face, and the dark-skinned

man holding it asked, "Were you able to talk to Coleman's ghost?"

They were guessing, just digging. I wasn't going to be the one to give them anything. I shoved the mic aside.

"No comment," John barked, guiding me down the first set of stairs.

The reporters made only a marginal path for us. Microphones cut between us, stranding me several steps down from John. I glanced back, but our goal was to reach the bottom. He'd catch up. More questions cut through the air, mics and cameras popping out of the crowd.

I was halfway down the stairs when the air behind me dropped ten degrees and corpse-cold fingers landed on my shoulders. The hands shoved, hard. I plummeted forward, throwing out my arms to break my fall. My wrist popped as I landed on it, but that didn't stop me. Momentum hurtled me ahead, and my skull cracked on the next step. My knee bounced off the cement. I rolled the rest of the way down the stairs and landed on my ass just in time to see a bullet sail through Death's incorporeal chest.

Chapter 3

※⟩◯⟨※

"**G**et off me." I shoved the EMT's hand aside, and a jolt of pain washed up my arm with the movement. Hot saliva filled the area under my tongue, bringing with it the burning taste of bile.

I swallowed it. There was no time to throw up, no time to let the pain pass. I had to keep moving. Keep pace with gurney. Keep the thread of magic steady. Something warm and sticky dripped into my eye. I wiped it away with the back of my hand, leaving a fresh streak of red on my forearm—the smear of blood was barely worth noticing compared to the other blood on me, most of which wasn't mine.

No, not my blood. John's. *From a bullet aimed at me.*

"Miss, please," the EMT hounding me said. He reached for my shoulder. "You need to follow me—"

I shrugged him off. "If I release this charm, we'll have an artery geyser. Again. Back off."

"You—"

I wasn't listening. All my attention was on keeping my fingers in contact with the charm. Thankfully, one of the reporters had been carrying a healing charm. The charm had kept John alive while we waited for the paramedics, but it wasn't designed to hold an artery intact. Above my hand, John's face was pale, damp. *Come on.* I milked my nearly depleted ring for more energy, boosting the borrowed charm.

Time moved in uneven jerks as I stumbled beside the gurney, away from the Central Precinct steps, toward the street. Then we were at the ambulance, John being lifted inside. I followed, sliding across the metal bench opposite the paramedic. The doors slammed and the ambulance lurched into motion, the screaming siren filling my ears.

As the medic strapped an oxygen mask over John's face, I siphoned the last drop of magic from my ring. Then there was nothing else.

Blood bubbled around the edges of the charmed disk.

Damn. "He needs a clotting spell."

"I thought—" The medic looked at the overloading charm, then grabbed a large adhesive bandage with an OMIH symbol stamped on the front. "On the count of three. One . . . Two . . ."

Three.

I jerked my hand away, taking the disk with me. The wound in John's throat oozed in the second before the medic slapped the charmed bandage in place.

It shouldn't have oozed. Arteries spray.

A monotonous screeching filled the air. The heart monitor—flatlined.

No.

The medic ripped John's shirt open, exposing his chest. Then he twisted, grabbing a pair of defibrillator paddles. He pressed them to John's skin. "Clear."

John's body jerked. Blood soaked into the gauzy charm at his throat.

My tongue filled my mouth, too big to swallow around, to breathe around. The monotonous beeping didn't let up. *Please no.* I couldn't watch, couldn't look away. I grabbed John's hand. It was damp, clammy.

"Clear!"

The medic knocked my arm aside, then pressed the paddles to John's chest again.

His torso vaulted a few inches in the air. The beeping broke, erratic sounds echoing in the small space. The electronic beep fell into a steady pattern again.

I let out a breath, and as if on cue, John's chest also lifted. The oxygen mask over his face fogged. His breath rattled, his chest lifting in shallow lurches, but he was breathing. I looked away.

"That bullet was meant for me."

"What?" The medic glanced up from where he was adding gauze to the charm on John's neck.

I shook my head. I wasn't talking to him. My gaze locked on the dark figure in the farthest corner of the ambulance. Death leaned against the back doors; his corded arms were crossed over the expanse of his chest. His eyelids hooded his gaze, but I could feel him watching me.

"Don't do it," I told him.

Death didn't move, but the medic leaned over John's body. He looked from me to Death's corner—a corner which probably appeared empty to him.

He pulled out a penlight, flashing it in my eyes. "Ma'am, can you please focus on my finger."

I did, but for only a moment before my gaze snapped back to Death. "He won't die," I said.

"We're doing everything we can," the medic said as he examined the gash in my forehead.

I met his eyes then, my hand gripping John's clammy palm. "He won't die."

*   *   *

"I tripped. I told you."

"You want me to believe you just happened to trip out of the way of a bullet?" Officer Hanson tapped his ballpoint pen against his notebook.

I tugged the pale hospital blanket tighter around me. Several hours ago it had been a heated blanket, but now the charm keeping it warm had given out, and it was an ineffective bit of fabric guarding me from the frigid hospital air. The blanket was doing better than the open-backed gown, though. Shivering did little to improve my already rotten mood, and I forced myself to take a deep breath before answering Officer Hanson.

"I fell. I don't know any other way to explain that to you."

"Ms. Craft, you had half the city's cameras pointed at you when the shot went off. I saw the film. You dove down those steps."

My head snapped up. "Do you think I'd have this"—I lifted my soft-casted wrist—"and a dozen stitches in my forehead if I 'dove' out of the way like you say?"

He leaned forward, towering over me, and tapped the pen to his pad, a staccato of cheap plastic hitting paper.

I wasn't impressed or intimidated. I was just irritated. In fact, I'd had enough with his looming.

I swung my legs over the side of the bed and stood. The muscles in my thighs ached, my back protesting. But, barefoot, I stood at eye level with Officer Hanson. "I told you. I. Fell."

His pen hung in midair a moment before tapping one more harsh note. Then his gaze dropped, and he closed the notebook. "Listen, Alex, we don't think you had anything to do with it. We're just trying to figure out what happened. Did you hear the shot? Did you see something? A suspicious car; a shadow on a roof? What made you dive down those stairs?"

"I—" What was I supposed to say: Death pushed me out of the way? That was a little outside a soul collector's job description. No one would believe it. Hell, I barely did. "I've told you everything I remember."

His lips pursed, but I was saved from his response by the arrival of my attending physician. He stepped around the curtain separating my bed from the rest of the ER and smiled. "Good news, Miss Craft. Your CT scan is clean, so I'm signing off on your release." He made a note in my chart. "I want you wearing that brace for the next few weeks. Your stitches are dissolvable, so they won't need to be removed. Just keep the wound clean. Any questions?"

I smiled. "Can you prescribe a ride home?"

I was joking—mostly—but Officer Hanson cleared his throat. "The sheriff thinks the shooting has something to with Amanda Holliday's trial. The idea of a shade on the witness stand has caused a lot of controversy. The sheriff's arranged for an officer to see you home and for an escort to the courthouse in the morning."

"Uh . . . Thanks?" *Could have mentioned that earlier.* You know, while he was grilling me like a suspect. I rubbed my good hand against my shoulder. The scratches still itched, but the doctor had assured me they weren't serious. I looked up at Hanson. Hopefully he wasn't my ride.

The doctor returned my chart to the foot of the bed and smiled. "A nurse will be by to check you out shortly. Have a good night, and try not to jump down any more stairs."

I showed some teeth. "Right." *Does everyone think I dove out of the way of that bullet?* I doubted I had the balls to take a bullet for someone else, but if I had known what was about to happen, I sure as hell would have warned John.

The doctor closed the curtain behind him, and I turned back to Hanson, waiting for the grilling to begin again.

He looked as weary as I felt. "If you remember anything, you'll call the station?"

"First thing," I promised, and I would. John was my friend. I'd do anything I could to help find who shot him. Hell, it was in my best interest for the shooter to be behind bars if he'd truly been aiming at me. I'd call if I came up with even the thinnest clue. Not that I'd forgotten anything, but the next time I caught up with Death, I had a bagful of questions for him.

Hanson rubbed his eyes and put the small notepad in his breast pocket. "Go home and get some rest. An officer is waiting for you in the lobby." His footsteps echoed on the linoleum as he disappeared around the curtain.

"Wait, what about some clothes?" Mine had been confiscated as evidence. I padded across the floor and ripped the curtain aside. "And I want to see John."

Hanson was nowhere in sight, but I startled a nurse heading my way. Her eyes flew wide, but her smile never slipped as she held out a small pile of fabric. "These will get you home."

Five minutes later I was dressed in purple polka-dot scrubs that fit like a pillowcase. At least the police had let me keep my boots. The knee-high black leather hid the fact the scrubs hit somewhere between my ankle and calf.

I signed the forms the checkout nurse handed me without reading them. Was this visit going to be expensive? *Of course.* Could I afford it? *Nope.* I scrawled my name by another red X.

"Ms. Craft, I'm sorry, but your insurance is being rejected."

I sighed. I assumed it would be—I'd stopped paying my insurance premium months ago. The attempt had been worth a shot, though. I took the worthless plastic card from her and dropped it in my purse. "You can bill me, right?"

She gave me even more forms. Once my signature was officially worn-out, I returned her clipboard. Only one more thing to do.

"Can you direct me to John Matthews's room?"

The nurse's smile wavered, and my stomach clenched. *No, he couldn't have . . . Death wouldn't have . . .*

He would. That was his job.

I swallowed around the lump in my throat. "Detective John Matthews. The cop I came in with. The one with the throat wound?"

She nodded, but the frown stayed firmly in place. "He's out of surgery, but I'm afraid visiting hours are over."

I let out a breath I hadn't realized I was holding. "You've got to be kidding me." *Who gives a rat's ass about visiting hours?*

Apparently my nurse.

"You're welcome to visit him tomorrow between nine a.m. and six p.m. Now, I believe the officer said your ride was waiting in the lobby." She pointed at a pair of double doors.

Right. I flashed her a tight smile before turning away. *I'll find the ICU on my own.*

I trudged toward the lobby on numb legs. John was out of surgery. That was a good sign. He'd be okay now.

I bit the inside of my lip and clenched the stiff hem of the scrubs.

Maybe he'd be okay. Only maybe. Death leaving a

soul in a body didn't mean the person stopped dying—
I'd witnessed that firsthand.

A shiver ran down my spine as I pushed open the
lobby door. A gleaming pair of elevators waited on one
wall. What floor was the ICU on? I could probably slip
in without anyone noticing. At the very least I'd get to
see John's wife, Maria. I needed to talk to her. To tell
her, to explain ... *what exactly? I dodged a bullet, and it
hit your husband instead?* Another shiver crawled over
my skin, tracing a clammy trail across the back of my
neck.

That was more than just drafty hospital air.

I flipped around, expecting Death's familiar form.
Boy, do I have questions for—

It wasn't Death.

A ghost stood behind me, his incorporeal form shimmering with unearthly light. A hospital wasn't a completely unexpected place to find a displaced ghost, all
things considered, but I recognized this ghost's slumped
shoulders, his unkempt hair, and his thick-framed
glasses. *The ghost from the morgue? What the hell is it
doing here?*

He frowned, his whole face pinching as he noticed
me looking at him, though by the intensity of his stare,
it was obvious he'd been watching me. *Was he following
me?*

I didn't have time to find out. He vanished, his presence slipping farther into the land of the dead. While
my psyche always gazed across the chasm separating
the dead and the living, I'd have had to drop my shields
to follow the ghost, and I was so not exposing my un-
shielded mind in a public place, especially a hospital
with hundreds of souls caught on the line between life
and death.

"Ms. Craft?"

I startled at the sound of the gruff male voice. Dismissing the ghost, I turned on my heels, searching for the speaker.

Oh no. My karma surely wasn't *that* bad.

Detective Andrews pushed off the wall where he'd been leaning. His stride consumed the distance between us, and he smiled, his full lips softening the severe angles of his face. But the smile didn't reach his eyes. I didn't bother returning the false-friendly gesture.

"I take it you're my ride," I said, attempting a cocky eyebrow lift. The sutured gash over my eye prevented the movement.

I received a grunt in reply as he strolled past me. Oh yeah, this was going to be a fun trip. I really shouldn't have hoped against Hanson being my ride. I shouldered my purse higher and fell in step behind Andrews. Since when did homicide detectives handle witness protection—or whatever I was considered? I still wanted to see John and Maria, but I got the distinct impression that if I told Detective Andrews to wait in the lobby while I snuck into ICU after hours, he'd haul me out of the hospital in handcuffs.

Detective Andrews's path bypassed the sliding glass entrance. Where were we going? *He can't seriously be about to interrogate me. Again.* I glanced back at the doors. "Aren't we leaving?"

He didn't slow down. "The last person who walked through a gauntlet of reporters with you got shot."

My shoulders lifted in an involuntary cringe, and I forced them back down. *Way to rub it in, jerk.* He couldn't have just said we were sneaking around reporters. Oh, no—he had to bring up John. I wrapped my arms around myself, bunching the oversized scrubs.

Andrews pushed open a door leading to a dimly lit corridor. Cinder-block walls lined the hall, and shadows ate away the corners. I hesitated. Years of using grave-sight had eroded my night vision, and navigating unfamiliar corridors shrouded in darkness wasn't high on my to-do list. Unfortunately, the detective continued without pause, and in a matter of steps the gloom swallowed his wide shoulders from sight. I hurried to catch up.

"So, how did you get drafted for escort service?" Not that I really cared, but I needed to fill the space with a sound other than the echo of our footsteps on the cement.

"I asked," he said without inflection. "This is our door." He pushed it open.

The door led to a multistory parking garage. A well-lit garage, thank goodness. As I stepped out of the corridor and the door swung shut behind me, the muggy air in the garage turned prickly.

A spell.

I skittered sideways, and my already-sore shoulder made impact with a body that hadn't been there the moment before. Or at least, hadn't appeared to be there.

Only I would jump *into* a spell, instead of away from it.

I reeled back. The concealment charm broke, and the petite woman who'd been hiding behind it—and whom I'd bumped into—narrowed her eyes before swiping a hand through her dark hair. It fell around her shoulders without a strand out of place, and she turned on her smile, thrusting a mic in my face.

"Ms. Craft, why do you think you were shot at today?"

I blinked dumbly at Lusa Duncan, the star reporter for *Witch Watch*. Behind her, her cameraman's red recording light blinked.

My first thought was to wonder if I'd thanked her for the healing spell she'd given me earlier. She was the reporter who'd had the charm that kept John from bleeding out on the Central Precinct steps. Then I registered what she'd asked, and I scowled. I was about to appear on the most popular news show in Nekros City wearing nasty purple scrubs.

I shot a desperate glance at Detective Andrews. He reholstered his gun and tugged his coat closed over the rig. Then he stepped between Lusa and me, knocking her mic aside.

"No comment," he said, throwing an arm over my shoulder and turning me to march away from the reporter.

Lusa didn't give up that easily. Her heels clicked on the concrete, trailing us. "Will you still be raising Amanda Holliday's shade in the morning?"

"Yes." No way in hell was I going to let some closed-minded gunman scare me into not raising Amanda.

My answer seemed to encourage Lusa to throw more questions. "Do you think the shooting had anything to do with what you learned from Coleman's body?"

Detective Andrews's fingers dug into my shoulder. A warning? I forced myself to keep moving, to not glance back. I wasn't an idiot. Lusa was digging. She had no idea whom I'd raised in the morgue. Only John and Andrews knew for certain that I'd so much as seen Coleman's body. John was in the ICU, and I had serious doubts Andrews had told anyone yet—especially the press.

Detective Andrews yanked a ring of keys from his pocket and hit a button. A car ahead of us flashed its headlights, chirping as it unlocked. My steps faltered. It gave Lusa a second to catch up, but I couldn't help it. The overhead lights reflected off the shiny finish of a red convertible, its top down, the black leather interior spotless.

That was so not police issue.

Unfortunately, I didn't have time to gawk. I slid into the passenger seat, the soft leather engulfing me. Andrews climbed into the other side, and the car cranked with the gentlest purr.

"Nice car." A major understatement.

Andrews threw the convertible in gear, and I trailed a hand over the bright red finish. *Probably fresh off the lot*—unlike my little hatchback, which had been factory assembled in the same decade witches came out of the broom closet.

The sharp echoes of Lusa's heels bounced off the cement columns as she rounded the car next to us, her mic extended. "Ms. Craft, did Coleman name his shooter? Do you think he was the same person who shot at you?"

Andrews reversed out of the parking spot in one fluid movement, forcing Lusa to jump back. Her mic hit the pavement, and Andrews switched gears.

The car zoomed forward.

"Call me!" Lusa yelled in our wake. I glanced at the sideview mirror in time to see her toss something.

No way would it reach us.

The small dot of what she threw grew larger in the mirror. It was catching up. The car turned the corner of the garage, and whatever she'd thrown followed a moment later.

I twisted in my seat. A pink origami crane flew over the back bumper and across the open rear seat. Its little triangular wings beat the air at a frantic speed, but Andrews was still accelerating, and the crane began to fall behind. I reached out, snatching it.

As I settled in my seat again the little crane unfolded, turning into a flat rectangle in my palm. In the center of the paper, in glossy black letters, was printed "Lusa Duncan, *Witch Watch*" and her phone number. A homing paper crane was quite an expensive spell for something as disposable as a business card, but I guess Lusa was used to her quarry running from her. I opened my other senses and scanned the card for additional spells. Nothing. It was just paper again. The fact that she hadn't tried to sneak a spy spell into the car, and that she'd helped when John was shot, improved my opinion of her. I dropped the card into my purse.

"I live in the Glen," I said as we reached the entrance of the parking garage.

Andrews made a left out of the garage without a word. The sky glowed rusty red from the city lights, but in my damaged vision, shadows clawed at the massive skyscrapers dominating downtown Nekros. I crossed my arms over my chest and angled my shoulders away from Andrews. There was only one reason I could think of for him to volunteer to drive me home, and I was *not* in the mood to answer any more questions.

Not that he cared.

"What did you see when you looked at Coleman's body?" Andrews asked before we reached the interstate.

Oh no, he did not get to pump me for information after kicking me out of the morgue. I readjusted my weight and stared at the darkness consuming the front window. "Do you know the corner of Chimney Swift and Robin?"

His eyes cut across the seat. "I know where you live. Tell me about Coleman."

"You want to know about Coleman? Watch the recording."

Light from a streetlamp trailed along his clenched jaw. "I've seen it. You lost control of one shade and claimed Coleman's body was enchanted despite the fact that a board-certified sensitive detected no spell. On top of that, you claimed the body might not be a body at all."

I cringed, but tried to hide it under a shrug. "You're right. I must be a hack magic eye. Why are you asking a hack questions?"

He slammed on the brakes, and the car jerked to a stop. My seat belt locked, but not before I braced myself on the dash. Pain spread along my casted arm. After the abrupt stop, Andrews rolled the car gently to the shoulder of the road.

We were between streetlamps, and the buildings around us were dark, so I could make out the man beside me only by the soft blue glow of the car's controls. I swallowed, hard.

Andrews regarded me with narrowed eyes that took on an eerie cast in the limited light. "Either you're a con artist who's been enjoying the limelight a little too much, or you found something everyone else missed."

I met his gaze. Held it. "Should I guess which you're inclined to believe?"

He frowned but didn't say anything, and the silence stretched. It filled the space between our seats, turned solid. A vehicle whizzed by, flooding us with its headlights, and I winced. When my vision cleared, Andrews had looked away.

"Let's try this again." The leather seat squeaked as he turned. "I'm Detective Falin Andrews, lead investigator on the Coleman case."

The shadowed outline of his hand appeared between us. Shaking hadn't gone well the first time we'd tried it. Still, I took his hand—his gloved hand, but in a car this hot, driving gloves were just another indulgence. His handshake was firm but professional.

"Falin," I said, since he'd given me his first name.

His fingers flexed around mine. "Alex." He dropped my hand. "Now, what can you tell me about Coleman's body?"

"Sorry. One handshake doesn't admit you to the good graces club."

"But one phrase said in anger—justified anger that someone was tampering with evidence in *my* case—is enough to bar me from it?"

I smiled at him. "First impressions suck that way."

His shoulders rolled back. "You have pertinent information about my case. I could arrest you for obstruction of justice."

And on to threats.

I sighed and glanced at the digital clock in the dash. "Late" had come and gone already. I definitely wouldn't be contacting Casey tonight. I'd have wait to tell her what I'd learned. For now, I just wanted to get home, feed my dog, and post a thread on the Dead Club forum to see if anyone had ever encountered a violent shade like Bethany's or anything at all like Coleman's body. Not to mention the fact I needed to recharge my ring before the trial, which was—I did the math quickly—in about seven hours.

Well, might as well get this over with. Suppressing a yawn, I rubbed the aching scratches made by Bethany's shade. Then, taking a deep breath, I tried to explain the spell I'd seen on the governor's body, describing as best I could the twisting glyphs and the way my grave magic slid around Coleman. As I spoke, Falin eased back onto the road.

"And you have no idea what the spell does?" he asked.

"I sort of got interrupted."

He let that pass. "Did Detective Matthews hire you to look at Coleman's body?"

I bit my bottom lip. Would John get in more or less trouble if raising the governor's shade had been his idea? I must have deliberated too long because Falin turned toward me.

I stared straight ahead. "Coleman was a favor. The only shade John asked me to raise was Bethany."

"The ritual victim."

Ritual? Did he mean like a methodical serial killer, or did he actually mean she was killed by a witch as part of a spell? John hadn't mentioned any magical connections, but something had seriously damaged Bethany's shade, so it wasn't much of a jump. I filed the information away. It might help me figure out how I'd "lost control," as Andrews put it.

We drove in silence for a while. As the skyscrapers vanished behind us the low hum of magic slowly infiltrated the air around the car. Not active magic, but the feel of the Glen.

The Glen, or Witches Glen, as it was called in some circles, was a clump of suburban sprawl surrounding Magic Quarter. The Quarter not only was the best place to shop for spells and supplies but also included the city's only private witchcraft prep school, a fae bar, and our local headquarters of the Organization for Magically Inclined Humans.

The convertible hit the bridge crossing the Sionan River, and the thrum of magic intensified. The Sionan River separated downtown Nekros from the Quarter and the Glen beyond. If you went west of the Sionan and weren't headed out of town, you were either magical or in the market for magic. Whether witches had originally built in the Glen because of the magical resonance, or the hum had grown from decades of magic being worked in a concentrated area, no other place in the city felt the same, and I relaxed as we drew closer.

"Who hired you?" Falin asked as he turned into my neighborhood.

"A client."

"His name?"

I didn't answer. Under normal circumstances, I didn't give out my client information. I definitely wasn't going to just hand Casey's name to Andrews. Not only was she family, but if word got out . . . My father and I might not see eye to eye on, well, anything, but I didn't walk around intentionally trying to cause scandals for him.

Falin pulled into my driveway, and I swung open the door before the car rolled to a stop. I didn't make it all the way out.

Falin grabbed my arm, his gloved fingers closing around my wrist. "Who hired you to examine Coleman's body?"

"That's confidential."

"Who knew you were looking at Coleman's body?"

"Besides you?"

His frown pulled his face down, making the shadows under his cheeks sharper. "Ms. Craft, while I'm sure your charming personality endears you to many people, is there anyone you know who would want to kill you?"

I froze, a chill crawling down my spine. "The sheriff thinks the shooting had something to do with the Holliday trial."

"That is one possibility. Who is your client? Who knew you were looking at either body today?"

I shrugged his arm away and climbed out of the car. The list of people who knew I was at the morgue was short: just the cops who'd given me a ride, John, Tommy, Falin, and, of course, Casey—and maybe my father, if she'd told him. No one on the list was likely to fire a gun into a crowd in front of the Central Precinct. The shooting had to be connected to the Holliday trail. Some nut didn't want a shade to take the stand.

"Thank you for the ride, Detective," I said, slamming the door behind me.

Unfortunately, slamming my door didn't keep him from opening his.

He slid out from behind the wheel. "Who hired you? Don't force me to get a warrant for your client list."

More threats? Okay, so I *had* been poking around his case. But, seriously?

I turned, ready to feed him a line of legalese about clients and privacy, but the words died on my tongue as a frigid wind lifted the hair off my neck. The temperature was still pushing the mid-nineties, with no breeze to speak of to cool the night. So, the tickling gust of cold air along my back was way out of place.

I spun around in time to see a shimmering pair of slumped, plaid-covered shoulders and thick glasses before the ghost disappeared. The ghost, the *same* ghost, from the morgue and then the hospital. Here. In my front yard. I cracked my shields just the slightest bit, so that my grave-sight overlay the world but didn't replace it. As the patina of decay washed over the yard the grass was simultaneously healthy green and withered brown, but there was no sign of the ghost. *He pulled back deep.*

Tightening my shields again, I frowned at the spot where the ghost had been. I was vaguely aware that Detective Andrews was speaking, but I waved him off and headed for the stairs to my loft.

"Ms. Craft!"

"Good night, Detective," I said, all but running up the driveway. I was thankful he didn't follow me.

I bypassed the front door—I rented the efficiency over the garage, so I had my own entrance. A path of evenly placed stepping-stones veered from the sidewalk, snaking around the side of the house. A spell on the flat stones made the pathway twinkle softly. As I stepped on the first stone the next lit up. The spell had been a birthday gift from my housemates last year when they realized how much damage my grave-sight had done to my night vision. I was more grateful than I let on.

The streetlights failed to reach the side of the house, and, as I hadn't planned to stay out so late, I hadn't turned my porch light on, so the glimmering stones were my only source of light. Two steps after rounding the corner of the house, I stopped. I couldn't have been far from the stairs leading to my loft, but the next stone was only a small sliver of light. I squinted. Something dark enough to absorb the spelled light covered the stone. The bit of light that escaped illuminated a pair of large paws sporting wickedly long talons.

"I've told you about blocking the path," I said, stepping off my stone.

The path dimmed, leaving me in what my bad eyes perceived as total darkness. I reached out, my hand finding the cool, stone head of our resident gargoyle, Fred, a three-foot, granite, winged cat. It had taken a liking to the spell on the stepping-stones, which was a real nuisance in a time like this. Using the gargoyle as a pivot point, I stepped around the hulking stone body until the path lit under my feet again. The glowing stones led right up to the base of the stairs.

My sore muscles protested the one-story climb, and by the time I reached my door, my body felt like an overstretched rubber band. A sticky sweat made the scrubs cling to my skin as I fumbled my keys into the lock. As I turned the doorknob a chill crawled down my neck. The ghost?

I spun around.

The ghost stood directly behind me, but I caught only a glimmer of his shape before he vanished again. *What is going on?*

Frowning, I pushed open the door, feeling my wards

slide over my skin as I stepped inside. PC, my loyal—
and recently very expensive—companion greeted me
with a wagging tail and an enthusiastic yip. Hairless
Chinese cresteds were pathetic in a cute way on good
days, but with one of his forelegs in a bright blue cast, he
was downright pitiable. I scooped him up awkwardly, my
own brace in the way.

"Sorry I'm so late," I said as he licked my chin. "But
look, we both have a cast now."

Okay, yeah, that wasn't really a selling point. I set him
down and watched him hobble around. He was moving
extremely well for having broken the leg only a week
ago. The cast would be off in a couple of days—long before the ER doctor would agree it was time for *me* to
take my brace off. Magically enhanced medicine worked
fast.

After watching PC a moment more, I turned back
to the door and twisted the bolt lock. My house wards
locked down with the bolt, buzzing lightly, and my
thoughts circled back to the ghost. *I wonder if the wards
will keep him out?* They weren't specifically designed to
keep out ghosts, though ghosts were mostly willpower
and energy, so if he was malicious, they just might bar
him. He'd tried to tell me something at the morgue, but
now he hid whenever I noticed him. What did he want?
And why the hell am I being haunted?

Chapter 4

ornamental divider

"**R**ise and shine," an overly enthusiastic voice announced as the inner door of my loft opened.

I pulled the pillow over my head. "If you aren't a sexy man bearing coffee, go away."

"Well, I don't think I'm bad," said Caleb, my landlord and good friend. "And this may be a fresh-brewed cup o' joe. Black. No sugar."

I pulled one side of my pillow away so I could peer up at him though sleep-blurry eyes. "Are you my fairy godfather?"

His lips twisted as he leaned down to scoop my robe off the floor. He tossed the robe at me. "Get up," he said in mock agitation, but I could hear the laugh rumbling under his deep voice.

Fairy godfather was a long-running joke between Caleb and me because he was, in fact, fae.

"So, what time is it?" I asked as I reluctantly rolled to my knees and shrugged on the robe.

"Eight forty-five."

I groaned. I'd been asleep less than four hours. When

I'd gotten home, I'd had to recharge my ring, and then I'd spent far too many hours searching the Internet for an explanation of the way Bethany's shade had acted and for any mention at all of glyphs like the ones I'd seen on Coleman's body—or whatever was posing as Coleman's body. Folklore was full of stories of the fae stealing a mortal and leaving a stock—wood or stone glamoured to look like a person—in their place. *But if the fae kidnapped Coleman...?* It didn't seem to add up. More sleep would probably help.

I collapsed back against my mattress. "Give me another hour," I whispered, my eyes drifting closed.

Caleb held the mug out, letting the delicious scent of dark-roasted coffee waft through my senses.

"You know," he said, "Holly left over an hour ago."

Holly, my final housemate and an assistant DA, believed in early mornings regardless of how late the night lasted. "Holly is a workaholic."

"And there is a cop downstairs who says he's your ride."

My ride? "Damn it—the trial! I have to get to the courthouse."

I rolled out of the bed, snagging the steaming mug of coffee from Caleb as my feet hit the ground. Not that I had time to enjoy the dark, bitter taste—I was too busy running around the one-room loft searching for the clothes I'd picked out to wear. Caleb at least had the decency not to laugh, much.

My introduction to Ms. Legal on the courthouse stairs consisted of an assessing glare under severely plucked eyebrows and the question, "Miss Craft, really—don't you own an iron?"

Twenty minutes later, I stood in the women's restroom, doused in dewrinkler, my hair pulled uncomfortably tight in a chignon, and with three inches of makeup caked on my face.

My OMIH-assigned babysitter, whose real name was Patricia Barid, dropped her blush brush and took my chin in her manicured fingers. "I think that's the best I can do," she said, but the corners of her eyes pinched together. "If you'd wear a complexion charm . . ."

I shook my head yet again. "I'm not raising a shade with foreign magic on me." I wasn't about to chance having my magic interact erratically in front of the entire courtroom, particularly after what had happened yesterday.

"Fine." She stepped back, her unimpressed gaze searching for something to pick at.

I fumbled for my hip pocket, but, of course, there wasn't one. Good slacks never had anything practical like pockets, and these slacks had been good once, before someone donated them to Goodwill and I picked them up. They were the best I owned, and I'd thought I looked pretty sharp. Right until I met Patricia Barid.

"It's not like anyone will be focused on me." After all, I was the wizard behind the curtain in this trial. The hard questions, like what was a shade, and why a shade couldn't lie, had already been addressed by an expert witness. I just had to raise the shade and then step back and let the attorney types grill her.

Patricia tilted her head and tittered. "That's what you think. This is history in the making, and you, my dear, are the face of the OMIH today." From the look she gave me, she clearly believed someone else should have been drafted for the job. Well, tough luck. I'd been part of this case since Amanda's body was found, and I was the one who was going to raise her for the witness stand.

It had been seventy years since the Magical Awakening, the day the fae decided to announce to the world that the good people of folklore truly existed. In an age of science and technology no one had believed in ghosts and goblins anymore, and there weren't even enough children clapping their hands and crying "I do believe in faeries" to sustain the fae. They had been fading from memory and from the world. So, they'd come out of the mushroom circle, as some say. Witches came out next and got organized. The folded spaces expanded. Magic blossomed. History had been made over and over since then—I just hoped my little piece of history was profitable.

A knock boomed on the wooden door, making me jump. We were out of time. I was expected in the courtroom. Patricia pursed her lips, but nodded.

"You'll do." She raked the cosmetics spread across the counter back into her oversized purse. "Don't use any flashy magic when you raise the shade. Just get the job done. And don't speak unless the DA asks you a direct question. And remember—"

I jerked the door open. "I got it." We'd been through this all already. Twice.

The bailiff waited outside the door, his hand poised to knock again. I gave him a tight-lipped smile and motioned him to lead the way. My boots made clunking sounds as I followed him down the hall, and then we were there, outside the courtroom.

I took a deep breath. *This is it.*

The bailiff opened a large oak door, and the courtroom fell silent as I stepped inside. People packed the rows of uncomfortable wooden benches, far too many for the AC—already overtaxed by the heat wave—to prevail against. A drop of sweat ran down my neck. Or maybe it wasn't the AC; maybe it was the fact everyone was staring at me.

A breeze picked up, to my relief, until I realized it wasn't an earthly wind. The ghost from the morgue crossed my path, his gaze sweeping over the courtroom before settling back on me.

What is he doing here?

I didn't have time to wonder.

The DA met me halfway across the room. "Doing okay, Alex?"

I nodded, smiling, and lost sight of the ghost. My gaze darted around the room. No sign of him. But I did spot several cops I knew, including Detective Jenson, John's partner. I nodded in greeting. I'd have to track him down after the trial to find out the latest news of John's condition. My gaze moved on but stumbled over a woman in the front row with puffy red eyes. Her clothes hung off her as though she'd recently lost a lot of weight. Despite her sallow cheeks, I recognized her face.

I almost swore; instead, I matched my pace to the DA's and dropped my voice to a whisper. "You're letting the family watch?"

The DA didn't even glance over his shoulder. "You'll be fine. Just do your thing."

He returned to his table, sitting down beside the journeyman attorney assisting him in the case. Holly, the assistant DA on the case and my workaholic housemate, had pulled her flame red hair back tight in a no-nonsense bun and was wearing a power suit. She looked imperturbable and stern, until she flashed me a double thumbs-up hidden from the crowd by her body.

That made me smile—Holly always could do that—and the rest of the walk to the front of the courtroom was a bit easier. I approached the stand but didn't take it. The chair had been removed to make room for Amanda Holliday's coffin. A witch, probably Patricia Barid or one of her PR minions, had sketched a circle around the stand and coffin before the courtroom filled this morning. All I had to do was activate it.

I closed my eyes. A soft murmuring spread across the courtroom, dozens of whispers wrapping together. I wondered how many of the spectators had known Amanda Holliday, and how many were here only to see her shade. Putting a shade on the stand had been discussed for years—after all, they were the perfect witness. Shades were just memories, with no agenda or self-awareness left in them. They couldn't lie, but would relate their life as they recalled it at the time of death. Despite that, no shade had made it to the stand. Until now.

I tuned out the crowd and focused on feeding energy into the circle until it sprang to life around me. Then I sank deeper, dropping my shields.

Amanda's next-door neighbor sat in the defendant's chair. Only two pieces of physical evidence put him there: a single blond hair found in his bed that was a visual match to Amanda but lacked a skin tag so couldn't be matched to her by DNA, and a receipt for gas in the county where her body had been found. The DA could prove he had the means and opportunity, but Amanda's eyewitness testimony was the only way the jury would be able to sentence him without reasonable doubt. The nature of the crime and the lack of evidence was what had finally convinced the DA to put Amanda on the stand. That, and the fact that if a jury sympathized with any victim, it would be with Amanda.

I poured my energy into her shade, trying to make her as physical, as real, as possible. A scream shattered the murmuring in the room, and my heart skipped a beat.

Did I raise another one?

No, it wasn't Amanda screaming. It was the crowd. People were screaming.

I opened my eyes. In my grave-sight, Amanda Holliday sat atop her casket surrounded by the rotted and pitted wood of the witness stand. She'd been buried in her Sunday best, but she'd died in a stained T-shirt, and that was what every cell in her body remembered and how her shade appeared.

The judge pounded his gavel, trying to restore order. Amanda's wailing mother had to be escorted out of the room. She wasn't the only one. Amanda's unseeing eyes appeared to watch them, her cherub face impassive. Being dead, she was no longer touched by the horror of her death. But it touched the jury, the crowd, and apparently the defendant. He'd turned paler than the shade, his eyes bulging as he stared at the five-year-old's body and the red gaping smile ringing her throat.

"To one of the shortest jury deliberations ever." Holly lifted her beer.

Tamara hoisted her own bottle. "To putting away the bad guys."

I clinked the rim of my bottle to theirs and took a deep swig of the room-temperature hops. As I set the bottle on the table, a shiver ran down my arms and I shrugged deeper in my blazer. I was probably the only person in the city wearing long sleeves, but I'd held the shade for over an hour. The chill had a way of clinging after that long.

Holly and Tamara had both abandoned the suit jackets they'd worn in the courthouse. And in a true show of celebration, Holly had let her red hair down from the stern bun she typically wore. She thought the bun helped her look more professional, but at five-two in heels and with her heart-shaped face, she always came off more cute than fear-inspiring—unless she caught you behind the witness stand.

In the corner of my darkened vision, I caught sight of a shimmering form hovering behind me. *That damn ghost.* I didn't bother turning around. No one else at the table could see him, and he'd just vanish if I did. It was what he'd been doing all morning. *Freaky haunt.* I ignored him.

"We make a pretty good team," I said to my companions, taking another swig of beer.

"I'll drink to that." Tamara brushed her long brown hair over her shoulder before lifting her beer bottle.

Holly nodded. "To teamwork."

We tapped rims again. Holly had worked in the DA's office to help prepare Amanda's case for trial, Tamara had performed the autopsy, and I'd raised the witness. Teamwork at its finest. All we were missing was our homicide detective. My stomach twisted at the thought of John. I'd talked to Jenson after the trial, and last anyone had heard, John was still unconscious. *How much blood had he lost?*

As if sensing my darkening mood, Holly leaned in and nudged me. "I think we're being scoped." She nodded over my shoulder.

It was early afternoon and the bar was mostly deserted, so there weren't a lot of options for who could be checking us out. The man at the table she'd nodded to had his back to me. In the dimness, and without my glasses—lost in my tumble down the stairs—all I could see of him was light reflecting off long blond hair.

My jaw clenched. *Why would . . . ?* I shook my head. It couldn't have been Detective Andrews. He wouldn't be in a little hole-in-the-wall bar like Mac's.

Mac's was the type of bar catering only to regulars. Situated in a little strip on State Street, several blocks from the courthouse, it had a used bookstore on one side, an artsy coffee shop on the other, and just a red door with no sign to mark the entrance. If Andrews had transferred in two weeks ago, there was no way he'd so much as *heard* of Mac's.

Still, how many men in this city had long platinum blond hair? I squinted, but my bad eyes couldn't make out any useful details. Not that it mattered. I twisted back around.

"You go for it," I told Holly as I drained my beer.

"Oh no." Tamara plunked down her empty bottle. "If I'd known this was a hunting trip, I wouldn't have come." Of the three of us, Tamara was the only one wearing jewelry serving no magical purpose, and that was a ring with a big fat diamond on it. As a charm witch she probably couldn't resist the temptation to enchant the engagement band much longer, but she and her fiancé hadn't even set a date yet, so she was still holding out. Holly and I had bets on how long she'd last before turning the diamond into a charm.

I smiled at Tamara. "Don't worry. This is a purely celebratory drink."

"Exactly. And it looks like we need another round." Holly waved a hand in the air, and Mac brought three more bottles as well as another basket of chips and salsa.

I lifted my beer. "To Amanda's testimony, the first of many victim voices heard in court."

"Good luck." Tamara tapped the rim of her bottle against mine.

Holly's bottle made a soft clink against mine, her movement restrained. "Alex, you know this will take time. The defense will drag this appeal through the courts."

The first guilty verdict based heavily on a shade's testimony? Yeah, I knew. In years to come this verdict would probably be a case lawyers cited, but no one would recall the details. Unfortunately, the DA wouldn't let me work another case until he learned what the higher courts decided. Which meant I was stuck with private clients a while longer.

I sighed into my beer, and the conversation moved on to what other cases we each had on our respective plates. I was probably a little too quiet and not as forthcoming as normal, because when the conversation paused, two pairs of eyes focused on me.

"Well, actually, I was hoping you could help me out with my newest case," I said, looking at Tamara. "I'd like to get a better look at Coleman's body. Think you can arrange a meeting?"

"It would be worth more than my job. Oh, and if that's why you were at the morgue yesterday, I don't want to know."

I paused with my beer bottle halfway to my mouth. "You didn't see the recording?"

"There wasn't one. I searched the hard drive. Not even a record of John turning the camera on." She frowned at her beer. "Which—if you did what I think you did—is a good thing."

I dropped my gaze to the salsa and concentrated on filling a chip. *How could the recording have disappeared?* I grabbed another chip. Falin had seen the recording; he'd admitted to as much.

Holly snatched the next chip I was reaching for. "Alex, tell me you didn't?" Her voice dropped to conspiratorial tones. "Coleman had a living will. No magic was to be used on him before or *after* his death."

I hadn't known that, though it didn't surprise me. I swirled the salsa. "I identified the Jane Doe vic. Her name was Bethany Lane."

"Thank goodness," Tamara said, obviously assuming— or at least, hoping—I'd been at the morgue only for John's case.

I didn't correct her misconception.

The silence built around the table. Tamara stared at her half-full bottle as if it held some secret deep in its depths. Shaking her head, she pushed it away.

"I should head out. I have several bodies on the table, and just because they're dead doesn't mean they should wait." She stood, her stool dragging across the scarred wood floor.

Boy, did I know how to kill a celebration or what?

Holly and I waved good-bye. Then Holly drained her beer. Setting it on the table with a hollow plunk, she leaned in and nudged my elbow. "You are still totally being scoped."

I glanced over my shoulder again. The man swiveled away as I turned, which was so not the most subtle move. *He does look a hell of a lot like Detective Andrews.* It couldn't be, though—could it? I frowned as I turned to face Holly. "I seriously doubt he's looking at me." *Unless it* is *Andrews.*

"He totally is. I've tried to catch his gaze—nothing. He is major eye candy. You should go for it."

"Are you forgetting?" I gestured toward my scraped and bruised face.

Holly twisted a ring off her pointer finger, and freckles crawled across her nose, up her cheeks, and into her hairline. I blinked. I'd seen her without the complexion charm before, but the mask of freckles she hid never ceased to amaze me. She pushed the charmed ring across the table, then dug a compact out of her purse.

When I didn't put on the ring, Holly frowned at me— one of those tight, disappointed frowns that rearranged her freckles. With a sigh, I slipped the ring on my pinky. The spell tingled, sliding over my skin, and I tried not to grimace—I hated the feeling of foreign magic on my body. Holly specialized in fire spells, but the complexion charm felt like her magic. Recognizing the spell and trusting the caster didn't alleviate my uneasiness with the magic washing over my skin. Holly's gaze moved in an assessing pattern over my face, and the way her eyes narrowed told me the charm hadn't worked as well as she'd hoped. She held out the mirror.

Between Ms. Legal's makeup miracle, and Holly's complexion charm, I almost looked normal. Almost. The stitches still trailed down my forehead, and there was swelling, but at least I looked less like the poster girl for domestic abuse.

Swiveling on my stool, I squinted. The man was facing the wall again. A gray jacket had been thrown over the back of his chair, and the sleeves of his oxford were rolled to just below his elbows. From where I was sitting, I could just make out the strap to a shoulder holster. *Damn. It is Andrews. Is he following me?*

Only one way to find out.

I slid to my feet, then hesitated, glancing back at Holly. "You won't leave without me?"

Holly was my ride home, and if she left me here I was screwed. My car was at the house. That whole not-being-able-to-see-after-raising-shades thing was a real downer when it came to keeping a two-ton chunk of steel between the yellow lines.

"Not unless you want me to." She flashed me a knowing smile.

I had a tendency to take guys home after raising shades. Nothing fought off the chill better than a stiff drink and a hot body against mine, but I was definitely not taking Andrews home. Holly flicked her fingers, urging me on. *If she only knew.* I wasn't going to tell her who he was, not yet. I wanted to find out where the video had gone first. My feet were overly heavy as I made my way across the room, but I'd pasted on a smile by the time I sank into the chair across from Andrews.

He looked up, his eyebrow lifting—a gesture I envied, as my sutures still prevented any cocky eyebrow lifting on my part—but his expression wasn't the least bit surprised that I'd invited myself to his table. "Miss Craft, is there something I can help you with?"

The smile that touched his lips was small, mocking. *How could Holly call him eye candy?* Okay, so he *was* easy to look at. But he was just so . . . irritating.

"Falin." I used his first name to annoy him. "I was actually wondering if there was something *you* needed? You appear to be following me." I flashed some teeth at him.

"Just stopped in for a drink." He lifted a glass, filled with more ice than clear liquid.

A twist of lime clung to the side of the small tumbler, but I doubted the contents were anything but water. Mac was a good bartender; you had to really piss him off to end up with that much ice. *Course, that's also a possibility.* I stopped forcing my smile.

"What happened to the recording?"

He didn't blink. His expression didn't change. His features just sort of stalled, as if he'd paused his face. Then his eyes narrowed, and his chin jutted to one side. "Of Coleman?"

I nodded. "The ME said there isn't even a log of John turning the camera on."

Falin slammed his tumbler on the table as he stood. He said nothing, but turned, grabbing his jacket in one movement. Then he marched toward the door.

I pushed out of my seat. "Hey, I wasn't done talking to you."

No response.

Had he seriously not known about the missing recording?

Holly made her way over, her eyes wide. "I take it that didn't go well."

I gestured to the door, which had just slammed. "That would be the lead homicide detective on Coleman's case."

Her lips formed an O, her brows scrunching together. *She doesn't know him either? Where did Falin transfer from?*

Wrenching the complexion charm from my finger, I handed it back to her. She'd already paid the tab, so I swiped the rest of our chips into a paper napkin. Then I made my way to the door. "I'll fill you in on the way home."

"Oh crap," Holly said, hitting the brakes.

I glanced out the front windshield. It didn't take a genius to guess what "crap" referred to. News vans lined the street outside the house. Reporters swarmed the sidewalk like mourners gathered around a celebrity grave. I saw several station call letters for national news channels.

"Caleb is going to kill me," I whispered, gaping at the cameras pointed at the house. Caleb enjoyed his privacy. My attracting a horde of reporters to his home wasn't going to make him happy.

I crouched lower in the passenger seat, trying to stay out of view. "There weren't this many outside the courthouse, were there?"

Holly shook her head and inched the car forward. As the car crept closer to the drive a couple of reporters caught sight of us. Then, as a whole, the milling mass turned and streamed forward, yelling questions at our closed windows. The car made slow progress, and Holly nearly committed vehicular homicide pulling into the driveway. The reporters obeyed the rules, though, and trespassed no farther than the front sidewalk. Of course, they didn't have to enter the yard to yell questions or point cameras at us.

"You get inside. I'll run interference," Holly said as she killed the engine. Her eyes darted to the rearview mirror, and her fingers brushed down the front of her immaculate courtroom power suit.

I only nodded. Holly was a lawyer: spin and PR were staples on her resume. We opened our respective car doors simultaneously. The assault of questions poured over us. Holly's smile was already working at full wattage as I ducked around the front of the car, headed for my loft.

"Miss Craft, do you have a statement about—"

"—first learn Coleman—"

"—you describe the pattern you saw on—"

"—fae responsible for the spell?"

I ground to a halt. I was catching only bits and pieces of questions, but it sounded as though they knew about . . . Whirling around, I spotted Lusa's face in the crowd. I pointed at her. "What did you ask?"

Lusa stepped forward, separating herself from the field of mics. "Can you guess the origin of the spell on Coleman's body? Is it fae or witch magic?"

The world tilted, and I could only stare at Lusa's perfect smile as my lips parted, my jaw going slack.

"Alex, go inside," Holly yelled.

I snapped my jaw shut and blinked at Lusa. *How the hell did Lusa know about the spell?* My gaze traveled over the mass of reporters. How did any of them know?

The recording.

I turned on my heel, running around the side of the

house and all but plowing over our friendly neighborhood gargoyle, Fred.

Fred wasn't the gargoyle's real name, but like most fae creatures, it wouldn't share its name. I'd started calling it Fred several years ago in an effort to irritate it into telling me something else to call it. To my dismay, the gargoyle seemed pleased with the name, or at least didn't care enough to object to it.

Though I'd never seen Fred move, it traveled the house perimeter, always staying near the garage. I typically left it a saucerful of milk, which the gargoyle seemed to like. I got the distinct impression it was guarding the yard from other gargoyles and that ours was a sought-after bit of territory. Magic called to magic, and Caleb used a lot of it. Of course, most of the diminutive fae living outside of the Faerie Knowe congregated in the Glen.

"*The green man will not like this attention*," Fred said inside my head.

"Tell me something I don't know," I muttered. "The green man" was what the gargoyle called Caleb. Without pause, I swerved around the stone creature. Then I took the stairs two at a time.

PC jumped at my feet—which he probably shouldn't have been doing no matter how well his leg was doing—but that didn't prevent him from begging for attention as I dashed inside. I didn't even pause. Crossing the room, I wiggled my finger in the hole where the TV's power button should have been until the screen buzzed and filled with color.

Lusa Duncan appeared on the screen, with my house as a backdrop. "—where Alex Craft has just arrived home. As of yet, we have received no answers about Alex's shocking revelation about the late governor in the video that appeared only hours ago on multiple Internet sites." The screen cut, and my face appeared. My eyes glowed with grave magic as I stared down at the bared head and chest of Coleman.

The TV image of me looked up at someone offscreen, voicing my words from the morgue the day before, but I could barely make them out. The static of panic filled my ears, drowning out sound. The screen changed again, this time showing the steps of Central Precinct as Detective Andrews stormed up them, lifting his arm to buffer the barrage of microphones.

"—As of yet, the Nekros City Police have issued no comment as to the validity of the video," Lusa's voiceover said as Falin reached the top step.

He looked back, and the cameraman zoomed, focusing on Falin's face. Icy blue eyes dominated the screen. Really pissed-off eyes.

Eyes I could have sworn were looking right at me.

Chapter 5

＂You stupid Web page.＂ I typed another command, but it was no good. I couldn't hit the back door into the site. Disgusted, I tabbed over to a new page. I'd been attempting to find the original version of the leaked video for almost two hours, but the file had spread like a virus over the Internet. News stations, blogs, boards, torrents—it was everywhere.

My phone buzzed beside my laptop, and I glanced at the display. The number wasn't familiar. I hit the button to send it straight to voice mail, which was probably full by now. Every reporter in the nation had apparently found my number. I was surprised I hadn't heard from Casey yet. With any luck, it would be a couple of more hours before she saw the video. I wanted more information before I talked to her.

PC, who'd been asleep in my lap, lifted his white-crested head and looked at me, clearly annoyed with my outburst. He stood and circled, but apparently couldn't get comfortable. His back legs bent as he prepared to launch himself from my lap.

"No, you don't," I said, almost absently, as I grabbed him and gently set him down on the floor. His nails clicked and his cast thumped on the hard wood as he moseyed over to check his bowl. His empty bowl—he'd already eaten all the chips I'd snagged from Mac's.

"Dinner later," I told him, then turned back to the computer. A chilled wind danced over my exposed shoulders.

That damn ghost.

I'd had about enough of his haunting gig. I flipped around. The ghost stood directly behind me, leaning forward as if he'd been reading my computer screen. My knees brushed his leg as my chair spun, and he jerked back, his eyes flying wide.

I expected him to disappear, to hide deep in the land of the dead as he had a half dozen times in the past twenty-four hours. Right now I was irritated enough to follow him across the chasm.

But he didn't fade. His gaze flicked from where my knees had brushed him, up to my face. Then his lips shot into silent motion. I shook my head. *Oh, so he's finally ready to talk?*

His hand shot out, and grave-cold fingers wrapped around the bones of my wrist.

I yelped, leaping off the barstool. It swayed and crashed forward through the ghost, slamming into my calf as it clattered to the floor.

The ghost's grip never wavered. He stepped sideways, out of the rungs of the stool. His mouth never stopped moving.

Not that I could hear him.

"Get your hands off me before I exorcise your ghostly ass." Okay, so I lacked the magic to back up the threat. But he didn't know that.

Or maybe he did. His grip tightened, his fingers pressing into my flesh. His lips moved in slow, exaggerated words, and he pointed at me with his free hand.

Right—he wanted me to do something. Well, I wanted him to *let go*.

I concentrated on my mental shields, focusing on the wall of living vines that enclosed my psyche and separated me from the land of the dead. There were always gaps between the vines, small holes that let me gaze across the chasm and interact with ghosts and soul collectors. Sealing my shields completely was exhausting and rather like closing my eyes and sticking my fingers in my ears. But it wasn't impossible.

I visualized the vines slithering tight around each other. In my mind's eye, dagger-length thorns sprouted from the green tendrils, the red-tipped barbs a clear warning.

The ghost's fingers slipped through my wrist, leaving grave-chill clinging to my bones. His shimmering form faded to translucent. He frowned, staring at his hand. He reached out again, and again his hand passed through my arm.

I smiled. Judging by the way the ghost backed up, it wasn't my most welcoming smile. He held up his hands, palms forward, and mouthed something, which could have been anything from "I'm sorry" to "please help."

One day I had to learn to read lips. But not today.

I crossed my arms over my chest and took a step back. "Let's establish some ground rules. First of all, I'm not in the business of helping wandering souls exact final revenge or pass messages from beyond the grave to loved ones. Got it?"

His frown deepened, but he nodded.

"Good. Now, I'm guessing you started following me at the morgue. Do you know something about one of the bodies?"

His lips parted and he nodded vigorously enough that he had to push his shimmering glasses back up his nose.

Okay; I was starting to get somewhere. "Which body?"

His mouth fell into motion, his arms emphasizing what was obviously a lively explanation. I held up a hand to stop the silent rant, and the ghost slumped his shoulders, an inaudible sigh disturbing his shaggy hair.

Right—yes-or-no questions, Alex. Duh. I cleared my throat. "Do you know something about Governor Coleman's death?"

The ghost cocked his head to the side, as if considering my question. Then he nodded, one slow rise and fall of his head.

Well, that wasn't the most reassuring or enthusiastic response, but it was better than nothing.

A drop of sweat dripped from my hairline, the moisture carving a line down to my chin. I couldn't keep my shields locked this tight for long. I nodded to the corner of the room and motioned for the ghost to follow as I made my way to the circle etched in the floor. Residual power buzzed at the edge of the circle, despite the fact the barrier was currently dormant.

"In you go," I said, pointing at the ghost.

He scowled at the etched line and shoved his balled fists into the front pockets of his baggy jeans.

"Hey, you want to talk to me? You go in the circle. That, or you find some other grave witch to haunt." I seriously hoped he didn't take me up on the latter if he honestly knew anything about Coleman, but he'd already learned I was tangible to him, and if I dropped my shields enough to hear him, we'd be very real to each other. I wasn't risking it if he wasn't trapped.

His inaudible huff made his shoulders slump farther, but he trudged into the circle. I channeled magic from my ring into the barrier before he could change his mind. As the translucent blue wall materialized between us I smiled and eased back on my shields. My mental vines uncoiled, and I coaxed them into opening more gaps than normal, enough so that while I wasn't straddling the chasm between the living and the dead the way I was when I raised shades, my psyche was still reaching pretty far across it.

I blinked as my grave-sight turned on, and the decaying world of the dead superimposed itself over my apartment. The purgatory world's crumbling plaster and weak gray light juxtaposed themselves over my solid beige walls, both real and not. I focused on the ghost.

His hair was a deep chestnut brown, and the frames of his glasses were the thick black plastic that tended to emerge and fade from fashion among sophisticates and emo kids alike. The flannel shirt he wore was almost as drab and colorless now as it had been when I was looking with my shields in place, but the baggy jeans were deep blue.

"What's your name?" I asked.

The ghost frowned at me, and at first I thought he wasn't going to answer, which would have been ironic considering how he'd been yelling while I couldn't hear him, but finally he shrugged and said, "Roy Pearson."

I nodded acknowledgment, but it wasn't a name I'd ever heard mentioned at the station. Not that there was any reason for me to know about most of the corpses that passed through the morgue. Ghosts were more adaptable than shades, their appearance often reverting to their perception of themselves as opposed to the actual state in which they died, but if Roy was truly a male in his early thirties in decent health—well, decent if he weren't dead—he'd probably wound up in the morgue by foul play.

It would have been polite to ask about him and how he'd died, but he'd been haunting me, I'd been shot at, and I had a swarm of reporters buzzing around. I wasn't feeling polite. "So, Roy, what do you know about Coleman's body? I'm guessing it's stock, right? Something glamoured or otherwise spelled to look like Coleman?"

"Coleman." His lips curled back as though he could barely stand the feel of the name passing over his tongue. "Everyone keeps going on about Governor Coleman." He looked at me, his eyes bright behind the glasses. "You bring justice to the dead, right? Like you did for that little girl."

I frowned. "Little girl" had to refer to Amanda Holliday. I'd already told Roy I didn't get involved in avenging the dead. For one thing, ghosts were sentient, so they had agendas and could lie. For another, they didn't have a currency.

"Listen; I'd like to help you, but—"

He cut me off. "That body everyone is so worked up about? It's real, all right. It just doesn't belong to Coleman. It's mine."

Chapter 6

"Back up. What do you mean, it's your body?" Even as I asked, possibilities were running through my head.

"Just what I said." The ghost shoved his fists in his pockets. "I'm the one who is dead on that damn slab."

I frowned. I'd had nothing but questions since I'd seen the spell on Coleman's body—not that I'd had much time to think about it. But my stock theory made the most sense, both because of the way my grave magic failed to latch on to the body and because of the basis of stock in folklore. Of course, most folklore was nonsense, but there were grains of truth in it. Even now, seventy years after the Magical Awakening and the fae coming out of the mushroom ring, stock had never been proven or disproven to exist. You can bet that every case of SIDS was carefully examined.

Though the stock theory did give me something to report to Casey to justify my fee.

But the problem with the theory kept circling back to the same question. If the fae were responsible for the assassination of the governor, why would they keep his body two weeks and then plant a fake? It didn't make sense. Of course, Roy wasn't disputing the fact the body was stock—or, at least, not disputing that it was something spelled to look like something else. He was saying it really was a body. *Just not Coleman's body.* Which still didn't explain why it didn't register as dead.

I chewed at my lip and looked up at Roy. He was watching me, as if waiting for my thoughts to settle before he said any more.

Whatever he saw in my face seemed to reassure him, because he let out a breath. "You believe me. Do you know how long I've been waiting to tell someone?"

"I'm guessing about two weeks?" That was when the surveillance camera caught the shooting. Now that I really examined Roy, he did look as though he could have been Coleman's unkempt younger cousin. His frame was right, and his hair, if cut, would have been identical. His eyes, too. It made sense that you'd find a body that already looked similar to the person you were making a stock of. Poor guy, murdered because of a vague resemblance.

Roy shook his head. "Two weeks? Try twelve years."

"Wait. What?"

"Twelve years that bastard has been walking around wearing my stolen body. Then he goes and gets it shot and just abandons it. But will anyone ever know what happened to me? No. They'll bury me under his fucking memorial, and my family, my girlfriend, will always be left guessing."

My head reeled, and I backed up. My thighs bumped into my bed, and I sank onto the mattress. *Twelve years?* That would be about the time Coleman showed up on the Nekros City political scene. If what Roy said was true, everything Coleman claimed to be, everything he claimed to believe in, was a lie. *That is, if I believe the ghost.*

"Prove it." My voice was low, contained, and I was proud it didn't waver with the uncertainty in my head.

Roy glared at me. "How the hell do I prove something like that?"

That was a good question. "How was it done?"

"I don't know. I'm—I was—human. Coleman—he went by Aaron then—put me in a circle and ripped a hole in reality. This ghastly specter of a girl walked through, and between the two of them, they cast the ritual. I don't remember all of it, just the shattering, tearing sensation as I was jerked from my body. Then Aaron collapsed, and my body stood up, walking around without me in it. Bastard is a body thief." Roy paced as he spoke, and in my grave-sight I could see the air around him contracting and sparking. I was glad I'd circled him. He was one strong ghost.

My brain felt as though it was one step behind in this conversation. Every question Roy answered created a half dozen more. Who was Coleman? Scratch that—more important, *what* was Coleman? And what kind of spell could possibly rip one soul out of a body and let another one in?

I took a deep breath, trying to realign my thoughts. Everything Roy had said was impossible, or at least highly improbable. *And before the Magical Awakening, science and logic were the only truths. Even children didn't believe in magic.* I let out my breath.

"Okay, say I believe you. Does that mean Coleman is really dead or that he switched bodies?"

Roy looked at his feet. "He conned another sucker out of a body."

"Who?"

He shrugged.

"Well, what did he look like?"

Roy's face scrunched up as if the effort of remembering was hard on him. Then he shrugged again. "Middle-aged guy. Brown hair."

Great. That described half the men in the city. I glanced away, and my gaze dragged over my television. It was hard to see the screen with my grave-sight insisting it was shattered, but I was still enough in the land of the living to make out the distorted image of my father, Lieutenant Governor Caine. *Actually, Governor Caine, now that Coleman's dead.* I'd muted the TV hours ago, but now I walked over and turned up the volume. *I can't wait to find out what Daddy Dearest has to say about my film debut.*

I didn't get a chance to hear. By the time I got the volume up, Caine had stopped speaking and the anchor reappeared, a photo of my father superimposed in the background.

The anchor smiled so hard at the camera, his lips barely moved as he spoke. "It sounds like Governor Caine is picking up right where the late Governor Coleman left off."

My mouth went dry as grave dust. My father was a middle-aged man. With brown hair. I whirled around, my eyes locking on Roy as I pointed at the screen. "Was it him? Was it Governor Caine's body?"

The ghost squinted at the screen. He shook his head, and the world righted itself. I hadn't even realized how worried I was until the weight lifted off my shoulders. My father and I had our differences, and we might not have been speaking currently, and well, we'd pretty much disowned each other, but that didn't mean I wanted his soul ripped out of his body and left to wander.

Roy finished his headshake with a shrug. "I don't know. It could have been."

The tension wrapped around me once again. "How can you not know?"

"I've been dead twelve years. After a while, the living I don't know all start looking the same." His bottom lip puckered out.

Perfect. A pouting ghost. Just what I need. The TV anchor had moved on to a new story, and I hit the mute button again. Then I walked to the bed and sat down. The mindless movement gave me a moment to collect my thoughts.

"Okay, so it boils down to this," I said, pulling my legs onto the bed and sitting cross-legged. "You have been following me because you want me to let people know your body was stolen. You say Coleman stole a new body before discarding yours, but you can't tell me more than a vague description of the new victim. I miss anything?"

Roy smiled. "I might not know anything about the victim, but I know where the recent switch occurred. I can show you."

I wrote down the address Roy gave me. I was vaguely familiar with the area, but when I cranked up my car, I didn't head straight for the building. After all, if Roy was to be believed, I was about to break into the scene of a crime. I needed to make sure the press didn't track me straight to it.

So I cruised downtown a while, constantly glancing in the rearview mirror to watch which vehicles were following me. Then I hit the interstate headed east toward Georgia. After about ten miles, I flipped around, passing Nekros to head toward the Alabama border. Once I was twenty miles away from the city proper, I made a quick exit and jumped on an old country road. There was no way anyone could follow me on the narrow unpopulated dirt road without my noticing.

They say that before the Magical Awakening, technology had made the world a smaller place. I think the saying had something to do with communication, and wasn't meant to be literal, but one thing was certain: the resurgence of magic made the world bigger. The fae called the new areas that appeared "folded spaces" and claimed the land had always been there—mortals simply hadn't perceived it before. Nekros City was built in the very center of such a space.

Inside the city and the surrounding suburbs, Nekros wasn't unlike any other city in America, but in the country, things were different. Wilder legends haunted the forests, and creatures of old were rumored to live in the floodplains below the city. The very air seemed untamed, as if it resented the growing human influence.

I kept my doors locked as my car kicked up dust on the dirt roads. After I crossed the Sionan River on an old stone bridge rumored to predate the Magical Awakening, I angled north, reentering the city. Then I took back roads into the warehouse district in the south of the city.

By the time I reached the address Roy had given me, almost two hours had passed, but at least I knew no one had followed me. I glanced at my phone as I climbed out of the car. I wished I could call John and run everything by him. *But I can't, and even if he were out of the hospital, he wouldn't know what to make of Roy's story.* I certainly didn't.

Looking up at the sprawling warehouse in front of me, I crossed the gravel pit I'd parked in. I kept telling people I was a PI, not just a magic eye, so it was time to start investigating.

Roy had told me that the loading docks were covered with aluminum siding, and that one of the sheets of aluminum in the center dock was loose, providing easy entrance to the bay where the ritual had been performed. Finding the dock wasn't a problem, but moving the panel with one hand in a brace wasn't the easiest thing I'd ever done.

The panel screeched as I dragged it across the cement dock bed, but I couldn't budge it more than a foot. *Well, here goes.* I shimmied through the hole I'd opened and was consumed by the gloom encasing the old warehouse. I blinked, trying to give my eyes time to adjust. Slowly, mounds of dilapidated and forgotten crates came into focus. I made my way around the closest. *There must be five years of dust on this thing. Could anyone have been here recently?*

I knelt, peering down at the dust around my feet. There were definitely more shoe prints than just mine in the room. *Could belong to vagrants escaping the elements.* Or, Roy could be telling the truth.

I crept around several more crates. Nothing moved in the gloom. No sound but my own clunky boots on the cement floor. I stepped over a rotted piece of plywood. Shadows clung everywhere, but the place looked undisturbed.

A chill crossed my neck, and I jumped. Whirling around, I found myself face to face with Roy.

"I was wondering if you'd join me," I said.

He smiled and said something I couldn't hear. It looked a lot like "This way," and considering he stepped around me and headed for the door set in the inner wall, I assumed that was it.

"Okay, you lead," I said, falling in step behind him.

I don't know what I expected to find in the next room. A body, maybe. Though I guess that didn't make sense, as Coleman/Roy's body had already turned up, and the other body was off walking around. What I didn't expect was to find nothing.

Literally nothing.

The room had no boxes. No scattered wood beams.

No broken crates. There wasn't even dust on the floor. The massive room was just a large empty cavern lit by a couple of skylights in the roof.

Roy walked to the center of the room and gestured to the floor as if to say "here." I frowned at him. This wasn't useful. This wasn't . . . anything. It was just a big empty room.

I stepped farther inside, and a tingle of magic brushed my bare arms. My breath caught in my throat. The touch of magic was oily, sinister, but it wasn't active. Whatever I was feeling was a residual taint left by a ritual. The magic brushed against me again, as if tasting me, and the scratch wounds on my shoulder ached. *Oh, I don't like the feeling of this.* Which, of course, meant I had to dig deeper.

I was a natural sensitive, nowhere near Tamara's level, but I had a knack for locating and deducing the purpose of spells. If only I could cast half of what I sensed. This spell, though, whatever had happened here, my mind tried to shy away from. *Maybe my subconscious is smarter than me.* I took several more steps into the room. The residual magic wrapped around me. It felt slimy, like being tangled in seaweed.

I crinkled my nose and closed my eyes, focusing on the spent magic that had been absorbed by the floor, the walls. The taint of magic swirled around me. More than one spell, one ritual, had to have been cast here. The chaotic jumble of magic battered my shields, each touch leaving behind a film of darkness. The spark of the inactive circle was directly in front of me, and I stepped across it.

I shouldn't have.

The magic, which had only tainted the air before, roared like a tempest inside the circle. Still inactive. Still spent. But it crashed over me. Terror tore at me. Not my terror, not yet, but something outside trying to get in. Echoes of screams roared in my ears, and the scratch on my shoulder turned cold, like a dagger of ice ripping into my flesh, hitting my soul.

The taste of bile filled my mouth, and my eyes flew open. I was still in the empty room. Nothing was here. Nothing but the memory of a spell that was trying to rip me apart. *And it's not even active.*

I backed up all the way out the door, out of the reach of the magic. My breathing was ragged, and I forced myself to draw in a lungful of air. Hold it until the count of three. Let it out. I repeated the exercise three times before I felt confident I could speak. "I've seen enough."

Roy frowned at me, and whatever he said was clearly a protest to my leaving.

I crossed my arms over my chest, feeling chilled despite the heat wave. "I believe you, okay? It's time to go." Because I wasn't going back in that room. Whatever magic had been worked in there had been big. Big and dark, and quite definitely evil.

PC met me at the door, his plumed tail wagging. I dropped my purse on the counter and scooped him up. He needed a bath; oil coated his gray skin, and the white crest on his head hung in limp clumps. I put bathing him on my list of things to do after I talked to Casey, saw John, and researched Roy's story. Oh, and tried to figure out what kind of spell would allow someone to steal bodies. Not necessarily in that order.

PC wriggled in my arms. I plopped him down, and he ran to his bowl, staring at the emptiness inside. He wasn't a fan of his recent switch from free feeding to rationed kibble.

"Yeah, I'm hungry too," I told him. It was early for dinner, but breakfast hadn't happened for me, and lunch had been chips. I grabbed the bag of far-too-quickly-diminishing dog food and measured out half a scoop for PC. Then I pulled open the fridge. I had an empty carton of cream, a pickle, and a single hot dog.

I grabbed the hot dog

PC had already finished his kibble, so I ripped off the top third of the hot dog and tossed it to him before taking a large bite of the remainder. *Mmmm, reprocessed and unidentifiable meat product.* I bit off another mouthful. At my feet, PC whined, yipping again.

"I outweigh you, mutt."

He lifted his front paws, crossing them in the air. One paw hung funny where it emerged from the bright blue cast.

"Fine." I tossed him another piece of the hot dog.

Stuffing the last bite in my mouth, I opened my laptop and typed "Roy Pearson" into the search box. I ran a records check, searching for speeding tickets, marriage applications, land purchases—anything that would have been uploaded to the net as public record. As I sifted through the mostly erroneous results, I couldn't help thinking that Rianna, my roommate and best friend from the best years I'd spent at academy, would have been thrilled by this case. We were both grave witches and had decided to open a PI business after we both graduated, but she'd been the one gung-ho about becoming some sort of super sleuth. I'd been the one who went along with the idea mostly because I couldn't *not* raise shades, so I figured I might as well get paid for doing it. But by the time I'd graduated from college, Rianna had disappeared. Searching for her had put everything I'd learned about being a private investigator to the test, but I'd never found a trace of her. Sometimes people just vanished—which usually meant they were dead. *Like Roy.* The only legitimate hit in my search for the ghost was a missing persons report. Filed twelve years ago. *Damn. Everything Roy said could be true.*

Three loud bangs on my door jerked my attention away from the computer screen. *If that's a reporter . . .*

PC growled, charging the closed door and barking—not that anyone would be afraid of a seven-pound hairless dog with a pretty white crest on his head and cute white puffs on his feet. PC didn't know that, though. I peeked around the curtain in the door and groaned. Pasting on a smile, I jerked it open.

"Can I help you, Detective?"

Falin stepped around me, shoving his way into my little loft. His eyes scanned the room.

"Hey, I didn't invite you in."

He grunted and walked a circuit around the room. His gaze traveled over the clothes piled in front of my dresser, my unmade bed, and the dishes in my sink, and finally stopped on my laptop. He stepped forward, tilting the screen back so the angle was better for a standing person.

"Hey!" I slammed the lid shut. "Was there something you wanted?"

I'd talked to Holly, and we were pretty sure I couldn't be arrested for attempting to raise Coleman's shade. Oh, the executives of his estate could sue me, though what would they take? My broken TV? But I didn't think Falin was here to arrest me. At least, I hoped not.

His jaw clenched, making his lips purse, and he looked around again. This was starting to feel a lot like an illegal search and seizure. PC sniffed Falin's leg, looked up at the tall man, sniffed again, and then apparently decided Falin was no threat and launched himself onto the bed. He curled up in the center of a pillow and closed his eyes.

Well, good to know my faithful companion isn't worried.

"Detective Andrews, what do you want?"

He finally turned and looked at me. "Stay out of the Coleman case."

"Okay." I'd learned about as much as I wanted about the body in the morgue. I definitely wanted nothing to do with the spell I'd felt. As soon as I confirmed that my father hadn't been the most recent victim, I was turning everything I'd learned over to cops in the Black Magic Unit, or maybe to the FIB, the Fae Investigation Bureau.

My phone buzzed, and I fumbled for the button to send it to voice mail without glancing at the display.

Falin scanned my face as if he was searching for a lie, but apparently I passed the test. "Are you going to tell me your client, or wait for the press to dig him up for me?"

"Why are you so convinced my client had anything to do with the" — *Oh crap* — "shooting?" If Coleman had stolen my father's body, and then Casey told him she'd hired me to look at the discarded body, he might have been afraid of what I'd find. Falin might have been right in disagreeing with everyone else in the police force about the shooter's motive. The shooting may have had absolutely nothing to do with the Holliday trial and everything to do with Coleman.

I tried not to let my thoughts show on my face. I was good at obstinate, and I pasted stubborn refusal all over my expression.

Falin frowned at me, but with a nod, he headed toward the door. He stopped before reaching it and turned back. "Keep your head down. You've attracted a lot of attention."

"Right." Like the mass of reporters circling my house hadn't alerted me to that fact.

The phone buzzed again. *Persistent much?* I glanced at the display, and my hot dog decided to disagree with my stomach. CASEY flashed in bold on the phone's screen. *Damn.* I had no idea what I was going to tell her.

Falin hadn't failed to notice the change in my face, and he looked a little too interested. I flashed a smile at him.

"Personal call, Detective. If you please." I gestured to the door.

His jaw clenched again, but he saw himself out. I locked the door behind him before flipping open my phone.

"Casey," I said in greeting, holding the phone slightly away from my head and fully expecting an earful.

She didn't disappoint me. "Alexis, what is the meaning of this? I haven't heard from you, but I saw the video on the news, and—"

I cut her off. "I think maybe this is something we should discuss in person."

Chapter 7

My old hatchback choked, sputtered, and then died in front of the wrought-iron security gate. I didn't bother cranking her back up, but leaned out the window and twisted so I could use my right hand to hit the button on the intercom. Again.

I waited, drumming my thumb on the steering wheel as I stared at the gate. I hadn't stepped foot on this property since the summer after I turned eighteen. That had also been the year my father joined the Humans First Party. Hopefully, my stalled-out hatchback was lowering his property value.

Finally the intercom squawked, filling with static before a gruff voice barked, "State your name and the purpose of your visit."

Friendly guard—just the way my father liked them.

"Hi, how are you?" I smiled at the monitor.

The guard didn't answer.

"Can you believe this heat wave? I have an appointment with Casey Caine."

The box squawked again. "Name?"

"Alex Craft."

The static cut off, and a sharp buzz announced the gate unlocking. Well, at least Casey had told the guard to expect me. I cranked my car and crept it up the magnolia-lined drive. The drive turned, and the house came into view. Scratch that; it was more a mansion than a house. After all, normal houses didn't have ballrooms.

I parked in the circle near the front entrance and pushed the car door, but it stuck. Again. I was going to have to get that looked at, you know, once I was eating regularly. I threw my weight into the door, and it swung open.

The butler, a graying man with a puffy red nose that betrayed his evening vice, answered the door. He stood out of the way, motioning me to enter in good butler fashion, but faltered in midstep, the door still only half open. "Miss Alexis?"

"How are you, Rodger? Father driven you insane yet?"

He smiled, and the smell of fermented fruit washed over me. Apparently Rodger no longer restricted his vices to his off hours. "Mr. Caine is his usual self. A busy man. He is at the statehouse this evening."

Thank goodness for small favors.

Sharp footsteps clicked on the marble floor beyond the door. "Alexis?"

Rodger straightened at the female voice and moved aside so I could enter. Casey, younger than me by four years, couldn't have been any more different. Where I was tall and sticklike, she was short and curvy. Normally she was all gloss and sophisticated charm, but today her blond hair hung limp around her face, and her blue eyes were red and swollen. Still, in her black silk top, black capri pants, and Gucci sandals, she looked like a fashion magazine had done a spread on a high-end mourners' line.

Despite the evidence of crying, she was the picture of poise. She stood with one hand on the balcony and the other on her hip. "Rodger, can you prepare coffee? We'll take it in my suite." She turned without waiting for his reply, her heels snapping softly on the marble stairs.

The old house hadn't changed much in the years I'd been gone. When we reached the second floor, I pointedly ignored the first door on the left, which led to what had been my rooms when I'd lived here. Not that I'd spent a lot of time in the suite even then. Once it became clear I couldn't hide my grave magic, my father had shipped me off to a wyrd boarding school. After that, I'd spent only summers at the house.

Casey ushered me into the sitting room in her suite, and I gaped. The last time I'd been here she'd been only fourteen, but no sign of the boy band–obsessed teenager she'd been was left in the room. Everything reflected a sophisticated debutante, which I guess was what she was.

The room catered to a minimalist's style. Everything was glass, black, or white, and the only decoration was a small black statue in the center of the glass coffee table. The blunt little statue appeared to be carved of petrified wood with an intricate symbol cut in the center. I reached for it, and Casey cleared her throat.

"Alexis, what is going on?" She lowered herself onto a white-cushioned love seat and motioned for me to sit across from her.

Casey watched me, waiting. I bit my lower lip and sank into the chair. *How am I going to explain?*

I'd thought about it on the drive but hadn't reached a satisfactory solution. I couldn't tell her that I suspected Coleman, the poster boy for the Humans First Party—a party that wanted to restrict the rights of witches and fae—of being something inhuman and full of dark magic.

Oh yeah, and when I asked "So, have you noticed Dad acting rather strange lately? Because I think Coleman might have stolen his body" I was sure to endear myself to her. Obviously, the truth just wasn't going to cut it.

Casey's eyes flicked to where my teeth worried my lip—a habit I'd had since I was a kid—and I forced myself to stop. While we were far from close, Casey and I weren't complete strangers. We'd spent every summer together until I was eighteen. She the perfect daughter who could do no wrong, me the one who accidently raised the shade of her pet parrot when I was twelve, and our older brother, Brad—well, we didn't talk about Brad. He'd disappeared when I was eleven. After I graduated from academy, changed my name, and left this house for what I'd thought had been for good, Casey and I had exchanged impersonal e-mails on holidays, and once, three years back on my birthday, we'd met for coffee. We didn't hate each other; we just didn't have much in common.

I took a deep breath before saying, "Someone or something tampered with the body. I couldn't raise the shade."

Her tweezed eyebrows pinched together. "Obviously. The whole world knows that. You made sure of it."

I blinked, lost for words. *She thinks I released the video?* I suppressed a groan. A lot of people probably did. Hell, that was probably what Falin was looking for at my house.

A knock sounded on the door, and I was saved from comment by Rodger's arrival with the coffee. He placed it on the glass table between us and excused himself without a word.

Casey leaned forward, scooping sugar into her cup. She lifted a small pitcher. "Cream?"

I rescued my coffee before she could dilute it. I inhaled the scent of the rich dark roast and all but melted with contentment against the plush white chair. Then Casey's gaze speared into me.

"What I want to know is what the spell you saw does. Who cast it? The fae, obviously, but what type?"

And just like that, she broke my moment of bliss. The Humans First Party saw the fae as public enemies: dangerous, unpredictable, and—most important to them if you actually read their propaganda—uncontrolled. They didn't paint witches as being much better. I took a sip of the coffee, but the contented moment had passed, and there was no recapturing the feeling. I set the cup on the table. *Time to play dangerously.*

"This goes no further than you, but I believe the body is a fake. It is only spelled to look like Coleman." Okay, that wasn't completely what I believed, but it touched the truth in quite a few places.

Casey's cup clattered against her saucer. The light brown liquid—too full with cream—sloshed over the edges. She looked down at it, then lowered the cup and saucer to the table.

"So what you're saying is that Teddy might be alive?"

"Yes." *Unfortunately.*

She collapsed into her seat as if she had deflated, but a faint smile clung to her lips. A smile so thin it seemed that someone had turned off her happiness and it was taking time to charge back up.

I shuffled in my seat, crossing then uncrossing my legs. I waited, expecting more questions, but they didn't come. I picked up my coffee and took the opportunity to redirect the conversation.

"How is Father handling Coleman's disappearance and presumed death?"

"He's distressed. We're all very . . . distressed." She stared off in the distance. "It seems so strange, the thought of him being dead. I saw him right before—you know? We were at Harriet's charity dinner. She's a state senator, by the way. It was some bleeding heart charity of hers for children displaced by magic or something. Anyway, I sat across from him at dinner. He was so alive, so brilliant."

Riiight. Sounded as if my little sister had a crush. "So, Father is handling the stress of taking over the governor's seat?"

Casey's eyes snapped into focus. "Why do you keep asking about Daddy?"

"I'm not. I'm . . ." *Caught. Dammit.* "Can't I be concerned?"

She stood. "I think it's time for you to go."

She swept across the room and held open the door, her lips pressed thin. I drained my coffee before following. She escorted me all the way to the front door. I reached for the knob but didn't turn it. Damn Falin for putting the idea in my head, but I had one more question to ask.

Casey saw me hesitate and huffed out a sigh. "I forgot, Alexis. Let me grab my purse." She walked to the side coat closet, the snap of her heels loud and harsh on the marble.

I waited for her to return before asking, "Who else did you tell I was going to see Coleman's body?"

"No one. Well, Daddy. But that was it. Why?" She didn't wait for me to answer but pulled the bills from her billfold and shoved them into my hand. "It's all I have in this purse, but since you couldn't actually raise the shade, it probably didn't take too much of your time. Now, please go."

I shoved the money in my bag and saw myself out. As I reached the bottom stair the sound of tires on pavement caught my ears. I looked up. A silver Porsche was winding up the drive. *Oh crap; Daddy Dearest is home.*

I darted down the walk and dove into my little hatchback. I slammed the door and shoved the key in the ignition simultaneously.

The engine sputtered.

Come on.

It sputtered again and then turned over. The Porsche pulled to a stop behind me. I threw my car in gear and gave her some gas. My little hatchback jutted forward, faithfully chugging down the drive. I wasn't going to come face to face with evil tonight, or Father either.

I stopped at a red light and tugged my purse into my lap. I'd thrown the money Casey had given me into the top of the purse when I'd taken off. Now I pulled the cash out, counting.

Thirty-two dollars.

An inappropriate giggle bubbled in my throat. I let it free until my whole chest shook and moisture filled the corners of my eyes. John was in the ICU; I had a dozen stitches, a sprained wrist, and a hospital bill I couldn't pay; and Casey thought my time was worth thirty-two dollars. I wiped my eyes and thrust the cash back into my purse.

I shouldn't have gotten involved in this madness. I should have told her no and gone home. What I needed now was a new client or two. Insurance cases were always good, or maybe one of those crazy shrinks who thought their patient needed closure with some deceased family member—those cases were weird, but they tended to last a while, which meant they paid well. Of course, I needed to start answering my phone again if I expected someone to hire me.

I drummed my thumb on the steering wheel and frowned at the red light. It was taking its sweet time to change. I reached for the radio knob—maybe I'd get lucky and it would work.

My car lurched forward, and my head bounced off the dash. Sharp pain tore across my forehead and tears welled in my eyes.

I jerked upright.

What the hell?

The front of a white van filled my rearview mirror. *How did he . . . ?* Something wet trailed into my eyebrow. *Oh crap.* I pressed my hand against my stitches.

My palm came away damp with blood.

This just made my crappy day. I threw the car in park and jumped out. My purse tumbled from my lap, hitting the pavement. *Great.* I brushed everything back inside and threw the strap over my shoulder.

My poor hatchback's bumper was crumpled under the huge steel front of the van. The other driver put the van in reverse and pulled back a foot. I stared at the damage. A hot tear sliced down my cheek. Dammit. I cried when I was angry, which only pissed me off more. I wiped away the tear and spun to face the man sliding out of the van.

"Sorry 'bout that, ma'am," he said, walking toward me. "Hey, haven't I seen you on TV? You're that dead witch."

I opened my mouth, but shut it before I said something I regretted. I took a deep breath. "Grave witch."

How the hell did he hit my car sitting at a red light? Hadn't he been stopped behind me? There was a line of stopped cars behind the van.

The old man grinned at me, flashing crooked teeth between loose lips. He took off his ball cap and scratched his head, leaning over my twisted bumper. "You can probably knock that out with a hammer."

Yeah, right. I fished my phone out of my purse. "I'm going to report the accident."

The grin faded from his face. "All right, all right. Let me get my insurance information." He leaned back inside the van.

The light changed, and cars careened around us. I stepped closer to the van to keep my toes from getting run over. If I'd been driving past the accident, traffic would have slowed to a crawl as people rubbernecked to watch the minor fender bender, but it was just my luck that since I was the one involved, people whirled by, the wind buffeting me in their wake. The old man, still leaning over his seat and digging in the glove box, glanced back and grinned.

Behind me a car door slammed. Wheels screeched, and I flipped around in time to see my little hatchback tear off down the road.

"What the hell!" I dashed forward.

Half the bumper fell, scraping along the ground and shooting sparks. The thief picked up speed.

I stopped at the edge of the intersection. "Get back here, you mother—"

The 911 operator picked up, cutting me off. "Are you in a secure location?"

"No, my car just got jacked on the corner of—"

The phone was wrenched from my ear.

Fingers with too many joints locked around my arm, and alarm shot through my body like an electric shock. I stepped sideways, trying to jerk free. The grip on my arm tightened like a vise. The old man grinned and hurled my phone into the oncoming traffic.

I swallowed hard. The shock that had run through me a moment earlier settled in my stomach and soured. To my credit, I didn't scream.

"What do you want?"

He grinned again, his crooked teeth straightening before my eyes, his wrinkles smoothing out, and his face taking on the hard angles of the fae. He flashed his now-pointed teeth and tugged on my arm, dragging me toward the van.

Now I did scream.

The sliding door of the van crashed open. Another fae stepped out. I screamed as if I had banshee blood and locked my knees, pushing my weight through my heels.

I lost more ground.

I jabbed the heel of my boot into the fae's foot. He yelped and jerked my arm hard, dragging me off balance. I crashed to my knees. The shadow of the van fell over me.

The second fae reached us. I swung my purse, the leather smacking him in the stomach.

It didn't faze him.

The new fae pressed something against my forehead, directly in the trickling blood from my split stitches. I tried to jerk back, but he barked a word in a deep guttural language, and a sticky string of magic wrapped around me.

My legs went numb, then my arms. My voice died in my throat.

The fae who had been an old man said something in the same guttural language. Not magic this time—a command. The second fae leaned down and grabbed me under the knees.

He lifted my legs, and I hung between them, unable to move as they carried me to the van.

Cars swerved around us. No one stopped. No one noticed. The Humans First Party claimed that the fae could commit crimes in broad daylight and no one would be the wiser because of their glamour—an illusion magic so strong it could reshape reality. I'd never believed it. Guess this was my wake-up call.

I couldn't blink. I couldn't even swallow as the fae with my knees lifted me into the stifling belly of the van.

"Freeze!"

They didn't.

"Let her go," a vaguely familiar voice commanded.

The fae glanced at each other but continued hauling me into the van. The loud bang of a gunshot crashed into the confined space. The fae holding my arms jerked back, dropping me, and a fountain of blood blossomed in the center of his chest.

My shoulders slammed into the floorboard, followed by the back of my head. I still couldn't move. The other fae released my legs. He lifted his hands and retreated into the gloom of the van.

"Alex, get out of the van," the commanding voice said.

Ha! I would have if I could have. I couldn't see my rescuer, but I could almost place his voice. He must have realized my predicament, because a hand dragged me, sliding on my ass, out of the van.

I landed like a lump on the pavement, and gloved fingers darted across my forehead, ripping the charm away. Feeling filled my body like dozens of needles pricking my skin.

"Get in the car," Falin commanded, hauling me to my feet. He shoved me toward his red convertible with one hand without taking his eyes, or his gun, off the fae.

I didn't need telling twice. Grabbing my purse from where I'd dropped it when the spell hit, I ran for the car. I jumped into the passenger seat, drawing my knees to my chest as the leather seat molded around me. My heartbeat thudded in my ears, pounding behind my eyes so hard it obstructed my vision—or perhaps those were tears making everything fuzzy. I scrubbed at my eyes with the back of my palm.

Falin stood in the street, his gun level. A pair of unmoving legs hung out the door of the van. I couldn't see the other fae.

"These are iron bullets," Falin said as he stepped toward the van. "So unless you want to end up like your friend, start talking."

Cars on both sides of the street slowed.

A crow's cry-laugh floated up from the bowels of the van, permeated the street. It drew an involuntary shiver from me.

"You'll be doing more explaining than me, I think," the fae said.

A black station wagon stopped, the woman inside craning her neck. The car behind her stopped as well. A man in that car pulled out a cell phone.

Clearly the glamour veil had dropped.

I slouched in the passenger seat, hiding from the prying eyes. Over the rim of the dash I saw Falin running for the car, his gun holstered.

He vaulted the door, twisting in midair to land in the driver's seat. In another situation, I might have been impressed. I swallowed around the lump in my throat, trying to make room for air. Falin threw the car in gear. It lurched into motion, and he swung a hard U-turn. My shoulder slammed into the door, and my already ragged breath burst out of me. Scrambling back into the seat, I clawed for the seat belt.

We swerved around the stalling traffic, and then Falin gunned it, going from twenty to sixty faster than I could blink. I twisted to glance back. The van jetted into motion, disappearing around the corner.

It was a long few minutes before my heart stopped pounding in my throat and I was able to speak.

"They tried to kidnap me."

Falin glanced at me from the corner of his eye but didn't say anything.

I looked up at him. "You shot him."

Still he said nothing.

I cleared my throat. "Shouldn't you, like . . . call it in and secure the scene? You shot someone."

Falin slammed on the brakes and spun the wheel. The car turned hard, tilting on two tires. I gripped the door, my knuckles white.

"What the hell is your problem?" I screamed as the tires jumped the pavement.

Falin straightened the car. "Most people say thank you when rescued."

I gritted my teeth, swallowing the scream bubbling in my chest. He swung the car into an empty grocery store parking lot and darted into a parking space. He pulled the emergency brake, and the car screeched to a stop.

Falin turned before the momentum of the stop snapped us forward. His gaze traveled over me, assessing, and his lips twisted in a grimace.

He leaned across the seat and fished through the glove compartment. Tugging out an unmarked red box, he sifted through the contents and pulled out an adhesive bandage the size of my fist.

"For your forehead." He dropped it in my lap, then leaned between the seats for something on the back floorboard.

I picked up the bandage. A faint tickle in the back of my mind warned me of the inactive charm. The dormant spell wasn't strong enough for me to feel what it did, but it was on a bandage, so probably it aided healing in some way. I lowered the visor and flicked open the vanity mirror. Only a few of the stitches had split, but I had small jagged tears where they'd pulled before snapping.

Removing the paper from the back, I pressed the bandage over the wound. My blood activated the spell, and warmth spread over my forehead, easing the sting of torn flesh. *Not bad.*

Falin straightened, a white oxford shirt in his hand. He tossed the wrinkled shirt in my lap, followed by a pack of wet-wipes that read G'S WINGS. "Change out of the bloody top."

I glanced at my tank. It was spattered in small red blotches. *Great. I'll never get the blood out.* I tugged it away from my skin. Oh yeah; I was damp from more than sweat. I cringed. Two days in a row I'd ended up covered in blood that wasn't mine.

I reached for the door and considered the grocery store facade. No signs, no lights—abandoned. Great—no chance of a bathroom there. I glanced back over my shoulder. Falin was cleaning his gun and not paying attention to me.

Well, hell. I tugged the tank over my head.

In the other seat, Falin made a half-choked sound. Guess he was paying more attention than I thought. Not that it mattered.

"Your timing, while opportune, was a little too convenient," I said, tearing open the foil on the wipes. "You've been following me."

Falin didn't answer.

The wet-wipe was cold, but I mopped up my chest and stomach even though I couldn't see any blood. Then I shrugged into the oxford. It was too big. I buttoned the two buttons between my breasts and tied the tails at my stomach. It was the best I could do.

When I turned, I found Falin staring at me. He cleared his throat and dropped his eyes. He held out his hand.

With a sigh, I handed over my tank. I guess it was evidence now. The police still hadn't returned my clothes from yesterday. *If I keep this up, they'll have my whole wardrobe in little paper bags.*

Falin propped open his door and dug a lighter out of his pocket. Without a word, he held the lighter under my tank.

"Hey! What do you think you're—"

The tank caught fire, filling the air with the scent of burning fabric.

I jumped out of the car. "You're crazy." I slammed the door. "What kind of cop are you? You shot a guy, fled the scene, and now you're destroying evidence. I should call nine-one-one." Except I couldn't. My phone was gone.

I tugged my purse strap higher on my shoulder and glanced around the empty parking lot. What was I supposed to do now? I stomped toward the street.

The convertible purred behind me, starting up. Gravel crunched under the wheels as Falin eased up beside me.

"I told you to stop attracting attention to yourself."

I blinked at him. *What, pray tell, had I done to attract attention to myself?* Well, except possibly reveal the existence of a really nasty spell that looked way beyond standard witchcraft. But since then? Okay, since then I'd investigated the site where a body switch had occurred. Oh yeah, and possibly visited the home of the latest victim. I cringed and kept walking.

"What did you tell the governor's daughter?" Falin asked, still crawling the car forward to keep pace with me.

"Casey had nothing to do with this."

"You don't find it the least suspicious that you were attacked minutes after leaving the governor's house?"

Yeah. I did. But I wasn't about to tell him that. Since my conversation with Roy, I was running on suspicions and questions. I guess I could have told Falin everything

I knew and thrown his case wide open—as if he'd actually believe me—but what if my suspicions were wrong? I didn't want to know what my father would do if I embarrassed him by falsely accusing him of dark magic. Besides, trying to explain my involvement might bring to light the deep dark secret that the esteemed Humans First Party member shared chromosomes with me, and my father had spent a lot of money—and if it were anyone else, I'd believe that binding oaths of silence were involved—to keep our relationship quiet.

When I didn't say anything, Falin rolled closer, angling his wheels. "Get in the car."

"I'll walk, thanks."

"Get in the car." He leaned over, opening the passenger door so it swung out to block my path.

I looked at him. The setting sun had turned his hair an eerie red, and the falling dusk did little to soften his face. He cocked an eyebrow and pointed to the seat.

He was dangerous.

He'd just saved my life.

I wavered, torn, and he smiled. It wasn't much of a smile, but it transformed his face, softening the edge that made me want to shy away and hide. *I do need a ride.*

I climbed into the seat.

"I'll take you to report your stolen car," he said once I shut the door.

"And the kidnapping?"

"Just the car."

Crap. He'd shot a fae. To rescue *me*. And he didn't want me telling anyone. I glanced back at the smoldering pile that was all that was left of my tank top. *What kind of detective is he?*

Chapter 8

The morning paper had a large picture of me on the front page. It must have been taken the second I realized the recording had been released because I had a rather stunned "oh shit" expression. Not flattering.

I folded the paper and tossed it on the counter, pausing to rub the scratches on my shoulder, which still ached. It was early afternoon, and so far I'd left the house only to take PC for a quick, and very tense, potty break around the backyard. Part of me doubted that the fae who'd tried to abduct me would try anything with a half dozen news vans around, but the other half of me — the paranoid side, which probably included my survival instinct — kept reminding me the first attempt had been on a busy street.

So, I'd stayed inside. With the blinds closed. And the doors warded. I'd even locked the door on the inner wall that separated my loft from the stair to the rest of the house — and I never locked that door. Now the biggest problem came down to one simple fact.

The pickle was gone.

The fridge was officially empty, and I'd fed PC the

last bit of his kibble for breakfast. If Casey's thirty-two dollars and I didn't make it to the store soon, PC and I were going to be very hungry.

"What do you think I should do?"

PC looked up from his pillow, confirmed that I didn't have food, and then closed his eyes again. I sighed. PC hadn't been a fan of our breakfast pickle.

"Okay. I'll go out." But I didn't move. *This is ridiculous. I can't hide forever.* I stood, but my feet felt heavy, and my knuckles were white where I gripped the counter.

Get a hold on yourself, Alex. I took a deep breath and pried my fingers from the counter. *It's just the grocery store.*

I grabbed a head scarf and huge sunglasses out of the bottom drawer of my dresser, then examined myself in the mirror. *I look like I'm trying to avoid the paparazzi.* If only the press were my major concern. I'd started to close the drawer when a bit of dark leather caught my eye.

I knelt, digging out the sheathed dagger. *I'd almost forgotten about you.* The enchanted dagger purred power across my hand, wanting to be drawn—that was one reason it was in the drawer. Fae-wrought, it was part of a pair and could pierce just about anything. Rianna had given it to me when she'd graduated from academy. She'd kept the mate. I ran my fingers over the charmed leather. I *would* feel better with a little protection.

I know I have an ankle holster in here somewhere. I dug through the drawer until I found the holster meant to conceal the dagger under my boot. After strapping it in place, I grabbed my purse and took the inner stair down to the main portion of the house.

"Holly? Caleb?" I called as I reached the bottom step.

"Workroom," a deep voice called back, and I headed down the hall to the garage Caleb had converted into a studio-slash-workshop.

His circle was up, so I couldn't step farther than the open doorway, but Caleb was in the center of the room with a chisel in one hand, a mallet in the other, and a hunk of marble in front of him. Stone dust covered his slightly green arms—his glamour was down—and when he glanced over his shoulder to look at me, it was with shiny black eyes. I'd been renting my loft from Caleb since my freshman year of college, but I'd never gotten used to seeing him completely in his fae-mien. After yesterday's kidnapping, it was more disturbing than normal.

He must have sensed my discomfort, or maybe he simply didn't like being seen for what he truly was— he rarely went without his glamour—but his green skin darkened to a well-tanned brown, and his eyes turned human. Suddenly, he looked not fae but like any average joe you might pass on the street whom you wouldn't glance at twice. Well, except for the fact he was covered in marble dust.

"New commission?" I asked, nodding at the block of stone. Caleb was an accomplished wardsmith and an artist. People commissioned his work not only for the power of his enchantments but for the aesthetics of his work.

He shook his head. "Just something I'm working on. There still cameras pointed at my house?"

"Uh . . ." I didn't even have to look to know the answer to that one. "Yeah? Sor—" I stopped myself before I finished the word. You weren't supposed to apologize to fae. "I was wondering. When you get to a stopping point, you think you could give me a ride to the store?"

"What happened to your car?"

"Gremlins, I think."

Caleb turned and stared at me as if to see whether I was joking. I wasn't.

He set down the chisel and mallet and brushed his hands on his jeans. "Yeah. Let me take a quick shower first. Did you say gremlins?"

PC pranced around my feet as I lugged in two bags of groceries.

"Hey, miss me?" I asked, smiling at him as I kicked the door closed behind me. I'd filled Caleb in on the abduction attempt during our drive to the store. He wasn't happy, and he wanted me to keep a low profile—which was already my plan, so I didn't disagree. He had connections in the solitary fae community, so he promised to keep his ear to the wind for me, see if he heard any chatter involving me. He didn't ask me about my case, and I didn't tell him.

Having survived my trip to the grocery store with nothing worse happening than a reporter accosting me in the cereal aisle, I was feeling pretty good. It had been foolish to hide in the house all morning. As Falin and Caleb said, I just needed to keep my head down. Which meant much more discreet poking into the whole Coleman thing, and just enough to find out whether my father was involved. But I couldn't stop living. Besides, after my shopping trip, I had only twelve dollars left, so I needed to find a new client.

PC bounced, his front paws working the air, his blue cast flashing, as he tried to entice me to pick him up. I dropped the grocery bags by my feet and reached for him. His ears perked up, and, forgetting all about me, he rooted through the bag.

Little traitor.

I rubbed his head as he whined and attacked the bag of dog food.

"All right, all right. Give me a second."

I filled his bowl, then left him to chomp happily as I unloaded the rest of the groceries. I'd bought the bare necessities of life, most overprocessed or freeze-dried to the point where they no longer resembled food, but they were cheap and edible. I grabbed two packs of ramen noodles and opened the cabinet.

If I wasn't looking further into Coleman, I needed to contact the FIB and tell them what I knew. I didn't have to tell them who I suspected was the next victim, though they would probably come to the same conclusion. I picked up the new pack of hot dogs and tossed them in the bottom drawer of the fridge. If I reported my outrageous story about a body thief, the FIB would start poking around. What if they discovered the fae Falin had shot? I hadn't done anything wrong. Hell, they'd been trying to kidnap me. But I hadn't reported the shooting. That made me an accomplice. The thought sent a shiver along my spine.

"If you weren't standing in the fridge, you wouldn't be cold."

I jumped at the voice, almost dropping the carton of milk I was putting away, and deep masculine laughter filled the air behind me. I turned.

Death leaned against my kitchen counter, his thumbs hooked in the front pockets of his jeans. Ben Franklin once said, "In this world nothing can be said to be certain, except death and taxes." Death was certainly consistent in my world. The black T-shirt that showed off the muscles on his chest, the chin-length hair, the dark eyes he watched me with that seemed to smile even when he didn't, all were exactly the same as the first time I'd seen him eighteen years ago. He came and went at apparent random, sometimes to talk, other times to tease. He kept his secrets tight, and he never interfered.

Until now.

He'd saved my life. Not just stalled on collecting my soul—he'd pushed me out of mortal danger. I had no idea what to make of that, or how to thank him.

I still had the carton of milk in my hands. I glanced down at it and turned back to the fridge. I set the carton on the top shelf and frowned at the fact the fridge still looked empty. Then I shoved the door closed. "I was kind of expecting you to show up sooner."

I knew he moved closer only because I could feel the chill of his skin in the air behind me. "I had to take care of some errands."

Errands. So someone somewhere had lost his . . . My mouth went dry, and I flipped around. "Not John?"

Death shook his head, and a breath I hadn't realized I was holding rushed out of me. I'd asked about John at the station last night, and they'd told me he was still unconscious in ICU. I hadn't liked the tones the cops used. John had been asleep too long. People were starting to whisper about brain damage.

"You should go see him."

"I know. I meant to go yesterday, but everything went crazy, and then today . . ." I looked down, away from Death's eyes. He knew me too well—which was totally unfair, as I didn't even know his real name, or if he had one. But he knew I avoided hospitals, particularly wards with comatose patients. "Thank you for"—I waved a hand in the air—"everything. But isn't it sort of outside your job description to save people from mortal harm?"

Death shrugged again, but he smiled, and while his lips lifted only a little, the full radiance of the smile escaped through his eyes. "I'll catch flak for it back at headquarters."

My gaze snapped up. Headquarters? Was he now giving away secrets, too? The mischief reflected in the crook of his mouth said he was teasing me, but I still pried. "So you'll get in trouble because of me?"

His smile grew wider. "You can make it up to me by giving me coffee."

I laughed. I'd introduced him to coffee as an experiment when I'd been a teenager. Rianna and I had noticed that my grave magic bridged the gap between the world of the living and whatever plane Death existed on. It was the one thing I could do that she couldn't.

Rianna, two years my senior, had been my roommate, my idol, my best friend, and my biggest competition. Where I had nearly flunked out of traditional Spell Casting, in academy she could work any spell her teachers assigned—and many they didn't teach her and probably would have wished she hadn't learned. But when it came to Death, she had to be in touch with the grave to see him, and even then he wasn't solid to her.

It was probably actually a negative point against me that I could see Death under normal circumstances. It probably meant I'd never learned to shield properly, to keep my psyche from crossing the chasm between the living and the dead. I didn't care. It was something only I could do. A kind of secret between him and me. And not only could I see him, but when I interacted with corporeal objects, so could Death.

One day I'd given him a mug of coffee. It turned out he liked it. A lot. If only he had let me take him to class as a magic fair project, I probably would have made better grades in academy.

I made two cups of coffee. Black for me, with milk for him. It wasn't until I picked up his full mug that I realized the problem. I had only one good hand. The other was sprained and in a brace.

"Uh, well, I guess I'll have mine later," I said, holding out Death's mug toward him.

Death wrapped both hands over the mug, his fingers covering mine. The heat of the coffee pressed into my palm, contrasting with the chill crawling over my skin from his fingers. He lifted the mug, with my hand still attached, to his lips. With those sparkling eyes locked on mine, he blew at the steaming liquid. His breath smelled of dew and freshly turned soil, and it mixed with the heady aroma of the coffee. "You can share mine."

I did a mental check on my heart. *Yup, still in my chest.* Though I was pretty sure it had spun a little. Tossing my head back, I crinkled my nose at him. "Your diluted coffee? Wouldn't touch it."

"Of course." He grinned, then drew his hands away.

I was tall, but he was taller. The height difference made it awkward for us to both hold the mug without him leaning and me lifting my arm uncomfortably high. His hands slipped to my waist, and he lifted me effortlessly to the counter. I shivered under his fingers, only half in reaction to his chill.

With me sitting on the counter, our heights were better matched. He cupped the mug again, taking a slow sip without looking away from my eyes. His skin was cold—not the chill of the grave, but an unnatural cold that burned as it settled under my flesh. I knew the reverse was true for him, my skin scalding his.

"So, you want to tell me anything about the shooter you saved me from?"

The shape of his smile remained the same, but I could tell the question dimmed it. He didn't answer, but closed his eyes and sipped the coffee. When he opened his eyes again, lights danced in his dark irises. His smile brightened again, as though it had only been dampened by a cloud that had blown away. His gaze traveled over me.

Then the humor bled from his face. He released the mug, his brows drawing to a concerned point over his nose.

"What happened?" His voice held no trace of teasing, and I frowned at him, not understanding. His fingers reached out, hovered near my collarbone.

I glanced at the scratches on my shoulder. "A shade attacked me. It was weird. When I was trying to raise her, it felt as if she'd been through a dicer. Then she came out screaming and violent. Have you ever seen a shade lash out?"

Death frowned and leaned closer, but he didn't touch the wound. "Alex, this is important. Where was she found? Was it a warehouse?"

"It was a body dump." I had no idea where the actual murder had taken place. The police didn't, either. I did know about a warehouse, though. Twisted magic had taken place there, and if that was the place he was referring to . . . "What do you know?"

Death didn't answer.

"You're scaring me."

He met my eyes, and there was no laughter in them now. "The wound is infected with a spell. It's spreading like a virus."

I nearly dropped the mug of coffee. *Infected with a spell? Virus?* Swallowing hard, I focused on turning and setting the mug beside me. The ceramic clattered against the countertop, and I drew my trembling hand away.

I took a deep breath. Let it out. *I can deal with this.* All spells had counterspells. I just needed to learn more about this one. "What is the spell?"

Death pressed his lips together, and for the first time

in my memory, he looked uncertain. He stepped back, his eyes pinched at the corners. Then he vanished.

I jumped off the counter. "Dammit! What does the spell do? How do I reverse it?"

PC looked up from his food bowl, but no answer came from Death. I didn't know if he had left or was simply invisible. I had no idea if he didn't know the answer or if he wasn't allowed to tell me. I didn't know anything. Because, as long as I'd known him, I didn't really know him.

Chapter 9

I sat in the center of my active circle, my legs crossed and my eyes closed, trying to find peace. It wasn't coming easily.

I used a meditative trance to reach the Aetheric, the magical plane, but at times like these I wished my ritual was more active, like dancing or chanting. Or screaming. I'd been shot at, a group of fae had tried to nab me, my father might have gotten his body stolen, and I had a spell spreading through my body. *Oh yeah—I could really get into screaming right about now.*

I concentrated on my breathing and attempted to clear my thoughts, but it was no use. My brain was buzzing. *Okay. Plan B.*

I channeled energy out of my ring and into an inert spell in my charm bracelet, activating it. A false calm descended over me, and my next breath was deep, slow. A bubble trapped all my thoughts, my worries, my personality, moving them out of reach. My mind went instantly blank, tranquil. I sank into a trance.

My next breath was full of color, light. I'd reached the Aetheric.

Wisps of magic floated on all sides of me. I ran my mental fingers through a strand of blue energy. It curled around my hand, and I drew it into my body. In the Aetheric, my body began to glow with magic and warmth. I laughed, giddy with the touch of it. The sound changed to bright blue notes in the air.

I danced through the swirls of energy, searching for blue and green threads, the colors that resonated with me. I drew magic until I glowed like a suncatcher. Only then did I remember why I was working magic. That was the problem with the meditation spell: the bubble didn't always pop once I hit my trance.

I moved outside of myself, looking at my Aetheric body. It was identical to my mortal body except for the whole glowing-with-energy part. The advantage was that I could see magic. All magic. The obsidian ring on my finger glowed teal with the energy I'd stored in it. The silver bracelet containing my shields was a mottle of colors because of the various inert spells I carried in the dangling charms. Both looked bright, clear, and healthy. My gaze moved on.

The scratches in my shoulder were black. They were like a void absorbing the glow of magic leaking out of the skin around them. I'd never seen magic so dark. Surrounding the scratches, dark tendrils grew like thirsty roots, digging over my collarbone, reaching down my arm. The skin around the tendrils was an angry, hurt crimson. As I watched, a thin tendril shot out of the scratch wound. It was only an inch long, but where it touched, the light died. Death was right: the spell was bad news, and it was growing.

I reached for a passing swirl of green energy and wrapped it around my hand. A thought turned it into a glowing green bubble. I concentrated on the dark spell, trying to pull it from my skin and force it into the

Aetheric bubble the way I would if I absorbed tainted magic.

The spell resisted, and I pulled harder. Red sparks of light ignited in the swirls around me, reacting to my strain. Still I pulled. Something dislodged, and the Aetheric spun in bright flashes of orange, red, and agony.

When the world righted, I looked at myself. The spell was still firmly attached to my shoulder, but I seemed slightly off center. I blinked, looked again. *How could I have pulled something inside myself askew?* Because the spell was holding on to . . . something. Something that made up my core.

I swallowed hard. I had no idea if Death could see magic, but I knew one thing he could see. Souls.

If this spell was sucking on my soul, I was so totally screwed.

I paced the narrow area between the kitchenette and my bed. It took only thirteen steps to cross from the boxy mattress to the other side of the small studio apartment—not nearly enough room to expend my nervous energy. PC watched from the safe perch of his pillow. I'd cast a healing spell on my wrist and on the scratches. Not that I was holding out a lot of hope that it would help, but I had to do something.

I had a malignant spell spreading and . . . I didn't even want to think about what it was doing, but sucking on my soul was at the top of the list of possibilities. I rubbed the cotton pad containing the healing spell I'd covered the scratches with. I'd known they burned more than they should.

I stopped pacing. The scratches had hurt the most when I was in the warehouse. *So, did the spell transfer to me from the shade, or did it somehow seep into the scratches at the warehouse?* Both options were ridiculous, maybe impossible; and yet, Death had said the spell originated from the scratches, and that had been my conclusion in the Aetheric as well. Too bad Death hadn't said anything else. *Damn him for disappearing when I asked questions.*

That wasn't really fair, and I knew it. If Death hadn't told me about the spell, I still wouldn't know about it. I just wished there was some way to contact him. My list of questions for him was growing. *Guess I could try for a near-Death experience.* The chuckle that leaked from my throat was rough.

I couldn't draw the spell out in the Aetheric. I needed a counterspell. There was an anticurse center in the Magic Quarter. Unfortunately, I hadn't paid my bill after I'd been cursed by an old widow who'd hired me to raise her husband's shade. She hadn't been thrilled to discover her late husband had been having an affair. Why she cursed *me* I wasn't so clear on, but needless to say, the center wasn't an option. If I could just figure out more about the spell, maybe I could research a counterspell myself.

Tamara.

Tamara was the most sensitive person I knew. If anyone could puzzle out the spell, it would be her. *That's if she's talking to me after this whole Coleman debacle.*

I rushed to my purse before remembering that my cell phone was crushed and decorating the pavement. *Right—no phone.* Holly was still at work, but Caleb was probably back in his studio in the garage. He'd let me use his phone.

I was headed for the inner door that led down into the main house when a loud bang sounded on the front door. I jumped, and PC launched himself from the bed. The dagger was in my hand before I realized I'd reached for it. I crept forward and peeked around the curtain.

Not again. "What do you want, Detective?"

I kept my foot wedged behind the door so Falin couldn't shove past me, but he didn't even try. Instead he smiled, his full lips curving around perfect teeth.

"Invite me inside, Alexis Caine."

"How did you learn my name?" No one should have been able to find my name change. I'd picked "Craft" for the irony and to annoy my father, but once the change was legal, my father had buried the paperwork. I had no idea how, or really *how deep*, but no one had ever found the connection before—not reporters, not Internet gossip groups, not even the investigators hired to find mud to sling during the campaign.

Falin frowned without answering and glanced at the dagger I was holding. I hid my hand behind my back, out of view.

"Well," he said, "I'm glad to see you're finally taking some precautions, but you weren't this tense when I dropped you off last night."

"But you were this annoying. At least one of us is consistent." I started to shut the door in his face.

His hand shot out, holding the door, but he didn't force his way in. "Let me in, Alex. Please."

It was the "please" that did it. I stepped back, letting him pass. After all, he might have been opinionated and bossy, but he *had* rescued me. I could hear him out. Besides, I needed to give him back his shirt.

He watched as I knelt and placed the dagger back in its holster, then gave himself a tour as I dug through the pile of clothes by the dresser. I ignored him as I searched for the oxford he'd let me borrow after he'd burned my tank top. *I should keep it as a replacement.* Of course, what I'd do with a man's oxford—especially one cut to cover Falin's broad shoulders—I didn't know. I finally found it and folded it, ignoring the wrinkles.

Falin was standing by my counter staring at the two mugs of now-cold coffee. I hadn't gotten around to dumping them yet. He lifted one mug. "Was someone here?"

"Is my personal life any of your business?"

"You should turn on the news."

Was that in response to my question? What have the reporters dug up now? He just smiled at me. Dropping the shirt on the counter beside him, I walked over and flipped on the TV.

The chief of police appeared on the screen. "—are currently searching for the source of the leak. But I will go on record to say that the city hired Ms. Craft because of the mysterious circumstances surrounding the late governor's death and disappearance. We acknowledge her as an expert in her field but will be flying in other grave witches from around the world to confirm her findings before we move forward. That's all." He turned, and the screen cut to Lusa's face in the studio.

She smiled at the camera, not glancing at the notes in front of her. "That was the official report given an hour ago in a press conference called by—"

I hit the MUTE button as I wondered which bean counter had determined the city would be better off claiming they'd hired me and having to face the financial consequences of breaking a "no magic" living will than to admit unauthorized magic was used in their morgue. I turned back to Falin. "So now I was officially hired? Do I get paid?"

His lips parted, but his face was torn between amusement and bewilderment. "You don't get arrested."

"Great. So you came by to let me know yourself. How sweet." I moved to the door, but he didn't follow.

"No, I'm here because you've been poking around in my case, and I think you know more than you're telling. Even if you don't, someone thinks you do." He hooked his thumbs in his belt, the movement making his jacket gape open and revealing his shoulder rig. "You have re-sources that could be useful to me, so I'm proposing we work together. A partnership of sorts."

If there was ever a time I needed to be able to cock my eyebrow in sarcastic disbelief, this was it. *Damn stitches.* I settled for leaning back and crossing my arms over my chest. "Sorry, I'm done looking into Coleman. I have other things to worry about." Like a creepy spell. "You'll have to find some other witch to help you find Coleman's killer."

"I'm not looking for the killer. I don't think Coleman is dead. I think he changed bodies."

I tried not to let my shock show on my face—really, I did—but I could tell by the sly smile that tipped his lips that he could read my surprise.

"You already knew that," he said.

Who the hell is this guy? He gave the impression of distrusting witches and fae, but he accepted magic that scared the shit out of me without blinking. How did he even know about the body thief?

And what else did he know?

My hand crawled to the cotton patch on my shoulder. A little information swap might be useful, but I needed to know more first. "What's your plan?"

"There's a charity dinner at the governor's home to-night. All the movers and shakers will be there. If Cole-man's new body is still in the city, he'll attend. I want you with me to help pick him out of the crowd and to shake him up a little."

"In other words, you want to use me as live bait." I shook my head. "I can't just crash a party at my father's house. I'd never make it past the front gate."

Falin only smiled and headed for the door. "I'll pick you up at six." The door shut behind him.

Damn. I hadn't agreed to anything, but I'd go. I knew I would. The party would give me a good chance to take a look at my father, too, though there was no guarantee I'd be able to tell whether he was possessed.

Now I really needed to call Tamara. And I needed to borrow a dress.

Chapter 10

❖⸺◦⊙◦⸺❖

"It's not a date." I growled and shook my head, vetoing the whore red tube of lipstick Holly pulled out of her makeup case.

"He's picking you up, right?"

"Yeah, but—"

She waved a hand through the air and then pulled a slightly less whorish red out of the bag. "And you're going to a fancy dinner?"

"It's business." I took the makeup case away from her and dug through her lipstick selection.

Holly smiled at me, the kind of smile that said she'd stopped arguing to amuse me. A knock sounded on the door, and Holly jumped to answer it.

Tamara bustled in, two dresses slung over her arm. "Sorry; I got here as fast as I could. I wasn't sure what you needed, so I brought a cocktail dress and an evening gown."

She held up my options, and I pointed to the slinky black evening gown. Accepting it, I hurried to the bathroom.

"I'm so excited. I've never heard of Alex having an official date before," Tamara said.

"It's not a date," I called over my shoulder. "Besides, I've been on dates before."

"Taking guys home from bars does not count as dating," Tamara yelled back.

"Neither does this." I closed the door on the sound of her and Holly giggling.

I slid out of the robe I'd worn while Holly fixed my hair and makeup. I still had the cotton patch on my shoulder. The dress had a halter top, so my shoulder would show. I pulled the patch off and examined the scratches underneath. They hadn't even had the decency to scab over. With a sigh, I tossed the patch in the trash, then stepped into the dress.

Tamara and I were the same height, but she was a full-figured woman with curves I envied—and clearly couldn't fill. What should have been a clingy dress fell shapelessly around me. I glanced at the clock: five thirty-seven. I didn't have time to beg another dress; besides, Holly and Tamara were my only girlfriends, and Holly was a good head shorter than me.

I stepped out of the bathroom. "Help?"

"Don't worry; we're on top of this," Holly said, hurrying forward.

"I have safety pins," Tamara added, and then they both escorted me back into the bathroom.

I posed like a mannequin as they filled the dress with black safety pins. "So, any news on how the tape was leaked?"

Tamara grimaced around the pins in her mouth and said, "Nothing official, but Tommy disappeared."

"Your intern?" Holly asked.

I nodded, only to get yelled at to stay still. "It couldn't

have been Tommy." *Though he was rather terse the last time I saw him.*

"I don't think so either, but his disappearance doesn't look good for him." Tamara motioned me to turn.

Stay still. Turn. Still. I sighed. "So, since the chief says I'm officially hired, when can I take another look at Coleman's body?"

Tamara gave me a sharp look through the mirror but didn't answer. I didn't really expect her to. We all knew my "hire" was a cover-our-asses move. I wasn't getting another look at that body unless Falin escorted me to the cold room himself.

Tamara stepped back. "I think you're done."

"We are awesome," Holly said, her reflection beaming at me from the mirror.

I made a full turn in front of the mirror. She was right. I could barely tell the dress was being held in shape with pins.

"My saviors." I pressed my hands over my heart. My fingers brushed the skin around the scratches, and pain shot through my shoulder. I winced. "Tamara, can I ask one more favor?"

A loud knock sounded on the door. *Damn. Falin couldn't be fashionably late, could he?*

"I'll get it," Holly said, scuttling out of my over-crowded bathroom.

"I'll do you a favor without you asking," Tamara said. "Wear this and lose the boots."

She held out a thin silver necklace with a delicate charm shaped like a ghost. The charm gave off a faint magical buzz.

I could feel the complexion spell, but it felt more specialized, as if it was designed for . . . "Bruises and cuts? Did you make this yourself?"

"Yes, and you'll need to personally activate it." She handed me a finger stick.

Ewww. I hated charms that had to be personalized with blood, but I wasn't about to turn down a gift like this.

Once the charm was activated, Tamara helped me fasten the silver chain, and I blinked at the mirror. The bruises, which had faded to green today, were completely gone. All traces of the stitches were absent, too.

"Impressive. I don't know how to thank you."

She smiled. "Just have fun." She pretended to flick away a tear. "I feel like I'm sending my little girl to the prom."

"Shhh. He'll hear you," I whispered. "It's not a date." I tugged at the skirt of the dress, then remembered it was held in place with pins and forced my hands off it. "There was something else I wanted to ask you. Can you look at the spell on my shoulder?"

Tamara frowned. "There's no spell on your shoulder."

I froze, my breath turning solid in my lungs. Then, as if trying to catch up for the lost moment, words flew from my lips. "There is. I saw it in the Aetheric. It had these weird dark tendrils and—" I trailed off at the increasingly confused—and alarmed—look on Tamara's face.

"Besides your jewelry, the only spell on you is the healing spell on the brace on your wrist. You've been using your hand, by the way. I don't know if you noticed."

I glanced down at the brace. Tamara had missed the dagger and the spell. I knew I'd seen something in the Aetheric. Death had seen the spell, too. How could she miss it?

"Alex?" Holly called from outside the bathroom.

"You better get out there," Tamara said, shooing me from the bathroom. "And lose the boots!"

"It's these or my sneakers," I muttered.

I wasn't sure whether she heard, because I'd just caught sight of Falin. He was studying the pictures stuck around the mirror on my dresser and hadn't noticed me yet, so I had a second to look him over. A second wasn't enough. His tux was black satin, fitted in all the right places so it showed off wide shoulders that tapered down into lean hips. If he was armed, he was hiding it well, because a shoulder rig wouldn't have fit under the tux jacket. His hair glimmered in the evening sun that streamed through the blinds, making it look as soft as a wisp of magic in the Aetheric. I had the ridiculous urge to walk over and run my fingers through the long strands.

Holly leaned close to me. "I'm so jealous," she whispered, then slipped her arm through Tamara's. They waved good-bye silently and nearly skipped across my small kitchenette to the door leading down to the main house. They'd be gushing about my yummy "date" before they reached the bottom step.

Falin didn't look up as the door closed, but lifted a white-gloved hand and pulled one of the photos off my mirror.

"Hey, what do think you're doing?"

He whirled around, the photo still between his fingers. He spared me a momentary smile. Then his attention returned to the photo.

Wow, I didn't even garner a second glance. I paused. *Oh, I hate how that irritates me.*

Falin flipped the photo over. "She looks familiar."

I marched over and snatched the photo from him. I'd clipped it out of the paper, and it was already yellowing with age. "Well, she should. She was all over the news for weeks."

He smiled, looking over the collage of photos around my mirror again. He pulled down another, this one a real snapshot. "This is her again? Rianna McBride, right? She disappeared about four years ago. Directly after raising shades on the site of a bombing to help locate and identify victims, if I recall the press coverage correctly."

I grabbed the photo from him and stuffed both it and the newspaper clipping into the top drawer of my dresser. "Can you not touch my stuff?"

Falin shrugged, finally moving away from the mirror. His gaze moved over me again, and his lips twitched, as if undecided whether they would smile or frown. I could feel heat crawling to my cheeks. Holly had managed to tame my hair into tight ringlets piled on my head, the charm fixed the bruises, and the dress wasn't that bad. I'd been mostly impressed, but he did look better than me.

I looked away and tugged at the sides of my dress. "How late do you think we'll be out?"

Now he did smile. "You have a curfew?" When I scowled at him, he laughed and shook his head. "Whose dress are you borrowing?"

"That obvious, huh?"

He nodded, and walked a full circle around me. Then he reached out and grabbed the side of the dress.

I jerked away. "Hey, what are you—"

"Stay still." His gloved fingers worked at the carefully concealed safety pins.

After a couple of seconds of destroying all of Tamara and Holly's hard work, Falin stood back. He nodded once and then motioned me to turn.

With a sense of dread, I stepped up to the mirror. My jaw nearly hit the ground as I stared at my reflection and the dress that now clung to me as though it had been designed specifically for me.

"Okay, you win. You have magic hands."

"Did you feel any magic?"

I shook my head and ran my hands over my waist and down my hips. I couldn't even feel the seams or bunched material. Tamara had done a good job, but this . . .

"Impressive," I said. I now looked the part for the party—as in I looked nothing like myself. Maybe it would be enough to help me get inside unnoticed. Just maybe. It was worth a shot, at least. I turned back to Falin. "We're going to be late."

"Stop fidgeting," Falin whispered as we walked into the Caine mansion ballroom.

I dropped the necklace and let my hand fall to my side. I'd taken off the wrist brace in the car. Tamara was right: I was using the hand. It was still tender, but at least I didn't stand out from the crowd any more than I had to. Not that I'd ever fit in here. Men in tuxes stood together making deals and decisions over Scotch. Women smiled at each other without any warmth as they chose their alliances based on the worth of each other's jewels. Okay, maybe I was being a little cynical, but these were the movers and shakers of Nekros City: the politicians, the CEOs of major conglomerates, and the slothishly unemployed.

I hadn't expected to get this far. I'd fully anticipated to be turned away by the guard at the gate, tickets or no. But he'd let us pass. As had the man at the door—who, I noticed, wasn't Rodger. Now here we were, in the ballroom.

"I thought this was supposed to be a dinner?" I whispered, leaning close to Falin's shoulder.

"We mingle first. Then dinner."

Great. Mingling.

Falin took my arm and led me farther into the room. I pasted on my smile. *Who exactly am I supposed to mingle with? Anyone I know at this party, I'm related to, and they may just kick me out.* Not that I thought anyone outside my family would realize who I was. Even with my face in the papers recently, only someone who knew me well would recognize me under all the makeup, with my hair up, and somewhat out of context at a Humans First dinner party. Hell, even my father probably wouldn't recognize me dressed like this. I certainly didn't feel like myself.

It turned out I didn't need to worry about finding someone to mingle with. Falin moved us around the room, stopping occasionally to speak to one person or another, taking me with him like arm candy.

"Detective Andrews," someone called out, and Falin steered me toward the voice.

"Chief Reynolds, how are you?" he asked, dropping my arm so he could clasp hands with the police chief.

The chief introduced him around the small cluster of men, mostly other big movers in the city. My face had been all over the papers, and the chief had mentioned me in a press conference earlier in the day, but after he finished his introductions, he looked at Falin expectantly. *Yup, makeup and a dress* is *a foolproof disguise.*

Falin didn't disappoint him. "This is Alexis Caine," he said, taking my arm again.

I blinked but managed to keep my smile from falling off my face. *What is he trying to pull?*

A woman with something dead wrapped around her throat leaned forward. "Any relation to our illustrious host?"

I turned my smile on full force. "Yes, on my father's side."

That caused a low murmur around the group, and I tugged Falin closer so I could whisper, "I need to talk to you."

He only smiled but didn't move. After a moment, the

sensation of my last name was forgotten and conversation moved on.

Chief Reynolds clapped Falin on the back. "Falin here just transferred into the department, and we're glad to have him. I've put him on the Coleman case. He has a very promising career in . . ."

I zoned out the conversation, smiling and mimicking body language without listening to what was being said. Instead, I focused on my other senses, scanning the crowd for magic. For a group consisting largely of Humans First Party supporters, there were a lot of vanity charms. Complexion spells, antibalding charms, even a couple of breast enhancements were active in the crowd.

"Sense anything?" Falin asked as he moved us on to mingle with another group.

I shook my head, gritting my teeth behind my smile. I wasn't a divining rod. I didn't even know what I was looking for.

A prickling sensation crawled between my shoulder blades, the kind of feeling that lets you know someone is staring. Then a wave of malevolent energy washed over my mind. I shuddered, my knees buckling. Pain cut into my shoulder as the soul-sucking spell reacted with an icy pulse. I gripped Falin's arm tighter. I did *not* want to fall out in the middle of this party. I swayed, and Falin's arm moved to my waist, kept me standing.

"Who is it?" he whispered.

As quickly as the feeling hit, it retreated, like a tide pulling back into the ocean. I braced for another assault, but it didn't come. I turned. Directly behind me was a large group of people, and in the center, surrounded by his aides, was my father.

His eyes met mine, then moved back to the person he was talking to, his expression never changing. He clasped the hand of the woman shaking his, the handshake lasting long enough to become personal and leave her with the impression she'd connected with him. Then he turned away. He touched the arm of one of the men beside him, leading him outside the group. My father said something, and the tall man's eyes moved to me.

Great. Security would no doubt find me soon. *Looks like I'll be missing dinner.*

My father smiled as he stepped back into the crowd, and already there were people vying for his attention. A rotund man who had the look of a businessman stepped in front of him, blocking him from my view. The man was middle-aged with brownish hair, though it was fading to gray. *Guess that makes him a suspect*—Roy couldn't have paid at least a smidge more attention, could he? I sighed.

"Who is it?" Falin asked again.

I shook my head. I couldn't be certain. I had fears, but until I confirmed it was my father, I wasn't saying a word. I scanned the crowd. I hadn't felt the darkness again when my father's eyes met mine, but I wasn't sensing it from anyone else, either. *So Coleman can hide.* That would make things harder.

"Who's that?" I asked, nodding at a man in his early fifties with light brown hair who had just broken off from the group around my father. He stormed across the ballroom and out the side door. Conversation paused as the door slammed, then buzzed around us once more.

Falin considered the door, then said, "Pratt Bartholomew, the new lieutenant governor. He's a good ole boy and a real hothead. Is he the one?"

"Back off. I don't know yet. I'm just looking for guys fitting the description."

"Description?"

Right—I hadn't told Falin about Roy yet. "I'll explain later."

Several stunned faces were still looking at the door. The businessman was slack jawed, but he'd moved enough that I could once again see my father. One of the governor's aides, a squirrelly faced man with thick glasses, leaned in, speaking quickly. Whatever was said, my father nodded, and the aide hurried away. *No doubt after Bartholomew.*

A man standing just beyond the group caught my eye, mostly because he was watching me. He was in his late forties with a full head of dark brown hair. When he noticed me looking, he lifted his brandy glass in a silent toast.

I gave him a tight-lipped smile and leaned closer to Falin. "Who is that?"

"Jefferson Wilks, III. A senator for the opposition party."

An Equal Rights Party member here? Of course, I was here, and I was currently the most famous — *or infamous* — witch in Nekros City.

Falin took my hand. "Should we go introduce ourselves?"

I shook my head and gestured to the table of hors d'oeuvres. I had a serious need to get my legs firmly under me again, and I wasn't up for fake smiles and small talk until I did.

Falin escorted me to the table, but as soon as we reached it, someone called his name.

"Just leave me here," I told him, waving him away.

His eyes studied me a moment; then he nodded. I almost sighed with relief. I was as alone as I could be in a room full of strangers. And there was food.

I grabbed several chocolate-covered strawberries from an arrangement in the center of the table, then moved on to the table crackers. *Too bad I didn't bring my purse.*

As I loaded a cracker with caviar, a familiar chiming laughter caught my attention. I followed it to a small group of debutantes, in the center of which was Casey. Gone were the black clothes and puffy eyes. Tonight she wore a brilliant red gown, bound to draw every male eye in attendance with its swooping neckline and gold cording. She laughed at something one of her companions had said, and it sounded real, full of life, and not the least forced.

I pretended to be fascinated with the ice sculpture so I could get closer. As I stared at the life-sized couple made of ice, I let my consciousness sink a little lower so I could reach out with my other senses. The first bit of magic I touched was a charm to prevent the sculpture from melting. I pushed forward. Each girl in the group carried at least one charm, but Casey wore the most. All were weak, rather feeble spells. *Where did she buy such shoddily crafted charms?* I scanned them again and hesitated. The large diamond that dipped into her cleavage held an attraction spell designed to make her noticed and adored. It was gray magic—illegal to buy or sell. Where the hell had she gotten it?

Out of the corner of my eye, I saw several men descend on the group where Falin was "mingling." One of the men in the invading group was my father. He zeroed in on Falin. *Ah crap.*

I glanced around. Security was easy to spot—thugs in tuxes still looked dangerous—and I spotted several conveniently mingling close by.

I moved away from the buffet table. It was too visible a spot. People looked up as I passed, and I smiled, forcing myself to slow down. If I ran out of the room, I'd draw even more attention.

I worked my way to the back of the room, where a curtain concealed entry into a back hallway the caterers

used to use. I assumed they still did. Without a backward glance, I swept into the hall, surprising a cocktail
waitress.

She yelped when she saw me, and tried to conceal a
half-empty glass of wine behind her back. The tray, with
the rest of the full wineglasses she had been hired to
give out, was balancing on the chair beside her.

I gave her my best airheaded smile. "I'm lost. Where's
the restroom?"

She slipped the half-empty glass of wine on her tray
as she gave me directions—bad directions at that—to
the bathroom. I dutifully ignored the fact that she'd
been sampling her employer's wares and hoped she
would similarly forget to mention me.

Once she picked up her tray and disappeared around
the curtain, I made my way down the hall. A couple of
turns took me into the living areas of the house.

Sneaking out to avoid being kicked out. Brilliant, Alex.
I shrugged the thought off. After all, if Coleman could
ward himself from my senses, there wasn't much point
left in mingling. I might as well snoop.

I took the stairs to the second floor. My father's office was my main target, but I stopped at Casey's suite
first. I didn't like the fact that she had a gray charm. The
doorknob turned silently under my hand. I scurried in,
shutting the door behind me.

I hurried across the sitting room. Nothing interesting
was hidden in the austere decorations. As I reached the
door to her bedroom I hesitated. A faint hint of magic
tickled my senses. *Residual magic? What is residual
magic doing in the heart of Casey's suite?*

I pushed open the door and flicked on the light.

Her bedroom was bigger than my entire apartment. A
canopy bed draped in gauzy cream curtains stood in the
center of the room, the red satin pillowcases on the bed

a shocking contrast to all the cream. A small plasma TV hung on the wall across from the foot of the bed, and to one side of the bed was a small corner table with a lamp. Aside from an oak chest at the foot of the bed, a dresser, and a small bookshelf, the only other furnishings in the room were candles on tall standing candelabra.

I frowned at the candles. The four candelabra were spaced evenly around the room, one for each cardinal direction. *What is Casey up to?* I crept closer. The tingle of residual magic turned thick, a low thrum I felt through my being. I'd stepped over the edge of the latent circle before I even realized it was there.

Okay, someone had definitely been doing magic here.

I walked to her dresser. The silver-framed photos on the dresser were the only personal touches in the austere room. One photograph had captured her with a group of friends wearing poufy dresses, one was of her standing between our father and Coleman, and one showed her standing in a group of senators. The last frame held a photo with a much younger Casey in it standing beside our older brother, Brad. I picked up the large silver frame, and the tingle of magic crawled over my fingers.

A charm?

A concealment charm. I frowned. *What is she hiding?* For a sensitive, concealment charms were basically a flashing light crying, "Something interesting here!" And once you knew they were there, they were terribly easy to circumvent.

Closing my eyes, I traced my fingers over the back of the frame. A pocket had been sewn into the back. I reached inside and pulled out a thin book about the size of my hand. The leather cover was unmarked and soft with age. It buzzed slightly, as though it had absorbed magic cast around it, but this magic felt sticky. I flipped the book open.

Handwritten lines filled the pages, the tight script small and too angular to be my sister's. I flipped the page and saw a diagram for an ornate circle with cardinal and guardian points marked. *A spellbook?* I flipped further on. The spell I landed on was designed to inspire fear in an enemy. *Not just any spellbook, but gray spells.*

The door behind me banged open. "What are you doing in here?"

I flipped around, hiding the book behind my back.

Casey stood in the doorway, her cheeks flaring angry red and competing with her scarlet dress. She balled her small fists against her waist, her elbows out to her sides as if she were trying to take up as much space as possible. "I'll ask again. What are you doing here?"

"Here as in the party or—"

"Here as in my room, Alexis." She swept into the room but stopped at the edge of the bed.

I still had the book in my hand. *What the hell am I going to do with it?* I cleared my throat, not meeting her eyes. "How did you find me?"

"I knew you'd crashed the party because I saw you. I knew you were in my room because you crossed my circle."

I glanced at the invisible circle with its candelabra cardinal points. "Then you're a—"

"Witch?" She lifted a perfectly sculpted eyebrow, crossing her lithe arms over her chest. "Yes. And if you tell Daddy, I swear I'll make your life miserable while I deny it."

"But ..." But I'd been disowned for being a witch. I'd been labeled a bastard. And now Casey, his favorite, the baby, was a witch in hiding. "How can he possibly not have noticed?"

She plopped herself down on her bed, the crimson dress even more garish against the cream comforter than the scarlet pillowcases. "Please. Daddy is the least sensitive norm in the world. Mom must have been practicing under his nose for years."

"What about Brad?" I asked, and she looked away.

Had he been the one to give her the spellbook? It *had* been hidden behind his picture. Casey still wasn't looking at me. I knelt and shoved the thin book into my boot. It was not a comfortable fit. I tried to shove it down farther, but the bed shifted as Casey moved. I stood, straightening my skirt and trying to keep my face blank.

"I haven't heard from Brad. No one has. Don't you think Daddy would have called you if we'd heard from him? So, wherever he is, he doesn't know, and I don't know whether he is a witch. After you, well, you know . . ."

Yeah, I knew. After my wyrd ability had made itself known, and I had proven unable to hide it, our father had sent me off to a wyrd boarding school as soon as he'd been able to enroll me. I'd been eight the first time I packed my bags and boarded a plane alone to head to the academy; Casey had been only four. It was an impressionable age.

"When did you realize?"

She shrugged, a small lift of her thin shoulders. "I guess I always kind of knew I was sensitive, but I didn't find a teacher until a couple months ago."

"Did you charm that diamond around your neck?"

Her hand moved to the necklace, but she didn't look at it. "Yes."

"Casey, that's gray magic. Whoever your teacher is should have warned you about the damage gray magic does to your—"

"Nobody asked you, Alexis. Stay out of my business." She gave me a petulant look, just like the way she had when we were kids. In the same tone she would have used then, she said, "And get out of my room."

"Casey, I—"

"I'm going to call security if you don't leave."

I considered not leaving. Just for the hell of it. But if she screamed "Daddy" now, I'd get escorted off the premises by guards. I turned, seeing myself out.

I didn't get far.

As I slipped back into the hall a beefy hand landed on my shoulder. I froze. *Busted.*

I didn't recognize the square-jawed man, but he clearly knew me. He shoved me forward, and I begrudgingly allowed him to march me into my father's office. Well, the office was where I wanted to go anyway—just not in this circumstance.

My father sat behind his huge mahogany desk, his fingers steepled before his lips. His dark gaze fixed on me as soon as I entered, but he said nothing. The beefy guard—or assistant or whatever my father called him— pushed me into the leather armchair in front of the desk. I leaned back, trying to look comfortable.

Still my father remained silent.

A game of nerves? I tried for an eyebrow lift, but even if my face didn't show the sutures, they were definitely still there. I ended up scowling instead. My father just watched me, his face impassive.

I shifted my weight, my dress rustling around my boots. *Fine; if we aren't talking, I'll do something else.* I focused on opening my senses and found—nothing. Not even a charm to make sure his suit continued to look perfect if he spilled food on it during dinner. I scanned his two goons, since they'd likely been in the group earlier. One carried a charm I couldn't identify on a casual pass, but it felt benign enough. The other had no magic on him.

Still no one spoke.

I shifted my weight again, wiping my palms on the skirt of my dress.

"Well?" I finally asked.

My father shook his head. "Always the impatient one." He dropped his hands and reached for a pen. He studied the document in front of him as though I'd been dismissed.

I wasn't fooled.

Without looking up he said, "This is the second time in as many days you've invaded my home. What is it you want, Alexis?"

I stared at the top of his head, not saying anything. The silence was sharp, cutting the air between us. Finally, he put the pen down and looked up. Impatient or not, I figured I was about as stubborn as he was, so I held my tongue.

Minutes ticked by, and his lips pressed into a thin line. "Alexis, I have a reason for my actions. A plan. Can you say the same?" He glanced over his shoulder and said, "See her out. And make sure the guards know not to let her back in."

That was my dismissal. The goon behind me squeezed my shoulder, and I stood without further prompting. As I stepped though the office door I turned back to face my father.

"By the way, George, great party, but one thing amazes me. Why is it Humans First Party supporters hate witches, but sneak in illusion charms for an instant face-lift or boob job?" Turning on my heel, I stormed out of the room, leaving the goon to catch up.

I shook my head as I took the stairs two at a time. *That was my great retort? A boob job?* After all these years, he still got under my skin. At least one thing was certain: that man was definitely my father.

Chapter 11

I leaned against the gate and smiled in the general direction of the guard's silhouette. I could only hope Falin saw me waiting for him, or I'd be begging for a ride. I had serious doubts I'd have much luck in that department.

I shouldn't have worried. Not twenty minutes after I was jettisoned from the party, Falin's convertible purred up to the gate. The stiff set of his jaw as he drove made me think he probably wasn't thrilled with leaving the party before dinner. What could I say? I'd never been on a date before. I didn't know the rules.

"Where did you go?" he asked as he took a turn a little too tight.

"Investigating."

"You got us kicked out."

I scooted lower in my seat, crossing my arms over my chest. "It was bound to happen anyway. Maybe you missed the memo, but my father and I don't get along. And what was with you using my real name? You were asking for my father to kick us out."

Falin grunted, which I interpreted as either amusement or disgust.

"Can I ask you a theoretical question?" I didn't wait for his answer. I was asking my question now, because after tonight, he might never speak to me again. "If there was a spell sucking on someone's soul, how would you stop it?"

He slammed on the brakes, and the car skidded to a stop in front of a red light. I waited.

The light turned green, but the car didn't move, and he still didn't answer. *Okay, what's with people not talking tonight?*

The plush leather groaned under me as I squirmed, and the driver in the car behind us blared his horn. The convertible jetted forward.

"You're not talking about a soul being ejected. You're talking consumption?" His voice was guarded, and deadly serious.

Considering it was my soul, so was I.

I nodded and waited, but he didn't say anything else. "Well?"

His cell phone chirped at his side, but he turned toward me, the streetlights highlighting the severe lines of his face. "Why do you expect me to know the answer?" The phone chirped again and he pulled it from his waist one-handed. "Andrews," he barked into the phone as greeting.

Because you seem to know too much? I didn't say it. Instead I rubbed the scratches on my shoulder and turned to look at the darkness outside my window, giving him as much illusion of privacy as I could in the small car. *If my father isn't Coleman, then who is?* There had been too many people too close together when I'd picked up that wave of dark magic. It could have been any of them. I shook my head.

"I'm not far. I'll be there in a moment." Falin's phone snapped shut, and he flicked a switch, filling the night sky surrounding the car with blue lights. "Change of plans," he said. "There's been a murder. I'll get one of the officers at the scene to drop you off."

I'd thought Falin's driving was reckless before, but the flashing blue lights freed him to press the car's speedometer to the max. In no time, we were pulling into a gravel pit filled with cop cars. I swallowed hard. My night vision was beyond wrecked from years of using grave-sight, and the flashing blue lights didn't help, but from what I could see, this place looked a little too familiar.

"Uh, Falin, is this an abandoned warehouse?"

"Yeah." He threw the car in park and jumped out, slamming the door behind me. "Stay in the car."

"Wait! I—"

"Stay in the car."

I slumped back into my seat, readjusted my skirt, and propped my booted feet on the dash. I fished the spellbook out of my boot and tossed it in my purse. Then I waited, counting under my breath. I hit number fifty. *He has to have made it inside by now.*

I looked around but couldn't see much. *Well, it's now or never.* I slipped out of the car and pushed the door closed silently. Then I walked toward the lights at the end of the gravel lot.

The building had enough security lighting around it that I didn't run into anything, but the corners where the light didn't reach were eaten by shadows. I avoided those as I made my way to the yellow crime tape.

"Alex, girl, is that you?"

I turned at my name. A man, probably a cop, swaggered in my direction. Or maybe it wasn't a swagger. Maybe his knees were weak. I stared too long, struggling to decipher the shadowed features into a familiar face.

"That is you, Alex. I hardly recognized you all dressed up."

The voice finally clicked. "Detective Jenson. How are you?"

He shrugged, but his face was paler than it should have been. Jenson hadn't been in the homicide unit for more than five years, but his eyes were already defeated. He'd been John's partner since transferring to homicide, but no one expected him to stay with the unit much longer.

"So, you're dressing up to see crime scenes these days? Touch of fame get to you?" Jenson said, and I couldn't tell whether it was the shadows that made his smile look like a sneer.

Generally I liked Jenson. He was at Tuesday dinner at John's once in a while, and he usually respected the help I provided the cops. The wind shifted, bringing with it the putrid smell of vomit.

I wrinkled my nose. "It's bad in there, isn't it?"

He glanced over his shoulder at the building looming behind him. "I saw Detective Andrews a minute ago. You screwing your way into crime scenes now that John's in the hospital?"

I blinked and curled my fingers into my arm to ensure I didn't slap him.

"I don't believe we were talking about my dating habits, Detective."

"I haven't heard much about you dating anyone." He leaned forward.

The scent of vomit wasn't just on the wind, it was on his breath. Whatever was inside the warehouse was bad, but I wasn't going to stand there being insulted just so he could block out what he'd seen. I stepped back.

"Good night, Detective." I walked away without glancing back. *The asshole—where did he get off thinking he could . . .*

I shook my head. I had too much to worry about to waste time thinking about Jenson. I needed a better look at the facade of the warehouse. But I knew already. The claws of dread had sunk deep into my skin, and I just knew. This was the same warehouse Roy had taken me to. And, I knew that whatever was inside was worse than Jenson imagined.

I stumbled around to the back of the warehouse. A security light buzzed in the humid air, illuminating three boarded-up loading docks—the center dock with loose paneling. I planned on turning back once I confirmed where I was. Really, I did. I'd felt the magic that had occurred in that warehouse. I didn't need to see whatever was inside. But standing in front of the middle dock were three people I could make out clearly, as if they were standing in bright sunlight. One of them was Death.

Considering that the cop standing between the three figures and me was shrouded in shadows, I was seeing Death's companions on a psychic level. Which meant they were all soul collectors. Death was the only collector I'd ever seen. I'd never even heard of a grave witch who'd had contact with more than one collector at once. I ducked under the tape.

I was halfway to the dock before I remembered the officer guarding the perimeter, and I remembered him only because he caught my elbow.

"I'm sorry, ma'am. You have to stay on the other side of the—oh, Miss Craft. I didn't recognize you."

I looked at the officer, who I guessed was younger than me and probably fresh out of police academy. New cops trended toward two categories: everything exactly by the book or unsure and wet behind the ears. I was seriously hoping this young officer was the latter.

"Evening, Officer," I said, smiling at him. "Detective Andrews brought me."

It was true. Falin had driven me here. The officer could take it any way he wanted.

The young officer released my arm. "Oh, I'm sorry, Miss Craft. No one told me you'd be on the scene. If you haven't seen her yet, it's easier to get in the front."

Her? "I'm just going to poke around a bit, thanks." I flashed the officer another smile. I had to say one thing about working a recent scandal—everyone in the department knew my name and that I raised the dead. But if he checked my story, I was going to be so busted. I quickened my steps.

Death looked up at my approach, but the other two collectors didn't appear to notice me. Or maybe they didn't care. *Well, if people can't see you, no point hiding.*

The three collectors couldn't have been more different. As usual, Death wore faded jeans with a tight black shirt. I'd always assumed black was the dress code for a collector, but the woman to his right wore a bright orange tube top with a pair of white PVC hip-huggers and knee-high boots. Her dreadlocks, dyed the same bright orange as her top, fell to the middle of her back. I'd heard of female collectors before, but she looked more as if she was headed for a rave than to collect souls.

In contrast to the raver's brightness, the third collector was drab. He wore a gray-on-gray suit complete with a wilted flower in his lapel. His gray hair was slicked back from his face, and at his side he carried a cane, a silver skull serving as a handle.

As I drew near, Death touched the woman's arm, silencing her before I was close enough to overhear their conversation. She glared at him and then followed his gaze to me. She dismissed me with less than a glance, but the man in gray strolled into my path.

I hesitated. Death had a tendency to walk through mortals, giving them a chill, but collectors were solid to me. Letting Mr. Gray run into me to prove the point wasn't a great a plan. I stepped out of his way, my eyes locked on his. His eyebrows lifted, and I noticed that the face surrounded by all that gray was youthful.

The woman put her hands on her waist, her bright nails pressing into her skin. She glared at Death. "What—did you advertise?"

He ignored her and held out his hand. Holding hands wasn't normally in our repertoire. *A social norm among collectors, maybe?* I didn't know, so I accepted his hand. His icy fingers closed around mine, his palm sending shivers up my arm despite the humid air.

He tugged me forward, closer to his side. "Why are you here, Alex?"

I could ask him the same question. Actually, I already had a pretty good idea. "Did you collect the victim's soul?"

The raver growled, a sound more at home coming from a tiger's throat than anything human-shaped. Of course, human-shaped didn't mean human. She looked down at my hand in Death's, and her lips curled back. "You're a fool." She stepped back and looked at the gray man. "You know what? I'm out of here. You fools can deal with it yourselves." She vanished.

What was that about? I glanced at Death. His lips, so often smiling, were drawn in a serious line, and his eyes held no spark.

I leaned close enough that his chill permeated the air around me, causing goose bumps to lift on my flesh. "What is going on?"

His tired eyes were a heavy weight on my skin as he studied my face. Then his gaze slid lower, tripped over the scratches on my shoulder, and hesitated before climbing to my face again. "I think you can help us."

The gray man shook his head. "I want no part of this."

"Then we all leave, and that's the end of it," Death said, but his fingers tightened around mine.

The cane swung like a pendulum below the gray man's clasped hands. He shook his head, but it was a slow, unsure movement. "No. No, I guess we can't do that." The cane stopped. "You'll take precautions," he said, his gaze flicking to me.

Death nodded, and his grip on my fingers changed. He stepped around to face me and guided my arm so our hands were clasped between our bodies. "I need you to swear you won't tell anyone our part in what will happen. What you learn tonight."

He leaned, his face only inches from mine, intimately close, but there was no hint of teasing in his eyes. "It might be dangerous. You don't have to agree," he whispered.

I swallowed. *Dangerous and I can't tell anyone?* The age of hiding and secrets among witches was supposed to be over. The OMIH encouraged sharing knowledge so we'd advance. But twice Death had stalled collecting a soul because I'd asked. And he'd saved my life. He'd never once asked anything of me. I could do this, whatever it was, and whatever the stipulations. I nodded.

Death smiled, but the way his lips tightened and the corners of his eyes pinched betrayed that it wasn't a happy smile, more concerned acceptance of my decision. His hand moved to my face, sending shivers down my neck. "Your oath."

I opened my mouth just as footsteps stopped behind me.

"Miss Craft, you okay?" the young officer from earlier asked.

Death frowned at him, which the officer couldn't see. I probably looked crazy standing here talking with invisible people. I turned.

"I'm fine, thank you. I'm ... preparing to go inside."

He nodded, but the suspicion didn't fall from around his eyes.

I waited until he was out of earshot before I turned back to Death. "I won't say anything."

The gray man scoffed, and Death shook his head. His hand fell from my face, wrapped around the fingers in my free hand, and then lifted it until I was staring at my own obsidian ring.

"A true oath, Alex," he said.

Damn. I hate binding oaths. Everything was in the wording. If I made the oath too encompassing, I'd be bound not to discuss anything I saw. Too limiting and we'd have to negotiate. Taking a deep breath, I tapped the power in the ring, then added the magic to my voice. "I swear on power not to discuss without your permission what I see tonight as it relates to the secrets of soul collectors."

He nodded. "I accept and promise to share what secrets you require to aid you this night."

His power met mine, cool mixing with heat. I could almost see it twisting, changing. Then the power-spun oath sank under my skin, and the binding settled on my mind, my heart, my soul. I closed my eyes and arched my back, feeling the slight heaviness of the oath. I'd get used to it soon.

Death dropped my hands and turned. He nodded to the gray man, and they both walked through the paneling and into the warehouse. *Yeah, great, guys. I can't exactly walk through solid objects.* Actually, I wasn't about to grumble much. I hadn't asked Death for anything in exchange for my oath, but he'd promised me aid. I could only hope that extended to the spell sucking on my soul.

The panel was still pried open from where I'd snuck inside before, and I wiggled through the opening, trying not to snag Tamara's dress. The last time I'd been in the warehouse, it had been midafternoon, and sunlight streaming in had illuminated the crates scattered in my path, but in the twilight, the warehouse floor was dark.

Death and the gray man were already on the other side of the room. A little bit of light leaked from the inner door where I guessed the body was located, but it wasn't enough to help. I reached out with my hands, taking slow steps, but I made it only a yard before bumping into a crate. *Dammit.*

Death looked up and, realizing the problem, moved to my side. He knew about my eyesight, though, in truth, even someone with great night vision would have had trouble in the dark warehouse. Death took my hand. "Step where I step."

Easier said than done. Not to mention that being led around by someone who normally didn't worry about solid objects meant he kept forgetting I needed to be warned when small objects I could step on or over were in my path. And he didn't take into account the fact that my dress would snag if I brushed against a crate. By the time we reached the door I was thankful my boots had saved my ankles and shins, but I had serious concerns about the condition of Tamara's dress.

The gray man waited right inside the door, twirling his cane as if it were a skull-tipped baton. "So, your little girl is going to go in there and work magic?"

Death frowned at him without answering. Then he looked at me. "Are you ready for this?"

I had no idea what I'd see inside, but I could feel the malevolence of whatever spell had been worked. It seeped out of the room like spreading darkness. It made my skin crawl, as though my flesh was trying to get farther away from the magic. Some part of me screamed to turn around, to run. I ignored it. Nodding, I stepped around the gray man, around Death, and into the scene of a dark ritual murder.

Chapter 12

⊸•≡◦≡•⊷

The cops were the first thing I noticed. They were moving. It's a survival instinct—when you're frightened, you always notice the moving things first. The cops were working in small teams to take pictures, put down markers, and bag evidence. Falin stood on the far side of the room, talking to the coroner.

Then I noticed the furniture. Yesterday this room had been deserted without so much as dust to disturb the emptiness. Today plush throw rugs covered the floor. On the rugs were dozens of large mood candles, most still lit. The candles were gathered around an ornate bed in the very center of the room. *And the center of the circle.* A small round table stood to the side of the bed, a bottle of champagne and two flutes on top. A white silken cord looped around the bedpost closest to me, the white turning scarlet where it was attached to a crimson object. I stared at it, knowing it would be bad when my brain took time to puzzle out the red lump.

A bloody foot.

I took a deep breath, hoping it would help the tightness in my stomach. It didn't, but I forced my eyes to move on. To move up the bloodstained leg, over the bare hip. My gaze snagged on what logic told me was a torso—all I saw were wet, dark shapes flowing from the crimson skin. Bile crept up my throat and burned my tongue, and I forced my gaze higher. The woman's face was washed in red. Her glazed, sightless eyes stared out at the room, her lips twisted in an endless scream.

It was too much.

I swayed. Only Death's arm sliding around my waist kept me standing as my knees gave out and I doubled over. My stomach heaved, and I gritted my teeth, fighting the convulsions in my throat. *I will not get sick at the crime scene.*

Death's cold hand moved to the back of my neck. "Breathe, Alex. Just breathe."

The cold helped calm the sick heat gripping me, and I nodded, obediently gulping down air. As I fought my body, the magic in the room grated against my mind, trying to worm its way inside my defenses. The circle was down, but the dark, cutting magic in the air was still very active.

I have to get out of here.

I straightened, ready to run as far as my shaky legs would take me, to flee and never look back. Death stopped me. His arms wrapped around my shoulders, dragged me against his broad chest.

"Come on, Alex. Deep breaths."

The gray man made a rude sound somewhere behind me. "This is your idea of help?"

The cutting iciness of Death's touch was fading, replaced by a growing numbness. It crawled over my cheek, across my chest, down my legs. *Numb is good.* Or it meant I was dying.

Death released me and stepped back. His hand moved to my numb cheek, and he tilted my head back.

My gaze dragged up to meet his. The cool depths of the grave reflected in darkness in his eyes. The chill, already saturating so much of my skin, seeped deeper, drawing out the part of me that touched the dead. My shields ripped away and my heat fled as a gray patina washed over the room. Without a circle, inside a room with malicious magic, I was now straddling the chasm between the living and the dead.

Death dropped his hand, a pained expression crossing his face. He didn't change in my grave-sight — he was exactly what he was — but the walls behind him crumbled, the rusting supports underneath revealed. I took a deep breath. The air was warm, but my breath condensed as I blew it out. I turned.

The gray man was staring, his cane suspended in midspin. "That was risky," he whispered, and I had no idea if he was talking to me or to Death.

Death stepped closer, but he didn't touch me. He pointed toward the center of the room. "You asked if we collected the soul of the victim. We did not. We could not. We need you to find what is left and pull it from the body."

I blinked at him. "The soul is still in the body?" I turned. In the center of the blood and entrails was the faintest glow of blue. A dim soul still locked inside dead flesh. Even filled with the calm chill of the grave, my stomach twisted.

I shook my head. "No."

Death raised an eyebrow. "No what?"

"She can still feel . . ." I couldn't finish the sentence. The woman — not breathing, her heart not in her body, her skin in threads — was somewhat alive. Somehow, on some level, she had felt everything that had happened to her.

I squeezed my eyes closed. That didn't help. I was

seeing things on a psychic level, so if anything, closing my eyes brought the faint pulse of her soul into sharper focus. I looked down at the floor, and as I stared at the crumbling cement under my feet I realized something was missing. The rugs.

I looked up. There were no rugs, no candles, no round table with a bottle of champagne on top. My gaze moved to the woman. She was very much still there, her soul pulsing weakly, but the ornate bed she'd been tied to was now a cheap folding table.

"I don't understand. What am I seeing?"

"You are Seeing," Death said, as if that meant anything. "You are looking through planes of existence, through truth."

Nothing in this room exists? Well, not nothing. There was the folding table and the markers the cops were setting down; while those were rotted in my grave-sight, they were in fact real.

I stepped forward but stopped before crossing the inactive circle. It had been broken, not released. I could feel the backlash still threading through the remnants. *The ritual was interrupted?*

I crossed the edge of the circle, and it was like stepping into a vortex. Every dark, angry wave of energy that crashed into me during my first visit was like a single raindrop compared to the tempest of what I stood in now. My body shook under the onslaught. I could see the sickly black strands and dangerous red knots of magic in the air, and for a moment I thought I'd been jettisoned into the Aetheric. But no. There was just that much magic here.

I took another step forward, and as if the magic could sense me, black and red tentacles of magic snaked toward me. A dark tendril reached me. It twined up my boot to encircle my bare calf.

Pain pulsed into my skin as the magic attacked what few personal shields I had remaining while consumed by grave magic. The pain turned to a burn, and I back-pedaled out of the latent circle. Death knelt, his hand moving to my leg, and the magic dissipated, leaving a dull throb behind.

"We'll have to get her through," Death said, looking at the gray man.

"I was afraid you'd say that." He lifted his cane straight in front of him as if it would ward off evil. Then he walked across the edge of the circle. "Come on, then. We're running out of time."

I shot an uncertain look at Death.

"Walk where he does, and stay close. I'll guard your back," he said.

Okay. Next time I was asking for more specifics before agreeing to any favors for Death. I fell in step behind the gray man, crossing the circle where he had. Again the onslaught of magic cozied up to my senses, leaving oily marks on my mind, but the tendrils of magic didn't attack this time. They flowed around us, opening like a tunnel before the gray man. Behind me, Death walked backward, his palm out. They looked as though they'd formed a protective bubble.

"Hey, who are you?" a cop yelled to my side. The collectors didn't stop, so neither did I.

"You two can't be in here!"

Two? They can see Death?

"Alex Craft!"

That voice was Falin. Definitely.

I kept walking.

"Sir, they just walked *through* the table."

Oops. He must have meant the table with the champagne I'd seen when I first entered. I couldn't see it at all now.

"What the hell is going on?" Falin again.

The cops closest to us drew guns.

"Don't shoot," Falin yelled. "Alex, get over here. Now."

We reached the bed, or table, as it now appeared in my grave-sight.

"Now what?" I whispered.

"Get her out of that body," Death said, still behind me.

How the hell do I do that? I looked down at the body and winced as I saw the glowing glyphs cut into her skin. When all I could see was blood and gore, I'd thought the attack on her had been savage, but now I saw it had been precise, each slice purposeful. One symbol was repeated over and over. The foreign glyphs were both similar to and different from what I'd seen on Coleman's body.

As I watched, the glow of her soul faded further as the crimson glyphs burned brighter.

The gray man grabbed my arm. "If you can free her, do it now."

I nodded, and I thrust my power into her. There was a struggle of life and death in the corpse, and life wasn't winning. I wished my power could heal her body, her soul, but it couldn't. My power was with the grave.

I could feel the spell on her body burning into my own skin. An icy, cutting spell. Pain stabbed through my shoulder, and I knew my personal soul-sucking spell was growing, devouring me. I recoiled, drawing my power back. Then I felt her soul.

In all the darkness of the spell, her soul was a thing of light and warmth. Like a moth drawn to flame, my power reached for her. But souls and the grave don't mix. The soul, weak from fighting the spell, sank deeper into her being. Hiding.

I poured everything I had into the corpse. My body

temperature fell, but I barely noticed. I had no more heat, no more life-power to feed the body, so I filled the body with grave-chill. My power chased after the soul as it retreated. Her soul sank into the space her shade should have filled, and I found a misshapen, shredded shade. *Just like Bethany.* My power flooded the space, and the soul retreated farther. I pushed on.

The spell was sluggish and methodical. I wasn't. My power swept deeper faster, both recoiling from the spell's touch and pursuing the soul. I reached the inner-most base of her being and filled it with everything I had, every ounce of power.

The soul sprang from the body, and I collapsed to my knees. Above me, glowing faintly blue where the dark-ness didn't touch her, was the soul. She screamed, still weak from fighting but filled with my power. I'd never understood how ghosts came to be, but I was looking at one. And this one wasn't sane.

The ghost wailed, lashing out at the gray man. The spell had come with her. The glyphs on her body were now dark patches surrounded by thick twisting tendrils. *Just like the scratches.* But unlike the spell on me, I could see this one growing, and it was growing fast.

The gray man reached out, and his fingers closed around one of the dark glyphs. He pulled, and the ghost screamed louder, tearing at his arm. He kept pulling, ripping the glyph free with all the tangled roots it had grown. Once free of the ghost, the dark glyph dissipated. The gray man grabbed another of the dark symbols, and Death joined him.

With neither of them guarding against the other magic in the circle, the knotted tendrils were gathering again. *It's time for me to get out of here.* I pushed to my feet. My knees buckled, and I stumbled, nearly falling again. Righting myself, I took another step. That one worked better. A dark tendril moved within a foot of me, and I broke into a jerky run.

I crossed the edge of the circle but didn't stop until I'd reached the far wall. Then I collapsed against it and drew my shaking knees to my chest. Death and the gray man were still in the center of the circle, still pulling dark glyphs off the ghost, but they were almost done. With each glyph they destroyed, the ghost grew brighter, more solid. But she didn't stop screaming.

Several cops were on their knees, their hands over their ears. Another had fainted. Two still had their guns drawn and pointed, but they were staring at the ghost. Falin was on the other side of the room, and he was the only person looking at me. My vision was starting to blank out, my grave-sight shutting down, so I could only just see the silver of his soul burning under his skin. But I didn't have to be able to see him to know he was pissed.

Death pulled the last glyph from the ghost. The gray man saluted him with his cane, turned, and then sank a hand into the ghost. She didn't stop screaming until both she and the gray man had disappeared.

Death turned and smiled at me, and the trance the cops had been in broke. One yelled for him to freeze. The other opened fire.

I tried to jump to my feet, but my legs didn't listen, and I slammed into the wall. My breath whooshed out, and I blinked. My vision was darkening. But I could see Death. He looked surprised, his hand covering his stomach. Time moved in slow motion as he pulled his hand away, his palm soaked in crimson.

"No." I meant to yell, but my voice barely carried. The sound of the cops yelling turned to a buzz in the back of my head as Death fell to his knees.

My body felt unreal as I struggled to stand. It took

three tries. I had no breath, no strength, but I had to make it to Death. *He can't die. He's Death.*

A shadow moved in the doorway beside me. "Damn boys can't do anything right."

The raver collector sashayed into the room, her nails clicking as she strummed her fingers together. "I guess this is your fault," she said.

I just blinked at her—I wasn't good for much else. I was out of magic, out of strength. The raver shook her head, making her neon dreads quiver. Then she marched across the floor. She pulled Death's arm over her shoulder and half carried, half dragged him out of the circle. Somewhere behind her a gun clattered to the cement.

"Come on." The raver grabbed my arm and dragged me, while still carrying Death, through the doorway and back into the dusty storeroom we'd entered when we first arrived. I stumbled after her.

"Well, get to it," she said, depositing me against the wall and, at least momentarily, out of sight of the cops.

"I, uh, what?"

"You swapped life essences. Take it back." She moved Death closer.

I reached out, brushing his dark hair back behind his ear. I'd always wanted to do that but never had the nerve. My fingers trailed over his cheek, and his skin was blisteringly hot to the touch.

His dark eyes opened and locked onto mine. "I'm sorry, Alex."

I almost laughed. He'd been shot and *he* was the one sorry? I shook my head.

His hand moved to mine, pressed my palm against his face. "You're trembling."

I blinked back the moisture blinding my eyes. "Don't worry about me." The words burned the back of my throat.

"Get on with it," the raver snapped.

I nodded. I had no idea what I was doing, but I hadn't with the soul, either. I could only hope I hadn't used up the last of my luck.

I didn't have any power to reach with, but it turned out I didn't need to. I opened my mind, myself, and just as it was with a corpse, my heat, my life essence, flowed back into me. Warmth filtered into my body. Not much warmth, just enough to accent the cold.

Then the pain hit.

My world went red. The pain was everywhere, everything. I was dying. I could feel every cell in my body dying, withering.

Strong arms wrapped around my body, and I realized I was shaking. *No. Convulsing.*

"It will pass," Death whispered, his hand pressed in my hair. "It will pass."

Death lowered me to the ground, and I lay there, gasping. The pain had passed, but I could still feel my body dying all around me.

I'm dying.

I must have spoken the thought out loud, because Death shook his head.

"You're mortal. You've always been dying."

"It's time to go," the raver said.

Death glanced over his shoulder at her. "I have something left to do." He turned back to me and smoothed away curls that had fallen in my face. His fingers, while not blisteringly hot, still felt warm. I was coherent enough to realize that Death feeling warm to me was a very bad sign.

"The consumption spell on your shoulder—" he started, but the raver cut him off.

"What the hell are you doing?"

"I'm oath-bound to aid her, like she aided us. Now lis-

ten, Alex. I can't pull the spell free while your soul is still
inside your body. You have to track down and destroy
the one who cast it. That is the only way."

Peachy.

He wasn't done yet. "The spell is malignant and contagious, but very specific in whom it targets. Your soul is
strong. It's fighting. But if the spell wears you down or
spreads too far, I'll come for you. I won't let it consume
you."

He'd kill me? Better than being eaten, I guess.

He leaned forward until my world was filled with his
face. His dark eyes were warm, his breath close enough
to caress my skin. "But please, Alex, find the one who
cast it."

The raver cleared her throat. "This is so sweet I'm
going to end up diabetic. Now let's get out of here."

Death frowned, but he stood. Then they vanished.

Chapter 13

I lay in the darkness trembling, trying to find the strength to sit up. I couldn't find it. So I lay there on the dusty floor. In a borrowed dress. With a roomful of pissed-off cops on the other side of the wall.

"What the hell are you doing in my crime scene!"

Scratch that. The most pissed-off cop of all was now in the room with me.

With my grave-sight gone, I was completely blind, but I didn't need my eyes to recognize that voice—Falin had yelled at me enough in our short acquaintance that it was ingrained in my memory.

I'd have liked to be nonchalant, but I'd exchanged essences with Death, been attacked by a malevolent spell, created a ghost, gotten my own essence back, and then had a seizure. The past ten minutes had been rough. I wasn't up for snappy comebacks. Hell—I was barely up to breathing.

So I just continued doing exactly what I had been doing. I lay there and trembled.

"Get up," Falin commanded. "Get up."

He reached down, grabbing my elbow, and his gloved

hand burned my arm like a branding iron. I yelped, the pain making my eyes sting with tears.

Falin jerked back. "Damn, you're freezing."

I heard his steps move farther into the room, circle back. When he spoke again, I could tell he'd crouched near me. "What the hell happened in there? Who was that man, and where did he go?"

I didn't say anything.

"Answer me, Alex Craft, or so help me . . ." He left the rest of the threat to my imagination.

"I can't."

There was a long pause after I spoke. Then he said, "Fine."

His hand locked on my arm again, but this time his touch wasn't blisteringly hot. *My temperature couldn't have risen that fast; how did he* . . . Body temperature wasn't what I should have been worrying about. Something hard and metallic snapped around one wrist, then around my other wrist.

Handcuffs? Oh crap, he's arresting me.

"Get up," he said again, and dragged me by my cuffed arms to a sitting position.

I tried to get my feet under me, but there was no doing it. My legs were like jelly, and I couldn't stop shaking. Falin seemed to realize the futility as well, because he leaned me back against the wall.

"I've seen you after raising a shade before. You weren't this bad off."

"Wasn't a shade." But I couldn't say anything more. The oath bound my tongue. I drew in a deep breath and leaned my head against the wall. My cheeks felt sticky. Tears were still leaking from my eyes, mixing with the dust. I moved to scrub the gritty mess away, but my hands were cuffed behind my back. The effort almost toppled me to the floor. Falin's hands steadied me.

There was a rustling sound in front of me; then fabric fell around my shoulders. *Falin's tux jacket?* He tucked it around me. I didn't feel any warmer for his effort.

"You can't see a thing, can you?" he asked.

"It's dark in here."

"Alex, I have my flashlight pointed at you."

I blinked. *He had light pointed at me?* All I could see was complete and unbroken darkness. I'd never been this blind after touching the grave. Never.

"I'm taking you to the hospital."

"No!" The last thing I needed was another hospital bill. I just wanted to be able to see again, and to not be cold, and to stand on my own, and . . . Besides, even if he took me to the hospital in the Magic Quarter, I doubted they'd ever treated anyone who'd exchanged life essence with a soul collector. "I just want to go home."

"You can't. Alex, you broke into a crime scene and tampered with evidence."

"I had to. The victim . . ." Again the oath bound my tongue. "I just had to. Believe me. And don't let anyone touch the body. You need an anti–black magic unit."

"They already cleared the scene."

My mouth fell slack. *How could they have cleared it?* "But the spells are active. And the furniture . . . nothing is in that room but the woman and a folding table." I hadn't been sure I would be able to say that last part, but apparently seeing through the illusion wasn't included in Death's secrets.

Falin's footsteps led away from me as he walked into the other room. Minutes passed. *If I stop trembling, I'll probably fall asleep.* Not that the idea of falling asleep on the floor thrilled me. But I was tired. More than that, though, I was cold. Had I ever been this cold before? Commotion picked up in the room behind me. People leaving. *Falin's clearing the scene?*

The other room was quiet by the time footsteps drew near me again. "The anti–black magic unit is on their way. I'm getting you out of here."

Then Falin picked me up. He carried me out of the crime scene, his jacket still draped around me and my hands cuffed behind my back.

"Where are we?" I asked as Falin's keys jingled. He'd taken the cuffs off me once we'd reached his car, and wherever we were now was too quiet to be a police station.

"My apartment," he said, and I heard the door open. He helped me hobble inside, then deposited me on a plush couch.

"And why am I here?"

"Because you won't let me take you to the hospital, and I'm not leaving you alone in your condition. Now, stay put."

I nestled into the cushy couch. I wasn't sure where he thought I'd go. I was in a strange place, I couldn't see, and I could barely hold myself up. Not exactly the perfect condition for snooping.

The smell of coffee permeated the air, and a hinge squeaked as a cabinet opened. The couch cushion moved as he sat. He lifted my hand, pressing a coffee mug into it.

The mug was hot. Way too hot. I winced, pulling back, and the couch cushion moved again. There was a soft clink as he set the mug on a flat surface.

A door opened somewhere to my left, and I jumped, blinking in the darkness that filled my eyes. Something large and soft fell around my shoulders. *Blanket?* Falin wrapped it around me, then pressed his hand against my forehead.

"This can't be natural."

"I'm okay. I just need ..." I wasn't sure what I needed. A couple of stiff drinks and another body against my skin to warm me would be a good start, but I couldn't really say that.

He moved away again, and I heard water running. When he returned, he pressed something wet against my cheek. I jerked back.

"Stay still," he said, and pressed the damp rag against my cheek again, wiping away the grit from the warehouse.

"I'm not an invalid," I said, trying to take the rag away from him. He was starting to freak me out.

"Fine." He gave it to me, and I scrubbed at my face until my cheeks felt raw. Then I shrugged out of the blanket and rubbed the cloth over my bare shoulders and arms.

When I was done, I realized I had no idea what to do with the rag now. Falin took it from my hand and replaced it with a dry towel.

"Why are you being so nice to me?" I asked.

He was silent a long time. "Maybe I just intend to get answers out of you."

Now, *that* I believed. I pulled my knees to my chest and dragged the blanket tighter. "I'll tell you what I can."

"Yes, you will." His hand moved to my face, his touch gentle as his palm cupped my cheek.

My first instinct was to pull away, but his hand was warm, and I so desperately wanted to be warm.

"Why did you break into my crime scene?"

"Initially because I recognized the warehouse. It is the same one Coleman used when he stole his new body."

"And how do you know that?"

I told him about Roy and my first trip to the warehouse. When I finished talking, I frowned. I'd said more than I wanted. A whole lot more. I'd practically put everything I knew on the table. "You're using a truth-seeking spell on me."

"Yes." He didn't pause. "You said that was only your initial reason. What were the other reasons?"

I opened my mouth. Closed it. The spell compelled me to answer. My oath bound my tongue. The words felt as though they were being forced up my throat and then tied in knots. I gritted my teeth. *How dare he use a spell on me?* But I couldn't not answer. Finally I said, "A favor for a friend. Why can't I feel the spell you're using?"

"It's my personal magic. You're not attuned to it," he said.

He answered truthfully? So the spell goes both ways.

He hurried on with his next question before I could say anything. "Was this friend the man in the warehouse?"

"I'm oath-bound not to say. How—"

He spoke over me, cutting me off. "Did this man have anything to do with the murder?"

"No. He was there to help. We helped her. How—"

His other hand covered my mouth. "Nod yes or no. The oath is preventing you from telling me about the man and what his purpose was there?"

My head nodded as if I had no control over it. *Damn.* I grabbed at his wrist, trying to rip it from my mouth, but I was trembling and weak. His hand didn't move. *Dammit. It's my turn to get some answers.* But it wasn't, not unless he could hear my question.

"Do you know what the ritual was for?"

I nodded, then shook my head. Finally I shrugged. How's that for indecision?

Falin growled with frustration and dropped the hand over my mouth. "Explain."

"I know what one spell was meant to do, but there

were more spells in that circle. And I don't know why the spell was cast." I stopped. I'd barely considered it until I said it, but there had to be a reason why someone would cast a soul-consuming spell. John had said Bethany was the third body they'd found with the same MO, and I was positive that if the ritual hadn't been interrupted tonight, this victim would have been cleaned up and dumped just like the first three. That was four victims in a short amount of time. It couldn't have been a coincidence that Coleman had used the same warehouse, *the very same circle*, for his body switch.

"The case John was working, the three body dumps—when was the first victim found?"

Falin was silent a moment, as though he had to try to remember. "He was working on it when I transferred into the department, so it was at least two weeks ago."

Before Coleman was shot.

His fingers on my face tensed. "Why? What are you thinking?"

"Those bodies probably had glyphs cut into them. You'll find that tonight's victim does as well. The spell—" The oath wouldn't let me say anything about the soul-consuming spell. But souls were full of life, energy. If that energy was being consumed, it had to be going somewhere. "I think the murders are preparation work. I think there will be a really big, really nasty ritual. And I think it will happen soon."

Falin's hand fell from my face, and the cushion moved as he leaned back on the couch. "I should never have called you a magic eye."

I smiled, stupidly pleased my deductions had impressed him. "That's almost an apology." *Hopefully I'm right.* I grimaced. Or maybe I didn't hope that. If soul-sucking spells were leading up to something really nasty, I didn't want to be anywhere nearby when it was unleashed.

I rubbed the scratches on my shoulder. Of course, that might not be an issue. I was running on a time limit now. *And fueling the killer's damn ritual.* I tugged the blanket tighter around myself.

"We should both get some sleep," Falin said, and I heard him walk across the room. A drawer opened and clothing rustled as he changed. "I have some sweats you can borrow to sleep in."

"Uh, thanks?" I accepted the clothes when he pressed them in my hands, but to my embarrassment, I ended up needing help getting into them and out of my dress.

Once I was clothed again, the silence stretched. *Did he go to bed already?* Then he spoke. "Would my body heat help you tonight?"

A sound broke from my throat that was half-strangled laugh and half choke. "Wow, that's awkward."

"Yes or no."

I nodded. "Yes." I really did need the warmth. It had been over an hour since Death left, and I was still trembling.

I felt Falin move onto the couch. His arm slipped under my legs, and he turned me, moving me lengthways along the plush back of the couch. He curled along my back, dragging me against his chest with a strong arm around my waist. He was warm, so very blessedly warm. But spooning with someone I hadn't had sex with? Majorly awkward. And the feel of the couch cushions in front of me and him behind? Slightly claustrophobic.

"Um, wouldn't this be easier in your bed than on the couch?"

"I don't own a bed."

"What?"

His jaw cracked as he yawned. "Got rid of it. Now, go to sleep, Alexis."

I jolted awake. A scene of myself, thin and vaporish outside my body with dark glyphs sucking away my soul, still played in my mind. *A dream.* But not one that faded in the weak morning light that streamed in through a large sliding-glass door. I rubbed my bleary eyes and then blinked, staring at the unfamiliar green microfiber cushion in front of my nose. *Where am I?*

Falin's apartment. But I was alone on the couch.

I sat up—probably a little too fast. My vision swam, but then it cleared again, bringing the one-room apartment into focus. A grin broke over my face. *Seeing is a glorious thing.*

I looked around. There wasn't much to the small apartment. The couch I'd slept on took up most of one wall; a dresser with a TV on top was directly across from it. A computer desk was tucked away in one corner, and a small card table with two chairs around it took up the other corner. There was a door on the opposite wall from the couch, and the smell of coffee—*and is that bacon?*—emanated from it. There was also a door on the same wall as the couch, and I hoped it was the bathroom.

I pushed to my feet. My legs protested, quivering under me, but they held. My whole body was tight, sore, as if I'd gotten a strenuous workout, and my movements were far from smooth. I wanted a hot shower, but I didn't think that was an option. I made a quick stop at the bathroom. After washing my face, rinsing my mouth, and trying to do something with my hair before pulling the mess of dirty blond curls back into a ponytail, I headed for the kitchen.

Falin was standing over the stove. He looked up as I shambled in. "Morning. How are you feeling?"

"Fine. I . . ." I stopped. Falin had showered, and his damp hair hung loose over his shoulders. The blond strands had seeped moisture into his oxford, which was unbuttoned and gave me a clear view of his chest. I couldn't tell if the skin over his cut muscles was as smooth as it looked or if he had fine blond hair, but I could imagine my hands sliding from his chest to his abs and finding out.

Falin frowned at me. "Can you see this morning?"

Oh yeah. I could see. I could definitely see. I nodded, tearing my gaze away and making a beeline for the coffeemaker so he wouldn't notice the color in my cheeks. I ran into a problem—I had no idea where the mugs were.

"Cabinet over your head," Falin said before I had to ask. "How do you like your eggs?"

I poured my coffee. "Listen, it was really nice of you to take care of me last night." *And to not arrest me.* "But I think this has gotten awkward enough. If you point me toward the bus line, I'll get out of here." I had a lot to look into, and PC had to be pacing anxiously, waiting for a walk and food.

"It's just breakfast. Have some food; then I'll drop you at your house before I head to the station."

The food did smell amazing. I couldn't seriously refuse real food, and having a full stomach could only help my investigation into Coleman. I rubbed the scratches on my shoulder. But after I changed and showered, there was a detour I needed to make. I was on an unknown timeline, and I had someone I needed to visit. Just in case.

I smiled at Falin around the rim of my mug. "All right—breakfast."

Chapter 14

An hour and a half later, showered and in clean clothes, I sat under the dim lights in the ICU.

"I could really use your advice," I whispered from the uncomfortable folding chair beside John's bed.

Pale and waxy, John made no response to my plea. Not that I expected him to. He'd been unconscious since Tuesday. It was Friday now. I sat there, gripping his hand, but it made no difference. He had no idea I was there.

I stood and laid his hand back by his side. "You'll wake up," I told him, but even to my ears my voice sounded uncertain.

I turned to go and nearly ran into Death.

I gasped, backing up a step. Not that being out of reach would matter if he was collecting souls. "Are you here for me or . . ." I glanced down at the bed.

Death shook his head. "I'm here for you."

For me, as in *for* me. Like *for* my soul? My hand moved to the scratches on my shoulder. I hadn't thought it had progressed that much.

Death shook his head again, and a small, sad smile

tipped the side of his mouth. He reached out, but his hand dropped short of touching my face. "I'm just moral support. I know how hard this is for you."

He stepped away, clasping his hands behind his back. I remembered to breathe again. The air rushed out of me in audible relief, and Death cringed at the sound. He stared at John.

I didn't want to stay. I didn't want to focus on John's lax features or his mustache, which wasn't betraying his emotions with small twitches.

I also didn't want to leave him alone, and Maria hadn't been in the waiting room when I passed through. *Has she given up hope?*

I sank back into the chair and took John's hand. Death said nothing. Neither of us said a thing.

A nurse walked by, jotting notes on her clipboard. She gave me a tight smile before moving on.

"Have you looked at him?" Death asked, breaking the silence.

I frowned at him. "What do you mean?"

"Look at him. See." He put emphasis on the word "see" just the way he had last night.

Which meant he wanted me to use my grave-sight. After the hours of blindness, I didn't want to. I didn't want to use that part of my magic again for a long time. We'd overloaded the shields in my bracelet last night, so I already felt brittle and could sense the corpses several stories below in the hospital morgue. But Death wouldn't have suggested it if it weren't important.

I opened my mental shield only the smallest amount. It was enough. The gray patina of grave-sight washed over my vision. John's soul glowed crimson with yellow swirls. I dropped his hand and jumped to my feet. His soul should have been pale yellow. Just yellow.

I stared at him and realized it wasn't his soul that

was crimson; it was his skin. The yellow of his soul was slipping through between crimson stains, and the darkest stain was around the wound in this throat. I reached with my senses, already knowing what I'd find. Darkness. Dark magic.

I looked up at Death. "The bullet was spelled?"

He nodded. Damn. Coleman—it had to be him. After all, both bodies I'd seen on Tuesday tied back to him. He'd well and truly intended that bullet to kill me, one way or another.

"If I find him . . ."

I didn't have to specify who "him" was. Death understood. He nodded. "If he's destroyed, all his spells will dissipate."

As if I needed another reason, another life, on the line. I sank into the chair beside John again. "I'm so sorry," I whispered.

Not that sorry mattered. What mattered was finding Coleman. I released John's hand and scrubbed the tears from my cheeks. I looked at Death.

"Do you know who he is?"

"Don't do this, Alex. Don't ask me."

"You do know. Please—"

He leaned forward, cutting me off as his lips pressed against mine. He touched me nowhere else. There was just the soft yet unyielding pressure of his lips on mine, and I felt as though every nerve had moved to my mouth.

Then he was gone.

I pressed the tips of two fingers over my mouth and blinked at the empty air in front of me. *He kissed me?* I stood there as though I was waiting for him to materialize again. But he didn't.

I knew he wouldn't. *The kiss of Death—a shut-up kiss.* He wouldn't, or couldn't, answer my questions.

I closed my eyes and pressed my lips together, remembering the feel of the kiss. He hadn't been cold. He hadn't been warm, either, but he hadn't been cold. It had been nice. A tingle of excitement trembled from my mouth down to my stomach. Okay, maybe it had been more than nice.

I let out a sigh and opened my eyes. It didn't matter. All that mattered was finding Coleman before he claimed another soul.

"You've been quiet," Caleb said as he pulled into the driveway. He'd been the only one at the house when Falin had dropped me off, so he'd gotten drafted into the job of driving me to the hospital, but I'd been too wrapped up in my own thoughts to talk to him most of the ride home.

"Yeah, sorry. I have a lot on my mind. Hey, if I ask you something, will you promise not to take offense?"

Caleb frowned at me, and I realized my mistake. Caleb looked as if he'd just graduated from college, but he was older—a lot older. I wasn't sure exactly how old because you just didn't ask things like that of a fae. You also didn't ask the fae to make a trivial promise.

"That's not what I meant." I took a deep breath. I'd been friends with Caleb ever since I'd started renting the upstairs loft from him my freshman year. He acted so witchlike, I sometimes forgot that the way I worded things could be very important. "What I meant to say is that I want to ask you something, but I don't mean any offense by it."

"Al, if it takes this much setup, you're probably going to have to trade for it."

I nodded. I'd been prepared for that. "If a fae was creating a dark ritual, and he was using glyphs I'd never seen before, like maybe they are particular to fae magic, would you be able to tell what the spell did by reading the glyphs?"

"Me? No."

Damn. Being fae, Caleb couldn't tell an outright lie, and there was no wiggle room in "no." Of course, he'd only said *he* couldn't.

"Would another fae be able to?" I wasn't sure the glyphs were of fae origin, but I'd never seen or heard of a witch spell that worked like the one Coleman was using, and I was pretty sure Coleman himself was something fae—something *other*.

Caleb's frown grew harder. "Maybe. Al, whatever you're tied up in, you need to walk away from it. These questions are dangerous."

"Okay, tha—" I caught the "thanks" before it slipped through my lips. One of the rules of the house when I'd moved in was that I was never allowed to thank him. Thanking a fae acknowledged a debt, and Caleb didn't want the temptation to collect. "I'll see you later," I said instead, sliding out of the car.

"Be safe, Al," he said, shoving his car door closed.

I waved good-bye as he trudged to the main part of the house and I headed for my loft. I was thankful it was Caleb rather than Holly who'd been around to drive me to the hospital. Holly would have wanted juicy details. *And would be sorely disappointed.* My mind flashed back to the expanse of chest that had been on display this morning. *Well, maybe not completely disappointed.*

I'd just let myself in after walking PC for the second time when movement in the corner of the room caught my eye. It was a man. I dropped to a crouch, pulling the dagger from my boot. Then I noticed the man was luminescent.

I sheathed the dagger. "Roy, what are you doing

here?" Which was a dumb question, as I wasn't going to be able to hear him. Adrenaline was still making blood pound inside my ears, so I could probably be forgiven a dumb question or two.

The ghost turned. "Alex, I've been looking all over for you."

I was too stunned to move. I just blinked. Then I pressed the heels of my palms against my eyes. My mental shields were in place, my extra shields were blown, but that shouldn't have affected how far across the chasm my psyche was reaching. I looked around. My grave-sight wasn't active, but I could see the fact that Roy's hair was brown, his jeans blue.

"I think I need to sit down," I muttered.

Roy frowned at me. Then he went into charades mode. He walked to my circle and stood in the middle. He threw his hands out as if to indicate all the area around him. Then he moved his fingers like a flapping duckbill, which I guess was supposed to tell me he wanted to talk.

I leaned down and released PC from his leash. The small dog immediately begged for lunch.

"Just talk, Roy. I can hear you." I didn't fully understand *why* I could hear him, but I could.

His thick brows scrunched behind his glasses. "Are you sure? Because before you—"

"Yes, I'm sure."

"Oh, cool. Well, I thought you should know that the police have brought in two more grave witches so far."

"Yeah?" I said, filling PC's food bowl. I'd already known the police were looking for second opinions.

"Well, both have disagreed with you."

I dropped the bag, and kibble scattered over the wood floor. "What? Who were they? What did they say?"

Roy shrugged. "They both agreed that the shade couldn't be raised, and that the body was resistant to grave magic. This morning's witch used that word—'resistant.' But neither found any trace of a spell or the symbols you saw on the body."

"Of all the incompetent—" I cut off because I didn't have words for the frustration I felt. Everything that had happened in the past four days had been balling in the center of my being, and the ball had just grown large enough to suffocate me. I couldn't breathe. My chest burned, like my lungs were clawing through my ribs, searching for air.

Roy's eyes went wide. "Maybe I should just . . ." He pointed over his shoulder and vanished.

Of course he fucking vanished. Roy could vanish. Death could vanish. Coleman could mask his dark, tainted presence. And what could I do? I could have a seizure and get my soul sucked out by a fucking spell.

Someone knocked on my door, and I jerked it open without looking through the curtain.

"What?" I yelled.

Falin cocked his head in confusion, his lips drawing together. "Did I come at a bad time?"

"No, I—" I cut myself off and massaged my temples with my thumb and pointer finger. "Sorry. It's been a long day."

"It's barely noon."

I glared at him "I suppose you're here to tell me the experts disagree with my analysis of Coleman's body and you want me to stay away from your case?"

"How did you—" He stopped. "Never mind. I think the so-called experts are wrong. May I come in?"

I gaped at him, and the pressure in my chest became more manageable. "Really?"

He frowned at me and let himself inside. After shutting the door, he turned and stared at the explosion of kibble that PC was doing his best vacuum cleaner impression on. There was way more kibble than one seven-pound dog could—or at least should—eat in one sitting.

"Oh, um, there was a . . ." I trailed off. Why was I trying to explain the condition of my house? *Because his apartment had been spotless.* I silenced the internal voice as I searched for where I'd stashed the broom last. "So, I'm guessing this isn't a social visit."

"No. You never saw any of the actual bodies in John's cases, did you?"

I shook my head and dumped kibble, with as few dust bunnies as possible, back into the bag of dog food. I'd seen Bethany's shade, but her body had remained inside the black body bag.

"You said I would find glyphs on the new victim's body. Can you describe them?"

I tossed the bag of dog food on the counter. "I can do better than that." I grabbed an unopened bill and a pencil off the counter. Then I sketched the glyph that had appeared most frequently on the victim. I'd had nightmares about the glyph last night. I definitely knew what it looked like. I left the last mark off. Some glyphs were powerful enough in their own right that norms could use them. As I didn't know what this glyph did—and it had been used in dark magic, so I was guessing nothing good—I didn't want to accidently cast it.

I held up the not quite finished drawing. Falin leaned closer. His brow furrowed as he looked at it; then he pulled an envelope out of the inner pocket of his jacket. He flipped through something inside and then withdrew a photo and tossed it on the counter beside us.

I picked it up and stared at it. The photo was a close-up shot of a torso. Carved into the exposed flesh was the glyph I'd drawn.

Falin took the photo back. "You couldn't have seen that under all the blood."

"Whoa—are you accusing me of something, Detective?"

His frown etched itself deeper into his face. "All the evidence from last night's scene disappeared. Every candle, both champagne flutes, the ropes she was tied with, the sheets from the bed, everything. Gone."

"I had nothing to do with that. Hell, you were with me all night."

"I know that!" He shoved the envelope back into his pocket. "What I want to know is this: what are you, Alexis Caine?"

Chapter 15

"That stupid, arrogant—" I wanted to scream. Except screaming wouldn't have been enough. The sound of the door slamming when I'd kicked Falin out still thundered in my ears—or maybe that was my blood pounding.

"What are you, Alexis Caine?"

Damn him.

I stopped in front of the mirror and stared at my face. "He thinks you're weird," I told the girl in the mirror. She already looked pissed, so my statement didn't change much. *Of course I'm weird. I'm wyrd.* I was the Caine daughter who was different, the one who couldn't hide what she could do. I was the one who couldn't not do magic, couldn't not raise shades. The magic exploded out of me and latched onto random corpses if I went too long between rituals. Wyrd.

And now Falin thought I was even weirder than wyrd.

"What are you, Alexis Caine?"

I was pissed. I was exhausted. I was . . . wasting time.

I inhaled a deep breath and let it back out. *This isn't helping you find Coleman.* No, but self-flogging was easy to do. But it wasn't just my life on the line anymore—I had to find Coleman for John.

My gaze moved to the corner of the mirror and landed on a picture of Rianna. As the only two grave witches at the academy we'd never been weird to each other. In the photo, she looked at the camera with her big green eyes peeking over the top of a paperback book—probably a mystery novel. A PI firm called Tongues for the Dead had been her dream, not mine.

"What would you do if you were here?" I asked the photo.

It didn't answer—not that I expected it to. Talking to the dead didn't mean I could make a photo answer. But I did know what Rianna would do. She would write a report about everything we knew, including all our suspects. I didn't have the patience for a full report, but a suspect list wasn't a bad idea.

I turned on my laptop and pulled up a blank document.

The party guest list was my suspect pool. I didn't know the names of all the men in the group where I'd sensed Coleman. From what I remembered, six men had met the description Roy gave me: the businessman, two aides, Lieutenant Governor Bartholomew, Senator Wilks, and, of course, my father.

In my opinion, my father was cleared—if not by his actions, then by the fact I'd seen him a half hour before Falin was called to the scene. That wasn't enough time for him to leave the party and commit the murder. Coleman probably wanted to get as close to the hot seat of power again, so I was betting on Bartholomew as the new host. After all, Bartholomew had left the party early on. That gave him the time and opportunity to get to the warehouse and conduct the ritual. I put a star beside his name and typed "prime suspect" in parentheses.

Now, the question was how to prove it.

I stared at the blinking curser. At my feet, PC whined. I glanced down at him.

"What do you think, PC?"

He thought he'd jump in my lap.

I needed to know more about Bartholomew. I hit the icon to bring up my Internet browser. My e-mail was set as my home screen, and I groaned at the number of unread messages in my in-box. I scanned, deleting as I went. As expected, most were from the press.

One wasn't.

I clicked to open the message. It was from a young couple who wanted me to raise the woman's parents. I read on. Apparently the couple had been having trouble with conception. They had an appointment with a fertility specialist but wanted to find out her family health history, which she didn't know because her parents had died in a car accident when she was a child.

It was a client. And it sounded like a good easy case. I frowned. I didn't really have time to work a case right now, but at the same time I couldn't just stop working. I was late on rent already, I had no car, and I had only twelve dollars to my name. None of that would matter if I didn't find Coleman.

I silenced the negative thought and glanced at the time stamp on the message. It had come in almost two days ago. Writing a quick response, I attached my standard contract, then added a line about half my fee being paid up front—I was tired of getting ripped off.

I hit SEND. Then I spent the next hour reading articles about Bartholomew. Falin was right: he was a hothead and occasionally stuck his foot in his mouth, but reading about his outbursts in the House and his views on this or that bill did little but make my eyes blurry.

I leaned back in my chair and stretched. My back gave a satisfying pop, and PC lifted his head.

"I think we've been sitting here too long."

He apparently didn't agree because he laid his head back down and closed his eyes. I scratched behind his ears and tabbed back to my suspect list, which now had a lot of useless information under Bartholomew's name.

If Coleman was stealing the energy from souls, he had to be storing it in something. Some material that could hold a high concentration of magical energy, like a gem, obsidian, or silver. No, not a gem. Not with as many souls as he'd drained. Whatever he was storing the energy in had to be large. There hadn't been any kind of magical receptacle at the warehouse, which meant Coleman probably had it at his host's home or office.

So, I was looking at breaking into the lieutenant governor's home or the statehouse. *Oh yeah, because neither of those will be a problem.* I slumped forward and propped my chin on my hand. The statehouse was a public building, at least, but the offices weren't, and they would have more security. Of course, magic could get around tech. I knew an excellent charm witch.

I hit the "home" icon to return to my in-box before closing my browser. I had one new message. I blinked. The couple had responded already.

I opened the message. The woman had signed, scanned, and returned my contract. Her appointment at the fertility clinic was first thing Monday morning, and she was anxious. She got off work at six and wondered if I would be available to meet her at Sleepy Knoll Cemetery at six thirty.

I chewed at my bottom lip and glanced at the clock. It was quarter to one now, and if I was breaking into the statehouse, I was going to have a busy afternoon. But I thought I'd be able to make it to the cemetery by six thirty. And how long could a family medical history take to convey? Half an hour? An hour? It would be easy money. As long as I didn't go blind again.

Considering everything that was going on, I'd make sure I didn't go alone.

I wrote her a quick message confirming that I'd meet her and reminding her I collected half my fee up front. Then I shut down the laptop, grabbed my purse and Tamara's dress, and went to beg another ride off Caleb. After I made a quick trip to the morgue, I'd pay a visit to the statehouse.

I dropped my purse on the conveyer belt, but I hadn't yet made it past the metal detector when the machine began beeping. The guard on duty dumped the contents of my purse and grabbed his spellchecker wand. *What could have . . . Oh crap. The gray spellbook.* With everything else that had happened last night, I'd forgotten all about the spellbook.

I glanced around, hoping Central Precinct's lobby was empty. Not only was it not empty, but because reality clearly hated me this week, one of the people present was Lusa Duncan, the star reporter for *Witch Watch*. And, of course, the angry beep had caught her attention, so she was watching me like a familiar monitoring a spell.

I turned my back to her and watched the guard work. As the wand crept over the book, the bead on the tip turned red. Crap. Not just magic. Malicious magic. As in illegal.

"Miss Craft, I'm going to have to ask you to wait right here." He reached for his radio.

"It's not mine."

The guard gave me a look that said he'd heard that one before. He barked into his radio, and I opened my mouth, closed it. *Now what?* I glanced back. Lusa wasn't watching me anymore. Instead, her eyes were closed and by the way her lips were moving, I guessed she was chanting. *Probably checking me out in the Aetheric. Will she see the spell on my soul?* That would certainly reflect badly on me. I turned back to the guard.

"I'd like to talk to Detective Falin Andrews."

Falin kept me waiting more than fifteen minutes. By that point I'd reclaimed the contents of my purse—except the book, of course—and been told not to move out of the uncomfortable orange chair the guard had pointed me to. Lusa was still haunting the lobby, watching, and I'd lost count of how many people had passed by me and stared while I sat there feeling miserable.

When Falin arrived, the guard tried to explain how he'd found the book, but with a terse "I'll take it from here," Falin plucked the book from the guard's hand.

I jumped to my feet as Falin stormed over. He wrapped a hand around my biceps and all but dragged me out of the lobby.

"I, uh—"

"Be quiet."

He marched me down a twisting hallway before pushing me into a room. The small room had a single table in the center with two chairs on one side and one on the other.

I clutched my purse to my chest. "Uh, this is an interrogation room."

"Yeah, it is." He slammed the door. "What the hell is going on? You're a gray witch?"

"No!"

"Then what's this?" He tossed the spellbook on the table.

"It's not what it looks like. I'm not stupid enough to

dabble in gray magic." Especially not while I had a dark spell sucking on my soul.

"Then why don't you explain it to me."

"It's complicated."

"Uncomplicate it."

I frowned and looked up at the large mirror covering half the far wall. *Two-way glass.* "Who's watching us?"

"That's not your concern."

"Then you might as well take off your gloves and use your truth-seeking sp—" I cut off as he stepped forward, his eyes wide with alarm.

In the next instant, his face regained its composure, or at least went back to just looking pissed. He crossed his arms over his chest and leaned back. "No one is listening."

"Really? So there's no issue if I talk about the illegal truth-seeking spell you used on me last night?"

No reaction this time, but I knew what I'd seen. He'd reacted first, thought second.

"Are you trying to goad me, Miss Craft?"

"No." *Just ensuring we're alone.* I sank into one of the chairs. "I stole the book from Casey's room last night."

He lifted an eyebrow. "The governor's daughter? Your sister?"

"As I said, complicated." And it had "scandal" written all over it. While I might enjoy putting my father in the hot seat, it would eventually turn out bad for everyone involved. "I'd planned to destroy the book, but after the warehouse . . . I forgot I had it on me."

Falin sat down in the chair opposite me and massaged the bridge of his nose with his thumb and forefinger. As the pissed look drained from his face he just looked tired. "Why are you here, Alex?"

"I was headed to the morgue to—"

"You are not allowed to raise shades here, not now."

I frowned at him. "I was just going to return Tamara's dress."

"Give it to me; I'll take it to her." He held out a hand.

"I, uh, it's not in the best of shape. I should probably take it myself." Which was true. It had been covered in dust and grit from the warehouse, so I'd thrown it in Caleb's washer when I got home this morning. Apparently it was dry clean only.

Falin pushed away from the table and pocketed the book. Then he opened the door. "Fine. That's where I'm going anyway. I'll walk you down. But don't go near any bodies."

"I'm really sorry about the dress."

"It's all right. We'll chalk it up as a casualty to improving your social life." Tamara gave me a weak smile. "But here is a tip from me to you: the night shouldn't end with you in handcuffs . . . unless you're into that."

"Tamara!" I hissed, but we both laughed.

We were standing in the basement corridor outside the morgue. Apparently that was as close to the bodies as Falin trusted me to get, as though I just wouldn't be able to resist raising a couple of shades if I went into the autopsy room. He, of course, got to go inside. If I were honest, with my damaged shields and the way the grave essence was reaching for me out in the hall, I was thankful for the extra space from the bodies. Not that I'd tell him that.

"I'll replace the dress," I said, avoiding looking at the shrunken black scrap I'd returned to Tamara. And I would replace it. Once the check from the city came in, the dress would be my top priority.

"Alex, don't worry about it. I've only ever worn it once."

"Strangely, that doesn't make me feel any better."

She shook her head and smiled. "Thanks for dropping it off, but I know you didn't come all this way just to bring me a ruined dress. What's up?"

Busted. "I need another favor." I ducked, mocking fear. She just rolled her eyes and propped a hand on her hip, waiting. I stumbled on. "Do you remember when you were having trouble with that video stalker and you crafted that charm that made you invisible on camera?"

She frowned at me. "What are you up to, Alex?"

"It's all this." I waved my hand around my head. "I'm sick of my face showing up on the evening news and the front page of the paper." Which was all true. It wasn't what I actually planned to use the charm for, but it was true.

She studied me and I gave her my most innocent smile. After a minute, she nodded and unclipped a small silver charm from her bracelet. It was shaped like a tiny lock.

"Use it responsibly, and if you get arrested, I didn't make it."

"Thanks! I'll get it back to you as soo—"

The morgue door opened and I fell silent. Falin strolled out, and I fastened the charm to my bracelet before he noticed. Not that I should have been worried about it; he was talking with a man about my own age whom I didn't know. The man wore street clothes, which meant he wasn't a beat cop. *ID-ing a body, maybe?* He squinted in the bright fluorescence as if he was having difficulty seeing. When his gaze landed on me, a dazzling smile broke across his face. He held up a hand, cutting Falin off, and walked over to where Tamara and I were talking.

"Beg pardon, may I presume you to be Miss Alex Craft?"

How am I supposed to respond to that? "Er. Yes?"

He bowed. "I am Ashen Hughes, and I am very honored to make your acquaintance." He held out his hand, but when I took it, he didn't shake. Instead, he lifted my hand and brushed his lips across my knuckles. "You have made great strides in our wyrd world."

A fellow grave witch? I looked him over again. I didn't know him, but that wasn't unusual. Even among wyrd talents, grave magic was rare—only premonition witches were less common—and it wasn't as though we had a national conference or anything. Ashen wasn't a bad-looking guy. The fact he was standing next to Falin was unfair to him, but he had nice eyes. Green, very pale green, as if using grave-sight had bleached the color out of his irises. His dark hair was just long enough to show a tendency to curl, and he wore it slicked back from his face.

"If I may be so bold," he said after releasing my hand, "I would be delighted to sit and talk with you for a while. It is rare to be in the presence of such talent. Or for that talent to be so pleasing to perceive. Would you be so kind as to join me for dinner?"

"Well, I, uh, I've actually already made plans." *Is he hitting on me?* My eyes flickered to Tamara.

She was standing a bit behind Ashen and clearly mouthing the words "Go." *Easy for her to say.* Of course, she *had* just sacrificed a dress to the improvement of my social life, as she put it.

Roy floated through the door. "I'd go," he said. "That one confirmed everything you said about the spell on my body."

Ashen's eyes shifted as though he'd heard Roy, but he didn't turn. Instead, he tilted his head, acknowledging my refusal. Then he said, "At the risk of making a fool of myself, may I ask if you have plans tomorrow around

lunch? I would love to hear your account of the Holliday trial, and of course discuss this rather baffling spell
on the late governor's body. Clearly fae magic, judging
by the glyphs."

He recognized the glyphs?

"Clearly?" I asked.

"Oh yes. You see, I'm quite enchanted by the fae
and have spent more time than I'd rather admit studying their magic and lore. Ancient glyphs are actually the
emphasis of my current research. I recognized a few of
the glyphs, though their arrangement and purpose on
the governor's body is beyond me."

"But the ones you recognized—do you know what
type of spells they are usually used for?"

"I can speculate." Ashen leaned closer. "Lunch, Miss
Craft? I would be delighted to speak of this at length,
but I'd like to consult some texts first."

Tamara was actually making hand motions behind his
head now. Falin leaned against the wall, his arms folded
across his chest as he scowled at me. *Ashen is some sort
of scholar in fae glyphs?* I couldn't pass up an opportunity to learn more about the spells I was up against.
Maybe he'd also be able to tell me something about the
spell used on the body in the warehouse. *Maybe he'll
even know how to counter the spell's effect—or at least
know a way to slow its progress.*

"Lunch sounds great. Should I suggest a place?"

His smile turned on high power. It was a nice smile
that went all the way to his pale eyes. "Actually, I've
heard a lot about the Eternal Bloom. I was hoping to
visit it before I left town."

The fae bar? Considering my current issues with the
fae, that sounded like a bad idea. Not that I hadn't been
there before, but if I went out for drinks, I preferred
Mac's. Usually the Eternal Bloom was filled with tour-

ists hoping to catch sight of a real fae, who, aware of that fact, were rarely present.

From his spot on the wall, Falin shook his head, his eyes drilling into me. *Not that it's his decision.* Apparently it wasn't mine either, because Tamara took that moment to jump into the conversation.

"Alex loves the Eternal Bloom, don't you?"

Uh. Crap. Tamara didn't know about the kidnapping attempt, and I obviously couldn't go into that here. I smiled at Ashen. "Okay, sure. Noon?"

"It's a date." He bowed again, then headed for the elevator.

Once he was gone, Tamara started gushing. "Oh, this is exciting. Do you need help deciding what to wear?"

"It's just lunch. Besides, you haven't even asked how last night went."

She glanced back at Falin, who was still leaning against the wall. She lowered her voice. "You ended up ruining my dress by collapsing on the dusty floor at a crime scene. I can guess it didn't work out. But this . . ." She smiled and gave me a hug. "Well, I should get back to work. I'm slammed here."

"Tommy still hasn't shown back up?"

Tamara shook her head. "And Sally—you remember her?"

I nodded. Sally was a wyrd empath who enjoyed working with the dead because she didn't have to shield from their emotions. Wyrd witches were few and far between, so I knew most of the wyrd residents of Nekros, but Sally and I were far from friends. She claimed I wasn't in touch with my feelings and that I projected like a bitch.

"Well, she worked night shift last night, and when she left this morning she said she was feeling pretty bad.

I won't be surprised if she calls out tonight." Tamara sighed. "So, I should get back to it."

I waved good-bye. Then I turned to Falin. "I suppose you plan to escort me out of the building?"

He lifted an eyebrow, and I hated him for that expressive eyebrow. This one was definitely a cocky *"Yes, and you can't do anything about it."*

I showed some teeth. "I have one more thing to do."

Roy was moping in the corner, and I walked over so Falin wouldn't overhear me.

Not that he wasn't watching. "Alex, are you planning to talk to that wall?" he asked.

"Yeah, it's a nice wall," I yelled over my shoulder, then turned back to the ghost. "Hey, Roy, I need a favor."

"Miss Craft, a moment of your time," Lusa yelled as I crossed the green space in front of Central Precinct.

I groaned and kept walking. Lusa and her cameraman followed. I was tempted to activate Tamara's charm, but if the statehouse had spellcheckers in use, having the charm active would make it a lot more noticeable, and I'd already had enough trouble with security for one day. So I just kept my head down and let my stride put sidewalk between us.

"Miss Craft, would you like to make any statement to the public about why you've decided to use gray magic?"

I stopped. I probably shouldn't have, but I did. "I don't use gray magic."

"I have video of a gray spellbook being confiscated from you, and you have a dark mark on your soul. The evidence is pretty damning."

I glanced from Lusa to her cameraman. The red recording light was blinking like a racing heartbeat. "Is this live?"

Lusa smiled at me. "It's for my Monday show. Unless I get a better story."

Crap. "How about if I can promise you an exclusive, but you have to wait?"

"I have deadlines, Miss Craft."

I frowned at her. I couldn't say anything, and I sure couldn't give her anything by Monday, but she was a reporter. If I dangled a big enough story in front of her nose, she'd bite at it. Without looking away from her, I said, "Roy, you want your story on TV?"

The ghost gaped at me. "Can I do that? I mean. No one can see me."

"Roy, give me your hand, and don't say anything confidential."

I reached out, and he took my hand. Then I grabbed the grave essence in the air around me. I channeled it through my body and into Roy. I'd never actually tried to make a ghost visible, but when Lusa gasped, I knew it had worked.

She took only a moment to recover and snap back into camera-ready professionalism. "Okay, a ghost. So, what's the story?"

"I know more about the body downstairs than any living person," he said.

"The late governor's body?" Lusa asked. At Roy's nod, she turned to her cameraman. "Is he showing up on film?"

The cameraman hit a button. "Yeah, he's a little shimmery, but he's there."

Lusa turned back to me. "Okay, so I get what—an interview with the ghost in exchange for not showing the footage I caught?"

I released my hold on the grave essence and Roy's hand. "His name is Roy Pearson, and the deal is this. Once everything comes out, and not before then, you get an exclusive interview. In exchange, I want the original of the footage from the station, and any copies in existence."

She nodded. "Deal. But I'm keeping the footage until after the interview, and if you back out, I can air it any time."

We shook on the deal. Hopefully, I'd make it through the Coleman ordeal and not give Lusa the chance to ruin my name posthumously.

Chapter 16

⋘══◉══⋙

"Over the House Speaker's chair, you'll notice the portrait of Governor Greggory Delane, our first governor after we were declared the fifty-fourth state. He was elected at a time when the populations in the newly discovered folded spaces had not yet diversified, and he was one of only three governors in our state's history to be fae."

Three they know about. I know at least one more. I didn't say it aloud as I hung near the back of the tour group. And by group, I meant the tour guide, a family of four, and me. It was going to be a lot harder to slip away than I thought.

"Is this really what the living do for fun these days?" Roy asked.

"Shh," I hissed, which was a little silly, since I was the only one who could hear him. I shuffled farther from the other members of the tour and kept my voice down. "Did you find the offices?"

"Yeah, she should walk you right by them if she takes the hall around this room. There are two people inside."

I nodded that I understood as the tour guide turned. "Try to keep up, everyone," she said in her crisp tone.

Everyone being me.

I followed the family out of the room. The couple had two young children. The oldest, a boy, was six at most. He poked down the hall, dragging his feet, then stopped and spit his gum in his palm. He looked around before trudging up to a marble statue of former Governor Delane.

"Danny, don't—" his father started, but it was too late. The boy squished the gum into the side of the statue at the same time the tour guide turned.

A look of horror crossed her face. "Did he just—?"

"He didn't mean any harm," the father said, but the tour guide was already running over to the statue.

She pulled a tissue out of her pocket and pulled at the sticky gum. "This statue was commissioned by . . ."

I won't get a better opening than this. I crept away from the commotion and followed Roy down the hall. I'd already activated the charm that blocked my image from cameras, so now I just needed to worry about the two people Roy had seen. He led me to a pair of large oak doors. He floated through them, and I waited outside, leaning against the wall and trying to look inconspicuous.

Roy stuck his head through the wood. "One went to the back. Just a receptionist left."

Okay, one door guard. Time to see what I was up against. I pasted on a smile and walked inside.

"Aunt Margie?"

The old woman looked up and adjusted her purple-framed glasses. Her thin lips parted into a smile. "Why, Alexis Caine, look at you. How are you, dear?" She stepped around her desk and wrapped her frail arms around me.

Margie wasn't actually my aunt. She'd been my father's personal assistant back when he'd been a big-shot defense attorney. After my mother was hospitalized up until the time I went to academy, and even after that during summer breaks, Margie was the one who took me to the doctor's office and helped Brad, Casey, and me pick out new clothes for school each year. She was probably one of the only people outside the family who knew my real identity, and she knew only because she'd already been a friend of the family before I'd been sent to academy. There weren't many people on that list.

"I'm good, I'm good," I said, still stunned to see her here. I hadn't known she'd stayed with my father all these years. How he'd earned her loyalty—not to mention her silence—was beyond me. I looked down at her desk and noticed a large brown box with pictures of her grandkids and a colorful mug in it. "Are you packing?"

"Oh. Retirement. It's time." She waved a hand in the air as if it was nothing, but the stony look that touched her eyes said otherwise. "The chief of staff and I had a falling-out, but that's not important." Her expression softened. "I've been watching you on the news. I'm so proud of you, out there helping the police with their cases."

I blushed. Yes, only Margie could be sitting in the middle of an office held by Humans First Party members and proclaim she was proud of a witch.

"Well, Margie, it's great seeing you again. I was wondering—can I head back to my father's office?"

"Are you two talking again?" Margie had always been an advocate for reconciliation. "I'm so glad to hear that, but he's not in the office, dear. I can't let you back."

Wow, I couldn't even get past the door guard, who'd known me all my life. She made a small comment about needing to finish packing. Then she picked up a small plaque from her desk and shoved it in the box, her movement more aggravated than her words had let on.

I stepped up to her desk and put my hands on the rim of the cardboard. "Can I tell you a secret you won't let get out?"

She leaned forward, always up for good gossip. I wondered once again if my father hadn't employed binding oaths to silence rumors about me.

"I'll be honest," I said, pitching my voice low in a stage whisper. "I'm here to snoop. You know I've been working for the police, right?" I knew she did because she'd just told me, but I wanted it fresh in her mind. "I'm sure you know they questioned my father in connection with Coleman's death. Well, I've been looking into the Coleman case, and I think it's possible the chief of staff could be involved. I'm looking for evidence."

All of which was mostly true. The chief of staff was one of the aides on my suspect list, but I was implying a lot I wasn't saying. I saw the missing pieces slide into place in her expression.

"Graham? That awful man could be behind it?" The way she said it wasn't a question, so I didn't answer. "He could even be framing Mr. Caine? I can't let that happen. So, you want to snoop?"

I nodded.

She looked around, looked down at her desk, and then picked up her box. "You know what? I think I'll leave an hour early today. What are they going to do? Fire me?" As she passed me, she whispered, "Mr. Graham and the governor's offices are through the door on the left." She winked, and then she let herself out the office.

"Okay, Roy; you said there was a second person back here?"

"Yeah, through the door on your right."

Damn. That was where the lieutenant governor's office was, and where I wanted to go. Regardless of what I'd implied, Bartholomew was the one I needed to check out. Still, it couldn't hurt to also check the chief of staff's office. *With any luck, by the time I finish, the person behind the other door will be gone.*

"Roy, keep watch here."

He nodded, and I let myself through the door on the left. I thought I'd have a hall with two offices, but the first room was Graham's office, with a door in the far wall that I assumed would take me to my father's office. I looked around.

There was nothing personal about this office. No photos on the desk. No stress breakers. No pens other than the standard blue and black. The desk drawers were locked, as were the filing cabinets, and nothing had been left in the wooden in-box on the side of the desk. I opened my senses, but aside from wards on the locks—pretty standard for any locking mechanism these days—no spells were present. Certainly nothing that jumped out as an artifact that could harbor stolen souls.

I checked in with Roy, but Bartholomew's aide was still in the other office.

Well, Coleman had been governor for longer than he hadn't. Maybe he'd left something behind. *Something that might still be in my father's office. Might as well take a peek.* After all, I had to do something while I waited for the aide to leave.

I headed back to my father's office. He'd been in it only two and a half weeks, but unlike his chief of staff, he at least had a photo on his desk. It was of Casey—not that I expected it to be a picture of me. A couple of files were on his desk, and I flipped through them. Reports. Budgets. Nothing useful.

Closing my eyes, I opened my senses. Coleman had sat in the office several years, so I expected some sort of dark-magical resonance in the room, but there was nothing. Not even wards. I frowned. Surely Coleman would have used spells in the room at some point during his time as governor. I walked the perimeter of the room, searching for traces of old magic. I even peeked inside the small bathroom tucked away in the corner. Nothing.

"Alex!"

I jumped as Roy materialized in the room.

"Don't do that."

"You've got to get out of here. Two men just showed up."

The sound of conversation drifted into the room, and I knew one of the voices very well. My father. *Oh crap.* They were in Graham's office, but I had no doubt they were headed to this room. I glanced around, then dived into the bathroom. I left a small crack between the door and the frame.

"—which is why I'm reiterating the fact I think you should cut him loose," the squirrelly faced aide said as he and my father walked into the office. *The chief of staff, no doubt.*

"You fully endorsed this plan when I made the decision, Graham."

The aide frowned as my father crossed around the desk, his frustration showing in the edges of his mouth. When my father sat, Graham lifted his hands, speaking with both palms up in a placating manner. "Yes, sir, but in light of recent circumstances . . . The man is a loose cannon. We have no idea what he'll do next."

"Which is why—" My father stopped as a knock sounded at the door.

"I'll see him in." Graham ducked out of the room.

I couldn't see my father's face, but his posture sagged

as he let out a deep breath, and I realized he looked tired. Which was weird, because I never thought of my father as being human enough to be tired. Footsteps sounded outside the door, and his back straightened. He opened a file on his desk.

The door opened, but my father didn't look up immediately. He waited a full thirty seconds, as if he couldn't rip his eyes off the page, and then slowly looked up. Whoever was there, I couldn't see yet. He must have stopped in the doorway.

"Come in," my father said, but he made no gesture of greeting. He just went back to reading the file in front of him.

The door shut, and in walked Falin Andrews.

I gasped and clamped a hand over my mouth, trying to muffle the already escaped sound. Falin's gaze flickered toward my hiding spot, and I backed farther into the darkness, trying to convince my heart to quiet down.

What is he doing here?

Falin sat, but didn't say anything. My father kept reading the file. When he finally looked up, he closed the file cover, and the impression was very much that Falin's visit was interrupting something far more important.

"I'd like a report on your progress," Father said, leaning forward and steepling his fingers.

Falin nodded, one sharp movement of his head. "I've been following some leads. There have been new developments."

"Developments. Like my daughter?"

"Sir?"

I frowned in the darkness. *What happened between Falin and Casey? Does Father know about the spellbook? How could he?*

"Your superiors spoke very highly of you." My father

opened the drawer and removed an envelope. "I must say I have not been impressed, particularly about the danger you put Alexis in." He tossed the envelope onto the desk in front of Falin.

Me? He was talking about me?

"I must be dreaming," I muttered, and Falin's eyes flicked to the crack in the door again. *Crap.*

I waited for one of them to walk over and rip the door off the hinges, revealing me, but Falin just grabbed the envelope. I couldn't see what was inside, but the lines in his face hardened. He looked up.

"I have certain expectations and—" A knock cut my father's words short.

The door opened and Graham said, "Sir."

My father stood. "Excuse me a moment."

He walked out of the room, and the door closed behind him. Muted sounds of him talking to his aide reached my ears, but no words.

Falin leaned back in his chair, his gaze fixed on the door of my hiding spot. He glanced over his shoulder in the direction my father had gone. Then he stood. He headed straight for me.

Oh crap.

The door at the front of the room opened, and Falin froze.

"I'm afraid I'll have to cut this meeting short," my father said from the doorway.

Falin turned and walked away from my hiding spot. *Saved by my father?* I couldn't say that often.

As the door closed I heard my father say, "But Andrews, do not disappoint me." Then the voices faded to a murmur and finally to silence.

I waited in the darkness. My calves and knees burned from crouching too long, and I stood, stretching my legs, but I didn't venture out of the bathroom.

"They're gone," Roy said, sticking his head through my door.

Thank God. "Let's get out of here."

I didn't even consider the fact I'd rushed out without checking Bartholomew's office until I'd crossed the main lobby. Well, no turning back now. I'd just reached the front stairs of the statehouse when a hand landed on my shoulder.

"Alex Craft, what the hell were you thinking?"

Chapter 17

⸺⫸⬤⫷⸺

I whirled around. "Get your hand off me, Andrews."

He didn't. Instead, he leaned forward and whispered through his gritted teeth. "You broke into the governor's office? Do you realize how stupid that was?"

"What are you going to do, arrest me? You're not even a real cop, are you, *Deceptive Andrews*?"

He jerked back as if stunned. Then his hand fell from my shoulder, and he released a deep breath around his frown. "Come on, I'll give you a ride home."

I stepped back. "I'm not going anywhere with you. I don't even know who the hell you are."

"You really want to have this conversation here"—his hand jerked, pointing at our very public location—"on the statehouse steps?"

I crossed my arms over my chest. "Yeah. Maybe I do. So you're working for my father? What did he hire you for?"

Falin glared at me, the muscles along his jaw bunching. Then he turned. His long legs took the stairs two at a time as he stormed away.

"Hey! Hey, I'm talking to you," I yelled at his retreating back.

He didn't stop.

Great. Now I had to either chase after him or let him go.

I was too pissed to let him leave.

I ran after him.

Protesters had rallied around the bottom of the stairs. They held aloft signs that proclaimed WITCHCRAFT IS THE WORK OF DAEMONS and COLEMAN MURDERED BY FAE! WHO WILL STOP THEM NOW?

Someone in the crowd recognized me.

"Leave our dead alone," she yelled, and someone else took up the cry. Soon they were chanting.

They surged forward, and I found myself swallowed by the yelling crowd. I ran, keeping my head down. A hand wrapped around my arm, jerked me back. The red face of an unfamiliar man filled the space in front of me.

"Police. Get your hands off her." *Falin.*

The protester growled at me, a savage sound that wasn't the least bit human, but he let go. Falin's arm slid around my shoulder. He steered me clear of the crowd and around the side of the building. I shrugged away from him as soon as we reached the parking garage.

He let me go and tucked his thumbs in his belt. "I'm not working for Caine."

"Oh, yeah, then what was that about?" I pointed back at the statehouse, but I was still breathless from my brush with the protesters, so my words carried a lot less sting than they would have on the stairs.

Falin frowned at me. "Caine signed off on the paperwork to put me in the department as lead investigator in Coleman's death. I'm FIB, Alex."

Fae Investigation Bureau? "And why should I believe that? The FIB have the authority to walk in and take over any case involving fae. John's bitched about it before."

He pointed back the way we'd just come. "You saw those protesters, Alex. Those people are scared. The governor was assassinated. What would have happened if it had become common knowledge the FIB had taken over the case? There are still people who remember the Magical Awakening. There are people who survived or lost friends in the riots afterward. Nekros has one of the largest fae and witch populations in the country, yet we haven't had an openly fae or witch governor in decades, and the Humans First Party are currently holding most of the important seats in the government."

And the Humans First Party probably had gained hundreds of supporters since the video of me declaring Coleman's body to be spelled hit the Internet. His supposed assassination was probably one of the best things to happen for his party. But . . . "But you aren't looking for the killer?"

Falin shook his head.

"Then the FIB knew what Coleman was—is?"

He just studied my face.

A white van turned into the parking garage. *The gloves, the truth-seeking spell, his knowledge about Coleman . . .*

"You're fae, aren't you?"

Falin frowned, not denying it, but not confirming either. His gaze flickered to the van rumbling toward us, and without warning he pushed me back.

"Get down," he yelled as the van door slid open and a dark gun muzzle appeared.

His body crashed into me, shoved me to the ground. Gravel bit into my palms, my cheek. His weight on top of me pinned me to the ground as the bangs of gunshots filled the air around me. One. Two. Three shots. A car window shattered, and glass tumbled down over my exposed hand.

Then Falin jumped up, his gun already in his hand. I looked back, between the tires of the car next to me, and saw the rear bumper of the retreating van. Falin fired. His shots pinged off the metal. The van's tire blew out.

It didn't stop but sped up, sparks flying. It turned the corner and jetted out the side entrance.

"You all right, Alexis?" Falin called back to me without turning around.

I pushed to my knees. My hands shook, adrenaline still flooding my system, but I said, "Yeah, yeah, I'm okay."

Something cylindrical rolled against my leg. Something that tingled with magic. I ripped my scarf off my head and scooped it up.

Without holstering his gun, Falin reached his free hand back toward me. "Let's get out of here."

"Yeah." I grabbed his hand and we ran for the car.

"Were they after you or me?" I asked, staring at the dart on the counter between us.

"You."

I frowned, holding PC tight enough to my chest that he squirmed. I didn't let go. "How can you be so sure? You're the one who shot one of them."

He removed one of his gloves and picked up the dart. He stared at the liquid inside and let the tube roll across his palm. "The draught in here includes a knockout spell and a complacency spell. They weren't after me." He slid his glove back on.

But how did they find me? I shivered, cold now that my adrenaline had dropped. Feeling a little dazed, I walked across the room and sank onto the corner of my bed.

Falin frowned at me. "You should probably eat some-
-thing."

I nodded blankly, though I couldn't have said whether
I was hungry. I glanced back at the clock. It was after six.
So yes, it was dinnertime. I stopped.

After six?

I shot to my feet. "Crap, I have a client."

"You what? Are you crazy? Cancel."

I wish I could. It was six seventeen, and my clients
were probably already en route to the cemetery. I
couldn't just not show up.

I set PC down on the bed and grabbed my purse.

"Uh." I stopped, looking at Falin. "Come with me?"

"As in you need a ride?"

Well, yeah. But more than that, I was a little freaked-
out right now. I'd feel a hell of a lot better with him there
than Holly or even Caleb. I winced a little. "Please?"

We pulled into Sleepy Knoll Cemetery fourteen minutes late. A large green sedan was parked in the visitor
lot, and a young couple stood near the gates.

"That must be the Feegans," I said, nodding to the
couple. But I didn't get out of the car. *Get it together,
Alex. Your clients shouldn't see you shaking.* I took a
deep breath. Let it out.

Falin killed the ignition, but he didn't open his door.
Instead, he watched me as if he was waiting for me to
take the lead. Which was good. I was raising a shade.
This was my territory.

I was still shaking. *Dammit.* I channeled magic into
my meditation charm.

My mind went blank, instantly clear, calm.

"Alex?" Falin shook my shoulder.

The bubble broke, and my head snapped up, but I was

calmer now. I could do this. I smiled at him and reached for my door. I stopped halfway out of the car.

"Who do I tell them you are?"

"I don't care." He frowned at me. "Make something up."

Right. I walked across the grass toward my clients with Falin at my heels. I hoped he didn't scare them.

They introduced themselves as Ann and Frank Feegan, and then looked expectantly at Falin.

"This is Falin Andrews. He's my . . ." *Bodyguard? Manager? Boyfriend?* ". . . associate. He'll just be observing today."

Ann nodded, her dark hair falling over her shoulders as she smiled at him. Frank held out a hand.

After going through the obligatory speech the OMIH forced me to recite, Ann wrote me a check, and we were ready to go talk to the dead. I let them lead the way to the grave. A couple of ghosts flitted along the path, so faded they barely existed. Not one was as powerful as Roy. I ignored them, letting them carry out whatever tasks kept them here in peace.

"This is it," Ann said, stopping before a double headstone with a fresh sprig of daisies in front of it.

I nodded, bowing my head for a moment of silence. Families tended to like a little reverence for their dead.

"If everyone can stand over by that grave, I'll draw my circle so we can get started."

The Feegans obediently walked over to the right, but Falin headed in the other direction. He hung back a couple of rows. I frowned at him but didn't say anything. It didn't matter where he stood, as long as he was out of the way of my circle.

Opening my bag, I dug for my ceramic knife. For indoor rituals, I always used my wax chalk, but that didn't work so well in dirt and grass. Outside I actually had to cut my circle. Which was why I always carried the knife. Except I couldn't find it. Frowning, I dug to the bottom of my purse and found a small claim stub. *Crap. I never got it back from the guard last Tuesday.*

"You're going to cast a circle?" Frank asked, and I couldn't tell if his uncertainty was on *why* I was casting it or *if*.

I smiled at him, trying not to let my nerves show. "Yes, I never work without one." *Unless there is a bunch of big nasty spells around and I'm with Death.* I masked my grimace by looking in my purse again. "Don't worry. It won't hinder your ability to speak with the shades."

What am I going to do without a knife? Actually, I did have a knife. I had the enchanted dagger in my boot. *That will have to do.* I didn't draw the circle yet, but dropped my purse by the headstone and let my awareness stretch out a little.

The bodies below me were little more than bone and dust, but I felt a small spark in them. Enough that I was reasonably confident that I could raise their shades. The couple's bodies weren't center with the headstone, but that was common. Of course, that also meant the graves around them weren't arranged quite correctly, either. I sent my awareness a little farther and plotted my path, walking the circle before drawing it. I didn't want to trap any of the other corpses in my circle. As I walked I left a small trail of power in my wake. The power would dissipate quickly, but it would help me guide my knife.

When I reached the start of the trail I'd dropped, I stopped and looked around. *More oval than circle.* It would suffice. Kneeling, I drew the enchanted dagger and went to work. The dagger liked to be drawn. It liked to be used. It did *not* like to be dragged through the dirt.

I ignored the feel of its displeasure in the back of my

head and finished tracing my circle. Then I stood, centered myself, and activated it. A blue barrier of power sprang up around me.

"I'm going to raise the shades now," I told the couple.

They were looking at each other, creases of concern written across their faces. I smiled, trying to look reassuring. Then I reached for the grave essence. It came easily, sliding along my skin like a cold but familiar lover, and I pushed it into the ground under me. I meant to raise the woman first, but I could feel both the bodies and the power moved through me, more than enough. Two shades sat up, out of the ground, their forms strong and crisp. *Well, okay. That works.* I tried to keep the stunned look off my face as I looked up. Any chance of controlling my face failed when I caught sight of the young couple.

"What's wrong?" Ann asked.

Through the patina of grave-sight, her smiling face was now a vastly different shape. The soft human woman was gone, replaced with a sharper, much more dangerous being. Her engorged black pupils left no whites or irises, and her hair was a snare of briars hanging to her knees. At her waist, Frank's fingers stroked her hollow belly. *Thorn fae.*

I looked at Frank. He had also transformed. No longer was he a small, homely man; his face had spread, flattened. His mouth was too wide, with thick calloused lips around pointed teeth. His small eyes were too close to the center of his face, and his large ears contained the only hair on his head. His body was bent, his knees bowed. I had no idea what type of fae he was, but I was guessing something in the goblin family.

He smiled, flashing his pointed teeth, and I winced. *Crap. What now?*

I glanced back over my shoulder. In my grave-sight,

Falin was standing in dead grass, staring down at the crumbled headstones. His hair was even paler than normal, like glistening snow. I ripped my gaze away from him and focused on the fae Falin was oblivious to.

Not all fae are bad, I reminded myself. After all, Caleb and Falin were fae.

But Caleb was my friend, and he hadn't deceived me. And Falin . . . well, I was still figuring Falin out. But he seemed to be one of the good guys. The Feegans—or whoever they really were—had brought me here under false pretenses. The two shades I'd raised were definitely human, not fae. I took a deep breath. *I'm inside a circle. I'm okay.* I just hoped everything stayed that way. I tapped into my ring and reinforced my barrier.

"Is there something wrong, Miss Craft?" Frank asked.

I shook my head. "You can question them now." My voice came out shaky. *Maybe they'll think it has something do with using my magic.*

The way they were both watching me, I didn't think they bought my bravado.

"You were staring," Frank said.

I tried to smile, knowing it came out weak. "Bad eyes."

"What's going on?" Falin asked.

Finally. I turned back to him and mouthed the word "fae." His eyes widened, and his hand moved to his gun.

"We hired the witch for a service," Ann snapped, watching his movement.

"Then ask your questions and be done with it," Falin told her.

The two fae frowned at each other.

"Do you See, Miss Craft?" Frank asked, emphasizing "see" the same way Death had.

I gulped. *See. As in see through glamour.* I didn't answer. Folklore was full of stories about people who had lost their eyes because they could see through fae glamour.

Again they looked at each other. Then Frank nodded. Ann stepped forward, her briars rustling with the movement. She walked all the way to my circle, and I stumbled back. I reached the back edge of the circle before forcing myself to stop. If I stepped through the circle or touched the barrier, it would snap. Then there would be nothing between the fae and me.

Falin pulled his gun and leveled it on the thorn fae. She ignored him.

Her fingers danced along the edge of my circle, sending flares of bright magic lacing through the blue barrier.

"The Shadow Girl sends a warning," she said. "A ghost girl of blood is worth treasure in silver chains, and if she is a fool, by commands she'll know my pains. She who sees knows the eyes' empty look, and seven times she'll know what it is he took. Blood Moon rises over my sorrow, and the Golden Halls are ruled by a nightmare on the morrow."

"What does that mean?" I asked.

The thorn fae only smiled. "Here is my advice. Run away, Alex Craft. Change your name. Change your face. Run fast."

Then she turned, and as if taking her advice, the two fae ran.

"You can't just decide you're staying at my house!"

Falin's mouth crooked, a hint of a smile. "I can. I am. In the past twenty-four hours you've trespassed on a crime scene, been caught smuggling a gray spellbook into Central Precinct, broken into the statehouse, been shot at, and decided to accept a couple of fae as clients. You're a danger to yourself when left alone." He closed the door behind him.

"That's not true." Or, at least, it wasn't completely true. I was quite obviously a danger to people with me as well. PC ran figure eights between our legs, and I scooped him up. "I'm not going out again tonight. I'll be fine."

"You're also chilled to the bone again."

Which meant he was also inviting himself into my bed.

"Just think of it as police protection." He gave me a full smile.

I rolled my eyes, but in truth, I'd rather not be alone. "I'm taking PC for a walk. We'll discuss it when I get back."

When PC and I walked back inside, I discovered Falin digging through my cabinets.

"How can you survive on this garbage?"

I unhooked PC's leash. "Hey, you're crashing my apartment. The food is what it is."

Falin slammed the fridge door closed. "Don't take your shoes off. We're going grocery shopping."

Two hours later, my house was filled with the mouth-watering scent of garlic and lemon. The delicious smell dragged me away from my computer screen. I shuffled into the kitchen, my hands in my back pockets as I tried to peer around Falin's shoulders.

"I thought you needed a grill to cook steak?" Which was the same comment I'd made in the grocery store when he'd picked out the thick cuts of meat. He'd only shaken his head and put them in the cart anyway. Not that I was complaining. Occasionally I ate with Holly and Caleb, but otherwise, the only meat I ate these days I poured out of a can.

Falin flipped the sizzling steaks. "I'm searing it, not

grilling it. Unless you want to cut the vegetables for the salad, get out of the kitchen."

I didn't pout. Not exactly, at least. By the time the salad was ready, Falin had the steaks off the stove and set on plates beside steaming baked potatoes.

"Where are we eating?" he asked, glancing around.

"Uh . . ." Crap, I hadn't thought about that. I usually ate in front of my computer or leaning against a counter. I didn't even have a second chair in the apartment. I shrugged. "Floor picnic?"

He shook his head, and his eyes swept over the small apartment again, as though if he looked hard enough he'd find a hidden table. After a moment, he huffed out his breath. "We'll have a bed picnic," he said, and set off with the plates.

PC danced around Falin's legs, jumping and begging. I hooked my foot around the small dog and dragged him backward. He whined, flashing big eyes at me. "No steak for you."

PC whined again, recognizing the word "no." Then he turned his attention back to Falin. As soon as Falin sat on the bed, PC jumped into his lap. *The little traitor.*

I grabbed silverware as Falin defended our dinner from one very hungry Chinese crested. "What do you want to drink?" I asked, opening the fridge.

"Beer."

I grabbed two bottles—another purchase Falin had made at the grocery store—and headed to the bed. I traded a bottle of beer for my plate. I was almost leery of trying the steak. After all, it smelled too good to believe—what if the taste didn't live up to the smell?

I gingerly cut a small piece. The knife slid through easily. And the meat—the meat all but melted in my mouth. I barely held back a moan. "I changed my mind. You can move in as long as you cook."

Falin's fork paused halfway to his mouth.

"Uh . . ." I looked away and grabbed my beer. "I'm kidding, of course. I just mean . . . dinner is great."

His lips curled into a small smile. "That is almost a thank-you."

"Don't let it go to your head." I focused on my plate, but a smile had claimed my mouth when I wasn't paying attention.

When I glanced up, he was watching me with a small crooked smile clinging to the sides of his lips. Okay, this was awkward, but the food was awesome. *Where had the man learned to cook?*

"So, uh, FIB, huh?" I said, feeling the need to say something in the uncomfortable silence building as he watched me eat—which was kind of weird. "What do they know about Coleman, or whatever creature was masquerading as Coleman?"

His smile slipped. "He's old. Very old. The fae were fading for centuries, but now that mortals believe again, the older legends, some forgotten in the sands of time, are reemerging. 'Coleman' was the body thief's most recent of who knows how many identities. I'm not sure what his original nature was."

I nodded. "So, do you—" I stopped myself. Falin was fae. That fact hadn't really had time to fully sink in yet, but it needed to. There were rules when talking to fae, taboos not to be broken, slippery wording. Caleb was my friend and would warn me if I blundered into a dangerous conversation with him, but even in our friendship, there *were* dangerous conversations. I had no such guarantee from Falin. "Can I ask you about the glyphs?"

He set down his fork. "I'd rather you didn't, but I doubt that would stop you. Whatever it is you can see on the corpse in the morgue, I cannot see, and I'm not familiar with the glyphs cut into the bodies of the ritual victims. Now, this is not exactly a dinner conversation."

"Right." I focused on my food and let the silence spread.

I'd meant to leave a piece of steak for PC, but before I realized it, my plate was empty. Leaning back against the pillows, I rubbed my belly. "That was amazing."

The thing about living alone is that you talk to yourself. A lot. For a very brief moment, I'd forgotten Falin was there. Of course, when he turned and flashed that lopsided smile at me, forgetting he was there was impossible.

Heat rose to my cheeks, and I sat up straight again. "Can I take your plate?" I asked, reaching toward the empty plate.

He held it out for me, but as I stood he also rose. "I'll help you clean up."

I'd intended to put the plates in the sink and leave them for later, but Falin insisted on helping me clean everything, so we ended up side by side. Me washing dishes and him drying them. He'd abandoned his jacket over the back of my one chair, and the sleeves of his oxford were rolled to his elbows. As we worked our shoulders brushed against each other. When I handed him a fork, his long fingers slid along mine, and my stomach somersaulted.

This was crazy. He was secretive, bossy, and regularly insufferable. He had also saved my life a couple of times. And he looked really good in my kitchen.

I cut off the water and dried my hands on the front of my jeans. "I'm going to . . ." *Run away? Hide?* I cleared my throat and pointed to the back of the apartment. "I'm going to take a shower before bed." Without another word, I retreated to the only other room in my loft.

Of course, that meant I'd forgotten to grab some-thing to change into. Wrapped in an oversized towel, I reached for my toothbrush and suffered a moment of confusion as my fingers landed on one that wasn't mine. Falin had picked up some essentials when we went to the store, and now his fresh new toothbrush was lean-ing against mine. I frowned at it, a chill sliding down my spine. I did *not* cohabitate. I hadn't even had a second date since leaving school. I quite preferred saying good-bye the morning after without ever learning the guy's name. Now I had a guy's toothbrush beside mine, and I hadn't even slept with him. Well, I'd technically *slept* with him, but we hadn't ...

I brushed my teeth until my gums bled. Then I brushed my hair, braided it, and unbraided it. *This is silly. I have to leave the bathroom sometime.* It was only going to get more awkward if I kept putting it off. I wrapped the towel tighter around myself and abandoned my hiding spot.

Falin was using my computer. He didn't look up as I stormed by, so I didn't pay him any attention. Ransack-ing my PJ drawer, I pulled out a plain camisole and a cute pair of silk shorts. They had been gifts from Holly last year, and the fact that I cared they were cute pissed me off. However, that didn't mean I wasn't going to wear them.

As I raided my top drawer in search of a clean pair of panties, Falin shut down the computer.

"I'll take a shower before bed, too," he said, stand-ing.

I nodded absently and turned my back on him so I could pull my clothes on. As I tugged the camisole over my head the bathroom door shut. I dropped the towel and stepped into the panties. Someone coughed behind me.

The world slowed to highlight every millisecond it took for my head to turn, my underwear still around my thighs. My cheeks burned as my eyes found Falin. He was leaning out of the bathroom, his eyes respectfully averted to the far wall but his lips curled in a grin.

"A clean towel?" he asked.

I yanked on my panties, glancing at the soggy towel by my feet. It *had* been the only towel left in the bathroom. Lifting a finger, I pointed. "Closet."

He pulled open the doors without further prompting, and I pulled on my shorts.

My cheeks were still burning as I climbed into bed and whistled for PC. He jumped on his normal pillow.

"I think Falin will probably want to sleep there," I told him and moved him to the end of the bed.

He gave me an indignant look, then turned three circles before settling down. He licked his casted leg, as if to point out he was injured and needed the pillow. Then his eyes closed, and he was asleep.

"Wish I could fall asleep that easy," I told the dog.

He didn't even look up.

I snuggled deep under my blankets and squeezed my eyes shut, but I was still awake when the bathroom door opened. The bed moved as Falin crawled into it, and the spicy scent of the soap he'd bought washed over me. Then his arm slipped around my waist. My heart made a simultaneous attempt to escape through the front of my chest and to cozy back against him. It left me breathless and trying not to gasp in the dark.

"Good night, Alexis," he whispered, his breath heating the skin on the back of my neck.

I didn't dare answer, or even move as his fingers splayed over my stomach. I lay in the darkness, listening. It was a long time after his breathing evened out with sleep that dreams finally found me.

Chapter 18

—◦—◦—❦—◦—◦—

"**B**ut what is the connection between the victims? Who were the first two women?" I asked, tapping my plate with the fork.

"Alex, you aren't working this case." Falin scooped another bite of eggs into his mouth, ignoring my frown.

"Why? Because my father said so?"

He almost choked on his eggs. Reaching across the bed, he grabbed his coffee from the bedside stand.

I gave him a moment to recover; then I asked, "Do you know the connection? I mean, I'm guessing Coleman didn't abduct them off the street and tie them to a bed. The scene was set for a romantic rendezvous. He knew the women before he killed them."

"We've seen only one crime scene. And, Alex, you're still not working this case."

"Fine." I passed my last strip of bacon to PC and carried my plate to the sink. Then I didn't know what to do. I wasn't used to sharing my space. The room was overcrowded but too quiet.

I flipped on the TV, and a local anchorman appeared

with the picture of a young woman in the background. I frowned. "I know her. That's Helena."

I pressed the volume button to turn up the sound.

"—was found two nights ago. Police are currently not releasing information but have confirmed that this is a homicide investigation. In other news—"

I flipped around to face Falin. "He's talking about the warehouse victim, isn't he? Was her name Helena Brothers?"

Falin frowned at me, and I tried to think back. I hadn't analyzed what I'd seen in the warehouse. What had been left of that woman had been awful, but now that I thought back to the glazed eyes, the pain-torn face, I could see Helena's features. I sank onto the bed.

"You knew her?" Falin asked, and I nodded. "You knew Bethany Lane, too. You're the one who initially identified her body."

"The wyrd community is small." I stopped and looked up, my eyes wide. "Have all the victims been wyrd?"

Falin didn't answer. He stood, avoiding me by carrying his plate to the sink. I frowned at his back.

"That's it, isn't it? Who were the other two vic—"

A knock sounded at my door, and I jumped. It wasn't my main door. It was the door leading to the rest of the house. Holly bustled in without waiting for me to answer.

"Tamara just called," she said, plopping down on the edge of my bed. "And she—" She stopped, her eyes wide as they landed on Falin standing in my kitchen in just a pair of jeans and his gloves. "Oh, uh, I didn't know you had company. I'll just . . ." She jumped to her feet and pointed toward the door.

"Holly, it's okay, really. What's up?"

She glanced at Falin again, and I followed her gaze. Falin was apparently trying to give us a measure of privacy and had busied himself with the dishes. There was an impressive view of his backside, which Holly was all but drooling over.

"Do I need to get you a bib?" I whispered, and she started. "What did Tamara say?"

"Oh, um. Tamara is having a hell of a day. She called crying. She's going to have to autopsy one of her coworkers who was found dead in her apartment this morning. I thought we'd go take her to lunch to cheer her up."

I frowned, a tickle of dread building in the back of my mind. "Did she say who died?"

"Yeah. Sally." She paused. "Oh, Alex, you probably knew her, too. I'm so sorry." She wrapped arms around my shoulders, but pulled back immediately. "Alex, are you okay? You're chilled to the touch."

I nodded absently. I was tired, but I'd had a rough couple of days and had barely slept last night. I was far more concerned with the fact Tamara had told me Sally was feeling sick when she came off night shift yesterday morning. A night shift that would have corresponded with Helena's body showing up in the morgue. It might have been completely unconnected, but . . .

"Did Tamara say what Sally died from?"

"No one knows." Holly pressed her lips together. "So, lunch this afternoon? My treat to both of you?"

I started to nod, then remembered I had a lunch date with Ashen. "Could we do an early dinner instead? I have lunch plans already."

"Really?"

I frowned. She didn't have to sound so shocked.

Holly glanced back at Falin. Then she nodded. "Yeah, dinner works. That will give us more time to talk and give everyone permission to cry over their beers. I'll see you about four o'clock?"

We said our good-byes, and I shut the door behind

her. I rubbed the scratches on my shoulder. I'd gotten infected with the soul-sucking spell from a shade who'd died from it. Now, Sally, another wyrd witch, had autopsied a victim and was dead. *But why is she dead and I'm not?* I'd checked the Aetheric this morning. The tendrils were now corded down my arm to my wrist and snaking through half my torso. It was spreading, but not fast enough to kill in a single day.

I need to see that body.

I turned around and discovered Falin watching me.

"I don't think you should go," he said from the kitchen.

I blinked at him, so lost in my own thoughts I couldn't follow where he was coming from. *He doesn't think I should go? Where—to see Tamara?* Well, so much for him giving me privacy during my conversation with Holly.

"One, it's not your decision. Two, why wouldn't I go see Tamara? I can't just hide in my house for the rest of my life." Though if I didn't find Coleman, the rest of my life would be a much shorter time than expected.

Falin frowned at me. He leaned against the counter, his hands braced at either side of him on the sink. He'd found yellow rubber gloves somewhere, and that would have been comical except for the rather distracting way sunlight played over his chest.

"I was talking about lunch at the Eternal Bloom."

"Oh. Yeah." Okay, awkward. Here I was staring at him, and we were talking about my lunch date with another guy. "Also not your decision."

"It's too dangerous," he said, and I felt a twinge of disappointment that the possible danger was the only reason he didn't want me to go.

Get your head on straight, Alex. Falin was an uninvited guest invading my space—and going to the fae bar *was* dangerous. The fae in the cemetery hadn't tried to hurt me. They'd just given me a cryptic message and told me to run away. But the fae in the white van were definitely bad news. At the same time, hiding in plain sight was sometimes the best course of action. And I wasn't going to be there alone. I was meeting Ashen. If I was lucky, his research had turned up something useful about the glyphs on Coleman's body. And if I could reproduce the glyphs from Helena's body, maybe Ashen could help me unravel that spell.

Falin watched my expression, a grimace engraving itself in his face. "You're going anyway."

"Yeah. Ashen could see the spell on Coleman's body. How many grave witches looked at Coleman?"

"Five."

"And how many could see the spell?"

Falin scowled. "Just two."

"Ashen mentioned that the glyphs appeared to be fae magic. He knows something. What did he tell you?"

"Clearly not as much as you're hoping he tells you," he said, but when I just stared at him he continued. "He confirmed what you saw, he indicated the spell was fae in nature, and he said he was unsure about the purpose of the spell. What does that tell us? Nothing we didn't already know."

I shook my head. "But he knows something about glyphs. You don't know what they mean, but he said he studies them. Plus he might have sensed more than I did. It's worth the risk." And he might know why the other three grave witches hadn't been able to see the spell, but Ashen and I had.

"You think it's worth risking your life to find out more about a spell you know is connected to Coleman's theft of the body? Alex, that's stupid."

I frowned at him. Okay, so when he put it that way,

it did sound stupid. But I hadn't told Falin about the soul-consuming spell. My life was just as much at risk if I stayed home and waited for my soul to get sucked out. If Ashen could decode the fae glyphs, he might be able to help me figure out Coleman's plans.

Falin must have read the determination in my face, because he shook his head but said, "Fine, but I'm going with you."

"Uh. No."

He pulled the rubber gloves off and tossed them beside the sink. Then he walked around the counter and opened my laptop.

"You're not going," I told him.

"It's a public place."

Great. I was going to have a babysitter. I changed the subject. "Sally autopsied Helena's body."

Falin didn't look up.

"She was a wyrd witch. Empath. She's dead. I told you the magic on Helena's body was still active."

His face pursed in a frown. "The anti–black magic, unit cleared the warehouse scene and Helena's body. Twice."

"Yeah, they did that before I saw all the active magic, too. I want to see Sally's body. I might be able to determine whether she died from the spell on Helena."

"A spell you can't explain to me."

I frowned at him, my hand moving to rub the scratches on my shoulder. His gaze flickered toward the movement, and I dropped my hand by my side. It was too late.

He stood and crossed the space between us in quick strides. I backed up, running into the counter, and Falin filled the space in front of me, blocking me in. He leaned forward, his gloved fingers running across the sensitive skin around the scratches. They still hadn't scabbed, hadn't started to heal.

"Stop."

He didn't listen. He pulled off his right glove and rubbed his thumb over the raw skin. Pain shot through me, a lightning-sharp stab that hit deep in my being, and my legs buckled. Nausea swam through me and filled my mouth with hot saliva. I closed my eyes, trying to swallow against the sickness, and Falin stepped back.

"That's black magic," he said. "How long have you been exposed to that spell?"

"Since we met. At the morgue. I caught it from Bethany's shade."

"I'm taking you to the hospital."

I shook my head, still fighting the sickness inside my body. "Won't help."

"Alex, do you know what the spell is? What it's doing?"

I nodded.

"What, then? What is it? How do you reverse it?"

I opened my eyes. "Have all the victims been wyrd?"

"No." He sighed and stepped back. Crossing the kitchen, he leaned against the counter opposite me. "The first victim was Rosa Hanks. She was a norm, an out-of-towner who had been making frequent visits to Nekros during the four months prior to her murder. The second victim, Michelle Ford, was also an out-of-towner. She was wyrd. Bethany and Helena you know about."

I nodded. So Coleman wasn't targeting only wyrd witches, but no one else in the ME's office had fallen over dead after examining one of the bodies. Death had told me the spell was contagious but specific. *Why did it spread to me?* What linked all the victims?

I needed to find out if Sally had died of the spell.

Falin pulled a shirt over his head and grabbed his shoulder holster and badge from the counter.

"Where are you going?"

He shrugged into his holster and grabbed his keys. "The station. I want to find out what killed Sally."

"I'm going with you." I grabbed my purse.

"No. You're staying here."

I crossed my arms over my chest. "You can't tell me what to do."

"Legally, I can stonewall any attempt you make to interfere with an ongoing investigation." One side of his lips quirked upward. "And I can deny you a ride."

I gritted my teeth. *Of all the insufferable . . .*

He reached out, and his gloved finger touched my shoulder, near the scratches but not close enough to hurt. "If the spell is still active, I don't want you anywhere near it."

I blinked at him, and he leaned forward. For one lingering moment, our eyes met and my breath caught in my throat. A dizzying flutter attacked my stomach.

His lips parted, and then he looked away. He cleared his throat.

"Stay here and out of trouble. I'll be back before you need to leave for the Eternal Bloom." His hand dropped from my shoulder, and he walked out.

Chapter 19

I stared at the closed door, still breathless from the prospect of a kiss that hadn't even happened. PC, misunderstanding my fascination with the door, trotted over, sat, and waited to go out. When I just stood there, he whined and pawed at the wood.

I scooped him up. "You're the only steady man I need in my life—right, PC?"

He wagged his plumed tail and licked my chin. He felt feverishly hot in my arms. *Is the consumption of my soul making me cold?*

I didn't know. I didn't even have anyone I could ask. I looked down at my dog, and he licked my chin again, then looked pointedly at the door.

"All right. A walk," I said.

His tail went into high speed at the w-a-l-k word, and I grabbed his leash. He charged out the door, doing his best to drag me down the stairs, but PC's seven pounds of enthusiasm weren't enough to accomplish the task.

At the base of the stairs, he stopped to sniff Fred, the cat gargoyal.

"*Don't you let that thing wiz on me,*" the statue

warned, its telepathic voice conveying alarm not evident on the snarling stone features.

I picked up PC before he could hike his leg. "Sorry, Fred. I didn't know you were so close to the stairs."

"The Sleagh Maith has visited you." Fred's voice wasn't alarmed now. It was just stating a fact. The fact happened to be that fae had been to my house. And not just any fae. No, a member of the Sleagh Maith, the good people, who from what Caleb had told me were typically court fae.

He could mean Falin, or . . . My stomach lurched, and not in the fluttery, awkward but excited way it had a few minutes ago. I glanced at the street, afraid I'd see a large white van headed for me, but the road was empty. The reporters had finally moved on to other stories, so for the first time in several days, the sidewalk in front of the house was clear. "When were the fae here?"

Fred didn't answer.

"I'll let PC pee on you." To mark my point, I lowered the wiggling dog toward the ground.

"While you're away, I miss cream."

The gargoyle's disapproval was obvious in my head, and I frowned at it.

It wasn't making sense. I hadn't been away, and I'd added milk to the saucer on the porch just last night. I waited, but Fred didn't say anything else. Gargoyles had a reputation for being precognitive. *Maybe he means I'm going away . . .* I didn't foresee a vacation in my near future. My mind drifted back to the fae in the van, and I shuddered.

"Come on, PC. Let's get this walk over quick."

I turned, heading for the backyard, and Fred's voice touched my mind again. *"You must See under the Blood Moon. You must know what you See is true."*

I whirled around. "What does that mean?"

Fred didn't answer.

"Dammit. What's the Blood Moon?" The thorn fae had mentioned the Blood Moon and nightmares in the golden halls. She'd called it a warning from the Shadow Girl. Then she'd recited a verse—a verse that didn't make sense.

I glared at the gargoyle. I was sick of cryptic messages. It was time to find some answers.

Falin returned at eleven, his eyes weary and his hair mussed as though he'd been running his hands through it. He tossed a white paper bag on the counter as soon as he walked in, and then kicked his shoes off by the door.

"You hungry?" He nodded toward the bag.

"I'm about to go to lunch," I reminded him. "What did you learn about Sally?"

He didn't answer but walked over and pulled a hoagie out of the bag. He unwrapped the silver foil on the Philly cheesesteak sub, and my mouth watered. I watched him take a bite of the sub, knowing my lunch wasn't going to be half as good. The Eternal Bloom was a bar with a very short order grill. Fries and hamburgers were about the extent of what I could expect real-food-wise.

I peeked in the bag. There was another silver-wrapped hoagie inside. *Maybe if I just eat half of it and then order fries when I meet Ashen . . .* As I pulled out the sub I noticed Falin grinning at me from behind his hoagie. I ignored him and enjoyed the food.

"So, as good as this sub is, it's not going to distract me. What did you learn about Sally?"

"I just got back from the station, Alex. Let me eat my lunch." He walked over to the fridge. "You want a soda?"

No, I didn't want one of *his* sodas that was in *my* fridge. I wanted him to answer my question or get out of my house. I wrapped the uneaten part of lunch and woke my laptop back up. If he wasn't going to tell me what he'd learned, I was going back to my research.

"The next full moon is next Wednesday," I said without looking up. Falin made a noise that didn't indicate whether he was listening or just enjoying his food. I continued. "There will be a full lunar eclipse. The moon will turn red."

He still didn't say anything.

"I think that's the Blood Moon in the warning. But what are the golden halls?" *The statehouse?* "Ghost girls could be exactly what it says: female ghosts. Or it could be grave witches." But the full first line of the verse was "A ghost girl of blood is worth treasure in silver chains," so if "ghost girl" referred to grave witches, what did it mean to be "of blood"? *Flesh and blood, maybe? As in living?* I frowned. The second half of that line was darker: "and if she is a fool, by commands she'll know my pains." Was that a threat from the Shadow Girl?

Falin walked over and glanced at the document on my screen. "Have you been working on that riddle since I left?"

"Mostly, yeah." After I'd found out about the lunar eclipse, I'd thought I might have a chance of decoding the verse. All I'd done was give myself a headache.

He leaned forward and put one hand on my back as he read. "Golden Halls would be the high court in faerie."

I blinked. "Seriously?" I jotted it down. If the golden halls in the line "The Golden Halls are ruled by a nightmare on the morrow" referred to the high court of faerie, I was even more confused why the Shadow Girl— whoever she was—would tell me in a verse. *Unless it's about Coleman's ritual. Is whatever he's doing going to threaten faerie?* But again, why tell me?

The second line was the most intelligible: "She who Sees knows the eyes' empty look." Death and the fae had both used "See" to refer to seeing through glamour. "And seven times she'll know what it is he took." If "he" referred to Coleman, I knew what he was taking: souls.

"The last half of the second line could mean seven victims," I said. Of course, there was no guarantee the verse had anything to do with the spell—or with anything. It could be nonsense.

Falin frowned at me and stepped back. "There was a trace of dark magic on Sally's body."

"Tamara sensed it?"

He shook his head. I frowned. Tamara hadn't been able to feel the spell in the scratches on my shoulder, either. If the soul-consuming spell had killed Sally, why had it worked so fast? I'd been infected for four days. She'd died after only one.

"What—" Falin cut off as his phone buzzed, alerting him to a text message. He pulled the phone from his belt and flipped it open. "I have to go. Don't go to the Eternal Bloom without me."

I glanced at the clock. It was already eleven thirty. "What's going on?"

"They found another body."

I hesitated as I climbed out of Holly's car where it idled in front of Eternal Bloom. "Do you want to come in and have a drink before you go?"

Holly shook her head. "Big case landed on my desk yesterday. I'm doing research for the DA, and I'm slammed, but I'll see you tonight. Have fun."

I closed the door, because short of begging her to come with me, I had nothing more to say. Now that I was standing outside the Eternal Bloom, I was seriously wishing someone else was going in with me. But I was here, I was going in, and I was going to learn what Ashen knew about fae glyphs. I hitched my purse higher on my shoulder and marched up the steps.

Beyond the main door was a small receiving room—too small, as the bouncer on duty was a troll. He stooped despite the nine-foot ceiling, his knuckles dragging the floor beside his bare blue feet.

"Please check all iron items," he said, his deep voice booming in the confined space.

I considered what I had on me. My car keys might have contained iron, but they'd been stolen with the car. I had the dagger on me, but it was fae-wrought, so not iron, and the troll hadn't said anything about checking weapons.

"No iron," I said, smiling.

He nodded his large hairless head. "Please sign ledger."

I looked around. No ledger. I did remember there being a podium the last time I came here. The troll watched me and frowned, his two lower tusks protruding. He shuffled to the side.

Right. That ledger. The one *behind* the troll. I scratched my name in the book, overly aware of the large fae breathing down my neck.

"Al-lex Ca-raft," the troll read aloud. He looked at a clipboard. "You have VIP status."

He shuffled some more and indicated a door I hadn't even known was in the room. I frowned.

"No, I don't," I said, but the troll only gave me a confused look. "I'm not a VIP here." Or at least, I didn't think I wanted to be.

The troll scratched the top of his head with a finger as thick around as my wrist. "Alex Craft. VIP."

"No, I'm not. Let me in the public part of the bar."

The troll frowned harder. He looked from the door,

to his clipboard, to the ledger, and then back to the clipboard. He shook his head.

Okay, then. It looked as if I was standing Ashen up. I didn't like my sudden elevation to VIP. I was getting the hell out of the Eternal Bloom.

I shoved the main door open, storming out of the bar—and plowed straight into someone.

I jumped back. "I'm so sorry; I—"

"No, please forgive me, Miss Craft, for keeping you waiting." Ashen bowed from the waist. "I am unfamiliar with these streets. I did not mean to be so tardy."

Of course, if I run over someone, it would have to be my date.

"You're not late. I just got here myself," I said, and then immediately regretted it as he smiled and motioned to the door.

"Should we find a table?"

"I, uh . . ." I glanced back at the bar. "Honestly, I'm having a bit of trouble with the bouncer. Why don't we eat somewhere else?"

"The bouncer? We'll see about that." He pulled out his wallet and wrapped his arm through mine. "I find the green speaks to fae as well as it does humans."

"Please check all iron items," the troll said as Ashen pulled open the door.

"No iron on me, my good fae," he said, and pressed a twenty into the troll's huge palm. "My lady friend and I would like a quiet spot in which to speak. That won't be a problem, right?"

The troll cocked his huge head to the side.

"See," Ashen whispered. Then he pulled me through the very door I'd been avoiding, leading me into the VIP area of the Eternal Bloom.

Chapter 20

❖═◉═❖

"**P**lease sign the ledger," a small voice said as the door closed behind Ashen and me.

I turned and discovered a small fae, her large wings shaped like those of a luna moth, sitting on the edge of a podium.

"I signed in outside," I told her.

"The ledger," she said again. "Name, date, and time."

I glanced at Ashen, and he shrugged. Okay, whatever; I'd sign in again. But as soon as Ashen got a look around, I was suggesting a change of venue—earlier if anything weird happened.

The VIP room of the Eternal Bloom was both more and less than I expected. It was certainly populated by more unglamoured fae than the regular part of the bar had been at any time I'd been there. But I guess that made sense. The fae in the public section were on display. Here they were relaxed. Most didn't look up as Ashen led me to an empty table in the corner. I accepted the chair against the wall—I didn't want my back to the bar's patrons. I watched the fae who'd noted our entrance, but there was nothing malicious about their glances.

I looked around, unsure what was real and what was glamour. The unadorned wooden walls were probably real enough, but I wasn't sure about the tables and chairs, which had been crafted with such skill that no metal screws held them together. Glamour was a belief magic so strong it reshaped reality. The basic principle was that I saw a chair, I felt a chair, and thus reality agreed there was a chair. My gaze landed on an ancient tree growing through the floorboards in the center of the room. *There isn't a tree growing out of the bar from the outside.* I looked up. Branches created a false roof to the room, starting twenty feet above my head. And between the branches, I caught the glimmer of stars.

"That can't be real," I whispered, staring. *Has to be glamoured.*

"It looks quite real," Ashen said, and I glanced at him. His eyes glowed pale green in the dim bar.

"You're using grave-sight?"

He smiled. "I find the world a more fascinating place when its corruption is fully revealed. Don't you?"

If I hadn't known I could see through glamour when I used my grave-sight, I'd have thought he was crazy. Now I wondered if he wasn't hinting at more than he was saying. *A dangerous thing to admit in a bar filled with fae.* To be sure, I edged deeper into the double meaning. "So, I take it you're not a fan of the pretty lies."

He inclined his head, which I took to mean we were talking about the same thing. He could See, too. Could all grave witches? Or was that why only the two of us had been able to detect the spell on Coleman's body? I added it to the list of growing questions in my mind.

"I imagine that is where the bar got its name," Ashen said, nodding at the giant tree. "Amaranthine. How lovely."

I looked at the large flowers far above our heads.

They glowed softly, swaying in a breeze I couldn't feel. As I stared I thought I caught an exotic scent perfuming the air. I inhaled. *Definitely flowers.* It was a sweet scent that filled my mind with moonlight and laughter.

"I wouldn't stare at the flowers," an old woman whispered as she walked by our table.

I ripped my gaze away, and the scent faded. *Flowers. Flowers almost enthralled me.* I opened my mouth to thank the woman, but the words died on my tongue as I got a good look at her.

She was bent with age, but she wasn't human. Her puffy skin was so fair, it was translucent. Not like a ghost's translucence, but as though her skin was only a thin membrane wrapped around a dark hollowness inside her body. She wore a plain black dress and carried a hand-painted sign that read DESIRES: BOUGHT AND TRADED. I recognized the sign. When I walked PC in the park in the Magic Quarter, I'd occasionally see her sitting on a bench, holding that sign. She'd always been glamoured to look much more human at the park.

I nodded to acknowledge her warning about the flowers, and she smiled, flashing the toothless hollow space behind her lips. Then she and her sign moved on, searching for an empty table.

"I don't think this place is exactly witch friendly," I whispered, leaning closer to Ashen. "Perhaps we should consider relocating."

"I am most amazed with this bar," he said as if he hadn't heard me. "Look there, in that small area. Do you see the dancers?"

I did. They moved in streams of motion, gliding and twirling in a circular pattern around a fiddler. When I heard the first note of music, I looked away—I didn't want to get caught the way I nearly had with the flowers.

"They dance the endless dance," Ashen said, still

watching. "And none will step out of that circle until the fiddle strings burst and the song is forced to end. Absolutely amazing." He turned back toward me. "Do forgive me, Miss Craft. I have a special interest in all things fae. I am probably boring you. We are here to discuss the late governor's body." He smiled.

"Please call me Alex. Actually, since seeing Coleman's body, I've developed my own interest in fae magic. You mentioned recognizing some of the glyphs. Did your research turn up anything about the spell?"

"No, unfortunately. The layers of spells on that body were intricate and topped with a distortion spell, making it hard to focus on. Quite bewildering." He looked around. "Can I order you something?"

As if summoned by the question, a fae with cloven feet showing under the hem of her long skirt walked up to our table. She placed two glasses of golden liquid before us. Then she turned to leave.

"I didn't order this," I said.

She glanced back over her shoulder, and her goat-slitted eyes narrowed. Then she pointed at a nearby table. A woman in a crimson dress sat at the table. She lifted her glass, also filled with the golden liquid.

Ashen picked up his glass, raising it in a silent toast.

I grabbed his forearm. "Are you sure about that?"

He glanced at the glass and shrugged. "It looks okay to me." He nodded at the woman. Then he took a long sip of the golden liquid. "Exquisite."

I picked up my glass and cupped it between my hands, but I didn't drink. The golden liquid looked thick, almost syrupy. *What is this stuff?* I put the glass back down and looked at Ashen. "So do you know many fae glyphs?"

"Quite a few, yes. I have been studying them for quite some time."

Good. The glyph from Helena's body that I'd drawn to show Falin was in my purse. I'd also sketched out what I could remember of a few others. I dug them out and tried to smooth the paper before passing it across the table. If Ashen knew something about the glyphs, I might be able to piece together more about the spells Coleman was using and what he was planning. I chewed at my bottom lip as Ashen picked up the paper.

His eyes widened. "Miss Craft, this is quite the diverse collection. You were able to See all of these on the late governor's body?"

"Uh, no. Not all of them." Or really, any of them. "Do you recognize any of the glyphs?"

Ashen flattened the paper between us and pointed at one of the glyphs. "This one is typically used for shielding spells, and this one is for a cage or trap of some sort. This indicates a link or a path. And this one . . ." He pointed to the glyph that had appeared most often on Helena's body. Then he frowned. He turned the paper.

"That is the soul," a harsh female voice said, but her accent made it sound like "dhe zoul."

I looked up at the woman in the crimson dress. She pulled back the chair beside Ashen and plopped into it. Setting her glass on the table, she plucked the page of glyphs out of his hand. He frowned, but he didn't say anything.

"I have not seen this glyph in a long time," she said. "This combination—I know this spell." She passed the paper back to me. "I hope that the body you found these glyphs on did not belong to a friend of yours."

I went still as ice landed in the pit of my stomach. "How did you know it was on a body?"

"This spell—you don't survive it."

"Then you know what it does?"

"Ya, I know. I know there will be seven victims. And I don't like seeing it this close to the Blood Moon."

The Blood Moon again. And seven victims, just as in the verse "and seven times she'll know what it is he took." The Shadow Girl's warning had to be about Coleman and the spell he was preparing.

I glanced at Ashen. He appeared to be hanging off the woman's every accented word. I chewed my bottom lip. The woman, while not overtly fae, had an otherworldly essence about her. She'd asked me no questions, while I'd asked two, plus she'd bought us drinks. If I wasn't careful, I'd end up indebted.

I smoothed the paper in front of me, buying time to consider my phrasing. *No questions. Just statements.* "I've been told the spell has a very specific target. I thought the targets might be wyrd witches, but it appears that isn't the connection."

The woman smiled, and it was the kind of smile a cat gives a mouse after the mouse has been cornered and the cat is content to play. "Wyrd witches? No, this spell's target is much more . . . genetic than that."

Genetic? She must have meant generic. English obviously wasn't her first language.

She was still grinning at me. *Even when cats play with mice, the mouse still gets eaten in the end.* It was time to go. I glanced over at Ashen. He watched her as if entranced, and I wondered what he saw with his gravesight. I reached across the table and touched his arm. His eyes snapped to me, clear and still glowing with power. *Okay, he doesn't look like he's under a spell. I don't feel bad leaving him here.*

"I really should be heading out," I said, pushing my chair back.

"Going so soon?" he asked. "You haven't even touched your drink"

I glanced down at the thick liquid. No way was I drinking that.

"You can have it if you like. I have to run." I started to stand, but my legs didn't respond. *What the—?* I looked down, wiggled my toes, and crossed and uncrossed my legs—everything worked, except when I tried to stand. I seemed to be glued to my chair.

"What's happening?"

"No one leaves until all drinks on the table are finished," the woman said, her smile practically cracking her face. "House rule. That is now three questions I've answered. What will you do for me, little witch?"

"I don't trade in retrospect."

She shook her head, but the jack-o'-lantern smile didn't dim. "That is a shame." She held out her hand, palm up as though she was offering something or panhandling.

I frowned. A shiver of magic brushed the air around me. "What are you doing?"

The magic crept closer, and a warm tingle slithered over my neck. I couldn't stand, couldn't back away from the table. I glanced at the glass of gold liquid. If I drank it, I could get up. Run out of the bar. *But maybe that's all the magic is for, to scare me into drinking.*

I didn't grab the glass.

The slithering magic tightened, bit into my neck like a too-tight necklace.

"Obey me," the woman said.

My eyes bulged as the compulsion to do just that flitted through my brain. I pressed the urge down and ripped at my throat. *Nothing. Nothing's there.* My heart beat against my lungs, knocking the air out of me as I fought the spell.

"She's too strong. Drain her," the woman said.

Ashen reached out, but he didn't touch me, not physically. Power crashed over me. Not a spell, just pure, raw energy. The rush of cold, of the grave, hit me hard enough to snap my head back. My shields shook, and I tapped the power in my ring. Then I remembered I had no extra external shields to reinforce. It was just me against the onslaught. *Oh crap.* Ashen thrust raw power at me. Not just magic; he wielded grave essence honed into a weapon.

My mental shield shook again.

"Obey me," the woman commanded.

"Go screw yourself."

Brave words, but I wasn't going to hold up much longer. If Ashen broke my mental shield, I'd be hurting and defenseless. I did the only thing I could: I opened my shields myself. He attacked me with grave essence. My talent reared up, drew on the chill he threw. There was no time for centering or guiding the energy. I just drank down the cold, the touch of the grave. Wind whipped my hair from my face. My own heat burned inside me, seeking a way out of my body.

Ashen grabbed that heat. I felt his power—even as I was making it mine—reach out and draw hard. He pulled the heat out of my body and then kept pulling, his power trying to drag me out of the land of the living, into the land of the dead.

Grave-sight filled my vision, revealing the corpse sitting across from me. The glow of a present soul lit his edges, but nothing living was so decayed. As I registered the body as a corpse, more heat leapt from me and seeped into him. The decayed skin of Ashen's face firmed, his rotted eyes rehydrating. Leathered lips cracked into a smile, and he breathed in deeply. Heat I didn't even realize was still in me seeped away, rushing across the space to him. He took that, too, and color lifted to his skin.

I trembled, the icy wind slicing into me. I had never

been this cold when still filled with the grave. Never. I felt as though I'd never be warm again. The ice in my limbs weighed me down. Made me slow. Tired.

The woman snapped her teeth like a shark catching prey and commanded, "Obey me."

Chapter 21

The words roared in my head. A force. A compulsion. I wanted to obey her. I *needed* to.

No!

I fought the urge, shoved it aside, away. She gritted perfect teeth at me. Unlike Ashen, her features barely changed in my grave-sight. If anything, she became more lovely, more enchanting. Court fae.

In her palm she held a coiled length of silver thread. She curled her fist around the string and jerked. My chest heaved in response to her tug, and in my grave-sight I could see the glittering silver thread stretching between us. I reached for it, but though I could see it, I couldn't touch it.

"Obey me."

I looked at her, the struggle fading from my limbs, and she smiled. She was beautiful and powerful. My mistress. I liked that she smiled. I wanted to please her.

"So strong," she whispered. "How . . . valuable." She pointed at the glass in front of me. "Drink, so we can go."

I picked up the glass, stared at it. My fingers were

trembling, making the golden liquid quiver. Suspended in the liquid, the blue swirls of a spell danced. I frowned at the spell. I didn't like spells used on me. I set the glass back down.

"Drink it."

My hand twitched. I didn't want to disappoint her. I didn't like spells.

"Alex!"

I looked up. Someone was running toward me, his hair glistening like fresh snow and his skin glowing in the dim bar. I knew him. But I couldn't think how.

"Drink," my mistress commanded again.

I picked up the glass. The man reached us, took the glass from my fingers. He set it on the table and wrapped his hand around my biceps.

"I'm getting you out of here," he said, but when he pulled on my arm, my body remained in the chair. "Alex?"

My mistress looked the man over. Falin. Yes, that was his name. She smiled at him, so I did as well. The corpse man even smiled.

"House rule," she said.

Falin looked down at the full glass. He lifted it, swirling the contents. Then he tipped it back and swallowed the spelled liquid in one gulp. "Let's go," he said, slamming the empty glass on the wood.

"Alex doesn't want to go; she wants to stay with me— don't you, dear?" My mistress reached out and ran a feverishly warm hand down my cheek.

"I—" Saying I wanted to stay with her tasted like a lie on my tongue. I knew she wanted me to say that, and I wanted to please her, but the words didn't make it out of my mouth.

She frowned, and Falin looked between us.

"You're a slaver," he said.

"And I just made my greatest catch." She stood. "Come, my pets, we have important buyers to see."

The corpse man rose to his feet immediately. I moved less quickly.

"Alex," Falin said. "Alexis, remember who you are."

I frowned at him. He made me feel confused. I didn't like it.

A tingling at my ankle annoyed me. The enchanted dagger wanted to be drawn. I could feel its desire in the back of my head.

"Come quickly," my mistress said, heading toward the great tree.

I blinked at her, feeling the command, knowing I had to obey it. But I could also feel the dagger. It wanted to be drawn. It would stop annoying me once it was drawn.

The hilt fit my hand, the tingle of magic crawling over my palm. The dagger knew what it wanted, and I let it guide my hand. With one smooth upward motion, the blade slid through the silver thread.

"No!" the court fae screamed, turning around.

The string sagged, severed. I gasped. My head cleared, adrenaline pumping through my senses again, washing away the fog of the spell. The dagger in my hand tingled. It wanted to sink through flesh, to draw blood. I gripped it tighter, holding it back, not letting it use me.

"What is it?" Ashen asked, staring at the court fae.

"I broke her toy," I said. "Falin?"

He was already at my side. I expected his gun to be out, drawn. It wasn't. He'd had to check his iron at the door. His hand moved to my shoulder. Was he holding me back? He swayed. No, he's holding himself up.

He'd drunk the spelled liquor.

"I suppose I've made an enemy," the woman said. "But you are not powerful yet, feykin. Come, Ashen."

They walked toward the tree. I trembled, the chill in my body threatening to tear me in two. No, Ashen couldn't leave. He still had my heat.

I reached with my power, sending the endless cold out like a giant hand. Ashen was an animated body, but he was still dead. I could see that. And I had an affinity for the dead. When he'd attacked me, he'd hit me with force, like a jackhammer against my shields. I reached like a specter, my power seeping through the seams of his shields.

He glanced over his shoulder, his eyes wide. His shields tightened. My power was already there. Pouring into him. Diving into his being. Searching for my heat. For the life force he'd stolen. Ashen yelped and began running. The woman reached the tree first. Then she vanished. A portal.

I couldn't let Ashen reach that tree with my heat. Desperate, I grabbed hold of his core with my power, and the dead body stopped, fell forward. Now instead of a man running for the tree, there was a running ghost.

It reached the tree and vanished, and my tongue curled in my mouth. I killed him? I swallowed. No, he was already dead. Or sort of dead. The now-empty body on the floor decomposed before my eyes, turned to dust. The fae at the surrounding tables were quiet. They watched me, their eyes cautious. Some scared.

I tumbled back a step and slammed my shields in place, pushing the grave away from me. My knees gave out, and my vision went black. I hit the floor, shaking. Cold. I could die from this cold.

I curled in a ball on the wood floor and pulled my knees tight to my chest, but I felt as if my organs had been swapped for icicles, my muscles for frozen wood.

"You're like ice," Falin whispered, his hands sliding

over my arms. "We have to get out of here." But he was too unsteady to help me up.

It took two tries, but I got my feet under me. I clung to Falin, and he clung back. We slowly made our way forward, me blind and shaking, him swaying and stumbling. No one stopped us, but no one helped us.

"Do you hear music?" he asked, stopping.

I did. A lively fiddle. One I could dance to. Falin turned our course, stumbling toward the sound. What had I heard about a fiddle recently?

The endless dance.

"No." I tried to pull Falin back.

He laughed, a full-chested sound of pure joy. "Dance with me, Alexis," he said. His hand around my waist slipped and slid along my arm as he ran forward.

I grabbed his hand. The fiddle music was all around me, and I could hear the dancers' laughter. Then my grip on Falin's hand slipped, and he was gone.

My head swiveled, and I searched the darkness before my eyes. The circle of dancers was just ahead. And somewhere inside it was Falin, spelled to be pliable and caught in the endless dance. He'd drunk the spell for me. I wasn't leaving without him.

I did the only thing I could do: I reached for power. My grave-sight filled my vision, and the dancers snapped into focus. The beautiful and the monstrous danced, twirling and gliding, and in the center was the fiddler, playing on a rotting fiddle. *They dance until the fiddle strings snap.*

I had to reach that fiddler.

I surged forward, ignoring the music, intent on the fiddle. But the dancers were dancing. A thorn fae smiled at me, his barbed fingers closing around my hand, and he dragged me with him, twirling with me before passing me off to a woman with hair that flowed around her as if alive. Hands touched my body—hands that were too hot, searing my frigid skin. I screamed, but no one noticed. The fae passed me to a dwarf half my size, who tossed me in the air. A troll caught me and spun with me before passing me to the next dancer. I was shocked to see a fully human face, one I recognized.

"Tommy?"

"You joined the dance, Alex? Isn't it amazing?" Tommy passed me off to another dancer, and the faces all began to blur.

Wide faces, thin faces, beautiful, terrible, blue, green, stone, bark. I was dizzy and no longer sure where the fiddler was. My skin burned from too many too-hot touches. I had to find the fiddler.

Glimmering hands landed on mine, but these hands didn't burn. I looked up at Falin's smiling face. "Alexis," he whispered, his arms sliding around my waist. He lifted me off my feet and spun in a tight circle. As he brought me back down he lowered me halfway, hugging my body to his. Then his mouth claimed mine.

His lips tasted of honey and laughter, and the first touch of warmth bloomed in my body, trailed from my lips to my core. Then he broke away, and new hands, hot hands, grabbed at me, tried to drag me to a new partner. Pain burst over my skin as a fae with hair of living flames grabbed me. I jerked away, stumbling back as welts lifted on my arm. I tumbled sideways.

Then I was in the center of the circle. The dancers flowed around me, but this small pocket was clear. Room for the fiddler. I jumped to my feet.

The fiddler's back was to me, but I could see the frail and brittle strings. I unsheathed my dagger and surged forward. I swiped the blade over the strings, and in my grave-sight, the strings crumbled.

The music died. The stunned fiddler looked down and studied his fiddle, and the dancers stopped. They laughed and clapped, and I ducked through the crowd, searching for Falin.

I found Tommy first. I grabbed his wrist. His skin burned against my palm, but I didn't let go.

"Come on, you have to get out of here."

"I only just got here, Alex."

"Really? When?"

Tommy frowned at me. "Maybe twenty minutes ago. I was having lunch with the lieutenant governor's chief of staff before I started dancing, and I danced to only one song."

"Right." I found Falin and grabbed him. Then, with shaking steps, I dragged both of them to the door.

"Sign out on the ledger," the little fae said from her podium.

I ignored her, dropping Tommy's arm to wrench open the door.

"Wait! You can't leave at this time," she yelled.

We did anyway, passing the confused-looking troll on our way out. Then we stumbled into twilight.

Chapter 22

Twilight? I frowned. It had been noon when I'd entered the bar.

Beside me, Tommy gasped, looking at the dark sky. "Um, guess I was in there longer than I thought," he said.

"Yeah, we all were." *How did I lose the entire afternoon in the bar?* "We should go."

After all, we couldn't loiter on the front stairs. I looked down. The steps were a treacherous obstacle in my grave-sight, the poured cement crumbled and the wooden rail rotted. The fact I was still trembling uncontrollably wasn't going to help me get down them. *Best to take it slow.*

I still had one hand locked with Falin, but he wasn't swaying anymore—the dancing appeared to have cleared his head a bit. I stepped down the first stair, and it crumbled under my feet. I grabbed for the rail. The rotted wood snapped as my weight hit it. Falin and Tommy grabbed my elbows and hauled me back up.

"Uh, Alex, I don't know how to tell you this, but you just broke a stair and the rail," Tommy said.

I blinked. "That's not possible." I looked back at the toppled rail and crumbled step. When I used my grave-sight, I interacted with multiple planes of existence, but they didn't touch. I stared at the destruction. *They do now.*

I glanced at Tommy, and he winced, dropping my arm.

"Your eyes are doing the creepy glowing thing," he said, taking a step back.

I frowned at his obvious distrust and turned away. *Weirder by the day—that's me.* I considered the stairs. There was no way I was going to make it down the full flight if every step crumbled under my feet. I was safer blind. I looked up at Falin. "I won't be able to see when I release my grave-sight."

He nodded, his hand moving from my elbow to my waist. I took a deep breath, preparing myself for the coming blindness, when Tommy cleared his throat.

"So, uh, since Alex obviously isn't going to introduce us, I'm Tommy."

"We've met," Falin said without looking up at Tommy. He wrapped his other arm around my waist and dragged me closer. Then his hands moved to my bare arms, rubbing them. "You're like a little ice princess." He leaned forward as if he was going to kiss me again, and I stepped back.

Tommy put a hand in his hair, scratching the back of his head. "Okay, I feel like a third wheel, so I'll leave you to it. Nice seeing you, Alex." He took off down the stairs and turned up the sidewalk without a backward glance.

"Call Tamara; she's worried about you," I yelled after him.

Falin's fingers traced a curl from behind my ear to my collarbone, and I shivered for a reason that had nothing to do with the cold. I turned toward him.

"You're drunk."

"Pixie brandy," he agreed.

Great—so how are we getting home? A yellow—and to my eyes rusted-out—car was parked up the street, a small taxi light glowing on the top. I pointed to it. "Get us in that taxi."

Falin nodded, and I released my touch on the grave, closing my shields. Darkness fell before my eyes, the chill wrapping tighter around me. I clung to Falin, letting him guide me down the stairs. I stumbled on the way up the street, my shaking too unstable to keep my legs under me. Falin wasn't completely steady, either.

A door opened, and Falin guided me into the backseat of the cab. He slid in behind me, and I drew my legs to my chest, trying to trap some body heat. It didn't help. My teeth chattered, shivers wracking my body.

"Where to?" a gruff voice in the front seat asked.

"Uh . . ." I mumbled as Falin rattled off my address.

"I charge the estimate up front in this neighborhood," the cabbie said.

Falin grumbled under his breath, but the seat moved as he reached for his wallet. "Keep the change," he said as he reached around me.

The cabbie grunted his thanks, and Falin tapped something plastic near my head.

"Close this partition, will you?" he said.

Another grunt issued from the front seat. Then a small motor cut on, and the noise from the front of the cab faded. The plastic seat squeaked as Falin settled back and dropped an arm around my shoulders.

"You stopped the dance," he whispered.

I shrugged, only half paying attention. Now that we were safely speeding away from the club, the adrenaline that had been spiking through me and providing at least a false source of warmth was fading, leaving me trembling harder than before. Falin's arm emanated heat where it draped around me, and I scooted closer to him, snuggling up to his warmth.

I'd planned on stopping there—really, I had—but his arms slid around my waist and gathered me into his lap. Loose tendrils of his hair fell forward on my cheeks, silky soft and warm from being close to his skin. They smelled clean, spicy. My hand rose to the hair, following it until I reached his face. My fingers traced the curve of his jaw up to his ear and then trailed the sharp angle of his cheek until I found the crease of his mouth. I traced the curve of his bottom lip, and his hand moved from my back to my neck.

With his fingers curling in my hair, he pulled me forward until I could feel his breath tumbling over my lips. Then he closed that space.

The kiss was gentle, his lips firm but giving, and warmth spread through me. I sighed against his mouth. The hand caught in my hair tightened, drawing me harder against him. His tongue dipped between my lips, bringing with it the honey taste of pixie brandy.

Pixie brandy?

I reeled backward, and he growled, dragging me to his mouth again. His lips were more demanding now, but as his tongue flicked into my mouth, it teased, taunting me to follow it into his mouth as it retreated. *I shouldn't be doing this.* But he was so warm.

And the hard planes of his chest begged to be explored.

My palms slid down, following the hard ripple of muscle until I reached the place where the shirt disappeared into his pants. Tugging the shirt free, I splayed my fingers over the warm skin of his stomach. He made a sound deep in his throat, and my heart skipped. Of their own volition, my hands moved higher, finally learning the answer to the question I'd had since seeing him in his kitchen. *Smooth*. The material of his shirt tangled around my wrists, stopping my progress. I tugged at the material in frustration. He shifted, and the movement freed the tension in the fabric.

I didn't realize he'd unbuttoned my shirt until his hand slid through the gaping cloth, his warm fingers gliding up the edge of my rib cage. The skin over my stomach tightened at his touch, awareness spiraling much lower than his fingers had traveled. As his thumb dipped below the top of my jeans I moaned into his mouth.

Rough fingers grabbed my shoulder, pulling me backward. I yelped, my back arching as the hand seared my skin through the thin layer of my blouse.

"Enough of that," the cabbie yelled without releasing my shoulder. "Wait till you get out the car."

The vehicle had stopped. I hadn't even noticed. The click of the door opening sounded from my left, and the cabbie finally let go. I was still sitting in Falin's lap, so I gingerly felt my way out of the back of the cab. The night breeze against my chest reminded me my shirt was still unbuttoned, and I gripped it closed with one hand, the other remaining on the side of the cab.

I could feel the familiar ambience of Caleb's magic in front of me, but without help, I wasn't going to find my way to the stairs without a lot of blind fumbling.

Falin didn't leave me lost. After slamming the cab door, he wrapped his arms around me.

I pushed away from him. "We should go inside."

His hair fell forward, brushing my cheek. *A nod?* He scooped me into his arms and swayed as he took the stairs one at a time.

"I can walk."

He didn't put me down.

I fidgeted with the buttons on the front of my shirt, trying to refasten them one-handed.

"Stop," Falin said, his voice barely a whisper. "I'm looking at those."

He shook me gently, and I threw my arms around his neck to steady myself. The fabric of my shirt slid back apart.

"That's better," he said, and heat rushed to my cheeks.

Is he really staring at my chest? I couldn't see, so I couldn't tell, but my traitorous body flooded with heat at the thought.

He lowered me to my feet at the top of the stairs, and I dug through my purse for my keys. I fumbled for the lock, the keys jingling in time to my trembling. He took the keys from me, unlocking and pushing open the door. The house wards slid over me as he dragged me inside.

His lips found mine before the door shut. He backed me against the wall, and his gloved hands roamed my stomach. Dropped away. Returned gloveless. His bare fingers roved my body, his mouth never leaving mine. His thumbs hitched under the wire of my bra, and I trembled. *God, I need this. But...* I pushed back, gasping for air as our lips broke apart. He didn't relent. When I turned away, his lips trailed up my jaw, leaving small kisses in their wake.

"You're drunk," I whispered.

"So?" He nipped at a soft spot of skin where my jaw and neck connected. His blunt teeth grazing the skin sent another tremble through me, my mind blanking out for a moment.

I pushed against his shoulders hard. With my back against the wall, something had to give, and he wasn't quite as strong as the wood.

"So, there was a spell in the brandy. It's affecting your judgment."

He swore under his breath and grabbed my wrists, pulling my palms from his shoulder. He leaned in until his words rolled across my lips in puffs of his breath. "You think I wouldn't do this if I weren't drunk?"

To demonstrate which "this" he meant, his lips closed over mine. The kiss was restrained, breaking almost before it began. My stomach flipped, craving the passion of a moment before. *Stupid, Alex. This is a bad idea.*

I shook my head. *No. If he weren't drunk, we wouldn't be here.*

He kissed me again, his tongue dipping in my mouth before he broke away. "I would." He whispered the words directly into my lips, and I moaned. We were close enough that I could feel his lips stretch into a smile at the sound.

His thumbs hooked under my bra and lifted so his fingers could trace the curves of my breasts.

"Stop." The word came out more a gasp than a command.

His fingers paused but didn't withdraw. "Why?"

"We shouldn't . . . If you weren't drunk, you wouldn't—"

"Are you telling me what I would and wouldn't do?" he asked, his lips dropping to my throat.

One hand slipped free of my bra and circled around my back. His fingers landed on the bra clasp and in one quick movement unsnapped it. His other hand took advantage of the slack and cupped my breast, his thumb circling my nipple.

I gasped again, my lips moving without words. Falin took it as an invitation, his tongue dancing into my mouth so there was no room left to protest.

I pulled back, wiggling away from where he'd pinned me to the wall.

"Coffee?" I asked breathlessly, desperate for a distraction.

He didn't give up but grabbed my arm. "You know, for someone with your reputation, you are amazingly difficult to get into bed."

My mouth fell open, and my hand shot out. My palm contacted his shoulder, doing no damage at all besides smarting my hand. He laughed, drawing me into the circle of his arms. Irritated, I shoved him for good measure, and he swayed. *Right. Forgot he's drunk.*

He righted himself easily and then scooped me off my feet. Air rushed around me as he tossed me; then I landed with a bounce on the bed. The mattress shifted as he crawled on after me.

"Does that mean I'm different from other drunks you pick up?" he asked, pushing the blouse off my shoulders.

His fingers brought goose bumps to my arm as he traced my collarbone. His lips followed his fingers, carefully avoiding the scratches at the far edge.

"No. It's—"

His teeth grazed my skin, cutting off my words. His fingers dug into my sides, then released one at a time, as if he was prying them off. Air moved by me as he looked up. His hand moved to my chin, tilting my head back as if my blind eyes could meet his.

"If I'm not different, then I'm just another man you've picked to chase off your grave-chill with my body heat. And you are just a woman whose body will help me ignore the spelled drink surging through my system."

My stomach twisted at the words. *Just a woman? Just*

a body? But he was right. We were exactly what each other needed at the moment. Nothing more.

I nodded, slipping out of my shirt. Then I slid to the edge of the bed and worked at my bootlaces.

His hands slid down my arms, stilled my fingers. "What are you doing?"

I frowned. "It's shoes—especially boots. There is never a good time to take them off during spontaneous sex. I'm getting it out of the way now. You should do the same."

"Alexis," he whispered, "shut up."

My eyes flew wide, but his mouth closed on mine, cutting off my protest—my will to protest. Then he broke off and his hands moved to my boots, removing them methodically and far too slowly. *The sooner we lose our clothes, the sooner the awkward part is over.*

With my boots off, he moved me to the center of the bed, the mattress creaking as he followed. My fingers moved to the button on my jeans, but Falin caught my hands.

"Let me do it."

He lowered the zipper, one small click at a time, and kissed a line down my body as he unzipped. His hair trailed over me, wrapping me in his scent. My heartbeat, which I'd almost gotten under control, picked up tempo again. He paused at my breasts, moving his hand to cup one as he caught my nipple between his teeth. I moaned and pushed at my jeans, eager to be rid of them. He caught my wrist, pulling my hand away from my jeans as he guided me back to the bed.

He pinned both of my hands by my sides without losing contact with my breast. He sucked my breast more, his mouth and teeth grazing against the sensitive skin just enough to make me gasp. I struggled in his grasp. I *needed* more flesh against my body, and we needed a lot less clothing. Fast. He didn't release me but kept my wrists captive even as he transferred his attention to my other nipple.

I was making low whimpering noises by the time his mouth left my breasts and traveled back to the center of my body. His tongue flicked out to circle my belly button and then moved downward. Tingles of awareness ran through me as his mouth moved to the swell of my hips, and he finally released my wrists so he could peel away my pants.

With my hands finally free, I wanted to touch him. All of him. But I could reach only his hair, his shoulders. I pulled at his shirt, my inarticulate words trying to command it to get off him. I pushed myself up, trying to reach the buttons, but he forced me back to the mattress.

"Stay still," he commanded. "I want to look at you."

"That's not fair."

He didn't answer. He slipped the last stitch of clothing off me, and I shivered. Without his hands on me, the chill he'd been holding off crept over me. I fought the urge to squirm.

"You're so beautiful," he whispered, his voice hoarse.

I blinked. This wasn't what I was used to, and I couldn't stay still any longer. I pushed myself up and rolled to my knees, reaching for him. I followed the line of his arms to his shoulders, then down his chest, pulling at the buttons of his shirt as I went. I was looking for flesh—as much flesh as I could touch at one time.

My lips trailed down the string of muscle in his neck. The button in the center of his shirt gave me trouble. I tugged until it popped free of the thread. Pushing the shirt down his shoulders, I let my hands rove over his sculpted chest.

Touching wasn't enough. Not nearly enough. My lips

found the hollow of his throat, and my tongue flicked out, claiming the soft skin. Falin made a sound low in his throat, and I flicked out my tongue again.

His hand caught in my hair, guiding my face up. Our tongues met, dancing in each other's mouths. I kissed him as if his mouth held my life. I'd abandoned myself to this, to him. *Tonight, only tonight.* I didn't think I could kiss him enough to satisfy me.

His hand splayed down my stomach, caressed my inner thighs, and then found the centermost part of me. His finger dipped into me, his thumb finding my nub, and I moaned. His mouth consumed the sound as he dipped another finger in me.

I was panting into his mouth. "Please," I whispered. I needed more. More touch. More of him. His finger pace picked up, making me quiver. His mouth drank my gasps.

I tugged at the button on his jeans, frantic as I rolled them down his hips. No boxers underneath. My fingers trailed down over his ass, and my nails raked lightly over the firm skin. Then my fingers glided up over the bones of his hips and down his flat lower abs. I reached curls. I wrapped both hands around him. The feel of him—hard, ready, in my hands—brought another sound from me. Falin matched the sound, his fingers losing rhythm for a heartbeat. I wanted this. I wanted *him.*

I dropped my shields, letting the grave back into my body. The world decayed around me, but Falin snapped into focus, his sculpted body glowing with ethereal light. He was handsome glamoured; he was almost too amazing to look at unglamoured. It wasn't that he looked different; he was just so much more. More real, more handsome. Just more. *Sleagh Maith.*

"What are you doing?" he whispered, his hand falling away.

"I want to see." I *needed* to see.

I trailed my fingers down his chest, watching the skin tighten in my wake. I reached the curls as light as snow and ran my fingers along his length lightly, using just the softest touch of nails. He groaned and grabbed my hand.

His fingers splayed through mine, and he brought my hand to his mouth, kissing my fingers lightly. "We're fighting the chill, remember? Not increasing it."

He didn't understand. I wanted to see. I needed to see him. I lifted my mouth to his, watching his eyes as we kissed, eyes so icy blue but so warm. When we broke away, I licked my bottom lip, still tasting him there.

He guided me back down onto the bed. "Let go. Trust me, and let go."

He kissed one side of my mouth and then the other side. "Trust me," he whispered.

I released my touch on the grave, surrendering to a darkness filled with his touch.

He kissed a line down my body until his breath rested against my thighs. Then his tongue flicked inside me. My heartbeat crashed in my chest, and warmth rushed low in me, building.

"Please, Falin, please," I whispered as his tongue flicked out again and again, sending my body spiraling.

"Please what?" he asked, once I was sure I would break in two at any moment.

I was beyond rational thought. Beyond complete sentences. "Please," I whispered again, breathless.

His smile stretched against my skin. "As my ice princess commands." His body crawled up mine. His kiss stole what little air I had left. The head of him pressed heavy against my opening, and I arched upward against him.

I was more than ready, but he slid in slowly, filling me. More than filling me.

Yes.

Heat surged through me, and he pressed himself deeper. I gasped, and he stilled above me.

"Am I hurting you?"

Words failed me. I shook my head. Arched against him again. "More."

He lifted his hips slowly, his pace too controlled. Too gentle. I dug my nails into his ass and dragged him into me harder. Moved to meet him. He made a sound like surprise in his throat, but he met my pacing.

My body clenched. Pressure built to pleasure so thick it could have been pain. My back arched, and his measured thrusts increased again.

The new pace sent me over the edge.

I came screaming. Wave after wave of pleasure surged through me. His mouth covered mine, drinking my cries. His pace faltered. Broke. He crashed into me one last time, pressing himself hard inside me.

We lay there, both gasping for breath. My body quivered, every nerve content. *The rest are ruined.* No fumbling drunk in my bed would top what I'd just felt. I kissed his shoulder, tasting the salt of the sweat on his skin. *Once in a lifetime.* Even sated in the aftermath of the best orgasm of my life, a twinge of sadness touched me. *Don't be stupid, Alex; it's just tonight. We both know it's just tonight.*

Then Falin's lips closed on mine, his hands trailing down my body. I traced the slick line of his spine. His body stirred, still inside mine. I felt him harden.

"Again?" I asked, my voice hoarse from pleasure.

His hands stilled. "Are you up for it?"

"Oh yeah." *Maybe more than once in a lifetime.*

Many hours later, we finally lay still in the bed, his body curled around mine. His fingers lightly curled a strand of my hair around them, but his breathing was shallow, even. I was close to sleep, happily exhausted and warm against his chest.

Then his words came, soft, barely a whisper as his lips moved across my forehead. "I'm not just a warm body."

After that, sleep was a long time coming.

Chapter 23

⟡

I blinked into the brightness of midday. A shadow hung over me, and it took me several blurry blinks to make out Falin's features.

"Were you watching me sleep?"

He smiled. "A little."

"Right." My eyes slid down his bare chest to the swell of his hips obscured by the sheet. I swallowed hard. "I'm going to, uh, take a shower." I rolled out of the bed, clutching the sheet to me as I rose. My legs trembled as I stood, and my hand flew to my pelvis. I hadn't been this sore in a long time. Blood rushed to my cheeks as I had a very vivid flashback of exactly how I'd ended up this way. I glanced around for clothes to grab. Articles of clothing, both his and mine, were everywhere, and none of mine was close to the bed.

Without a glance back, I dragged the sheet off the bed and stalked out of the room. Falin said something under his breath as I left, but my ears were stinging too badly to hear.

I dropped the sheet just inside the bathroom door and turned the shower on full heat. Billows of steam rolled off the water. I turned the knob on the heat down a full rotation before testing it. Snatching my hand back, I cradled it against my chest. *Still way too hot.*

"I don't like him," a deep voice said behind me.

I whirled around. Death was leaning against the bathroom sink, staring at me.

Flexing my stinging hand, I grabbed a towel and wrapped it around myself. "What?"

He motioned outside the door. "I don't like him."

I shrugged, trying for nonchalant, but the girl reflected in the mirror behind him looked a little too wide around the eyes. "I don't question your sex life."

And he'd kissed me, then vanished, so he sure as hell didn't have a right to judge mine.

He smiled as if I'd made a joke, but the smile didn't reach his eyes. Then his gaze dropped, traveling casually down my body. I was glad I'd opted for the towel.

The look changed, lost its teasing edge. "It's spreading." His fingers alighted on my shoulder. He touched the skin just outside the edge of the scratches.

"You're not cold." He wasn't exactly warm either, but just as it had that day at the hospital, his temperature matched mine.

He frowned, his hand moving up to cup the back of my neck. "You're not blisteringly hot. Do you feel chilled?"

I shook my head. I'd woken up contentedly warm in Falin's arms, and the loft wasn't cold. I was pretty comfortable—mortified, but comfortable.

"A side effect of my soul fueling Coleman's spell?" I guessed.

Death shook his head. "Your soul will never reach him. I will dispel it by force before letting him have any of you."

I looked up. *Before?* Then the spell wasn't an active

transfer. It had to finish before returning to its master. *Good to know.*

A knock sounded on the wooden doorframe. "Alex, you okay in there?"

I jumped. "Uh . . ." The girl reflected in the mirror turned pale. I scowled at her and cleared my throat. "I'm going to be in here a while. You probably need to head to the station." I could only hope he worked today. I hugged my arms across my chest. "You should go home to get ready."

I waited, expecting him to argue. He didn't say anything. I didn't even hear him walk away. After several moments, I turned back around. Death was beside me, a small private smile on his lips. He reached out and placed both his hands on my shoulders. His thumbs moved over my bare skin, and he stared as if amazed he could touch me.

I frowned. "I need you to answer a question, and I swear if you just smile and disappear, I will never speak to you again."

His lips curled upward. "Your question?"

I stared at his hand. He was Death. He should have been cold to the touch. The living were supposed to be warm. I met his eyes. "Do souls recover? Or, after I find Coleman, will I always have a huge hole in my soul?"

The smile slipped from his lips, and we both stood staring at each other. After a moment, he dropped his gaze, looking away. "It depends on the soul."

And he doesn't know if mine will or not. I nodded and forced myself to take a deep breath, let it out. Death stepped back. His hand fell from my shoulder. Without another word, he vanished, leaving me alone in the bathroom.

I remained against the counter, watching the mirror fog over with steam. The gray vapor crawled over my reflection, blocking the unsure eyes and startled lips. Finally I dropped the towel and climbed into the shower, letting it scald my skin until I turned pink.

The smell of strong coffee drew me out of the bathroom. It had been contending with the fruity scents of my hair products for nearly an hour, and I couldn't take it any longer. Besides, if Falin hadn't left yet, staying in the bathroom made it appear I was hiding—which I wasn't. Okay, well, not much.

Once again, I'd fled to the bathroom without clothes. I wrapped a towel around myself and peeked around the corner. Falin was in front of the sink wearing only his jeans and those ridiculous rubber gloves. I needed clothes. I couldn't face him in only a towel.

I made a beeline for my dresser and grabbed the first pair of jeans and shirt I could find. When I turned, Falin was staring at me, his face tight with emotion I couldn't read. I clutched the clothes to my chest, ducked my head, and then dashed back to the bathroom.

Fully dressed, I felt more prepared to face the day. *And Falin.* I touched the charms on my bracelet. I needed to get my shields fixed.

I slunk into the kitchen, creeping to the coffeepot. My mug was beside the pot, filled to the brim with black coffee. Cupping it in my hands, I took a long sip.

"It's cold by now," Falin said without looking up.

I jumped, sloshing coffee over my fingers. It wasn't exactly cold, but it could have been hotter. Falin stripped off the rubber gloves and dropped them on the counter before wrenching open the stove. He pulled out a plate stacked with pancakes and set them on the bar. Turning, he crossed his arms over his chest.

"I made breakfast. An hour ago it might have still been good. Not sure if it's even edible now."

"I told you I'd be a while," I mumbled into my coffee mug. "I'm not hungry."

"Well, I am."

He pulled two plates out of the cupboard and divvied up the pancakes. I frowned at the short stack he pushed at me. Despite his claim, they smelled delicious, which made me want to eat them even less. I focused on my coffee and set the plate on the counter.

Falin cocked an eyebrow as his fork hung in the air between his mouth and his plate. "Not hungry?"

When I didn't answer, he grimaced. "Fine, let's get this over with." He set his plate aside. I fought the urge to step back as he moved into my space, towering over me. "You want to talk about it? Or do you want to forget it happened? Either way, you still have a black spell spreading through you, so I doubt you're giving up your search for Coleman. We are working together. Quit trying to brush me off."

He leaned as he spoke, the movement making him both ominously looming and almost close enough to kiss. I clenched my fists and ducked around him.

"I have to feed PC," I said, grabbing the bag of dry dog food off the counter.

"Alex . . ." he started.

I froze, my eyes sweeping the apartment. "Where's PC?"

"What?"

My heart crashed into my stomach. "Where's my dog?" I ran to the bed and dropped to my knees. Pulling the bedskirt aside, I looked under the box springs. "PC?"

He wasn't there.

Did I see him when I woke up? I couldn't remember. My head snapped back and forth. My eyes took in every cranny of the small apartment.

I rounded on Falin. "Have you seen him?"

He shook his head.

"Well, don't just stand there!"

He turned, pulling open cabinets. No little gray and white dog popped out.

Dread caught in my throat, solidified. *How could I lose PC?* Had I been that out of it last night? Had he run out when we'd first come in? I threw open the door.

Fred the gargoyle was on the doorstep, but not PC. He knew to come home if he was outside alone. He *knew*.

"Have you seen PC?" I asked, tapping Fred's stone head.

The gargoyle didn't answer. I slammed the door, reeling back around to scan the apartment again. Falin was on his knees looking under the bed.

The solidified dread expanded, sank, filling my stomach, entering my blood. PC wasn't here. PC wasn't anywhere.

I sprinted the short distance through the apartment and jerked open the inner door leading down to Caleb's house. My feet barely touched the stairs as I took them three at a time. The downstairs door clattered against the wall as I burst through it.

"Caleb!"

Metal clanged in the workroom. A tool hit the ground. A dog barked.

Caleb didn't own a dog.

I rounded the corner in time to see PC hurl himself through the edge of Caleb's circle. The heavy dread filling my body retreated under a wave of relief so fast I stumbled from the sudden weightlessness. I dropped to my knees, and PC soared into my lap. His ears were perked straight up, his tongue hanging out of his mouth. In a matter of seconds my cheeks had a thorough tongue bath.

Caleb appeared at the edge of the circle. "Al?" His hand passed though the circle, dispelling it, and in two large strides, he was in front of me. Hauling me up, he enclosed me in a long bear hug. "Holly is almost out of her mind with worry, and PC, well . . ." He gestured to the dog, who was panting in my arms. "Where the hell have you been, girl?"

I frowned at him. Caleb never cursed. What had happened yesterday—?

I'd missed the dinner with Tamara.

No wonder Holly was worried. "I'll apologize to her," I promised. I didn't apologize to Caleb. He was fae; you didn't do that. "Why is PC down here?"

Caleb's eyebrow quirked upward. "Girl, what were you—" he started, but cut off. His head shot up, his gaze moving over my shoulder as his brows creased.

I turned, staring at the empty doorway. *What does he . . . ?*

Falin stepped out of the hall, still shirtless, the button on his jeans undone to show a maximum amount of flat abs. His gaze scanned the room and landed on Caleb and me. His lips tugged down as his eyes strayed over Caleb's hands on my shoulders, but he didn't comment. Instead he nodded at PC. "You found him, I see."

I clutched the small dog tighter to my chest. "Yeah, he was with Caleb."

PC's tail wagged in greeting to Falin, but I turned away from him. I was hoping that if I didn't offer to introduce anyone, Falin would go back upstairs and Caleb would forget about him. I should have known better. Caleb stared at Falin, a frown etching itself deep in his face. His lips stretched farther than humanly possible and then curled back, revealing green teeth.

His glamour is failing. Or he was dropping it intentionally.

"Caleb?"

He pushed me behind him, his fingers bending strangely with an extra joint, his complexion turning vegetative. "Get in my workroom, Al. Activate my circle."

"Caleb, what —?"

"Just do it," he snapped, his teeth gnashing.

I stumbled back from him, and PC whined at the rising tension in the room. I clutched the small dog tightly and glanced between Falin and Caleb. Falin stood with his hands in his back pockets; his posture was relaxed, but his gaze was as hard as ice. Caleb took a step forward, his lips twisted in a snarl. I rushed between them.

"It's okay, Caleb. He's with me."

Caleb only shook his head. "Do you know what is standing in my house?"

I looked over my shoulder at Falin. His eyes met mine, and the question was repeated in their icy depths. Something inside him seemed to cry out, "Do you know me?" and wherever that small voice hid in him was a place filled with pain. It hurt to see. I knew voices like that. I *had* a voice like that. And I knew that whatever I said would be heard by that voice and would echo in that sad place.

But do I know who Falin is? I knew he was court fae, most likely winter court. I knew he had secrets. I also knew he'd saved my life more than once. That he was intense but could also be tender.

I backed up until my shoulders and back brushed his chest. He tensed behind me.

"I trust him," I whispered and felt a startled breath jerk through him.

Then Falin's hand moved to my waist, his touch tentative, unsure. I did my best not to flinch, both for his sake and for Caleb's. I wasn't sure of all the dynamics flowing through the room, but I knew Caleb was on the defensive. He was an independent fae with alliances to no court, no season. This was his territory, and Holly and I were his friends, his witches. I needed to prove to him that Falin meant no harm.

Caleb shook his head, his dark eyes hard. "Move away from him, Al. He's bewitched you."

"He hasn't, Caleb. I promise."

"No bit of tail ever comes between you and Prince Charming. He must have entranced you."

"Prince Charming?" Falin asked, the question barely a whisper.

"What did you think PC stood for? Politically Correct?" I answered without glancing back. To Caleb I asked, "What are you talking about? How did Falin come between me and PC? Why is he even down here?" I realized something else was off. "And what happened to his cast?"

"The vet removed it. And he's down here because someone had to take care of him while you were gone."

"He was alone for only ten hours, Caleb."

"Al, you disappeared on Saturday. It's Wednesday."

Chapter 24

I didn't drop PC, but it was a near thing. *Wednesday?* I'd lost three days?

"That can't be true," I whispered, and then shook my head. It *couldn't* be false. *Caleb can't lie.*

"Step away from him, Al. He's charmed you."

"No." I lowered PC to the floor. "It wasn't Falin. I was at the Eternal Bloom."

"Holly checked the Bloom. You weren't there."

"VIP section."

Caleb's elongated jaw dropped. "Are you crazy? The VIP section is a pocket of Faerie."

"Yeah, I figured that out." What had the door guard said? It wasn't that we couldn't leave, but specifically that we couldn't leave at that *time*.

"I suppose he took you there." Caleb nodded at Falin.

"Actually," Falin said, entering the conversation, "I tried to convince her not to go. Then I told her not to go without me, but she is stubborn."

Caleb stared at him. Then his frown softened and

morphed into something human. "Yeah, she's pretty stubborn."

And as though my stubbornness was a point they could bond on, the tension dissipated. Caleb's eyes didn't lose their distrust, but he nodded and walked back into his workroom, dismissing us.

He paused before reactivating his circle. "I reported you missing to the OMIH yesterday. You'll need to contact them. I don't suggest sharing where you've been."

Great. I was a missing person. *With a secret about Faerie.*

Wednesday. Even after I made it back to my loft, it didn't seem possible. *Wednesday.* The day of the Blood Moon. And it was already late afternoon. We had to find Coleman before he unleashed whatever nightmare he was collecting souls to cast.

I used Falin's phone to call Tamara and Holly while he showered. Both calls went to voice mail. I'd just updated my suspect list when Falin walked out of the bathroom, dressed but still towel-drying his hair.

"Last night Tommy said the lieutenant governor's aide took him to the bar," I said, looking up from the computer. And Lieutenant Governor Bartholomew was already my prime suspect for Coleman's new body—Tommy's story was a damning point against Bartholomew. I was sure of it. "Bartholomew's aide doesn't meet the description of the body Coleman stole because she is, well, a she. I think Coleman, in Bartholomew's body, found out I raised the shade. He had his aide talk Tommy into stealing the recording. Then the aide lured Tommy to the endless dance."

Falin frowned and shook his head. "How did Coleman find out you were at the morgue?"

"Because of the—" I was going to say shooting, but

that couldn't have been it. The bullet had been spelled, so Coleman had to have known I was at the morgue. To spell the gun and set the trap, he would have had to have been waiting for me to leave the building. I shook my head.

"Tommy is the one who told me you were raising Coleman's shade," Falin said as he sat down on the bed and slipped on his shoes. "Last night Tommy acted like he'd never seen me before. I've been with the department since two days after Coleman was shot. When I started, Bartholomew hadn't been named lieutenant governor yet."

I frowned. Tommy couldn't have been at the Eternal Bloom for over two weeks. I'd seen him the day Casey hired me. *It could have been Coleman glamoured to look like Tommy.* That would explain why he acted so out of character. "Okay, Coleman wraps himself in glamour and becomes Tommy to watch his old body and make sure no one gets close to the truth." *Except I did.* "So when he recognized me, he tattled to you, and then went outside to plan an ambush for when you kicked me out." It was a stretch, but the events did add up. Only one thing didn't work. "You're fae. How did you miss that Coleman was posing as Tommy?"

Falin frowned at me. "Coleman is a master at glamour. Even for fae, glamour isn't always easy to detect or see through, once reality has accepted the illusion as true."

"Oh." I turned back to my suspect list. Bartholomew hadn't been in the office yet; that meant the chief of staff Tommy had mentioned was Graham, my father's squirrelly faced aide. I'd already cleared my father.

But we hadn't cleared Graham.

He was the right age to meet Roy's description, and had the right hair color. I knew from his conversation

with my father that he'd reversed his opinion about
Falin's being assigned to the Coleman case. He'd been
standing right next to my father when I'd felt Coleman's darkness, and he'd left the dinner party directly
after Bartholomew, giving him the opportunity to meet
and murder Helena. The pieces fit. My heart tap-danced
around my chest, pounding out little triumphant beats.

I knew whose body and identity Coleman had stolen.

I repeated the idea to Falin, and he punched in num-
bers on his phone before I finished my list.

"Hi, yes, this is Detective Andrews with Nekros City
PD. I'd like to speak to Chief of Staff Tolver Graham,"
he said. Then his face darkened in response to whatever
the person on the other side of the line had said. He
scowled as he hung up. "Graham left for the day. Sup-
posedly he had a family emergency."

The triumphant beats of my heart died. The next dull
thud hurt, echoing in my chest. "He's preparing for the
ritual?"

"Probably."

"Should we check the warehouse?" But even as I
asked the question, I knew Coleman wasn't going to
return to the warehouse. Not now that the police had
discovered it.

"I'll call the station to learn what we missed while
in Faerie and see who I can rally to help flush out
Graham."

I nodded. *So, what do I do?*

Where would Coleman go?

I pulled up a Web browser. Finding out what had
happened during the past three days wasn't a bad idea.
The news reported two more bodies. I assumed the first
woman, Emily Greene, was the body Falin had been
paged about Saturday before I went to the Eternal
Bloom. The second body, Caitlin Sikes, was found Mon-

day. I scanned the page. The article didn't include much useful information. Both women were norms, though apparently Emily had recently begun taking a class on magic for the non–magically inclined.

That made six victims, seven including Sally. *She who Sees knows the eyes' empty look, and seven times she'll know what it is he took.* Seven was the number of souls in the Shadow Girl's warning and the number the slaver had confirmed. *But he hasn't stolen seven.* I'd helped free Helena's soul—the gray man had collected her once the spell had been removed. A collector had probably also come for Sally, since her soul hadn't been shielded and caged with glyphs. That meant Coleman had five out of his seven souls. *If he hasn't already killed again.*

Falin's phone snapped closed, and he snatched his holster and badge from the counter. I turned, ready to update him on what I'd learned. Then I saw his face.

"What happened?"

He looked at me, his eyes narrowed and his lips tight. "I've been summoned to the chief of police's office. Immediately."

"Hey, Craft, we've been trying to reach you," the desk sergeant called out as I entered Central Precinct's main lobby.

I'd hitched a ride in with Falin, hoping to catch Tamara at the morgue before she left for the day. I needed to apologize for disappearing and let her know I was okay. I also planned to pump her for information. With Graham missing, our only chance of finding Coleman was to figure out where the ritual would be taking place. Finding out as much as we could about his recent victims was our best chance for doing that.

I stopped at the desk and waved good-bye to Falin. Or really, to Falin's back, as he didn't pause but stormed through the station. Then I turned to the desk sergeant, whose name I was pretty sure was Holt.

"Where you been?" he asked. "I've been trying to reach you."

"My phone got stolen, remember," I said to him.

"Yeah, well, we found your car—"

Finally something good. Maybe my luck was turning around.

"It turned up in a scrap shop. There wasn't much left, but your insurance should be able to confirm it was the old clunker."

I'd clearly thought positive too soon.

"That's just great," I said behind a drooping smile. If I'd had any insurance on the thing, that might have even been helpful information. Sighing, I forced a better, more hopeful smile onto my lips. "Have you heard anything new about John?"

Holt frowned. "Still unconscious, but last I heard, they did a brain scan and it lit up with activity. He could wake up any day now." Despite the optimistic words, his gaze dropped, his lips tugging downward.

I nodded to acknowledge the news. *He's still alive. That is what is important.* But I had to find Coleman. Waving good-bye to Holt, I said, "I'm headed down to the morgue."

I passed through a security check—no gray magic this time—before making it down to the basement. Tamara was leaning over a body when I walked into the morgue. She looked up, her eyes widening and her lips parting as she saw me. To her credit, she didn't drop the heart she was lifting out of the open chest cavity.

"Alex!"

"Hey, Tamara," I said, shoving my hands in my pockets and rolling my shoulders in. Knowing people thought you were missing or dead and then just walking in was awkward. I hadn't realized exactly how awkward it would be. I pressed the toe of my boot into the ground. "I, uh, I'm okay."

Tamara looked around as if she was trying to figure out what to do with the organ in her hands. Her eyes had a frantic edge to them, which was strange to see mixed with relief. She placed the heart in a tray and stripped off her gloves. Then she stepped around the table and gripped my shoulders.

"I was so afraid you were going to come here in a bag." She didn't hug me, not exactly. She was still dressed for autopsy. But she squeezed my shoulders as if touching was the only way she could reassure herself I was really standing there. She pulled back, dropping her feverishly hot hands from my skin. "You're cold enough to be on my table. What happened? Where have you been?"

"Well, it's kind of complicated."

The relief in Tamara's face hardened. "And you couldn't pick up the phone? Alex, there's a madman killing women in their beds. Didn't it occur to you to let someone know you were all right?"

I winced. For quite a large portion of my time in the Eternal Bloom, I definitely hadn't been all right, but I didn't say that. Instead, I looked down and stared at the drain in the linoleum floor. "I wanted to come by, say I was sorry for disappearing. I didn't mean to. I honestly had no idea how long I was gone."

I glanced up, and Tamara twisted her lips, turned away. She grabbed a new pair of latex gloves out of the box, snapping them as she pulled them on. Then, without a word, she leaned over the body again.

I didn't follow. I had an affinity for the dead, but I didn't have the stomach to do Tamara's job.

As the silence stretched I looked around. Even with my mental shields held tightly in place, I could feel the bodies nearby. Without drawing grave essence, I let my awareness sink into the female body on Tamara's table. I found exactly what I expected—a mostly empty cavity with a shredded shade inside.

"Another ritual victim?"

"Found by her sister this morning." Tamara looked up, her eyes narrowed. "Do you have any idea how worried I was? You're gone for four days, and then you walk in here and say, 'Sorry. It's complicated.' That's just not acceptable. Friends don't do that. They don't—"

"I was in Faerie."

"—just disappear and—" She stopped. "You what?"

"I told you it was complicated. I was in Faerie. I was there for only a few hours, but I lost three days." I'd told Caleb I wouldn't share with the OMIH and the public where I'd been, but Holly and Tamara were my best friends. I'd been keeping a lot of secrets from my friends recently. Too many. Tamara was staring at me, so I stumbled on. "Everything is a mess right now. When this is over, I promise I'll tell you everything I can over a couple beers."

"That's as crazy as Tommy's story."

Oh crap, Tommy. He'd lost close to three weeks in the Bloom. He was likely more than confused—and no one had warned him not to talk about what happened. "What he say?"

"Oh, I've only heard rumors. Security stopped him on the way in, and he claimed he had no idea what recording they were talking about. Then he had no idea Governor Coleman had been assassinated. He's been up in interrogation all day."

Poor Tommy.

I gave Tamara a weak smile. Then I nodded at the body in front of her. "Who is she?"

"Oh no, you're not changing the subject that easily."

She bent her wrists and pressed them against her hips. I just stared at her, and she blew air between her teeth. "You were really in Faerie?"

I nodded.

"Girl, what have you gotten yourself tied up in now?" She shook her head and bent back over the body. "This was Julie Staton, a precog, but I hope she didn't see this one coming."

I grimaced, agreeing with her. Precognition, the ability to foresee future events, was the rarest wyrd ability. There were no shields to block out precogs' visions. They were just taught how to cope with them, and then they spent a lot of time in counseling because their visions were always the future. If they saw a horrible event and tried to prevent it, the vision had already taken their actions into account. If Julie had foreseen ending up a soulless husk on Tamara's autopsy table . . . I shivered.

Tamara shook her head, staring down into Julia's chest cavity. "For the life of me, I can't figure out what killed this poor woman."

"No glyphs were carved into her?"

"Oh, there are the same glyphs cut into her as all the rest, but all the wounds are shallow, superficial. There isn't even enough blood loss to explain her death. It's like he cut her up and she gave up the will to live. The last three have been like this."

"Emily, Caitlin, and Julie?"

Tamara nodded, and I frowned. I knew how Julie had died—her soul was sucked right out of her body. *Like cracking open an oyster.* I rubbed the scratches on my shoulder. So Coleman had six souls already. That left one more, and I had a feeling he'd take that one during the Blood Moon.

"You know the strangest part about these victims?" Tamara asked, and whatever she did inside the body made a slurping, squishing sound. I cringed and looked away as she continued. "It's the glyphs. They are all nonsense. No trace of magic at all."

"So, you don't think a spell killed the women?" I asked because she'd paused and I had to say something, and I couldn't just say, "Sorry. You're apparently not sensitive to fae magic. And, oh yeah, by the way, that's a soul-sucking curse."

"A killing spell would stain black. There's nothing here. Now, Caitlin was wearing more gray spells in her necklaces, rings, and bracelets than I've ever seen in one place, but that wouldn't have killed her."

No, it wouldn't have, but . . . "Caitlin was a norm, wasn't she?"

Tamara's answer was drowned out by the morgue door banging against the wall. I whirled around as Falin stormed into the room. His eyes landed on me.

"Let's go," he snapped, and then turned on his heel, shoving his way back through the door.

Okay. Guessing it went less than well with the chief.

"I've got to, uh . . ." I glanced at Tamara. Her eyes were wide again, but her mouth was screwed tight, concerned. I pointed in the direction Falin had gone.

"Alex," she called after me, and I turned back as I reached the door. "Whatever mess you're in, be careful."

Chapter 25

━━━◦◉◉◦━━━

Roy ambushed me outside the morgue doors.

"Alex, where have you been? I've been looking all over the netherworld for you."

Of course he had. Because if I disappear for three days, I have to answer to everyone. Even the dead.

I pasted on a smile I didn't feel. "Hi, Roy. Now isn't a good time."

"But you've got to do something. They're talking about releasing my body for burial."

And how exactly was I supposed to prevent that? "Believe it or not, I have more important things to worry about right now than a body that's already dead."

Roy shoved his glasses farther up on his nose. "I watched him inside my body for twelve years. Twelve years." Roy stepped forward, accenting the words with his hands. "And now they are going to bury me under his name. No. No—I refuse." One gesture went wild, and his hand shot out, wrapping around my wrist. "You have to do something."

My eyes flickered to where he gripped my arm. "Let go of me."

He didn't.

I locked down my shields, closing every small gap. The color didn't fade from Roy, and he didn't become any less solid. *Crap.* Apparently I was way too close to the world of the dead.

Does that mean I'm only partially alive?

"Roy, I'm going to say this once, and only once." I kept my voice level, quiet. If I started screaming at someone no one else could see, I'd attract attention. "They are not going to release your body this evening. If I don't find Coleman today, if I can't stop him before the Blood Moon, he is going to complete his ritual. Then he'll take whatever nightmare he creates and conquer Faerie. I won't be able to reach him in Faerie, and I will die. Who will help you claim your body then? Huh? Who will get your story told?"

His hand dropped from my wrist. "You're going after Coleman?"

"Yes." I knew my face looked exasperated, and I didn't care. Roy was wasting my time. I headed for the elevators. Falin had already left me behind.

Roy fell in step beside me, and for the first time, his shoulders rolled back and he stood straight. "Then let's kick some body-stealing ass."

My ghostly sidekick and I caught up with Falin in the parking lot, and I noticed Falin was missing two very important things: his badge and his gun.

Oh crap. "I take it we lack police support?" I asked.

"Get in the car."

Right. I slid into the passenger seat, and Falin threw the car in reverse before I got the door closed. The car careened out of the lot, and he made a hard left, swerving into traffic. My hand flew to the armrest, my nails scoring the leather.

"Maybe I should drive? Just until you calm down?"

He glanced at me from the corner of his eye but didn't say anything.

Roy whooped from the backseat, though I wasn't sure what he was experiencing, as the car wasn't actually tangible to him. I pried my arms off the armrest as Falin's speed leveled out. He was still pushing a good twenty over the limit, but at least he stopped gunning it.

"So, are you going to tell me what happened?" I asked, trying to sound casual.

"Power came from the top to get me on the case, and power came from the top to have me removed from it."

As in my father had demanded he be suspended.

Crap. "Where are we going?"

"To Graham's condo."

"Do you really think he'll be there?"

"No." His lips tightened, but I knew he was right. We had to find out as much about Graham as possible, and we couldn't ignore the chance he was preparing for the ritual at his condo. "After we eliminate the condo, we'll take a closer look at these."

He grabbed an envelope from between the seats and dropped it in my lap. Inside were several brown folders. The tab on the side of the top folder read STATON, JULIE.

The most recent victim.

"Should I ask how you got your hands on the case files?" I asked, counting the folders. Seven, including Helena.

Falin's smile crooked at the edge of his mouth, but he didn't answer. It was just as well; I knew a suspended FIB agent couldn't walk out of Nekros City's Central Precinct with seven active case files—legally.

I flipped open Julie's file. There wasn't much inside. Mostly just crime scene photos and handwritten notes by the lead detective. Detective Jenson. I frowned. Seriously? They gave the ritual serial murder case to Jenson? I deciphered what I could of his notes and studied the photos.

Julie had been found in her own home, with evidence indicating she'd been tied to her four-poster bed. The setup was similar to how we'd found Helena only in the fact that the bed was in the center of the circle. No candles or champagne at this site. At least, not by the time she was found. Glamours created with the purpose of being temporary tended to last only until sunrise.

The file for Caitlin Sikes was next on the stack. Like Julie, she'd been found in her own home, in her bed. Emily, too.

So Coleman was committing the rituals in his victim's homes now that the warehouse had been discovered. That meant tonight's ritual would be in a private home. Some woman, somewhere in the city, was slated to die. But who?

"What's the connection?" I asked, though the question wasn't directed at anyone in particular.

Falin shook his head. *No one knows.* Well, that wasn't completely true. The slaver had known, but she'd had her own agenda.

Four wyrd witches and three normal, nonmagical humans. Seven targeted victims, plus two more wyrd witches, counting Sally and me. What do we all have in common?

The car slowed, and Falin pulled up to a gated parking lot. Beyond the gate, Nekros City's most elite condominium complex was visible over the manicured landscape. Falin stopped before he reached the guardhouse in front of the gate. His hand moved to the empty spot on his belt where his badge usually rested. His lips tugged downward.

No badge meant he couldn't play the cop card and

bully us into the building. He was just a citizen now, and I doubted the guard was going to let a PI and a private citizen through the gate.

I twisted in my seat so I could see beyond my headrest. "Roy, you ready to do some scouting?"

"Alex?" Falin made my name a question. When I looked over at him, I found him staring.

Right. He couldn't see ghosts. "Um, Roy, give me your hand."

Just as I had for Lusa, I channeled a small bit of energy into Roy. Falin started, his elbow hitting the steering wheel. The horn beeped, and the guard stepped out of his box.

"Falin, Roy," I said by way of introduction. Then I turned back to the ghost, speaking quickly. "We need to know whether Graham is home. If he is, come get us, and we'll find a way past the guard. If he isn't, poke around for any indication of where he might have gone."

Roy nodded. He vanished, pulling deep into the land of the dead, where he could move faster. I turned back around.

The guard swaggered toward our car. *Okay, how do we explain what we're doing here?* I had the feeling that explaining we were waiting on a ghost wasn't going to cut it.

Falin pointed to the glove compartment. "Hand me the badge."

Badge? I opened the compartment. A leather badge case sat on top of the car registration. Inside was a very authentic-looking badge. I rubbed my fingers over the lifted print. "I didn't think you could have duplicates."

"You can't." He accepted the badge and strapped it to his belt. "And we will be in trouble if he touches it to anything iron."

It was a glamour construct? I didn't have time to ask.

Falin stepped out of the car and approached the guard. Maybe I'd been a little premature in sending Roy out scouting, but I'd thought it was a good idea.

The guard rested his hands under the wide girth of his belly, the gesture clearly meant to draw attention to the stun gun strapped to his belt. He shook his head at whatever Falin told him, his loose jowls shaking. I couldn't hear what was said, but judging by Falin's face as he turned, the conversation hadn't gone well. Falin slid back into the car, slamming the door behind him.

"What happened?"

"He's refusing to let us through without a warrant."

So sending Roy hadn't been all that premature.

Falin reversed the car, scowling.

"We can't just leave," I said. "Roy won't be able to find us."

Falin hit the brake. The guard, who had started back to his little guardhouse, turned back, his thin lips tugging downward. I ignored him. Roy would be back soon.

I focused on the case files spread over my lap and frowned as I scanned the crime scene photos from Caitlin's house. For a norm, she had a lot of spell-crafting paraphernalia. Tamara said she had come in with gray charms. Had Caitlin made them herself? Not all norms were complete nulls; some could be taught to reach the Aetheric.

I moved on. I'd been present at Helena's crime scene, and I remembered it a little too clearly. I quickly flipped through the photos, but my hand paused on one shot. The photographer had caught an image of me in the circle with my eyes glowing bright enough to overexpose my face, so I looked as ghastly as the ghost Death appeared to be battling behind me. No wonder the norms had no idea what was going on.

I flipped through Bethany's file before moving on to

Michelle Ford, the second victim. The file listed her as a telekinetic wyrd witch, though beside that, in handwriting I recognized as John's, was the word "uncertified."

How could a wyrd witch end up uncertified?

We all came out of wyrd academies certified. Unless she didn't attend a wyrd academy. Or she flunked out—the way I almost did because of my Spell Casting grades.

"That can't be it," I whispered.

"What?"

I looked up at Falin, opened my mouth. I snapped my teeth shut. *That can't be the connection.* It would be too hard to trace. I shook my head.

Falin's brow creased. "We're not exactly rolling in ideas, Alex. If you've got a guess on the connection, I want to know."

"It could be a coincidence, but the second victim was an uncertified wyrd witch, and Bethany and I knew each other from academy where we were in Remedial Spell Casting together. Helena used to tease that she couldn't even cast a circle. The fourth victim was a norm taking magic for the non–magically inclined. And the fifth victim was a norm who apparently was dabbling in gray. Including me, that's six out of nine people infected by the spell who use magic at lower than average magical aptitude."

Falin's eyebrow lifted. "I've seen you working magic. You do not have a lower than average aptitude."

I was pretty sure that was a compliment. A small, silly smile spread over my face. Unfortunately, it wasn't true. "You've seen my grave magic, my wyrd ability. I'm talking spells that any wyrd or normal witch should be able to cast, but I usually blunder."

He frowned at me, and I shrugged. "Like I said, it might just be a coincidence. I mean, exactly how does one single out a group of the magically inept?" I looked at the papers spread across my lap and closed Michelle's file. "Even if we do find the connection, how do we know who he will target next? There are thousands of people in this city."

I clenched my fist, bending the file in my hand. We weren't going to find him. Not in time. We had less than five hours before the Blood Moon.

Falin held out his hand. I glanced down at the crumpled paper. Crap. I made a half-assed effort to smooth the report before giving him the file, assuming that was what he wanted. It wasn't. He took my hand, his fingers lacing through mine, his gloves rough against my skin.

I stiffened, surprised. I stared at my hand caught in his. "What are you doing?"

He reached out and tilted my head back so I met his eyes. "We're going to find him." His gaze was intense, as though by his will alone we would find Coleman.

"Um, okay." I wasn't used to this. I wasn't sure how to respond.

"Is this a bad time?" Roy asked, appearing in the backseat.

I jerked back, pulling away from Falin.

"Roy—" I started, and realized I had no air. How did I end up breathless? I tried again. "What did you find? Was he there?"

The ghost shook his head. "The place is spotless. Looks like a model home or something. Furniture is still there, but not a personal item in the whole condo."

I repeated Roy's observations to Falin.

"Coleman took anything of importance. He doesn't intend to return," he said, cranking the car.

I nodded. It looked that way. Turning around, I grabbed Michelle's file off the dash where Falin had tossed it. Now the only lead we had left was whatever we could learn from Coleman's victims. For the first time since my grave magic emerged, the dead weren't talking to me; they weren't sharing their secrets. But we had to learn their secrets, had to find the connection, had to find the next slated victim. Coleman still needed one more soul.

Chapter 26

I paused on the top step of a small blue duplex. "Tamara said Julie was a precog."

"Yeah?" Falin said, clearly not following.

I frowned. "There are no wards on her door."

Almost all witches warded their thresholds. Of course, most witches in the city lived in the Glen. Julie's house was miles from the Magic Quarter and Witches Glen, in a norm neighborhood, but it was still odd for her to have skipped warding her door. *Unless she didn't have the magical aptitude.* I didn't. Caleb maintained my house wards.

"Shall we?" Falin asked, slicing through the police seal on the door. He turned the doorknob, and I felt a flicker of magic as the lock tumbled.

Useful trick.

He pushed the door open, and I stepped into the dim house. It was sort of ironic, us breaking into a crime scene after he'd considered arresting me for the same thing a couple of nights ago. *Probably best not to mention that fact.*

"So, what are we looking for?" Roy asked, floating through a door in the side wall.

I headed for the door in the other wall. "Anything to tie the victims to each other."

I knew before I opened the door that I'd found the bedroom—the tingle of dark magic seeping through the wall was unmistakable. The police had stripped the bed of linens, and fingerprint dust still covered most surfaces, but very little else in the room looked disturbed. Pictures still sat atop the dresser, and a small stack of books leaned against a chair that faced a window.

I closed my eyes, sensing the course of magic in the air. The spells that had been worked in the room had left an oily taint. It wriggled under my skin, making my shoulder burn, but nothing malicious was active.

Rubbing my bare arms as if I could wipe off the foul residue of magic, I stepped farther inside the room, Falin at my heels. He moved to the pictures, using a pen to turn them in his direction. I walked the circuit of the room. I used the edge of my shirt to open the closet. It was a small walk-in with clothes on only one side. The other side had been cleared, and a circle had been drawn on the floor. *She worked magic in the closet? Like she was hiding.* I looked over the limited collection of spell-crafting materials. They resonated with a hint of used magic, and I frowned. *Gray magic?*

I backed out of the closet and walked the rest of the room. My shoulder burned, the dark magic clearly calling to the spell devouring my soul. *I can't stay here.* I let myself out of the bedroom and found Roy in the corner of the den.

"Did you find anything?" I asked.

He turned, stepping aside so I could see the wire cage he'd been staring at. "She had parakeets. I think we should let them go."

"Do they have seed and water?"

His shimmering head nodded.

"Then leave them alone."

"But—" he started.

I cut him off and walked over to point at the blue and gray birds. "They have lived their whole lives in that cage. You release them into the wild and they'll die. We'll call animal control."

His bottom lip extended, and I rolled my eyes. *Pouts from beyond the grave don't work on me.* I started to walk away, but a faint tingle of magic caught my attention. I opened my senses, trying to distinguish the black seeping out of the bedroom from the signature of a— concealment charm? *What was she hiding?*

The spell clung to the birdcage. I reached out, running my finger under the plastic base. My nail caught in the edge of a small envelope taped to the bottom.

Pulling it free, I flipped it over. "AC" had been written on the front. *A letter?* Whatever was inside felt thicker than just paper, but it wasn't lumpy. I opened it, pulling a tri-folded piece of stationery free.

Dear AC:

   You don't know me, so let me start this by saying that I Saw you. You came here looking for something. I'm not sure why, but the answer is blood. If you show the enclosed photo to the blond with you, he'll understand what that means. Maybe he can explain it to me too—he's cute.

                                        Good luck,
                                        Julie

I stared at the short letter, reading it over three times. Julie was a precog, so "Saw" probably meant she'd had a vision. AC had to be Alex Craft, but how could the answer be blood?

Was the spell transferred through the blood? I'd gotten it from a scratch, and the spell had spread through Helena's soul from where it had been carved into her skin. *But what about Sally?* Perhaps she'd cut herself while performing the autopsy? A blood-bound spell?

Death had told me it was contagious only to a specific target. Of course, the slaver had said it was more generic than wyrd witches. *Actually, the word she used was "genetic."* I'd thought she'd made a mistake, but another interpretation of "blood" was the family line.

The Shadow Girl's warning also mentioned blood. *A ghost girl of blood is worth treasure in silver chains.* I had a good idea what "silver chains" were, thanks to the slaver, but I'd thought "blood" meant flesh and blood. Maybe it had something to do with ancestry?

I reached into the envelope and pulled out a photo. Julie, wearing a graduation cap, stood between an older couple, probably her parents. Were all of the victims descended from nonmagical parents?

"What did you find?" Falin asked as he entered the room.

Well, the note says to show the photo to Falin. I handed it to him.

He glanced at the photo, shrugged.

"She said the answer is blood."

His eyes narrowed, and he stared at the image. Then he looked up at me, his gaze running over my face as though the answers were there.

"Blood," I said. "Genetics. Family line, right?"

"It's feykin," he said. "All the victims are descended from the fae. First-generation, maybe second-generation bloodline."

"Bullshit. I caught it, remember." And I knew damn well my father wouldn't have married a fae. I shook my head. "I've heard the word feykin before. The slaver called you that at the Bloom."

"Not me, Alex. You."

Me? I laughed, but it was an ugly sound.

Falin stepped closer. "It fits. It even fits what you said in the car. Humans with fae blood would have a harder time manipulating Aetheric energies because fae do not craft magic in the same way. I've known two of the victims were feykin, and Julie is a third. If we look hard enough, we will probably find fae ancestry in all of them."

"Except me." Wasn't I weird enough without him thinking I had mixed blood? "My father would never willingly have anything to do with the fae. He's in the Humans First Party, for fuck's sake."

"So was Coleman." Falin reached out and plucked a curl from the side of my face. "Alexis, you can see through glamour. I can't even see through glamour unless I know it's there."

I stepped back, shrugging him off, and crossed my arms over my chest. "I think you need another theory."

I stormed back into the bedroom. *Black magic is safer than his theories.* I walked over to a bookcase filled with knickknacks, only half paying attention to what I was looking at. *How could he think . . . ?* I could see through glamour. But that was a new development. *There has to be some other explanation.* A small piece of carved, petrified wood caught my attention. I recognized the glyph cut into the statue. It had haunted my nightmares. *The fae symbol for a soul.*

Why would Julie have a statue with a fae glyph on it? Where would she have found it? The glyphs weren't exactly common, and this one was apparently less common than most, based on Ashen's reaction when I showed it to him. *So where did Julie get it?*

From the killer? It was too big a coincidence otherwise.

I frowned at the little statue. It looked familiar. Had I seen one in other crime scene photos? I seemed to remember just the statue, in the middle of a glass table. In an austere room.

I dropped the statue.

"Falin!" I ran back to the den. "I need your phone. I need your phone now!"

His brows creased, but he handed the cell phone over. I stared at the display, my mind going blank. *Come on, remember the number.* I punched keys and hit the call button.

It rang.

And rang.

And went to voice mail.

"You've reached Casey Caine—"

I snapped the phone shut. She hadn't answered. Now what? It could be nothing. It could be she'd found the statue . . . somewhere. *Where would you find a statue with a magical fae glyph for a rare kind of soul?* It could be nothing . . .

Or it could be everything.

The feykin aspect aside, if being susceptible to the spell was genetic, then she was predisposed. Plus, at least two of the victims had been using gray magic. Casey had recently found a witch mentor. He was teaching her gray magic.

"We have to get to my father's mansion," I said, already headed to the door.

"What's going on, Alex?"

"Please. I just . . . I think my sister is the next target."

To his credit, Falin didn't ask any more questions. We sprinted to the car, and I twisted the strap of my purse around my hand as the car soared over the asphalt. I tried calling again.

No answer.

My thoughts sped around my brain, urged on by the racing beat of my heart. *What if he harvests the last soul before the Blood Moon?* The sun was already sinking behind the taller buildings of the city. *It could already be too late.* I couldn't think like that. I couldn't.

The squeal of tires drew my attention to a white van careening out of a side street. It charged forward. As if in slow motion, I saw Falin look up, floor the gas. It was too late.

Falin grabbed my arm. Cool magic coursed through the air. Then the van plowed into Falin's door.

My scream blended with the crunch of metal, the whoosh of the air bags. The world filled with motion. The car spun. A lamp pole slammed into my door. Glass shattered.

The world stopped on its side.

Shit. Caleb will kill me when he has to watch PC again.

There was blood.

"Falin?" My voice broke, no air in my lungs.

I tried to move. Groped for the seat belt.

"Falin?" I said again.

No answer.

I twisted, trying to distinguish up from down. The convertible roof ripped open. I blinked into the orange glow of the setting sun. *We'd stopped. How—?*

Hands locked around my arms. Hands with too many digits. They dragged my legs free of the crumpled car, and a face with sharp teeth came into view.

The tingle of a spell hit my neck.

Then there was only darkness.

Chapter 27

"Alex."

Darkness swirled around me.

"Alex, wake up."

Beyond the darkness was pain. Thundering, searing pain. I clung to the cool darkness, but the voice dragged me forward, into the pain.

"Alex, now would be a good time to wake up."

I pried my eyes open. Roy's face slowly emerged from the red haze.

"Go away."

"Shhhh," the ghost hissed, clapping a hand over my mouth.

He woke me to tell me to shut up? I groaned and rolled over. *Why do I feel like I've been hit by a truck?*

The van. The wreck. I *had* been hit by a truck.

I jolted upright. "Falin?"

The world spun, black dots filling my vision, and my stomach flipped. Roy caught my shoulders before I collapsed.

"Maybe not quite so fast," he said. "And keep quiet. They are fifteen feet away."

They? I blinked, pressing the heel of my hand against my forehead. "What happened?"

"Well, you abandoned me in a stranger's house. I caught up just as a big van full of nasty fae plowed into you. They dragged you out of the wreckage, spelled you, and then brought you here. I followed, and I've been trying to wake you for the past hour. I finally figured out I had to take that damn disk off your neck."

But where is here? I looked around.

A thin barrier of red stretched beyond my feet, surrounding me on all sides. I reached out, feeling the tingle of magic. I pushed through the feeling and met solid resistance in the translucent light. *I've been circled.*

The world beyond the circle was hard to make out. I thought I saw the edge of a bed, and I was sure I could see a large candlestick. Another barrier flashed beyond that. *I'm in a circle inside a circle?* I rolled to my knees and leaned into the barrier, ignoring the biting tingle of magic that crawled over my skin as I cupped my hands over my eyes and peered through the magic.

Definitely a bed. I was in a bedroom? Something moved on top of the mattress. A loud moan trembled through the air, making the skin along my spine itch.

"Hey!" I yelled, slamming my fists against the barrier.

"What was that?" a female voice asked. She sounded familiar.

"Nothing," a man answered. "I have a surprise for you."

An arm appeared over the edge of the mattress, followed by a man's sweat-soaked bare back. He twisted, his gaze cutting into me, and I found myself staring into the face of the late Governor Coleman.

I reeled back, landing on my ass. Roy's body was dead. Coleman's face had to be glamour. I *knew* that.

But the man *looked* like Coleman. He reached down, grabbing at nothing on the floor, and white silk cords appeared in his hand.

Oh crap.

Bed. Silk cords. Woman. *He's going to kill again.*

"Stop." I beat my fists on the barrier. I focused on the only part of the woman I could see, a bare leg. "Run, dammit!"

"Are you crazy?" Roy pulled me back from the edge of the circle. "The bad guy is out there, and you can barely sit up straight."

"He'll kill her."

"I heard something." The woman pushed up to her elbows. Blond hair fell over her shoulders.

Casey.

"I'm sure it's nothing," Coleman said, crawling over her. His hand moved to her face, turned her away from me.

My stomach twisted, and I ripped free of Roy's grasp. Pushing up to my feet, I rammed into the barrier. Pain exploded through my body as every ache from the car wreck intensified. Casey didn't even look up. *She can't hear me.*

Coleman wrapped the cord around her wrist and guided her back down on the mattress. *Dammit.*

"Casey. Get out of there."

She didn't react. Coleman moved to tie her feet.

Okay, Alex, think. I looked around. I was in a nearly soundproof circle with a ghost. I was clearly glamoured to be invisible, because Casey didn't know I was there. Coleman did; he'd looked directly at me. *Why did he bring me here?* I had to get out. I had to reach Coleman before he began his ritual.

"Help me overload this circle," I said to Roy as I tapped the magic in my ring. I couldn't draw outside magic through someone else's circle, but no one had taken my charms.

"I don't think—"

"That's my sister with that killer."

Roy frowned, but he joined me at the edge of the barrier. He pressed against the red haze separating us from the rest of the room, and sparks ignited in the barrier. His face contoured—ghosts were pure energy held together by will and personality. I'd asked something dangerous from him, but I had to reach Casey before it was too late.

I channeled the raw magic from my ring into the barrier. More sparks appeared. I drained the ring. The haze wavered. It didn't break. *Damn.* Sliding off my charm bracelet, I pressed the sliver charms into the barrier. *If I can hit it with enough magic . . .*

It didn't fall. *What else can I hit it with?* I glanced down. A small circular disk was on the floor—the spell the fae had used to knock me unconscious. I pushed it with the edge of my boot, shoving it into the barrier.

Still not enough.

Roy pulled back, more translucent than normal. My ring was empty. The charms in my bracelet had overloaded. *What else do I have?*

The dagger.

I could still feel the enchantment tingling at my ankle—Coleman hadn't taken it. Bending made my ribs protest, and my vision spun as I crouched, but my fingers found the hilt. Drawing my hand back, I jabbed the enchanted steel into the circle.

The blade sank in up to the hilt. Streaks of lightning shot through the barrier. The dagger began to glow, searing the skin on my palm. I jerked back. The dagger hung in the barrier, angry flashes of light cutting through the air around it.

"Get back," I yelled to Roy—not that either of us had much room to go anywhere.

I crouched as close to the center of the small circle as possible and covered my head with my arms. Magic zinged through the air, making my hair stand on end. Then the circle imploded.

The magical backlash tore around us, knocking me to the ground. A woman screamed. Coleman cursed. The dagger hit the carpet.

I grabbed it. The hilt burned in my grasp, but no magical resonance emanated from the blade. *The enchantment overloaded.* At least it was still a weapon.

I crawled to my feet, my body protesting. I ignored it. I forced my legs under me.

"Alex?" Casey tried to sit up, but she had only one hand left free.

"Damn you," Coleman said. He grabbed Casey's wrist and strapped it down. Then he turned to me. "Obey me."

Fear clutched at my throat as his voice crashed through my consciousness. *No.* The dagger slipped from my fingers. I couldn't see the slave chain, but I could feel Coleman's will battering mine. I fell to my knees, my arms wrapping around my bruised ribs—maybe if I could only hold on tight enough, I could keep myself inside me and Coleman's commands out. It didn't help.

I gasped and embraced the pain in my body, letting it remind me I was alive and I was me. I needed to focus. Casey yelled something, alarm tainting her voice. I had to get Coleman's attention off her until . . .

Until what? There was no guarantee help was on the way. *Falin—* A new ache, one that had nothing to do with my body, ripped into me. I didn't know what had happened to Falin. I didn't know if he was alive or dead. The back of my throat burned. No help was coming. No one knew Casey was in danger. No one knew where I was. Still, stalling was my only option. At least until I had the strength to sit up straight.

"What do you want?" I whispered, my voice shaking as I fought to keep my thoughts my own.

Footsteps scrunched in the carpet, and a large hand wrapped itself in my hair, jerked my head back. I blinked at Coleman, his face only a foot from mine.

"What do I want?" he repeated. He laughed, but the sound was rough, and his thin lips curled back in rage. "What do I want? I want the fear and respect I deserve. That the fae deserve. The King of Faerie is an old fool. His stand of equality and harmony with humans is preposterous. It is time for his rule to end, and you, my dear, are going to help me."

I shook my head, my hair pulling with the movement. "I won't. Even if I could." I'd die first.

"Oh, you can," he said. Dark light reflected in his pupils, and his mouth twisted into a cruel smile. Nothing sane looked out at me from those eyes. He leaned closer. "You can. And you will."

Coleman released my hair, shoving me back to the ground. Then he held up a hand and ripped a hole in space. A gray-cloaked shadow stepped through the opening. "Don't let her interfere," he told the cloaked figure.

"It's her," Roy whispered.

I looked up as the specter of a woman approached. She held up a dull hand, and I could feel the static of magic crackling around her skin. I swallowed. *The Shadow Girl.*

"Teddy, what's going on?" Casey jerked against her restraints. "Let me up. Let me go."

Coleman ignored her. He pulled a curved blade from a bag beside the bed. *No!* I struggled to my feet. The

Shadow Girl stepped forward. She pressed two fingers against my forehead, and pain laced through my body. My muscles turned to jelly. I collapsed. The air rushed out of me. Drawing in more air was hard, requiring more strength than I possessed.

Coleman looked up. "It's time. Open the gate."

The Shadow Girl nodded. She lifted her hands, and magic leaked over my skin, wrapped around me. Sinister strings slithered across my throat, my chest, threatening to crush me. I couldn't imagine anyone channeling so much magic, but it poured out of her, through her. Darkness crawled over the ceiling above us. Then the darkness split like a rift. The night sky appeared. The moon, full and closer than I'd ever seen, hung directly over the room. The shadow of the eclipse bled over one side. *The Blood Moon.*

But it was more than that. I was looking at stars I'd never seen. At a sky close enough to reach. *The sky of Faerie.*

Coleman returned to the edge of the bed. He chanted, lifting the wickedly curved knife, and Casey screamed. I squeezed my eyes closed and pushed up to my hands and knees. The Shadow Girl surged forward. I rolled, trying to get out of reach. It didn't work. Her hand still caught me, and pain ripped through my body.

I found myself panting into the carpet. Warm moisture dripped onto my hand. I blinked at it.

Water? *No. Tears.*

The Shadow Girl was crying silent tears. *A ghost girl of blood is worth treasure in silver chains, and if she is a fool, by commands she'll know my pains.* Her verse wasn't a threat. It was both warning and explanation. She was a slave.

Casey screamed. Blood trickled down her ribs. I had to do something, and I had to do it now.

"Help me," I whispered.

The Shadow Girl's cloaked head dropped. Her hand lifted. Magic sparked around her fingers. The message was clear. *She couldn't help me.* Whatever was left of her, of whom she'd been once, was buried, and she couldn't disobey Coleman. Which meant, slave or not, as long as she was between me and Casey, she was my enemy.

I opened my senses. The dark magic in the air clawed at me, trying to worm into my mind. I ignored it. *Let it do its worst.* I could fight only so many battles. I would either win or die in this circle.

I was out of magic, cut off from the source, but I reached with my senses. There had to be something I could use trapped in the circle with me. I opened my shields. There was grave essence in the air. Bodies. Bodies hidden from sight by glamour, but I could feel them.

I let the power sweep into me. Let it fill me with the chill. My vision changed. The world decayed, magic became a physical substance swirling in the air around me, and the glamour vanished. The dead bodies that had been invisible snapped into focus. Rodger I knew, but the other two I'd seen only from a distance. *Father's guards.* I didn't have time to focus on those already dead.

My gaze snapped to Coleman. Without the glamour, his body was Graham again. Lines of glyphs covered the stolen skin. He turned, a smile cutting his face.

"Yes, Alex Craft," he said, his manic eyes glittering. "Yes, grab your power. Merge realities. I will transcend all planes. They will be mine to rule."

Chapter 28

--•=◉=•--

Shit.

I tried to cut off the flow of grave essence, but the chill continued to pour into me. *No!*

"Cross the planes, Alex. Merge realities."

Coleman's command crashed through my mind, vibrated through my body. A cold wind raked through me, the grave drawing itself into my being. I couldn't stop it, couldn't control it. The power clawed into me, and I screamed, squeezing my eyes closed.

"Alex?"

Roy. My power reached to him. He was dead, a ghost, a familiar aspect, and I had too much grave essence. *Way too much.*

He backed up as if he could sense the reaching power, but it wrapped around him anyway. I siphoned chill into him, made him a repository for power I had no ability to stop drawing.

The Shadow Girl's head snapped up, her attention torn between the now-visible ghost and me. Roy looked down at himself. He lifted his hand—a hand that wasn't translucent—and a grin crawled over his face. He hurled himself at the Shadow Girl. They went down in a tumble of limbs.

I didn't have time to watch. I needed something else to do with the power surging through me. I reached out, searching. Shades rose from the three bodies on the ground.

Still the power burned.

"Freeze, Coleman," a voice shouted as a door banged open.

Falin? I turned. In my grave-sight, he shone, his silver soul glowing below his skin. He limped as he entered, but his gun was drawn. *He's alive.* Relief surged over me, made me feel lighter, as though a space inside me that had crumpled had opened again. That new space was quickly overwhelmed by waves of power with no-where to go.

A bang crashed through the air, and I ducked, throwing my hands over my ears. The bullet, having no magical properties, passed through the circle. Coleman jerked.

Blood blossomed across Coleman's chest as he fell. He hit the ground. Falin dragged himself toward the edge of the circle. The Shadow Girl broke away from Roy. She ran toward the edge of the circle as if anticipating it would collapse. It didn't. She stopped, turned, and we all stared at the corner of the bed.

Was it over? Was that it?

Coleman's laugh crawled over the carpet. He pushed himself off the floor. Blood no longer spurted from the hole in his chest.

How . . . ? His heart wasn't beating. *He's dead.*

Being dead didn't stop him.

He glared at Falin. "The Winter Queen's lover and as-sassin? She always did oppose me." A dark smirk spread over his face. "I'll bring your mistress to heel once I'm King."

The Winter Queen's lover? I glanced at Falin, but he didn't look at me. Wouldn't look at me. His face was hard, not denying Coleman's claim.

I squeezed my eyes shut. The cold tore into me as if I were an open wound filled with ice. I embraced it, wishing the chill would numb me. It didn't. It just built. And built. More power than I could contain.

I needed release.

Falin leveled his gun. Three more shots sounded. Coleman stumbled, but he only laughed.

"Go ahead and destroy this body, assassin. In a few minutes, I will have a body of energy, of power." Coleman turned to me. "Alex, merge this world with the Aetheric."

Power hemorrhaged from my body. I screamed, and the sound ignited into sharp sparks of color. Swirls of spells became tangible. A blue thread of raw magic appeared, then a green, then a purple. *Oh crap. The Aetheric plane.*

Coleman reached a hand toward a raw string of magic and drew it inside his body. "Magnificent." The black wisps of magic swirled closer to him, seeping below his skin.

He's high on power.

But he wasn't done. Casey still struggled under him. Her soul, a pale blue glow, already had several dark spots expanding over it. I had to do something. I had to stop him. The moon overhead was more red than not. Time was running out.

Magic poured through me, still seeking an outlet. *Coleman's body is dead.* I reached out, guiding the power. In my grave-sight, the body was already decaying, but my power slid over the spells on his skin, not touching. *Dammit.*

"Alex, I think now might be the time to do something," Roy whispered.

"I'd never have guessed." I climbed to my feet.

The Shadow Girl turned to me again. She rushed forward, her hand lifting. Magic gathered around her fingers.

Inside Coleman's circle the Aetheric was part of reality, and I drew power, gathering blue swirls from the air. I'd never held both grave magic and Aetheric energy inside my body at once. The raw energy burned, its heat fighting the chill of the grave for dominance. It felt like blistering steam replacing my blood. My skin glowed, and the Shadow Girl hesitated. Without any elegance, just a hell of a lot of pissed-off will, I released the power.

It burst from my body and crashed into the Shadow Girl. It caught her in the torso, lifting her off her feet. She flew backward, and I sagged from the rush of power moving through me. She landed a yard from the bed. Her hood fell back, revealing lank red curls, sunken and bruised green eyes.

Rianna.

No. It can't be.

My old roommate stared at me. Tears wet her cheeks, but she held up her hand. Power gathered around her fingers. Roy jumped forward. Whatever spell she'd prepared fizzled, sliding off the ghost. I tensed as his fist hit her in the jaw. *She's not my best friend right now*, I reminded myself.

She was Coleman's Shadow Girl.

I looked away. I'd expended a hell of a lot of power with that blast, but the grave essence kept pouring into me. *I have to stop it.* The only way to stop it was to stop Coleman.

Falin banged on the barrier, his cell phone gripped in his hand. "Alex, how do I get inside?"

"You don't." If the circle failed, I didn't know what would happen. Would realities continue to merge throughout the city? The country? The world?

Grave essence seeped into my body. It had to go somewhere. I reached out, searching for a vessel, something I could siphon off the power into. I couldn't touch Coleman. I'd already raised the shades in the bodies. I could feel Casey's soul struggling against the spell, but I forced the power away from her. I needed something else, some other source.

My power trailed over something I couldn't see. Then it latched on, and I let it flow through me. A new scream tore through the room, followed by a second, a third. Six vaporous women escaped from an item near Coleman's feet. *The souls.* Or really, six pissed-off and insane ghosts.

Filled with my power, the ghosts solidified. Their screams of terror and hatred erupted as red flashes in the Aetheric. As one, the group turned. Like a half dozen angry cats, they tore into Coleman, ripping at him with ghostly nails.

"Stop them," Coleman yelled.

His words tumbled through my mind as a command, but I only smiled.

"I can't stop them. They exist in our reality now."

And they certainly didn't like Coleman. Their rage emerged without words as they gouged his flesh. Their screams snapped and cracked in the magic-laced air.

"Alex!"

I turned. Death stood outside the circle, the gray man and the raver at his side. His dark eyes were wide as he scanned the bubble of chaos around me, but he didn't enter the circle. *He can't pass the barrier.*

"Alex, you're running out of time." He pointed at the bed.

Casey lay amid the decayed cream sheets, unconscious. Not yet dead, but close. Her soul was only a dim glow inside her body. *No.* I looked up. The moon hung swollen and red above us. *The Blood Moon.*

Coleman looked up as well. Then the magic he'd been gathering swept out of him. It bound the six ghosts in chains of darkness. "It's time."

No.

I looked around. Falin and Death were both stuck outside the circle. Roy still struggled with Rianna. The ghosts were bound. I was the only one left. *What can I do?*

In my grave-sight, Coleman was a decaying corpse now that Falin had killed Graham's body. He obviously hadn't had time to bind all the spells he'd cast on Roy's body on Graham's, but that didn't help me. I couldn't reach inside him the way I had Ashen. Not with the spells on his skin. *What if he didn't have skin?* If what I was seeing was true, if he really was just a corpse . . .

"You must See under the Blood Moon. You must know what you See is true," the gargoyle had told me. *Fred, I hope you were foreseeing this.*

I rushed forward. *Coleman wants me to merge realities; I'll merge realities.*

My hand landed on his wrist, and I pushed with power. The chill burst out of me, rushed into him. Dead skin sloughed off under my fingers.

"No!" Coleman's other hand angled toward me, his knife clenched in his fist. Pain exploded in my stomach.

My vision went red with agony, and air suddenly wasn't there. But Coleman's strike was too late. The decay spread up his arm, his skin withered, and his bones crumbled to dust.

"Welcome to the land of the dead," I whispered, gasping for air I couldn't find. I looked down at the hilt of Coleman's ceremonial blade where it emerged from under my ribs. Seeing it made the pain worse. I stumbled back, collapsing onto the bed. *Don't pull it out. Don't pull it out. You'll do more damage.* But I wanted it out of me.

There wasn't time. Destroying Graham's body wouldn't kill Coleman. As the body dissolved, the black stain of the true Coleman, of an unguarded soul, was revealed. With my mind, I reached out. Instead of pushing power into the soul, I drew energy out.

Coleman screamed. His essence felt like sucking sludge from the bottom of the swamp into my body, but I didn't dare stop. Casey's soul was almost gone. I had to stop Coleman, and I had to stop him now.

I drew harder, and Coleman's soul thinned, fading from existence. *Existence on any plane.* He diminished to a shadow, his scream an echo. And then there was nothing left.

The chill he'd commanded me to draw stopped. I let go of the excess, letting it flow out of my body. I didn't release it all—I didn't want to lose my sight, not yet.

Coleman's circle shattered, his spells dissipating. The six souls screamed again, freed but with no target for their desired vengeance. Rianna tore herself away from Roy. I heard her say something about being under Coleman's control, but I was beyond following her words. I curled in a ball around the dagger in my stomach, trying to remember how to breathe. Casey was unconscious beside me, but the glow of her soul was brighter, stronger.

"Alex!" Two male voices yelled my name simultaneously.

Death reached me first. He knelt beside the bed, his face level with mine. "Alex . . ."

"I stopped him," I whispered.

Death's dark eyes creased with concern, and his hand moved to my face. His skin felt warm—which meant I'd taken way too much chill. "You did," he said, his thumb stroking my cheekbone.

The gray man appeared behind Death. "It's time."

Death jumped to his feet. "No. No, leave her."

The gray man tapped the skull on his cane against his arm. "We'll take care of the others first. But we have to take her." He turned away, spinning his cane as he walked toward the displaced souls. The raver followed. They began collecting the screaming ghosts.

Death knelt in front of me again as Falin reached the bed.

Falin's expression was ragged. He stepped around Death, scowling at the collector as he moved to the head of the bed.

"Alexis." Falin's hands hovered above me, as if he was afraid I might break if he touched me. He sank onto the mattress near my shoulders. "An ambulance is on the way," he whispered.

"They won't make it." The world was becoming fuzzy. I looked at Death. "Will they?"

Death shook his head and squeezed his eyes closed. He took my hand, pressing his lips against my skin. "There is no pain in the end," he promised.

Good to know. I blinked and lost time in the darkness.

Falin's hands were on my face when I opened my eyes again. "Stay awake. Stay with me."

I tried to smile at him, but my lips cracked into a grimace I couldn't control. Breathing was becoming too much of a chore.

"It can't wait any longer," the gray man said, appearing behind Death.

"No."

Falin's hand moved to his gun. He drew it, leveling it on the gray man and then swinging the barrel to Death. "Stay away from her."

"You can't shoot them," I whispered.

He looked as though he wanted to. Needed to. But there was no one left to fight. His arm sagged, and his fingers moved to my hair.

I closed my eyes. I was tired. So very tired and hurt.

"It's time," the gray man said again, placing his hand on Death's shoulder.

"No. I love her. I won't do it."

My eyes snapped open. *Death loved me?*

The gray man's fingers flexed on Death's shoulder. "Then stand aside, friend."

"No," a female voice said. "Get away from her."

The two soul collectors turned. Falin stood. He drew his gun again and stood between Rianna and the bed, the gun leveled at her chest.

Rianna glanced at the gun. "Please, I can help her." Her eyes moved to the collectors. "Give me a chance."

"You were working with Coleman," Falin said, not blinking. His finger hovered over the trigger.

"Not by choice."

"Rianna." Her name emerged from my throat as a rasp instead of a word.

"Alex." She swept around Falin and his gun, moving to my side next to Death. "I tried to warn you, to tell you. I'm so sorry. Coleman forbade me from telling anyone his plans, and from warning you in particular. Coming up with a verse cryptic enough to get around his command was a bitch. And don't even ask how I talked a thorn fae into delivering it."

"Time is an issue," the raver said, turning from where she'd collected the last ghost.

Rianna looked up. "I'm going to need someone to pull out the knife and someone to hold her shoulders."

"I'll hold her," Death said, moving around the bed. He lifted Casey, sliding her farther to one side. Then he climbed on the mattress beside my shoulders.

Falin frowned at Rianna. "She needs a healer."

"Well, I'm all she has. You take the knife. Be ready when I say." Rianna motioned for him to move to her other side.

He walked around her and climbed on the bed near my hips. He grabbed my hand, squeezing it once before his fingers moved to the hilt of the knife.

Rianna looked down at me. "Sorry, Al—this is going to hurt." The Aetheric and reality were still merged, and Rianna gathered pale blue strands of magic around her. Then she placed her hands on my ribs.

"Now."

Falin pulled the knife. I screamed. The knife sliding free was like a hot poker dragging through my body. My back arched as I twisted in pain. Death held me. He pinned me to the bed, but I thrashed in his grip. The knife pulled free. I sagged on the bed, damp with sweat.

Rianna's cool magic pumped into me, dulled the searing pain to an ache. Blue swirls of Aetheric energy swirled around all four of us. It sank into my body along with Rianna's will-turned-magic. She'd always been a master spell crafter—I didn't remember her being a healer, but when she pulled back, only a memory of the pain remained.

Falin slid my shirt up my torso, his hand exploring my stomach. A smile broke over his face, melted the tension in his icy eyes. He leaned forward, and his lips moved to mine without ever losing that magnificent smile.

"You'll be okay," he whispered when he pulled back.

I looked at him. At the relieved smile claiming his

entire face. *He's the Winter Queen's assassin? Her lover?* Then my gaze moved to Death. He glared at Falin, his hands pressed possessively over my shoulders.

How did things get so complicated?

But we'd won. Over my head, the first sliver of pale moon appeared around the red shadow. Coleman was gone. John would live. I'd keep my soul. Casey was alive. Rianna was free. *We won.*

A small smile crawled over my face. A siren sounded in the distance. Rianna looked up, her face alarmed as the siren hurtled closer.

"I have to go." She backed away.

"Go? Go where?" I asked. I'd only just found her again, and she was going? I struggled to sit, but I didn't have the energy.

Rianna's pale lips tugged down at the edges. "Back to Faerie. I'm a changeling now, and so many more years have passed for me than for you. I'll turn to dust if the moon sets and I'm still here." She gathered magic to herself and then ripped a hole in space. "Visit me at the Eternal Bloom, Al. We have a lot to talk about." She stepped through the rift and was gone.

The sirens stopped outside. A door burst open downstairs.

"Alex?" both Falin and Death said at the same time.

I just closed my eyes. I was so tired. "I think I'll pass out now."

Chapter 29

I spent the night in jail.

I probably should have gone to the hospital, but Rianna's spell had fixed most of the damage I'd taken. I'd been found with a suspended FIB agent, my unconscious and brutalized sister, and three dead bodies. I probably should have been glad I didn't end up somewhere worse than jail.

I sat in the tiny isolation cell, waiting for them to decide what to do with me. I slept intermittently. Each time I woke, I found Death sitting across the room, his eyes pinched tight as he watched me. When he noticed I was awake, he'd disappear without a word.

Sweet, but sort of creepy. *He'd said he loved me.* The thought made me smile—and want to run.

I lay on the unpadded cot and stared at the ceiling—or at least stared at where the ceiling should have been. I'd been completely blind since releasing my hold on the grave—and apparently on reality. I hadn't noticed at first because I was experiencing the world on a psychic level. Currently the Aetheric swirled around me, illuminating the room with threads of magic. When I blinked, the color disappeared, the room turning gray as the walls crumbled. The land of the dead. I blinked again, and the room glowed with remembered energy, the walls radiating the frustration and anguish of those who had been in the cell before me. I didn't even know the name of that plane of existence. I sighed.

The vision thing was disconcerting, but I'd screwed with reality and channeled way too much power. This was clearly the backlash. I just hoped it wasn't permanent.

"Alex?"

Roy? I sat up and stared at the ghost. "Where did you go last night? I didn't see you after Rianna broke away from you."

He shrugged and pressed his glasses up with a finger. "Those soul collectors were gathering up ghosts. I had to get out of there." He smiled. "But guess what? My body looks like me again. I just checked out the morgue, and I'm there! I mean, I look like what I should."

"Congrats. Guess that means you'll be moving on soon? Go wherever ghosts go next?"

His shoulders hitched forward. "Well, you see, about that . . . I still have that TV interview, remember? And then I was thinking I might hang out for a while. I mean, now that I have someone to talk to, being a ghost isn't so bad."

"Someone to talk to" being me. *Great—I really do have a ghostly sidekick.* If I got out of jail anytime soon.

As if summoned by my thought, an electronic buzz sounded. Roy vanished as a cop stepped up to the cell bars.

"Alex Craft, you're free to go," he said as the door slid open.

I unfolded from the small cot and followed the waiting officer into the hall. He led me down a cement-floored hall to a door, where another officer returned my personal effects in a brown paper bag.

"That's it? I can go?"

The uniformed officer pursed his lips. After where I'd been found, I hadn't expected to see daylight for a long time. But the door buzzed in front of me, and I walked into the lobby.

A man waited for me just beyond the door. He tugged awkwardly at the front of his expensive suit. "Alex Craft?"

The officer nodded. "She's good to go."

The man frowned at me but said, "Please follow me."

I glanced at the officer who had escorted me to the lobby. Exactly whose care was he releasing me into and under what conditions? The officer's face gave away nothing.

Well, I can't stay here forever. I followed the nervous man.

He led me out of the building. Then he walked up to a limo and opened the door for me.

Okay. That is not normal.

I leaned down and peeked inside. My father sat on the seat, a document in one hand, a glass of red wine in the other.

He looked up and tucked the file aside. "Come in, Alexis."

I almost didn't. I almost turned around and walked straight back inside. But curiosity won me over, and I climbed into the seat across from him. *This ought to be good.* If nothing else, I had some questions for him.

My vision peered into the Aetheric plane. My father was a silver soul of light surrounded by swirls of color, but none reached for him. The magic threads almost seemed to be avoiding him. *Fae?*

I blinked. *He's the fae in my blood?*

"Your sister has asked about you," he said, steepling his fingers and balancing his elbows on his knees.

I shook my head, too shocked to process his words. I had to blink several times—and watch the world change drastically before my eyes—before I figured out what he was talking about. "What did Casey say?"

"Just that you saved her. She is refusing to talk about what happened. Are you going to ask how she is?" When I didn't, he continued. "She is confused and will probably need counseling after this traumatic event, but she is a resilient girl. She will have scars, but she can acquire complexion charms to cover them. Otherwise, she is fine."

She was cut up and needed counseling, but yeah—no problem; she was *fine. Clearly using a different definition of the word "fine" than the rest of the world.*

He leaned back, watching me. I waited. He'd gone out of his way to see me, so I assumed he had a reason, but he didn't say anything. I shuffled in my seat, overly aware that I'd been through a car wreck, a magical battle, and a night in jail, while he looked fresh enough to have walked off a magazine cover.

When he still didn't say anything, I grew annoyed. "So, were you ever planning to tell us you were fae? Court fae from the look of it."

My father didn't even have the decency to look shocked that I'd figured out his secret. He just sat there, watching me.

Under his glamour, his short, professionally cut hair was longer, paler. His features were sharper—not grossly inhuman, but striking. And he looked young. My father didn't look much older than me. His fae-mien also looked extremely familiar.

I frowned, trying to place this face that he kept hidden. Suddenly it clicked. The portrait of Greggory Delane at the statehouse. *My father was the first governor of Nekros?* That was over fifty years ago. My already aching head began to throb, and I shook it as if the movement could help settle my thoughts in place. It didn't. Still my father said nothing.

I glared at him. "You didn't think being feykin was something your kids should know?"

"Feykin." His lips twisted around the word as though he disliked the taste, and he shook his head. "There are humans with fae blood, Alexis. Then there are fae with human blood. The difference is the soul." He leaned forward. "The Blood Moon called to the soul of Faerie. It woke many who were still sleeping, but its approach only quickened the inevitable."

And just when I thought I was done with cryptic riddles. "What's that supposed to mean?"

"This is the long game, Alexis." He smiled as if amused by my confusion. Then he reached into his breast pocket and pulled out a small piece of paper. He passed it to me. "I'd like to hire you retroactively for your part in uncovering the murder of my chief of staff and disrupting the plans of a megalomaniac."

I plucked the slip of paper from his fingers and unfolded it. It was a check. A check with a lot of zeros on it. *Do I accept this?* It was hard to refuse money, especially since I'd been working for free the past week and a half. But I didn't trust his motives. "What do you want?"

"The money is for services rendered. Nothing more."

I stared at him. He was fae. He couldn't lie. I pocketed the check. "Fine."

He said nothing else, so I let myself out of the limo. As I turned to slam the door his voice followed me out.

"Alexis, can you fix the rift in my house? Or should I lock the door and toss the key?"

I cringed. I hadn't been able to fix reality, so a circular area in the middle of the Caine mansion was now a crossover point for the Aetheric into our plane of existence. There were also a couple of spots of decay where the land of the dead had merged with reality. It probably wasn't safe to leave it the way it was, but I didn't know how to put things back in the right plane.

I met my father's eyes. "Call a good locksmith."

I stood back as the limo took off. Then I didn't know what to do. *Wonder if the cops will let me call home for a ride?* I turned to head back up the stairs.

"Al!"

I turned as a car stopped on the curb. Caleb jumped out of the front passenger side. His huge arms wrapped around me, all but squeezing me in half. "We've been so worried about you, girl."

We?

Holly and Tamara were right behind him, and I found myself in the center of a giant hug sandwich. They were warm, nearly too hot to touch comfortably, but right at that moment I didn't care.

"Thanks for coming for me, guys," I said, blinking back tears.

"We're not the only ones here," Holly said. "We brought you a surprise."

She opened the back door of the car, and a smile cracked across my face. "John!"

He moved slowly, stiffly, but his mustache twitched in a smile.

"You're awake," I said, trotting up to him.

"Woke last night. Maybe it was the full moon." He winked at me.

Yeah, the moon. I tried to hide my wince behind a cough that was only half forced.

John squeezed my shoulders. "I'd say good to see

you're okay, but you look rough. How you holding up?"

I forced a smile. "I'm good."

"Well, we thought we'd take you to lunch, but . . ." Tamara trailed off, her eyes taking in my fresh-out-of-a-horror-movie outfit.

Yeah. All I really want is to go home.

"Alex," Holly whispered, nudging me with her elbow. She nodded to the top of the stairs.

Falin had just walked out. His hand was still on the door, but he'd stopped, his eyes on our group. I looked around. There was no one here to meet him or take him home.

"I'll be right back, guys," I said as I headed for the stairs.

Falin met me halfway. He wrapped me in a hug both tender and world-encompassing, but when I tensed in his arms, he pulled back.

He stared at my face, and whatever he saw there didn't make him happy. "Guess we don't have a reason to work together anymore?"

I shook my head. "No, we don't."

Coleman had said Falin was the Winter Queen's lover. The thought made my chest hurt as though I had another knife digging into me. I didn't like the feeling. It would be smarter to say good-bye now. To not see him again. But that idea didn't make me feel any better.

I don't have to decide right now never to see him again. Yeah, he'd lied by omission, but it wasn't like I didn't have secrets myself. I had to stop sleeping with him, though—in any sense of the word. That just muddled everything.

And everything was confusing enough, what with seeing different planes of existence with each blink, blending reality, and finding out my father was fae. The one constant in my life, Death, had been terribly inconsistent. *And he'd said he loves me.* I still didn't know what to think of that, or how I felt. Keeping Falin around was a recipe for disaster when what I really needed was normalcy.

And yet, I didn't want to say good-bye.

"You need a ride?" I asked, nodding at Holly's car.

"I need lunch. You?"

I was hungry but . . . "What I want is a shower."

"You can shower while I cook." His smile was bright enough to thaw the ice in his eyes.

Already trouble. "You'll have to make enough for six." I wrapped my arm around his and led him down the stairs toward my waiting friends. "Oh yeah, by the way—get your toothbrush out of my bathroom."

Read on for a taster of the next instalment
in the Alex Craft series:

Grave Dance

Coming in February 2012.

Chapter 1

When I first straddled the chasm between the land of the dead and the world of the living, I accidentally raised the shade of our recently deceased Pekinese. The former champion dog floating around our backyard resulted in my father shipping me off to a wyrd boarding school. Seventeen years later, I still reached across that chasm, but now I got paid to do it.

"That isn't a body, John," I said, staring at the open black bag. "It's a foot." A pale, bloated, waterlogged foot.

John Matthews, personal friend and one of the best homicide detectives in Nekros City, nodded. "It's a left foot, to be precise, and I have two more back at the morgue. What can you tell me?"

I frowned and nudged the toe of my boot at a clump of grass sprouting between chunks of loose gravel. My business cards read: ALEX CRAFT, LEAD PRIVATE INVESTIGATOR AND GRAVE WITCH FOR TONGUES FOR THE DEAD. I was actually the owner and only employee of the firm, but that was beside the point. I raised shades and gave the living a chance to question the dead—for a fee. My work tended to take me to a lot of graveyards, the occasional funeral home, and to the Nekros City morgue. The parking pit for the Sionan Floodplain Nature Preserve was most definitely *not* my typical working environment. Nor was a single severed appendage my typical job.

"Sorry, John, but I need more than a foot to raise a shade."

"And I need some better news." His shoulders slumped as if he'd deflated. "We've been scouring this swamp for two days and we're turning up more questions than answers. We've got no IDs for the vics, no obvious causes of death, and no primary crime scenes. You sure you can't give me anything?" As he spoke, he shoved the flap on the body bag farther open with the butt of his pen.

The foot lay in a sea of black plastic. The sickly scent of rot filled the humid afternoon air, coating the inside of my nose, my throat. The bloodless skin had sloughed off the exposed ankle, the strips of yellowish flesh shriveling. My stomach twisted and I looked away. I'd leave the physical inspection to the medical examiner—my affinity for the dead was less for the tangible and more for the spectral. Memories hid in every cell of the body. Memories that my grave magic could unlock and give shape as a shade. Of course, that depended on having enough of the body—and thus cells—at my disposal for my magic to fill in the gaps. I didn't need to cast a magic circle and begin a ritual to know I couldn't pull a shade from the foot. I could sense that fact, the same way I could sense that the foot had belonged to a male, probably in his late sixties. I could also sense the nasty tangle of spells all but dripping from the decaying appendage.

"The foot is saturated with magic. Some pretty dark stuff from the feel of it," I said, taking a step back from the gurney and the sticky residual magic emanating from the foot. "I'm guessing you already have a team deciphering the spells?"

"Yeah, but so far the anti–black magic unit hasn't reached any conclusions. It would really help if we could question the victim."

But that wasn't going to happen with such a small percentage of the body. "You said you had a matching foot back at the morgue? Maybe if we assemble all the parts, there will be enough to—"

John shook his head. "Dancing jokes aside, unless this guy had two left feet—literally—neither of the other feet belong to him."

Three left feet? That meant at least three victims. "You're thinking serial?"

"Don't say that too loud," John said, his gaze flashing to a passing pair of crime scene technicians headed toward the dense old-growth forest. "No official determination yet, but, yeah, I'm thinking serial." His grizzly bear–sized form sagged further and his mustache twitched as he frowned. The mustache had been a thick red accent to his expressions as long as I'd known him, but in the weeks since he'd woken from a spell-induced coma, slivers of gray had joined the red. He pushed the flap of the body bag closed. "Park rangers found the first foot yesterday morning when they were checking the paths after the recent flooding. We got wardens and cadaver dogs out here, and the second foot turned up. When we found the third, I pulled some strings to hire you as a consultant."

"Do you want me to stick around? Wait and see if your guys find more of the body?"

"Actually"—John rubbed a hand over his head, wiping away the sweat glistening on his spreading bald spot—"I was hoping you'd join the search."

I hesitated. I probably even blanched. Wandering around with my shields down sensing every dead creature most definitely was *not* my idea of a good—*or safe*—time.

John didn't miss my pause. "You've located DBs before," he said. DBs as in *dead bodies*. "And the paperwork you signed covered the possibility of searching the swamp, so you'll be paid for your time."

I opened my mouth to respond—while I might have qualms about opening my psyche to whatever might be in the floodplain, we both knew I'd risk it—but I was interrupted before I could answer.

"What's wrong, Craft?" Detective Jenson, John's partner, asked as he stepped around the side of a black SUV. "Don't want to get those tight pants dirty tramping through the swamp? Got another TV appearance to run off to? Or maybe your magic eye license doesn't allow you to do any good old-fashioned legwork."

I glared at him, and I had to unclench my gritted teeth to answer. "Way to be hypocritical, Jenson, insulting me and in the same breath asking me to use magic to help." The term "magic eye" was derogatory slang for a witch PI.

"I'm not asking you for anything." He leaned back on

his heels and crossed his arms over his chest. "And I think this city has seen enough of your magic lately, what with the way they keep rebroadcasting that interview with you getting all touchy-feely with a ghost."

"What's wrong? Jealous?" I asked, cocking a hip and tossing curls out of my face. Okay, so I was goading him, but he was being an ass. A few days ago I'd participated in the first studio interview of a ghost, and to keep said ghost visible I'd had to remain in contact with him, but I'd most certainly not gotten "touchy-feely" or any such crap.

John cleared his throat. "That's enough." He glanced between us, then turned to his partner. "Get Alex some hip waders and let the wardens know we'll be joining them."

Jenson sneered at me—an expression I returned—and said, "Sure. Boots for the two-legged corpse hound. I'll get right on that." He disappeared around the side of the SUV.

I stared at the spot where he'd been standing. "What a jerk." Things hadn't always been so antagonistic between us. In fact, we'd almost been friends. Then a month ago his attitude had gone to shit. The change coincided perfectly with John's taking a spelled bullet aimed at me. Coincidence? *Doubtful.*

"I don't know what's going on between you two," John said, turning back toward me, "but let's not forget we've got three severed feet and no leads. Now, before we go in there, I suggest turning your shirt inside out."

"You what?"

John waved a tech over to take custody of the bagged foot; then he scooped my purse off the ground, where I'd set it earlier. He handed the red bag to me and nodded toward his car.

"The park rangers warned us when we started searching that the local fae delight in leading hikers astray. The unwary can end up wandering through the same patch of land for days. Pixie-led, they call it. Turning your shirt inside out is supposed to confuse their magic."

I glanced down at my tank top, the shirt clinging to me in the afternoon heat. "Are you thinking fae are involved in the murders?"

John's mustache twitched. "That's another thing you shouldn't say too loud."

"Right." I ducked inside John's car to shimmy out of the top. Not that I thought reversing it would really protect me against fae magic. The fae relied mostly on glamour—a belief magic so strong, it could reshape reality, at least temporarily.

By the time I'd re-dressed, Jenson had dropped off a pair of hip waders for me. They were a thick, waterproof one-piece with suspenders and attached boots. I stepped into them, pulling the brown material up over my clothes. They nearly reached my collarbone.

"We aren't seriously planning to wade chest-deep, are we?" I asked as I adjusted the suspender straps.

John, who'd also suited up in a pair of waders, handed me a plastic bottle of water. "Nah. With the speed the water is retreating, we'd be in danger of getting swept away. If you sense the bodies in the deep water, we'll have to send a team out. Ready?"

I nodded and followed him toward the closest path into the floodplain. John collected a couple of officers as we trekked into the forest, and I wasn't the least bit disappointed when Jenson didn't join us. The forest canopy filtered the sun, but the humidity under the trees hung heavy, making the air thick. Sweat coated my skin, and my blond curls clung to my cheeks and neck. I cracked the seal of my water bottle, but took only one long swig—no telling how long we'd be hiking.

"That is where the first foot was found," John said after we'd been walking for half an hour. He nodded ahead of him to where yellow crime tape ringed the path. "The second was found about a quarter mile farther up the path; the third a mile or more to the south. We're not sure yet if the recent flooding unearthed shallow graves or if the bodies were dumped farther upstream and floated into the floodplain, but with the speed the water is retreating, every passing minute increases the chance of our evidence washing away. We need to find those bodies."

And that was my cue.

I unclasped my silver charm bracelet. Among other charms, the bracelet carried the extra shields that helped buffer the excess of grave essence always trying to drag my psyche across the chasm to the land of the dead. Of course, that was the very chasm I now needed to traverse. As soon as the silver charms lost contact with my skin, a frigid wind lifted around me—the chill of the grave clawing at my remaining mental shields. I cracked those shields, imagining the living vines I visualized as my personal mental wall slithering apart, opening small gaps to my psyche.

The world around me lost the rich hues of life as a gray patina covered everything. My vision doubled as I saw both the land of the dead and the land of the living. In my gravesight, the trees darkened, withering, their thick green leaves turning brown, and the officers' clothing decayed, the cloth becoming threadbare and moth-eaten. Under those mottled rags, their souls shimmered bright yellow. I looked away.

Unfortunately, opening my shields exposed me to more than just the land of the dead. The Aetheric—the plane in which raw magic existed—snapped into focus around me in swirls of brilliant red, vivid blues, and every other color imaginable. The magic twisted, tauntingly close, but I ignored the raw energy. It wasn't supposed to be visible, even with my shields open. Witches didn't physically interact with the Aetheric plane. It wasn't possible. Or at least it shouldn't have been. But I'd been able to see the Aetheric, to *reach* it, ever since the Blood Moon a month ago.

Being able to do something didn't mean I should. Or that it was safe.

I ignored the colors, forcing my eyes to focus on the decaying forest as I reached out with my senses, feeling for the grave essence leaking from the dead. And there was no shortage of dead in the floodplain.

The grave essence from a dead doe reached for me like cold wind trying to cut into my skin. *And to think I was hot a minute ago.* Her remains were no more than fifty yards from where I stood, but I pushed my senses farther, skimming over the traces of small animal bodies and not letting the grave essence sink into my being. I trekked deeper into the floodplain, my magic flowing around me.

The path washed out not far from where the first foot had been found, and the mud made squishing, sucking sounds under my boots until even that gave way to dark water. Foliage, simultaneously healthy and decaying, with-

ered as my gaze moved over it, and I hoped my attention
didn't damage the plants. I'd once crumbled a set of stairs
when my powers pushed the land of the dead into reality.

"Anything?" John asked, trudging behind me.

Yeah, lots of things. Small animals mostly. Not exactly
what we were looking for. I waved him off and kept walking. The water splashed up to the knees of my waterproof
suit as I waded through it, my steps slow, both from the
water rushing around me and because I was concentrating
on feeling the grave essence while holding it at bay so I
didn't accidentally raise any shades.

Something ... I turned in a small circle, reaching with my
mind, my power. Yes, there was something. My power told
me it was touching a body, a human body. Male. And I felt
a female too. And ... two more males?

"This isn't good."

John stopped beside me. "You found something?"

"Bodies. And I hope I'm wrong, but I'm sensing four
different essence signatures."

"A fourth victim?"

I wasn't sure, so I didn't answer. I wished I could close
my eyes and concentrate just on the feel of the bodies, to get
a better sense of where they were located, but it was hard
enough to navigate the flooded forest with my eyes open. I
waded farther in, the water lapping up to my midthighs. I
slipped once, and only John's quick reflexes kept me from
landing on my ass in the murky water.

"We might be getting too deep," John said as one of the
officers, the shortest in our group, lost his footing and
slipped forward in the current. He dug in his toes and
righted himself a moment later.

I shook my head at John. "We're almost there." I could
feel the bodies just ahead.

The rushing water broke around a fallen tree a couple of
yards in front of us. The ancient hardwood's giant roots
stretched out in every direction, dirt still covering them, so
the root-ball formed a massive mound. The tree hadn't
fallen in this particular flood—moss covered the mound
and saplings clung to the root-packed earth. The grave essence emanated from somewhere around that tree, and not
only grave essence but a dark knot of magic.

I stepped closer, searching with both my power and my eyes. Then I saw them.

"Feet."

"Where?" John asked, looking around.

I pointed. In a hollow near the base of the tree was a neatly stacked pile of bloated and decomposing feet. John's bushy eyebrows drew together, his mustache twitching downward as he frowned. He mopped sweat off his forehead before tilting his head to the side and giving me a confused look.

He doesn't see them? I pointed again, but I wasn't wearing gloves, so I didn't want to contaminate the scene. Trying to figure out the differences between what I could see and what he could see was impossible while staring over multiple planes of reality, so I closed my mental shields, blocking my psyche from the land of the dead—and whatever other planes it touched. My grave-sight faded. The gray coating of the world washed away, as did the swirls of the Aetheric. And so did the feet.

I blinked as I clasped my shield bracelet back around my wrist. Releasing my grave-sight made dark shadows crawl over my vision—I couldn't peer across planes without paying a price—but when I squinted I could make out the hollow where I'd seen the feet. An empty hollow. Or, at least, it *looked* empty, but I could still feel the grave essence and the taint of magic lifting off the dead appendages. The essence raked at my shields like icy claws, trying to sink under my skin, into my mind. I shivered. The feet were definitely there.

"John, we have a problem," I said, leaning back and trying to shove my hands in my jean pockets—which were blocked by the rubber hip waders. I dropped my hands by my side as everyone looked at me. "There's a pyramid of feet stacked in that hollow. I counted four and at a guess, they are all lefts."

One of the uniformed officers stepped forward. He lifted a long sticklike object with a glass bead on the end. *Spellchecker wand.* He waved the wand over the hollow. The bead flashed a deep crimson to indicate malicious magic, but the glow was dim, the magic only traces of residual spells.

Stepping back, the officer shook his head. "No active spells, sir."

I stared at the empty-looking hollow. "If they're not hidden behind a spell, it has to be glamour."

"Crap," John said, and turned toward the cop beside him. "Someone get the FIB on the phone. We've got a situation."

The FIB, as in the Fae Investigation Bureau. Glamour was exclusively fae magic, which meant John had just lost jurisdiction.

I slouched in the front of John's police cruiser, one foot on the dash, one hanging out the open door. I'd rather have been out of the car—or more accurately, out of the floodplain. The FIB had arrived and ruffled the cops' feathers. In turn, the cops dashed around, trying to look busy. I was just trying to stay out of the way. But being in the car made me claustrophobic. Actually, if I was honest with myself, it was more than that. Ever since the Blood Moon, being locked inside a car made me jumpy and made my skin itch. I had a sinking suspicion the sensation had something to do with the iron content in the metal. *No wonder Falin drove that hot plastic convertible.*

The thought of Falin Andrews made my gaze twitch toward the rearview mirror and the two FIB agents reflected in it. I'd met Falin a month ago when he'd been working undercover as a homicide detective on the Coleman case. In truth he was a FIB agent—and a fae—and during the course of the case he'd ended up under my covers as well. But I hadn't heard from him in several weeks. As the two FIB agents approached, I could see there was no shock of long blond hair or a towering swimmer's build among the agents who'd responded to John's call. I wasn't sure yet if I was grateful or disappointed.

"Miss Craft?" A woman in a tailored black power suit approached the car.

Here we go. I nodded, jerking my foot from the dash as I stood.

"I'm Special Agent Nori." She didn't extend her hand. "You were the one who found the remains in the hollow?"

Again I nodded, sliding my hands into my back pockets. It had been nearly an hour since I'd released my grave-sight, and my vision was returning to normal, but I still squinted as I studied Agent Nori. She was a couple of inches shorter than me in her fat-heeled pumps, but she stood completely straight, making the most of her height. She wore her dark hair slicked back like shiny black armor and her piercing eyes were set close enough that her sharp features seemed to come to a point in the front of her face. Or at least, that's what she looked like currently. Being an FIB agent meant she was probably, but not necessarily, fae. What she might look like under her glamour was anyone's guess. I could have dropped my shields and found out, but one, it would have been rude, and two, and perhaps more important, my eyes glowed when my psyche peered across planes, so she would have been able to tell. I wanted to get out of here without any trouble.

"Can you tell me how you were able to pierce the glamour?" she asked, which was exactly the question I'd feared. Luckily I hadn't been waiting idly. I'd been planning my answer.

"I was helping the police search for the remains of the . . . remains, by using my grave magic. The glamour didn't hide the grave essence emanating from the feet." I left out that I'd been able to see them. Fae didn't tend to like it when people could see through glamour. You could lose your eyes for less.

She pressed her lips together and jotted something on her notepad. "So you followed this . . . essence? Then what?"

"I tracked where the grave essence originated. I could feel that the body parts were there. That no one else was able to see the feet was a good hint we might be dealing with glamour." All true—just not all of the truth.

Agent Nori clicked her pen closed. "Miss Craft, when you realized glamour was involved, you didn't for a moment think it might have been more prudent to inform the FIB rather than let the mortals blunder around the scene?"

I bristled at the insult toward John and his team. I had a lot of friends in the Nekros City Police Department. Placing a hand on my hip, I lifted one shoulder in a shrug. "They hired me."

"Yes, well, I'm sure they appreciate your help, Miss Craft. Your services will no longer be needed." She turned, gravel crunching under her pumps as she walked away. A few feet past the car, she glanced back over her shoulder. "You realize, of course, that this means we'll have to look into the independent fae in the area." The smile that spread across her face made her brilliantly red lips stretch to flash a lot of white teeth, but it wasn't a happy smile.

I didn't balk. I'd recently learned I was feykin, but she couldn't know that. *Could she?* Plastering on my own smile, I said, "I guess so."

She left the small gravel parking lot, no doubt headed back to the place where I'd found the pyramid of feet. As I turned to slide into the car again, movement at the tree line caught my eye. While my eyesight had recovered significantly, I'd been in touch with the land of the dead and the grave quite a bit, so at first all I could see was a moving man-shaped mesh of colors. But as the figure drew closer, I quickly realized that while *male* was the right gender, he wasn't hu*man*, but fae.

He hunched, his stringy legs never fully straightening as he slunk closer. Even bent, he stood a head taller than me—and I'm not short. He had the same features as a human, but they were all slightly off. His wide eyes were dark, and overly recessed in his skull, but not from illness. His pale skin was the color of a worm's belly, as if he had never been exposed to daylight, and his hawkish nose extended nearly a hand's width from his face, almost hiding the thin lips and pointed chin.

Even now, seventy years after the Magical Awakening, it was rare to see an unglamoured fae. The fae had come out of the mushroom ring, as some put it, because they were fading from memory and thus the world. They needed human belief to anchor them to reality, but aside from the fae celebrities and politicians, a human was likely to see an unglamoured fae only in a venue that profited from showcasing the fae's differences. Most of those places were little better than tourist traps.

I glanced behind me. Across the parking pit, two officers huddled around the van that had been established as a temporary headquarters for the investigation. *Well, at least I'm not completely alone.* Of course, just because the strange fae looked creepy and was near the place where we'd found feet masked in glamour, that didn't make him guilty. It did make him a suspect, though. Or possibly a witness.

"Can I help you?" I yelled the question louder than needed, but I wanted to ensure that the officers also heard me. They would want to question the fae.

He paused, then hurried forward in a blur of movement. He crossed from the far edge of the parking lot to the front of John's car before my heart had time to crash in a loud, panicked beat. The cops yelled something I didn't catch above the blood rushing in my ears.

"Can I help you?" I asked again, not daring to look away from someone who could move as fast as this fae. I slid back a step, and then another, the movement far too slow.

"Are you daft?" he asked, his thin lips splitting with the words to reveal pointed teeth.

I blinked at him, startled, but not because of the implied insult in his words, or because of the threat in his expression. No, my shock came at the sound of his voice. The voice that emerged from that thin, awkwardly threatening body was a rich, deep baritone that made even such an angry question sound musical. He had the kind of voice that, in the old folktales, would have drawn children and young women from their beds. Unfortunately, most of those stories didn't end well.

"I don't know what you mean," I said, taking another step back. Across the parking pit, gravel crunched under the cops' running steps. Close. Maybe not close enough.

"Those feet were hidden for a reason." The fae's gaze moved over my head, and his eyes narrowed. "This is your fault, and you will regret your actions," he said. Then, as the cops neared us, he turned, dashed back to the tree line, and disappeared.

He just wanted a decent book to read ...

Not too much to ask, is it? It was in 1935 when Allen Lane, Managing Director of Bodley Head Publishers, stood on a platform at Exeter railway station looking for something good to read on his journey back to London. His choice was limited to popular magazines and poor-quality paperbacks – the same choice faced every day by the vast majority of readers, few of whom could afford hardbacks. Lane's disappointment and subsequent anger at the range of books generally available led him to found a company – and change the world.

'We believed in the existence in this country of a vast reading public for intelligent books at a low price, and staked everything on it'
Sir Allen Lane, 1902–1970, founder of Penguin Books

The quality paperback had arrived – and not just in bookshops. Lane was adamant that his Penguins should appear in chain stores and tobacconists, and should cost no more than a packet of cigarettes.

Reading habits (and cigarette prices
Penguin still believes in publishing t
enjoy. We still believe that good desig
and we still believe that quality books pu
make the world a

So wherever you see the little bir
prize-winning literary fiction or a cele
de force or historical masterpiece, a se
world classic or a piece of pure escapis
the very best that the g

Whatever you like to r